Double Crossed

a novel by

Darrien Lee

Q-Boro Books
WWW.QBOROBOOKS.COM

An Urban Entertainment Company

Published by Q-Boro Books
Copyright © 2008 by Darrien Lee

ISBN-13: 978-1-933967-60-8
ISBN-10: 1-933967-60-9
LCCN: 2007940326

First Printing October 2008
Printed in the United States of America

10 9 8 7 6 5 4 3 2 1

Cover Copyright © 2008 by Q-BORO BOOKS, all rights reserved.
Cover layout/design by Candace K. Cottrell
Editors: Melissa Forbes, Candace K. Cottrell

Q-BORO BOOKS
Jamaica, Queens NY 11434
WWW.QBOROBOOKS.COM

Acknowledgments

First I would like to thank God for his everlasting love. I also would like to thank my church family at Olive Branch Missionary Baptist Church in Antioch, Tennessee under the leadership of Pastor Vincent Windrow and First Lady Stacy Windrow for their support and prayers.

I want to express my gratitude to my entire family for the joy and love that you bring into my life each and every day. I can't list you all, but I had to include my mother Ines, sisters Emily and Phylishia, brother Edward, nieces Marquita, Ashley, and Jessica, Paige and nephews Tylan and E.B. I also want to send love out to my great niece Kenya and great nephews Ty and Emmanuel. I also want to send love and appreciation out to my mother-in-law Sylvia, brothers-in-law Lee, Troy, and Patrick, sisters-in-law Sheledia and Juanita. To my devoted cousins Rolanda and Venus, I thank you for the love, laughter, and the quarterly brunches.

To the ladies of Sistahs Keeping It Read of Tennessee Book Club, Ties That Bind Book Club, and Ebony Pages Book Club, I applaud what you do for the community and I appreciate your continued support. A special note of appreciation goes out to the entire staff at the Smyrna, Tennessee Public Library and for providing me with a platform to showcase my novels.

Much appreciation and thanks goes out to my editor, Melissa Forbes of Carbon Copy Editing for the awesome job you did on my novels. Melissa, you are da bomb! Seriously, though, I appreciate your advice and for being the best critic and editor an author could have. I don't want anyone touching my novels but you.

To my dear friend and fellow author, V. Anthony Rivers, thank you for the motivation and being a great friend and brother.

To my lifelong girlfriends, Tracy Dandridge and Buanita Ray, I love you guys! You know our years at Tennessee State University are infamous. To the rest of my Divalicious partners in crime, Brenda Thomas, Robin Ridley, Monica Baker, Angie Burum, Sherrie Davis, LaTonia Davenport, Vanessa Maston, Sharon Sutton, and Sharon Nowlin, I blow kisses to you and want you to know that each one of you has a special place in my heart.

A special thanks goes out to my beautician and dear friend, Ronda Gilbert, for always making sure I look fabulous. To Rita Rippy, thanks for the reviews and the love! Next time, lunch is on me! To James Davis, words can't express how much your friendship and support means to me.

My undying appreciation goes out to my wonderful publisher, Mark Anthony. Mark, you are the best, and words can't express my admiration for you and all that you've done for my career. I thank you for allowing my voice to be heard. To Sabine Holsey, Candace Cottrell, and the entire Q-Boro staff, I thank you for your hard work in making sure my work as well as others' is presented in pristine condition.

Lastly, to my husband Wayne and daughters, Alyvia and Marisa, I love you a million times over. Without you, I couldn't do what I do. I lift you up with love and joy in my heart every second of every day.

Dedication

This novel is dedicated to **Police Officers**, **Fire Fighters**, and **Paramedics** for your undying bravery and dedication to public safety.

Prologue

Damon gave Nichole's hand a gentle squeeze each time the airplane hit a series of turbulence. They were flying in and around a thunderstorm, and Damon could tell that Nichole was affected by the bumpy flight as well as the tragedy awaiting her in Philadelphia.

"Nichole, are you OK?"

She turned to him and tried to smile.

"I'm as well as to be expected under the circumstances. Look, Damon, I really appreciate you flying back with me to Philly on such short notice. I'll pay you back."

Damon waved her off.

"There's no need to pay me back. I got this. Besides, it's an emergency situation and I didn't want you to go alone."

When the lightning flashed through the window again, Nichole flinched. Damon noticed the tears on her cheeks.

"I'm so scared, Damon," she whispered.

He took her hand into his again and caressed it. "I know you are. Would you like me to pray with you?"

Nichole froze. Damon noticed her body language as she tensed up.

"I'm sorry. I didn't mean to . . ."

"It's OK, Damon. I think it's sweet and considerate of you to offer to pray for Deacon. I haven't prayed in a long time, so I don't know if God will even listen to me." Damon smiled.

"Nichole, let me assure you that God answers all prayers in one way or another. I know he answered mine."

She nervously played with a Kleenex and lowered her head.

"I hope you're right," she said in a voice barely above a whisper.

At that moment there was a loud clap of thunder and a series of lightning flashes. The pair heard a loud popping noise just before the small jet went into a steep nosedive.

Nichole immediately screamed out in fear.

"Oh my God, we're going to die!"

Damon pulled Nichole over into his lap and buckled her into his seat with him.

"We're not going to die," he said as he caressed her cheek. "Just hold on to me, Nichole."

Chapter One

By the time the airplane finally landed, perspiration had soaked through Nichole's blouse.

"Nichole?" Damon whispered.

Nichole was silent as she remained in his arms with her face buried against his neck and a death grip around his waist.

"Nichole? We've landed. See, I told you we weren't going to die."

He gently titled her chin upwards. Nichole slowly opened her eyes and shook her head in disbelief.

"I can't do this. I hate flying. I'm not strong enough to handle this thing with Deacon."

"Yes you are. You just have to have more faith in yourself," he replied.

"That's easy for you to say. I can't believe how calm you were when the plane was going down."

He unbuckled the seatbelt and helped Nichole out of his lap.

"I was calm for you. Let's go so I can get you to the hospital so you can check on your friend."

Nichole smiled and then hugged Damon's neck. Before releasing him she planted a tender kiss on his cheek.

"You are my angel, Damon."

He blushed. "Nah, I'm just a good Samaritan."

Embarrassed, Nichole giggled nervously. "I guess you think I'm some kind of maniac, huh? I didn't mean to fall apart like that."

"You're no maniac, Nichole, and just for the record, my lap is available for you anytime you want to sit in it."

Nichole put her hand over her mouth and giggled. Damon seemed to always say the right thing at the right time to make her feel better. She picked up her purse and took a step toward the restroom.

"I appreciate your offer, but hopefully I won't be in a situation like this again. I wouldn't have made it here without you, Damon. Thank you. I'll be ready to go as soon as I freshen up."

"I already have a car waiting for us," he said as he opened the overhead compartment, "so as soon as you're ready, we can leave."

Once again, Damon had surprised her. He was very organized and it didn't hurt that he was so attractive, but unfortunately she was unavailable. Deacon was her man, and at the moment he needed her.

It only took Nichole a few minutes to return to the cabin of the airplane. When she stepped out of the restroom Damon could tell she had reapplied makeup that she really didn't need in the first place. She was also wearing a heavenly scent, and it was one that he wouldn't forget for as long as he lived.

"Are you ready to go?" he asked.

Nichole sighed. "I know it seems like I'm hesitating, and I am. I don't know what I'm going to find when I get to the hospital. I'm so scared."

He reached out and put his hand on her shoulder. "It's understandable, Nichole. I know you're scared, but try not to worry. Just pray."

She pulled her purse up on her shoulder. "You're right. Let's go."

Damon and Nichole exited the plane and found the Infiniti QX56 awaiting their arrival. Damon got behind the wheel, and within minutes they pulled off and raced toward the hospital.

It took the pair nearly forty-five minutes to reach the hospital. Traffic was at a stand still, which frustrated and worried Nichole even more. Damon, who also lived in Philly, was able to maneuver through a few side streets, and finally they reached the parking lot of the hospital. Damon turned off the ignition and looked over at her.

"Are you cool?" he asked.

She nodded without speaking as the pair exited the vehicle and hurried into the hospital.

Once inside, Damon stood aside as Nichole asked a receptionist for information on Deacon's whereabouts. The receptionist directed them to the elevator and the eleventh floor, which was the site of the surgical waiting room. When they stepped off the elevator, Nichole was greeted by a couple of Deacon's fellow officers. As soon as they made eye contact, she knew it was bad. Her heart sank as Deacon's partner, Riley, approached her. He quickly pulled her to the side and away from the others.

"Nichole, I'm so sorry about Deacon."

She put her hand over her heart. "Is he . . ."

"No, he's still in surgery, but I'm not going to lie to you, Nichole, it's bad. The bullet nicked an artery. He lost a lot of blood," Riley revealed.

"What happened?" she asked as she tried to come to grips with the severity of the situation.

Riley went on to explain the botched police sting and the fact that Deacon wasn't wearing his bulletproof vest.

"What was he thinking, Riley? Deacon knows better than that."

Riley leaned against the wall and sighed. "He was trying to keep his cover from getting blown."

Nichole shook her head in disbelief. "What is he doing working undercover anyway?"

"We work the gang unit. I thought you knew."

"No, he didn't tell me. As a matter of fact, he hardly ever talks about what you guys do. I guess he doesn't want to worry me."

"Well, Deacon got a tip from one of his informants and wanted to check it out."

"Were you with him when he was shot?" she asked as she leaned against the wall for support.

"Nah, he called me right before he met up with the informant. I begged him to wait for me, but you know how he is."

Nichole shook her head in disbelief. "Stupid!"

Riley pulled Nichole even farther away from the group of officers who had gathered in the surgical ward.

"Nichole, listen to me, there's something else you need to be aware of while you're here."

She pulled out a tissue and wiped her eyes.

"What is it?" Riley hesitated and stumbled over his words.

"I didn't expect to be the one telling you this, and I don't think you already know, but—"

Before Riley could finish his sentence, the surgeon walked out and addressed the group.

"Officers, could you please point me in the direction of Deacon Miles's family?"

Before Nichole could step forward, a tall, statuesque woman stepped through the crowd of officers.

"Hello, doctor, I'm Lala Miles. How is my husband? Is he OK?"

Nichole was shocked. Her knees became weak and she grabbed onto Riley for support. She stood there unable to speak as she watched the surgeon lead the woman over to a nearby chair where they sat down.

"Husband?" she asked in a trembling voice. "I've only been out of town a couple of days, Riley. When the hell did Deacon get a wife?"

Riley turned to Nichole. "That's what I've been trying to tell you. Deacon's been married for about six years."

Nichole was beyond angry. She couldn't believe her ears or her eyes. Deacon never mentioned a wife or ever being married.

"I'm sorry about all of this, Nichole. Deacon planned to tell you about her."

"When!"

Riley didn't know what to say. All he could do was apologize. "I'm sorry you had to find out this way, Nichole."

"Sure you are!" she replied with an elevated tone.

"Listen to me, Nichole. He wanted to tell you. He just didn't know how."

As Riley and Nichole continued to talk, Damon stood several feet down the hallway, but even from his vantage point he could see that Nichole was in distress. As he studied the situation he noticed that the man seemed to be restraining Nichole. He had her by both arms, so Damon hurried through the crowd to Nichole's side.

Damon got right in Riley's face. "I think you need to take your hands off of her," he said calmly.

Riley released Nichole. "Look, I don't know who you are, but you need to back up. This is between me and Nichole."

"Are you OK?" Damon asked Nichole as he slid her to the side.

"I'm fine," she said as she grabbed Damon's arm.

Damon backed Riley against the wall. "If I ever see you put your hands on her like that again, you're done," he said.

Riley's fellow officers saw Damon's aggressive behavior and started to intervene, but Riley held his hand up to keep them at bay. He smiled.

"Are you threatening a police officer?" Riley asked.

"That doesn't matter to me. What matters to me is how you were manhandling Nichole."

Riley chuckled. "Bro, I didn't do anything to Nichole. We're old friends. Tell him, Nichole. And who are you anyway?"

She blew her nose into the Kleenex. "He's my friend, Damon Kilpatrick," she answered. "I thought you were my friend, Riley, but now I don't know."

Riley nodded in the direction of the waiting room. "Nichole's upset because she just found out that Deacon is married."

Damon looked into the waiting area and then back at Riley. "Married?"

Riley lowered his head. "Unfortunately it's true," Riley answered.

"You knew all along, didn't you?" Damon asked.

"He's my partner. Besides, he said he was going to tell Nichole. It wasn't my place to tell her."

Damon looked at Nichole, who was still wiping away tears.

"What do you want to do?" he asked.

She linked her arm with his. "Get me out of here, Damon."

He started to lead her away, but before they walked away, Damon turned to Riley and said, "Some friend you are."

As they made their way to the elevator, Riley yelled, "Nichole! I'm sorry!"

Damon pushed the buttons on the elevator and when the doors opened, they stepped inside, leaving Riley, Deacon, his wife, and all the other officers behind. As the elevator descended, Nichole whispered, "I've been such a fool."

"You're not a fool, Nichole. You loved and trusted him, that's all. He should've been honest with you."

She turned to Damon and let out a breath. "It doesn't matter. I know about her now. I would like to find out why he kept this from me. I didn't even know he had been transferred to the gang unit."

"If you want to stay and see what his prognosis is, I don't mind. We can wait in a waiting room on another floor if you like," Damon offered.

The elevator doors opened and they stepped out into the lobby.

"No, it's OK. It looks like Deacon is in good hands with his wife and all the rest of those other lying bastards up there he calls friends."

The two were silent until they climbed back into the SUV. Once inside, Damon turned to Nichole.

"Look, I didn't mean to interfere up there. From where I was standing it looked like you were being mistreated, and I couldn't stand back and not say or do something."

"I'm glad you did, Damon. Riley always acts so smug. He needs to be held accountable for his lies too."

"I hope the guy lives to answer to you and anybody else he's hurt with his lies."

Damon put the key in the ignition and started the vehicle. He was pissed! It was guys like Deacon that made it hard for decent guys like him to be trusted by women like Nichole.

Nichole leaned back against the headrest. "Damon, could you do me one more favor and drive me home?"

"Are you going to be OK?"

"I have no other choice, do I?"

"See, that's where you're wrong. You have plenty of choices, Nichole. I know we just met and we don't know each other very well, but for some reason I feel like I've known you for years. Don't let this incident mess with your head. You're bigger than this."

She smiled. "Now how would you know?"

He looked over at her and smiled. "Trust me, I know."

Nichole giggled, and for the moment she believed that everything was going to be OK.

Damon made his way across town after obtaining directions to Nichole's neighborhood. He pulled into her driveway and put the car in park.

"Nice house."

"Thank you," she said as she opened the car door.

They climbed out of the car and walked over to her garage. Nichole punched in a series of numbers and the garage door slowly lifted. Once it was up, Damon and Nichole walked past her silver SL-Class Mercedes Benz Roadster and a black Cadillac EXT truck.

"Nice vehicles," Damon acknowledged.

Nichole put her key in the door. "Thanks. I've always wanted a Benz, but I'm a truck girl at heart."

Damon followed Nichole into her kitchen, which was decorated with shades of lime green, black, and white. It was spotless and gave off a warm feeling.

"Come on in, Damon. You can put my luggage there. I'll get it later."

Damon sat her luggage on a window seat as instructed. "Can I get you anything before I leave? Are you hungry?" he asked.

She opened her refrigerator and pulled out two bottles of water. "No, I'm not hungry, but thanks for asking. You want some water?"

He held out his hand and took the water. "Thanks."

"Have a seat, Damon. Take a load off."

He opened the bottled and took a sip before sitting down next to her at the bar in her kitchen.

"Are you sure you're not hungry?" he asked again.

Nichole took a sip of water and smiled. "I'm sure, but if you're hungry I could fix you something."

"No, I'm fine," he said and smiled.

Nichole tilted her head and admired him. "Damon, I've taken up enough of your time. Don't you have to get back to Houston? I don't want to hold you up. I'll be fine, Scout's honor."

Damon swallowed the rest of the water and then turned to her.

"I'm good. I don't have to be anywhere until Wednesday."

"I'm sorry you had to shorten your trip on account of me."

He shook his head. "No, I welcomed the opportunity to come home early. Don't sweat it, Nichole." He looked at his watch and stood. "Look, I'd better get out of your way so you can have some privacy."

Nichole stood and gave Damon a warm hug. "Thank you, Damon. All I'm going to do is take a hot bath and crash."

Her body felt fabulous against his and he savored every second.

"Sounds good."

After releasing her he walked toward the garage and reached for the doorknob. Nichole put her hand on top of his.

"You can go out the front door."

They walked to the front door together and she opened it. Damon stepped out on the porch and handed her his business card.

"Call me if you need anything or want to talk."

Nichole took the card out of his hand and smiled. "I will. Good-bye, Damon, and thanks again for being there for me."

"No problem. Good-bye, Nichole."

As soon as Nichole closed the door she sunk to the floor and burst into tears.

Chapter Two

Damon made his way home, and as soon as he got settled in, he called Arnelle, who was still in Houston visiting with her brother, Keaton, and his wife, Meridan. The entire family was in Houston to celebrate the birth of Arnelle's nephew and to attend his baptism. That was where Damon and Nichole had just come from. Nichole and Meridan were best friends.

Damon used to have strong feelings for Arnelle a couple years earlier, but it didn't work out. They'd been close friends ever since. Damon just happened to be in Houston scouting for the Philadelphia Eagles, so it was only natural that he was invited to the celebration as well. Damon was an assistant coach with the Eagles, and Arnelle was a sports medicine doctor, which allowed them to work together occasionally. Damon wanted to call to apologize for his sudden departure from the festivities, and to explain what happened with Deacon and Nichole. He quickly filled Arnelle in on the news.

"I'm worried about Nichole," he revealed to Arnelle. "You should've seen her. She was trembling and everything. I almost lost my temper at that hospital when I thought one of those cops had done something to her."

Arnelle leaned back in the recliner and crossed her legs. "You're so thoughtful, Damon, and I'm glad she didn't have to go through this alone. What is she going to do now?"

He sighed. "I don't know. I want to call her to check on her, but I don't want to crowd her. Maybe it's best I give her some space to deal with her situation."

"Is he going to live?" Arnelle asked.

"We left the hospital before we could find out. You know it's true when they say policeman have a code of silence. I'm sure all of his friends knew that guy was married and was using Nichole on the side."

Arnelle smiled as her two-year-old son walked over and put a stuffed Teddy bear in her lap. She leaned down and kissed him on the cheek before returning to her conversation.

"You don't know the full story yet, so don't be so quick to judge him. Is it possible he and his wife are separated or going through a divorce?"

"It doesn't matter. There's a wife that Nichole didn't know about, and that makes it wrong."

Arnelle giggled. "Look at you. You're so protective of Nichole, and you guys hardly know each other."

"I know her type, and I know his type. I see it every day. Even some of my players are involved in drama like this, and it's uncalled for. What's wrong with being honest?"

Arnelle played with the Teddy bear her son had put in her lap as she thought about what Damon said.

"I agree with you there. So, did you get finished here in Houston before you jetted back to Philly?"

"Pretty much. I was kind of ready to get back home anyway. When are you and Winston coming back?"

Arnelle's husband, Winston, ran past the family room playfully chasing their screaming four-and-a-half-year-old daughter, MaLeah. Arnelle looked at them curiously and then shook her head before continuing her conversation with Damon.

"Do you want me to see if I can find out how he's doing?"

"Would you? I mean, I would hate for the guy to die, but what he hid from Nichole was foul. She's been dating him for a while, hasn't she?" Damon asked.

"From what Meridan told me, yes. She also mentioned something about them discussing marriage at one time."

Damon poured himself a glass of milk. "That's odd. Do you think he was playing Nichole intentionally?"

"I don't know what to think. Meridan told me Nichole has a terrible temper. There's no telling what she'll do to Deacon once she gets over the shock," Arnelle revealed.

"Does she own a gun?" he asked, concerned.

"I don't know, Damon. Look, Deacon is a cop and all his friends are cops. They're going to protect their own and I would hate for you or Nichole to get mixed up with any drama. It's not worth it. Deacon has a wife, so he's her responsibility, not Nichole's. I hope she just lets it go."

"Maybe you should get your sister-in-law to talk to her," Damon said as he sat down at his kitchen table.

"I will, but you know it's not easy to just walk away from someone you love. I'm not so sure Nichole is willing to just let it go."

"Finding out something like this would actually make it easier for me to walk away," Damon replied. "I don't think I would snap, but you never know how something like this affects a person."

Arnelle giggled. "You're too sweet. I can't see you doing anything like that. So what are you going to do?"

Damon put his empty glass in the sink and leaned against the countertop. "I'm going to try to be Nichole's friend, but I'm not going to lie to you. I'm very attracted to her, but she's vulnerable and it's not good to start a relationship under those circumstances," he announced.

"I know you wouldn't. Just be careful. I don't want you to get hurt."

He chuckled. "Now you sound like my grandmother."

"I'm serious, Damon. You never know. Nichole might somehow work this mess out with her boyfriend. We'll just have to wait and see."

Damon chuckled again. "I don't see how it's possible, but stranger things have happened. I didn't want to disturb her but I would like to check on her; however, I forgot to get her number."

Arnelle smiled and said, "I normally don't do this, but I'll give Meridan a call and get her telephone number for you."

"Thanks, Arnelle. I owe you."

Arnelle's son Fredrick crawled up in her lap and smiled. Within seconds she smelled a very unpleasant odor. She frowned.

"You don't owe me, Damon. I'll call you back shortly."

"Thanks," he answered. "I really appreciate you doing this for me."

"You're welcome. Well, I have to go, Damon. Fredrick has messed on himself, and I need to get him cleaned up."

He laughed. "I can't wait to have an experience like that with my own children."

Arnelle held Fredrick out like he was a bomb waiting to detonate as she rose from the recliner. She laughed.

"Children truly are a blessing, but when they blow up their pants like Fredrick just did, you have second thoughts."

"I'm sure it's challenging, but you're right. It is a blessing. I'll talk to you shortly."

"Good-bye, Damon."

Damon hung up the telephone and headed upstairs to shower and change clothes.

Nichole stared up at the ceiling from her bubble bath below. She couldn't believe what she had experienced over the last twenty-four hours. She wasn't a woman who let someone kick her when she was down, but at the moment, she didn't have an ounce of fight in her. Deacon meant the world to her. At least he used to until he betrayed her.

"Why didn't you tell me you had a wife, Deacon?" Nichole mumbled to herself. She splashed the water in anger. "Don't you dare cry, Nichole."

Deacon had committed the ultimate betrayal, but for some reason she wanted him to look her in the eyes and explain himself. The ringing of the telephone shattered her thoughts. She really didn't feel like talking to anyone, and the number on her caller ID was not familiar. Taking a chance, she answered it.

"Hello?"

"Hello, Nichole. Did I disturb you?" Damon asked.

Nichole let out a breath and relaxed. "What a nice surprise. No, you didn't disturb me. I'm just soaking my sorrows away."

"I hope you don't mind me calling. I was worried about you so I got your number from Arnelle."

Nichole was actually flattered that Damon went through those lengths to get her number.

"It's OK. I should've given you my number anyway. I could use a friend right now. I've never felt so foolish, Damon."

"Everybody's been there in one way or another," he softly replied. "Have you talked to your friend, Meridan?"

"No, I can't right now, and I don't want to put my dark cloud over her head either."

"She's your friend, Nichole. I'm sure she's worried about you, and you'll probably feel better after talking to her."

Nichole played with the bubbles in silence. "Maybe you're right. I'll think about calling her later."

Damon took a deep breath before speaking. "Listen, Nichole, if you feel up to it, would you like to grab some dinner later?"

Nichole thought for a moment before answering. "I really don't feel like going out, but I could use some company. If you want to come over, we can order in and maybe watch a movie or something."

"I'd like that, and don't worry about dinner. I'll take care of it. Is there anything you don't like?" Nichole laughed.

"You don't know me that well, do you?"

He wasn't sure what the joke was, but he was curious to find out. "What aren't you telling me, Nichole?"

"Well, I've been known to have a hearty appetite, and it's one that surprises most people, especially men."

Damon chuckled. "That's hard to believe with a gorgeous physique like yours."

She blushed. "Thank you, Damon, but believe me, I have to work hard to maintain it."

"On that note, I'll be very selective with our order," he joked.

"Seriously, though, there's nothing I don't like, and all this food talk is making me hungry, so hurry up," she teased.

"In that case, I'd better get moving. Looks like we're going to be having an early dinner, huh?"

She giggled. "I guess so."

"It sounds good to hear you laugh."

Staring up at the ceiling once again, she said, "I hope it lasts, Damon."

"So do I. I'll see you shortly, Nichole."

It didn't take long for Nichole to get dressed and curl her hair. She lit some scented candles and shuffled through her library of DVDs. She preferred a comedy to lift her spirits, but if Damon wanted to watch a movie full of action, she was open to that as well. Nichole was actually happy that Damon was coming over, because he seemed to be a great listener with constructive advice.

The doorbell rang sooner than she expected, and when she opened the door she found Riley standing on her porch with an arrogant look on his face. Seeing that it wasn't Damon, she became angry.

"What do you want, Riley? I don't remember inviting you over."

"May I come in?" he asked as he took a step toward her. "I need to talk to you."

Nichole blocked his path and folded her arms. "You men are all alike, and as far as I'm concerned, we have nothing to talk about, so there's no need for you to come into my house."

"Come on, Nichole. Don't be like that," he begged as he leaned in closer to her.

She sighed and then allowed him to enter. "Say what you have to say so you can leave. Nothing's going to matter anyway."

He pointed to the sofa and asked, "May I sit down?"

She shrugged her shoulders and sat down in a nearby chair.

Riley sat down and sighed. "Look, Nichole, I'm here because I know Deacon would want me to come.

"So he's OK?" she asked out of concern.

"Yeah, he made it out of surgery. You need to go see him. I know your face is the face he wants to see when he wakes up."

"Forget it! His wife is there for him."

Riley scooted out on the edge of the sofa. "Listen, Nichole, if you don't go see him, I don't think he's going to recover as quickly without you."

"That's his fault, not mine," she softly replied without looking at Riley.

"Nichole, Deacon's lucky to be alive. It was touch and go there for a minute, but he's a fighter."

"Yeah, and he's obviously a lover too, since he tricked my ass."

Riley stood and walked over to where Nichole was sitting. He put his hand on her shoulder and said, "It's not what you think. Look, I know you're pissed and I know you're hurt. Just go see him, Nichole."

"No. I'll think about it, but right now it's out of the question."

"Deacon's going to be just as upset as you are over how this went down."

"What reason does he have to be upset? Oh, wait! It's because I found out that while he was screwing me, he had a wife at home?" she asked sarcastically.

"Once again, it's not like it seems. Deacon's been good to you. Go see him. The surgeon talks like he could wake up from the surgery at any time. You owe him, Nichole."

A feeling of rage overtook her as she stood. "I don't owe him a damn thing, Riley," she yelled, "so go back to the hospital, and when your boy wakes up, tell him I said go to hell. Now get out of my house!"

Riley put his hands up in defense. "Nichole, calm down and try to be reasonable. You know you love him."

She walked over to the door, opened it, and screamed, "I think I asked you leave. Get out of my house!"

Damon stepped onto the porch just as Nichole screamed at Riley. He was standing there confused with a bag of takeout food in his hand. When he saw Riley, he frowned.

"What the hell is going on here? Nichole, did he hurt you?"

She shook her head, but Damon could see she was clearly upset. He looked at Riley. "What are you doing here?" he asked.

Riley stepped out onto the porch. "That's none of your business."

Damon sucked in a breath before handing the bags of food to Nichole.

"Nichole, take these into the kitchen. I'll join you in just a minute."

With tears in her eyes, she looked over at Riley and whispered, "Just go, Riley, please."

Once Nichole was out of sight, Damon approached Riley.

"Look, bro, I don't know what kind of game you and your partner are playing, but whatever it is, it ends now. Nichole's been through a lot and I'm not going to sit back and watch you or anybody else hurt her anymore. So I suggest you leave and don't come back unless you're invited."

Riley eyed Damon in silence. He didn't know it, but Damon wasn't a man he wanted to tangle with, cop or no cop.

"Whatever, man," Riley replied as he stepped around Damon. "Nichole is wrong if she doesn't go see Deacon."

"What's wrong is that he took advantage of her in the first place. Now get the hell away from here and don't come back."

Riley stopped walking and turned to look at Damon. He laughed as he opened the door of his car. Before sliding in he said, "If I was you, I'd be careful who I threaten."

"Bring it on, Officer," Damon calmly replied.

Riley got in his car, started the engine, and squealed his tires as he backed out of Nichole's driveway and disappeared down the road.

Chapter Three

Damon entered the kitchen and found Nichole preoccupied with the takeout food. She looked up at him when he entered the room.

"I'm sorry about Riley."

He walked over to the table and took the food containers out of her hand.

"What do you have to be sorry about? He was the idiot."

"I just wish everyone would leave me alone," she whispered.

Damon put his hand over his heart. "You break my heart, Nichole."

She turned and rolled her eyes. "I didn't mean you," she apologized. "I meant Riley, Deacon, and any of the rest of their lowlife friends."

He picked up a plate and winked at her. "I was hoping you weren't putting me in that category."

"I don't know you well, but I have a feeling that you could never be like them, Damon."

He pulled her chair out for her. "That's one thing I can guarantee you. Would you like me to bless the food?"

She looked at all the delicious food in front of her and said, "That would be nice."

Damon held her hand, blessed the food, and he and Nichole started putting the pasta salad, grilled salmon, corn on the cob, and stir-fried vegetables on their plates.

Back at the hospital, Riley walked into Deacon's room and found him asleep. He made eye contact with Deacon's wife, Lala. She smiled.

"He woke up a little while ago. He's been asking for you."

"How long has he been asleep?" Riley sat down and asked.

"I'm not asleep," a groggy voice replied. "Lala, I need to talk to Riley alone for a minute. Why don't you go home and relax for a while? I'm OK."

She stood up and picked up her jacket. "Are you sure?"

"You've been here since they brought me in. The doctor said I'm going to live, so you don't have to sit here twenty-four, seven."

Lala leaned down and gave him a kiss on the lips before leaving the room. "All right, but I won't be gone long. Riley, don't tire him out. He needs his rest."

Riley stood and slid his hands inside his pockets. "I won't. One of the officers outside can drive you home."

"Thanks. I'll be back shortly," she replied as Riley helped her into her jacket.

"Take your time," Deacon mumbled.

She exited the room and Riley took the seat she had just vacated.

Not wanting to waste any time, Deacon asked, "Where's Nichole?"

Riley sighed. "She's at home now, but she was here

several hours ago. I'm sorry, Deek, but she knows about Lala. I've never seen a woman so angry."

Tears filled Deacon's eyes. "Does Lala know about her?"

"I don't think so, but there was a lot of commotion and people up here."

"Is she coming to see me?" Deacon asked.

Riley looked over at Deacon. "Didn't you hear me? I said she was pissed, so why would she come? I did my best to cover for you, but it's hard to cover up a marriage."

Deacon drifted in and out of consciousness, talking to Riley when he could. Riley looked out the window.

"Get some sleep, Deacon. We'll talk more when you're feeling better. I'm glad you're OK, man."

Riley took his seat and stayed by Deacon's side for the rest of the night.

Damon watched with amazement as Nichole ate. She wasn't lying when she said she had a huge appetite. He shook his head.

"I don't know where you put it."

"I told you I have to work hard in the gym to keep it off. I eat a lot! I have to have my three meals a day. If I don't, I get sort of crazy," she teased.

"Well, I'm glad I didn't have to witness that today," he responded. "Do you have room for dessert?"

Her eyes widened with excitement. "What did you bring?"

He stood, walked over to one of the bags, and reached inside. He looked back over his shoulder at her and winked. Then he slowly pulled the tempting dessert out of the bag.

"How does caramel pie sound?"

Nichole started clapping. "Oh my God! I love caramel pie!"

"Before I let you have some pie, you have to tell me one thing about you that would surprise me," Damon challenged. "Don't worry, you'll get to quiz me too."

"I already revealed that if I don't get three meals a day I get crazy."

He shook his finger at her. "That doesn't count. The game starts now."

Nichole put her hands on her hips and smiled. "Let me see. I guess if I had to choose one thing, it would have to be that I'm a golf fanatic."

Damon pretended to get weak in his knees and staggered backward. "Tell me you're joking."

Nichole greedily reached for the pie. "No, it's the truth. I play hard, Damon. It's an obsession."

He walked toward the table with the pie. "That's interesting, because I happen to be a pretty good golfer myself. I can't wait to see if you got game."

"Be careful what you wish for. I've been playing since I was seven years old."

"Are you trying to tell me you're the female version of Tiger Woods?" he asked curiously.

Waving him over closer with the pie, she blushed. "I don't like to brag, but people have compared me to him."

Playfully holding the pie out of her reach and over her head, he said, "Look at you! OK, I'll bite. You know we could always make this interesting," he proposed as he finally sat the pie on the table.

"And just what are you suggesting?" she asked with a raised brow.

This time, Damon raised his brow and smiled. Nichole giggled as the ringing of the telephone interrupted them. She walked over to the telephone and answered without looking at the ID.

"Hello?"

"Nichole, baby, please don't hang up," Deacon pleaded. "I really need to talk to you, please.

Nichole gripped the telephone. "I'm glad to see you're OK, Deacon, but I would appreciate it if you wouldn't call me anymore."

"Nichole, it's not like it seems," he tried to explain.

"Are you married, Deacon?"

"Legally, yes, but—"

"Then there's nothing to discuss. You kept something very important from me and I deserve more respect than that."

Deacon coughed and grimaced in pain. "Please, Nichole. I need to see you so I can explain. It's really not what it seems. I love you."

"Well, you have a funny way of showing it. Listen, I wish you a speedy recovery, but as far as what we had, it's over. Good-bye, Deacon."

Nichole hung up and stood there in silence for a moment. Deacon's telephone call had made her mood do a one-eighty. She turned to Damon. "Would you excuse me for a moment?"

He took the top cover off the pie and softly replied, "Sure. Are you OK?"

She nodded without speaking as she leaned against the wall.

"Are you sure?" Damon asked again.

She smiled. "I'm fine. Go ahead and cut me a piece of pie. I'll be right back."

Damon picked up a knife and said, "Take your time."

Nichole excused herself to go to the bathroom. She felt like the room was closing in on her. She sat down on the toilet seat and bent over to get some air into her lungs.

"Hold it together, Nichole. You can get through this," she told herself. "Don't let him do this to you."

Minutes later, Nichole returned to the kitchen and

found Damon pouring two cups of milk. He looked up at her and smiled when she walked back into the room. Nichole sat down.

"I'm sorry I ran out on you, Damon."

"You didn't run out on me. This is your house. You're free to do whatever you want in it."

She reached across the table and took his hand. "How is it that you know how to say the right things all the time?"

He caressed her hand."I hate seeing you like this, Nichole. I hate seeing any woman in pain. Don't let this guy mess with your head."

Nichole stared at him and then released his hand. "You know, Damon Kilpatrick, I barely know you, but you make me feel like I've known you for years."

"Well, maybe we can get to know each other on the golf course," he said as he took a bite of pie. "But I'm going to warn you, I stay very busy during the football season. The off-season is not so bad, but I still have to work. It's been hard for me to find a friend to hang out with who can deal with my hectic schedule."

Nichole took a bite of the caramel pie and closed her eyes to savor the taste. She opened her eyes. "I would love that. Besides, I could use a friend right now, especially with Meridan in Texas with Keaton and their new baby. I don't want to bother her too much with my problems."

"I would bet you anything that Meridan would be upset with you if you didn't let her know what was going on in your life. You should call her," he suggested as he took another bite of pie.

"I'll call her later," she replied as she finished off her pie and sat down her fork. She leaned back in her chair and patted her stomach. "That was delicious! Now, are you up for a movie?"

Damon finished off the rest of his pie and put their empty saucers in the sink. "A movie sounds great."

He stood, and just as he was about to wash the saucers, Nichole said, "Leave those. I'll get them later."

"Are you sure? Because I really don't mind."

"I'm sure."

"In that case, lead the way to the theatre room," he joked.

Nichole smiled and motioned for Damon to follow her into her family room where she popped in *Madea's Family Reunion* for a good laugh.

Deacon handed the cell phone back to Riley. "You're right. She's not coming," he said.

"I tried to tell you," Riley replied as he tucked the cell phone back on his belt.

Deacon coughed and grabbed his shoulder in pain. "If she won't come on her own, you're going to have to make her come."

"How am I supposed to do that?" Riley asked.

"Whatever it takes. By force, if necessary," Deacon demanded.

"I can't bring her kicking and screaming into this hospital in front of Lala," Riley explained.

"I don't care what Lala thinks!"

Riley stood and put on his jacket. "You're not thinking straight, man. I can get Nichole for you, but I'm not going to bring her here. Give her some time to cool down, and when you get out of the hospital and back home, I'll deliver her to you myself."

Chapter Four

Nichole and Damon laughed throughout the movie. When it was over, Damon looked at the clock on the mantelpiece and asked, "Is that the right time on your clock?"

She giggled and said, "Of course it is."

Damon looked at his watch to verify the time. "I guess you're right. I can't believe I've been over here this long."

Nichole walked over and removed the movie from the DVD player. As she was putting it back into the case she turned to Damon.

"Time flies when you're having fun, huh?" she asked.

He stood and yawned. "You got that right, but I'd better get going. I have a lot of work waiting on me at home."

"You really should get some rest."

He straightened the pillows on the sofa. "There's not much rest for the weary. The Eagles organization keeps us pretty busy. As a matter of fact, I'm off to Atlanta next weekend."

"Sounds exciting. I envy you, Damon."

He chuckled and asked, "Why?"

"You get to travel all over the country meeting interesting people in exciting places."

He picked up his jacket and laid it across his arm. "It's not as exciting as it sounds. I'm usually in meetings or at a stadium all day. I hardly ever get to enjoy myself when I travel because the days are so long. When I get back to my hotel, all I want to do is eat and sleep. I'm just as content at home, but I have a job I love and it pays the bills."

Nichole folded her arms and blushed. "I admire you, Damon Kilpatrick."

He walked over to her and kissed her on the forehead. "I admire you, too, Nichole Adams, and with that said, I'll get out of your way so you can go to bed."

"You know you don't have to leave. We could watch another movie or something."

Damon made his way over to the front door and opened it. "That's a sweet offer, but I don't want to wear out my welcome. I'll take a rain check."

Nichole followed him over to the front door and stood next to him. "Well if you change your mind and want to come back, just give me a call."

He laughed and said, "I'll keep that in mind. Good night, Nichole."

She gave him a loving hug.

"Call me any time if you feel like talking," Damon said.

"Thank you, Damon. I will."

"Good night, Nichole"

"Good night," she replied as she watched him walk down the sidewalk to his car. She really did enjoy his company and wished he had stayed a little longer. Being alone wasn't something she really wanted to be right now. After closing the door, her telephone rang once again. She ran over and answered it.

"Hello?"

"What is this I hear about Deacon having a wife?"

It was Meridan.

"Damn! News sure does travel fast, especially when it's bad news. I was going to call you later and tell you about it, Dee.

"What happened?" Meridan asked.

Nichole lay down on the sofa and sighed. "I don't even know where to start. I've never felt so hurt and betrayed."

"How is Deacon?" Meridan asked. "He's not dead, is he?"

"No, he's not dead, but at times I wish he were."

"You don't mean that, Nikki," Meridan replied. "Arnelle told me that Damon called and told her there was an ugly scene at the hospital. What happened? You didn't show your tail, did you?"

Nichole giggled. "No, and it's only because I didn't have a chance to. Everything happened so fast, and I guess I was in shock. You should've seen her, Dee. I felt and looked like a fool."

"Deacon's the fool for hiding the fact that he was married."

Meridan's husband, Keaton, yelled from the background, "Tell Deacon I'm going to kick his ass when I see him."

"Be quiet, Keaton!" Meridan yelled. "You're not going to do anything to Deacon or you'll wind up in jail, and you know it."

Nichole laughed. "Tell Keaton I appreciate it, but I can handle Deacon."

"What are you going to do, Nikki? Don't do anything

stupid because I don't want to see you on *America's Most Wanted*."

"I'm cool. I'm just glad Damon was there. He helped me through the whole nasty ordeal. As a matter of fact, he just left. He brought over dinner and we watched a movie together."

Meridan cleared her throat after hearing that piece of news. "Speaking of Damon, what's going on with you two?"

"Nothing's going on," Nichole answered while playing with the tassels on a pillow. "He's a sweetheart, though, and so fine. Why isn't he married?"

"I don't know. I think it has something to do with his busy lifestyle. From what Arnelle told me, being an NFL coach is very demanding. It doesn't leave them a lot of time for family or a social life during the season," Meridan said.

"That's a shame, because he's seems so compassionate and attentive."

"From what Arnelle told me, he is. You know he and Arnelle kind of dated for a hot minute."

"Really?" Nichole asked.

"Yeah, but it was during the time Winston was acting stubborn and stupid. Luckily, he came to his senses. I think Damon's ego was a little bruised, but they continue to work together, and they're still close friends."

"So how does Arnelle's husband handle her remaining friends with Damon?"

Meridan giggled. "Winston's OK with it now. He finally started using the good sense God gave him and married Arnelle. She wasn't serious about Damon, though. Winston was the man she was in love with, and they already had a daughter together at the time."

"Wow," Nichole responded. "I bet Damon was heartbroken."

"Maybe a little, but he realized that Arnelle wasn't into him on that level. Damon's a strong man. He'll meet the right woman one day, or has he already?" Meridan asked.

"Starting another relationship is the last thing on my mind, Dee. Deacon's lies have destroyed me. I don't know if I'll ever be able to trust another man," she admitted.

"Give yourself time, Nikki, and I'm not saying Damon will be the one, but if not, you already know he has the friend gene. Just chill for a while," Meridan suggested.

"You know, I think I will. By the way, how's my godson?"

"Jeremiah is doing just fine."

Nichole smiled with pride. She was so happy for Meridan and Keaton. Just when Meridan thought she would never be able to have children, God blessed them with Jeremiah.

"Well, kiss him and tell him his auntie loves him and hopes to see him again soon."

Meridan smiled. "I will. Now back to you. Make sure you call me and keep me posted on Deacon."

"There's not going to be anything to keep you posted on. I'm through with Deacon," Nichole announced.

"Are you sure? Have you at least seen him?" Meridan asked.

"No, and I don't want to. He has a wife and he's a liar, so there's no room for me in his little equation."

Meridan chuckled. "Well I can't say that I blame you."

"Oh! Can you believe his partner, Riley, came over here to try to convince me to go to the hospital, but I wasn't hearing it. The next thing I knew, Damon was here. They exchanged some words, and before I knew it, Damon was in his face."

Meridan gasped. "Nichole! Don't you let Damon do

anything that could make him lose his job or end up in jail!"

"I had no control over him. Besides, everything happened so fast. Anyway, it's late. I'll try to be a good girl," she joked.

"You'd better be!"

"I'll also try to keep Damon out of this. Tell Keaton good night, and don't forget to kiss my godson. I'm getting ready to go to bed so I can get up for work in the morning."

"Call me tomorrow. I love you, and take care," Meridan replied.

"I love you, too, sis. Good night."

Nichole hung up the telephone and lay there in deep thought. Seconds later she got up off the sofa, set the alarm, and climbed the stairs to her bedroom.

Damon drove across the city reminiscing about his evening—first going toe-to-toe with that renegade cop, and then relaxing with Nichole. It was evident to him that she had the strength to bounce back from her adversities, and he enjoyed spending time with her.

It didn't take Damon long to get home, and when he walked inside the house he was greeted by his youngest brother, Zel, a twenty-five-year-old career college student.

"What's up, bro?" Zel yelled as he gave Damon a loving handshake and hug.

"What are you doing here?" Damon asked as he studied his baby brother.

"Well, I'm happy to see you, too," Zel replied sarcastically.

Damon threw his keys on the table in the foyer and hung his jacket in the hall closet. He turned to Zel.

"You know what I mean. Why can't you call ahead instead of just showing up on my doorstep?" Damon walked into the kitchen with Zel following closely behind.

"You know how I roll, Damon. I do things on the spur of the moment. I'm a spontaneous kind of guy."

"What's her name?" Damon asked.

Zel's laugh indicated that Damon had hit the nail on the head.

"See what I mean?" Damon said. "You need to get some structure in your life and stop messing around with so many different women. You're going to mess around and get one of them pregnant if you're not careful," Damon warned his brother.

"You're crazy as hell. There's no way I'm going to let a shorty jam me up like that," he assured Damon. "I'm not about to go out like that."

"How's the new job coming?" Damon asked as he opened the refrigerator and pulled out a bottle of cranberry juice.

"It's great. Right now it's part time, but after I graduate it's full time all the way," Zel answered as he picked up an apple and bit into it.

"That's great, Zel. You made yourself marketable by having a double major in electrical engineering and business, and in a few months you'll have your master's in electrical engineering."

"I know," Zel said, looking Damon directly in the eyes. "And I owe it all to Nanna, Papa, and my brothers, but especially you, Damon."

"We're family, and education has always been important in our family. We want you to be successful in life."

Zel watched as his brother took a sip of juice. Damon's words touched him.

"Thanks, bro, and while we're on the subject, here's the first payment of what I owe you. I promised you I was going to pay back every dime I owed, and this is a portion of my first paycheck."

Damon took the check and glanced down at it. "Not bad. They must be paying you very well."

"They are," Zel replied as he picked up a *Sports Illustrated* magazine from the table and opened it. The next thing he knew, Damon was ripping up the check.

"What are you doing?" he asked, startled by Damon's actions.

Damon walked over and put the tiny pieces of paper into Zel's hand before giving him a hug.

"I'm canceling your bill."

"Are you serious?" Zel asked as he looked down at his hand.

"Of course I'm serious. Consider it my contribution to the Zel Kilpatrick Education Fund."

Zel's eyes widened in disbelief. "I don't know what to say, bro."

"Thank you would be a good start," Damon answered as he straightened up the magazines on his coffee table. "I never meant for you to pay me back, Zel. I just wanted you to learn some responsibility and see if you would stay true to your promise of paying me back."

Zel couldn't help but wipe his eyes. He didn't want Damon to see his tears, although he knew Damon wouldn't tease him about them.

Damon sat on the sofa and began to open his mail. Zel sat down across from him and tossed a miniature basketball up in the air.

"Since you're being so generous . . ."

"No," Damon casually replied.

"You don't even know what I'm going to say."

"I have a good idea," Damon said as he opened another piece of mail.

Zel continued to toss the basketball in the air as

Damon looked through his mail. As they sat there in silence, Zel tossed the ball over to Damon, nearly hitting him in the face.

"Watch it, Zel! You almost broke the vase."

Zel held up his hands in defense and laughed. "My bad. Damon, go on a double date with me tonight. You look like you could use a night out with a fine lady."

Damon tossed the ball back over to Zel. "Thanks, but no thanks. I have too much work to do, and it's late."

"You never want to have any fun when I come to visit," Zel mumbled. "You need a woman because you've forgotten how to have fun."

Damon sat his stack of mail on the table and stretched his arms. "Are you my matchmaker now?" he asked.

"Somebody needs to be before you dry up."

Damon stood and laughed. "You're funny, Zel. I'll be in my office working if you need me. Don't trash my house and don't bring any women in here. Help yourself to whatever you want in the kitchen, but clean up after yourself."

"Cool!" Zel replied.

As Damon walked out of the room, Zel yelled, "Can I borrow your Lexus?"

"Hell, no!" Damon yelled back at him.

"I'm telling Nanna!" Zel jokingly yelled back at Damon as he turned on the TV.

Minutes later Damon walked into the living room and tossed Zel the keys to his Infiniti QX56.

"I'm going to let you use my truck, but you'd bet' not get a scratch on it. Do we understand each other?"

Zel smiled as he walked toward the garage.

"Thanks, bro. I'll take real good care of it. I'll be back later."

"Drive carefully," Damon softly responded as he turned and walked back toward his office. Before he could sit down at his desk, he could hear Zel backing out of the driveway with the music thumping loud.

Damon loved his brother, and he finally had to admit to himself that he had a hand in spoiling Zel. Now it was time for Damon to cut Zel loose so he could be a man and support himself in the corporate world. Their grandparents had raised three boys, Damon being the oldest. Their grandfather had been a great role model and instilled in them to be upstanding gentlemen. Damon had done his best to set the same example for his brothers and walk in the footsteps of their grandfather.

Damon, Zel, and their other brother, Anthony, all had different fathers. They were raised by their maternal grandparents, who saw to it that they had a stable, clean home and received a good education with a strong Christian upbringing and plenty of love. If Damon didn't pass anything else on to his future children, he wanted to make sure he showed them how to love.

Chapter Five

Lala returned to the hospital the next morning and found Riley asleep in the chair. Deacon was still asleep as well, so she gently touched Riley's arm.

"Riley, wake up," she whispered. He sat up and wiped his eyes.

"Hey, Lala. I didn't realize you were back. What time is it?"

She hung her jacket in the closet. "It's around eight. Thanks for staying with him last night. I really did need to get some rest."

He stood and yawned. "No problem. It's hard to get any sleep here anyway with the nurses coming in and out."

"I thought you would like watching the nurses up close and personal," she said as she sat down.

"You're right," he replied as he looked at his watch. "I'd better get going. I need to check in at work."

"Was he in much pain last night?"

"He did OK. When it got too bad the nurses gave him more medication to make him comfortable, and it made him sleep most of the time."

Lala looked over at Deacon, who was still sleeping, and then walked closer to Riley.

"Who is she, Riley?" she whispered.

"Who's who?" he asked as he laughed nervously.

She touched his hand gently. "I'm not stupid, Riley. I saw her yesterday."

Riley put his hands up in surrender. "I'm not going to get in the middle of this, Lala. If you want to know something, wait and ask Deacon."

"I knew you wouldn't tell me anyway. You men stick together like Super Glue, and even though Deacon and I haven't been living as a couple for a while now, I still love him, and I believe he still loves me."

Riley folded his arms. "Just talk to him when he's able to hear you and explain things."

She looked over at Deacon. "I'm really glad he's OK, but I really would like to know who that girl is that he's been sleeping around with."

"What difference does it make?" Riley asked. "Just leave it alone, Lala."

"I can't and I won't."   .

Riley stared at her in disbelief. She wasn't going to get any information out of him. Not now and not ever. "Lala, can I talk to Deacon privately?" Riley asked when he glanced over and saw that Deacon was awake.

She walked over to Deacon, kissed his lips tenderly, and caressed his face. "Are you in any pain, baby?"

"I'm fine," Deacon said after he cleared his throat. "I need to talk to Riley."

"OK, I'll leave you two guys alone. I'm going downstairs to grab a cup of coffee, but I'll be back," she replied before walking out the door.

Riley walked over to Deacon's bed. "How are you feeling?"

Deacon tried to sit up in the bed, but Riley stopped him.

"Hold on, Deek. Let me raise the bed up for you. Let me know if it hurts and I'll stop." Deacon grunted a little bit and it caused Riley to stop raising the bed.

"Maybe you should stay where you are before you bust something."

"I don't care. I want to sit up," Deacon replied and he continued to struggle through his pain. Riley pushed the button on the bed to elevate it, and adjusted the pillows behind Deacon's back.

"Thanks, partner. That's much better."

"Can I get you anything? Some water, shot of vodka?" Riley teased.

Deacon laughed and then grimaced in pain. "No, I'm cool. Have you seen Nichole? Has she been here?"

Riley sat back down and sighed. "Not today. Lala saw her here. She tried to ask me about her a few minutes ago, but I wouldn't tell her anything. I told her if she wanted to know, she needed to ask you."

"I was afraid something like this was going to happen," Deacon whispered as he looked up at the ceiling. "What am I going to do, Riley? I was planning on telling Nichole about Lala when she got back from Texas. You know that Lala and I have been separated for a long time."

Riley could hear the dryness in Deacon's voice. He poured him a cup of water and put a straw in it so it was easier for him to drink. Holding the cup in front of his friend, he said, "But you weren't divorced, dude, and that makes you a married man. You really should've told her. Now Nichole's pissed at me because I knew about it and didn't tell her, and Lala's cornering me asking all sorts of questions. Y'all need to leave me out of this."

Deacon took another sip of water. "I don't know why Lala's tripping. She knows we haven't lived as husband and wife for a long time."

"None of that matters now. She almost lost you, and correct me if I'm wrong, but if anything does happen to you, she's gets everything, right?"

"Yeah," Deacon solemnly replied, "but she should know it's over."

A nurse walked in and greeted Deacon and Riley. She checked Deacon's blood pressure, his IV bag, and his incision. After changing the bandage, she told him the surgeon would be in soon and so would breakfast. After she left the room, they continued their conversation.

Riley pulled some of the cards off the many flowers that had been delivered to Deacon's room and started reading them.

"Deek, you have that huge insurance policy and Lala knows it. Our line of work is high risk, and she's not going to let you leave her out in the cold. She's going to stick with you like white on rice."

Deacon laughed. "Are you saying you think Lala is hoping I die before I divorce her?"

"No, I'm saying she might not sign any divorce papers too quickly, especially after she got a good look at Nichole at the hospital. And, bro, you have to admit, Nichole is hot, but Lala's no skank either. Women hate when their man leaves them for a beautiful woman."

Deacon motioned for Riley to pass him the cup of water once again. "Lala needs to just give it up."

"Lala has the upper hand on Nichole right now," Riley said as he held the cup for Deacon. "And with Nichole out of the picture, she might try to wiggle her way back in."

Deacon frowned when a pain hit him. A nurse walked in and sat his breakfast tray in front of him. It was Jell-O, oatmeal, and milk. Once she was gone, Deacon looked at the tray and shook his head.

"This is breakfast?" he asked.

Riley walked over and picked up the bowl of oatmeal. "Are you going to eat this?"

"Nah, you can have it," Deacon replied as he ate a spoonful of Jell-O. "Lala has to understand that we're cool and all, and I appreciate her being here for me, but I'm not in love with her anymore."

"It didn't look dead to me when she kissed you a minute ago," Riley pointed out as he watched Deacon eat.

"That was only because I got shot. Any other time, I wouldn't hear from Lala. I'm in love with Nichole and have been for some time now."

"That may be the case, but I think this incident made Lala look at your marriage in a different light. I have a feeling she's going to be sticking closer to you from here on out. Nichole won't be able to get within ten feet of you," he joked as he watched Deacon maneuver with his breakfast. "Do you need any help with that?"

"I got it," Deacon replied as he used his good arm to feed himself. "Riley, I need to talk to Nichole. I have to make her understand my circumstances."

"I think you need to talk to Lala first so things won't get out of hand."

"I never hid my relationship with Nichole from Lala. It just appears that way."

"I know you didn't, Deacon, but you hid the most important information from what you say is the most important person."

Riley sat down the oatmeal and pulled out his cell phone. He dialed Nichole's number. "You're going to get me cussed out for this," he said.

"Thanks, Riley," he replied as he sat his spoon on the tray and took the telephone out of Riley's hand.

Riley went back to eating Deacon's oatmeal. "I think you're wasting your time calling Nichole, but knock yourself out. I doubt she answers, especially since she's with that guy."

"What guy?" he asked curiously as he hung up the telephone.

"I'm working on it. I don't know the nature of their relationship, but I found out a little information on him. He showed up at the hospital with her."

Deacon was angry and jealous that Nichole had been seen with another man. "Who is he?"

Riley sat back in his chair and laughed. "I ran his license plates. His name is Damon Kilpatrick and he's a coach for the Eagles."

"Where did he come from?" Deacon asked, clearly agitated.

Riley put a toothpick in his mouth and answered. "I don't know. I can check him out further if you want. They must've known each other for a while, because he got in my face and told me not to ever come back to Nichole's house."

"Her house? When was he at her house?"

"I'm sorry to have to tell you, Deacon, but I went by Nichole's house yesterday to check on her. Nichole got upset when I told her she needed to come see you, and as she was throwing me out of her house, he showed up and got in my face," Riley revealed.

Deacon lay there in deep thought. He was confused. Nichole had never mentioned anyone named Damon Kilpatrick before, so where did he come from, and what was he doing with *his woman*?

"I guess she got one over on you, like you got Lala over on her," Riley joked.

"That's not funny, Riley. Nichole and I were doing just fine before this happened. I still can't figure out where this Kilpatrick guy came from."

Riley stood and put the empty bowl back on Deacon's tray. "That was nasty. I need to get out of here and get me some real breakfast since it looks like you're OK."

"I'm not OK, Riley, especially when I find out my baby is hanging out with another man. It doesn't make sense."

Lala walked back into the room and smiled. "Are you guys through talking?" she asked.

Riley looked over at Deacon. "Are we, Deek?"

Deacon coughed and grimaced. "For now. Go get yourself some real breakfast and see if you can find out who the shooter was. We'll finish talking after you get more information for me."

Riley knew exactly what Deacon was talking about, and it wasn't about the shooter, because he already knew the suspect.

"Is there any new information on the shooter?" Lala asked as she refilled his cup of water.

"No, but detectives are working on it," Riley said.

Lala sat on the side of the bed and caressed Deacon's arm. "Sweetheart, you don't remember who shot you?" Without making eye contact with her, he shook his head.

"Nah, I don't remember much of anything. Could you ask the nurse to give me something for the pain? It's starting to get worse."

"I knew you were trying to do too much," she answered as she pushed the call button on his bed.

A male voice boomed over the speaker. "May I help you?" he asked.

"Yes, my husband is in pain. Could you please bring him something to make him more comfortable?"

"We'll be right in," the nurse replied.

"Well, I'll leave you two alone," Riley said as he reached for the door. "I'm going to run home and shower before going into the office. Deacon, I'll be back to check on you later. Lala, until the shooter's caught, we're going to keep an officer at the door for protection. Make sure you keep him posted on your whereabouts."

"I will, Riley. Thank you, and thanks again for keeping Deacon company last night."

Nichole rolled over in bed and stared at her alarm clock. She had already hit the snooze button twice and still couldn't get up. She sighed, picked up the remote, and turned on the TV. The aroma of freshly brewed coffee made its way upstairs from the automatic coffeemaker. Still dragging, she made her way into the bathroom and then into the shower. After showering she sat on the side of the bed in somewhat of a daze. As she sat there she realized she didn't feel like going to work. Without giving it a second thought, she picked up the telephone and called her office to let them know she wouldn't be in. Relieved, she checked the weather report and saw that it was going to be a gorgeous day.

Her ordeal with Deacon had been a nightmare. Now she was ready to wake up and get on with her life. She put on her warm-up suit and laced up her Nike tennis shoes before hurrying downstairs to the kitchen. There she turned on the TV, poured herself a hot cup of coffee, and toasted a couple of bagels. As she spread strawberry cream cheese on a bagel, the news anchor caught her attention. He was giving an updated report on the police shooting Deacon was involved in, although they didn't mention Deacon by name. As she listened to the report she found out that Deacon had shot and possibly wounded his attacker, who still on the loose. The news anchor reported that the officer involved was in serious but stable condition at an undisclosed hospital.

Nichole turned off the TV and pulled Damon's business card out of her purse. After studying it for a second, she picked up the telephone and dialed his number.

"Hello?" Damon answered.

"Good morning, Damon."

"Good morning, Nichole," he replied with a smile in his voice. "What a nice wake up call."

"Did I wake you? I'm so sorry. I didn't know what time to call, or if I should call at all. I just thought if you weren't too busy today, you might want to play a few holes of golf, but if you're busy, I understand," she nervously babbled.

He chuckled. "Slow down, Nichole. First of all, you didn't wake me up. Secondly, today I'm only as busy as I let myself be, and thirdly, I'd love to beat you at golf."

Nichole giggled. "I'm sorry. I bet I sounded like a babbling idiot, didn't I?"

"You could never sound like an idiot. How soon do you want to hit the golf course?"

"How quickly can you get dressed?"

Damon checked his watch. "I'll pick you up in an hour."

"No, I'll pick you up. That way you won't have to rush. I have some errands to run anyway," she replied.

Excited to have another opportunity to spend some time with Nichole, he quickly agreed.

"In that case, let me give you my address."

Damon proceeded to give Nichole his address. She wrote it down and tucked it inside her purse before hanging up the telephone.

Chapter Six

Nichole finished her errands and arrived at Damon's house right on time. She made her way to the front door and rang the doorbell. The door swung open and Zel looked her up and down.

"Good God almighty! I hope you're here to see me," he yelled.

Nichole backed up and pulled the address she wrote down out of her purse. She studied it and asked, "Is this Damon Kilpatrick's house?"

Zel licked his lips and smiled. "Who wants to know?"

"Never mind," Nichole said as she backed away. "I must have the wrong address. I'm sorry I bothered you."

"Don't leave!" Zel yelled. "We haven't been properly introduced!"

Nichole hurried to her car. Just as she was about to get inside, she heard a familiar voice.

"Nichole! Wait!"

She turned and saw Damon running out of the house in his bare feet. He yelled out in pain and then cursed as he stepped on a rock. Nichole had to stifle her laughter as she watched him hop up and down on one foot.

"Damon, are you OK?" she asked as she made her way over to him.

He gritted his teeth and said, "I will be as soon as I get my hands around that fool's neck."

"I thought I was at the wrong house."

"I'm sorry about that, and please excuse my idiot brother for being so rude."

She pointed to Zel and giggled. "Oh, that was your brother?"

He limped back to the house. "Unfortunately it is. Come in and have a seat. I'll be ready as soon as I put on my shoes."

"Are you sure you're OK, Damon? I don't want you using your foot as an excuse for losing to me at golf."

"I said I was fine," he said with a smirk on his face as he turned to look at her.

Nichole giggled as she followed him into the house. When they walked inside, Zel was standing in the foyer grinning. He put his hands up defensively because he already knew he was in trouble

"I'm sorry, bro. I didn't know she was here to see you."

Damon frowned as he closed the door. "You knew she wasn't here to see you. Stop acting so asinine. Nichole, this is my brother, Zel. Zel, this is Nichole Adams."

"Nichole. That's a beautiful name," he responded as he took her hand and kissed the back of it.

Damon took a step toward him. "Zel!"

Zel backed away from Damon playfully. "OK, bro. You don't have to get hostile."

"I want you to apologize to her . . . now!" Damon ordered.

Zel smiled and took a step back because he thought Damon was going to take a swing at him.

"OK, OK. Look, Nichole, I'm sorry for scaring you." After looking her body up and down, he continued. "You're just so fine, and I haven't seen a beautiful woman at my brother's door in such a long time that I was caught off guard."

Openly frustrated with Zel's behavior, Damon moved toward him, causing him to back up a few more steps.

"Hold up, bro. I'm not through apologizing to Nichole."

Damon folded his arms and stared at Zel, letting him know his patience was wearing thin. He made it obvious to Zel that he was not amused by his behavior.

"Nichole, if I said or did anything to offend you, I apologize."

Nichole blushed. "Apology accepted," she said.

Zel cautiously approached Nichole, and without taking his eyes off Damon, he took her hand again. "I'm also sorry that you're here to see my big brother and not me, because if you were here to see me, I would—"

Damon didn't let Zel finish his sentence. He immediately chased him down the hallway and out of sight. Nichole couldn't help but laugh as she heard Zel pleading for mercy. She couldn't hear what Damon was saying to Zel, but she could tell he was reprimanding him for his antics. When he returned he saw that Nichole was clearly amused by what had just taken place.

"What are you laughing at?" he asked as he sat down and laced up his shoes.

She giggled again. "You guys are typical brothers."

He opened the hall closet and pulled out his golf clubs. "Nichole, he drives me crazy. If he wasn't my brother, I'd kill him."

"You love him. Admit it."

As he checked to make sure all his golf clubs were accounted for, he looked at her and responded. "I do, and that saves his life every time."

"Well, I think it's sweet."

"You're delusional right now," Damon said as he opened the front door. "But once you get to know Zel, you'll think differently."

"He's young, Damon," she pointed out as she opened her hatch.

"It's time for him to grow up. Forget Zel for now. Let's play golf."

The pair climbed inside her truck, and as she turned the ignition, she asked, "Are you ready for your spanking?"

"I'm not going to go out like that, Nichole. Talk is cheap. I'm going to save all my talk for after I beat you."

She smiled as she backed out of his driveway. "Have you had breakfast?" she asked.

"I did. What about you?"

"Of course. I wanted to check with you, because I don't want you to use that as an excuse either."

Damon chuckled. "You aren't joking, are you?"

She glanced over at him. "I told you I was a golf fanatic. I want your best game, too, Damon, so don't hold back."

"I'd never hold back with you, Nichole," he replied with a sensual tone to it. Shivers ran over Nichole's body. She cleared her throat and continued to drive toward the golf course.

It didn't take long for the pair to reach the golf course. After checking in at the clubhouse, they drove over to the first hole where there was a lot to park the truck.

"I'm glad you blew off work today," Damon said.

"I wouldn't have been able to concentrate anyway. I need to breathe in some fresh air and to clear my head."

"Playing golf is a good way to relax, but I don't want you crying once I beat you."

"Oh, it's on, Damon Kilpatrick," she teased.

Just then, blue lights flashed behind them.

"What the hell?" Nichole mumbled as she looked up in her rearview mirror.

Damon turned and looked out the back window. "Were you speeding?" he asked.

"No, I didn't do anything. I don't know why I'm being pulled over."

Nichole pulled the car to the shoulder of the road and put the truck in park. Within seconds a patrol officer approached the driver's side.

"Good morning, ma'am, sir. I need to see your license and registration, please."

Nichole opened her glove compartment to retrieve her registration. She also pulled her license out of her purse and handed both items to the officer.

"Why did you stop me, officer?"

Without answering, he walked back to his vehicle to check her registration. Nichole turned to Damon.

"Am I dreaming? What is going on?" she asked. Damon frowned.

"I don't know, Nichole. Just be cool."

The officer returned to the car and handed Nichole's license and registration back to her.

"Ma'am, I stopped you because you seemed to be weaving in your lane. Have you been drinking this morning?"

Agitated, Nichole frowned.

"No, I have not, and I was not weaving! What's your name, officer?"

"Officer Graham, ma'am."

Nichole grabbed a pencil and jotted down his name and badge number.

"This is ridiculous," she mumbled.

"Take it easy, Nichole," Damon cautioned her.

"This is some bullshit, and you know it, Damon," Nichole mumbled again.

"I know, but don't say or do anything to make this any worse. The sooner he can finish with us, the sooner we can get out of here."

The officer leaned down and said, "I'm going to let you off with a warning this time. Drive carefully and have a nice day."

Nichole pulled away from the curb and sped off to the golf course.

Damon looked over at her and smiled. "You'd better slow down before you get pulled over again."

"These cops around here are a joke. I hate all of them."

"That's a strong word, but I guess you should know since you dated one, huh?" he teased.

"What is that supposed to mean, Damon?" she asked, frowning.

Damon put his hands up in defense. "I was just joking. I didn't mean anything by it. Forget I said anything. It's over. Don't let this ruin our day. OK?"

She sighed. "You're right. I'm sorry for snapping at you. I guess the truth hurts."

"Don't be sorry. I was wrong for saying anything."

She laughed. "OK, we're both sorry. Now with that settled, let's play golf."

Nichole pulled into the golf course parking lot and put the car in park.

"Do you need to warm up or anything?" Damon asked before getting out of the car.

Nichole opened her car door and giggled. "I don't think so, coach. You might know football, but I'm about to teach you a few things about golf."

"Well, bring it on!" he replied as he climbed out of the car. They grabbed their clubs and headed toward the course.

*　*　*

By the time they reached the ninth hole, Nichole had a two-stroke lead over Damon. He watched her as she pulled her nine iron out of her bag and walked over to the ball. Damon coughed as she aimed her club at the ball.

"Are you trying to distract me, Damon?" she asked without looking up from the ball.

"Can you blame me? You said you weren't going to hold back, and I see you meant it. It doesn't help that you sway your hips every time you get ready to drive the ball. You're playing dirty."

She looked over at him and blushed. Seconds later she hit the ball with excessive force, sending it far away onto the green at the next hole.

"Damn, Nichole!"

She picked up her golf tee and jokingly said, "Don't hate."

By the time they were finished, Nichole had put a serious hurting on Damon. As they walked back to the parking lot, Nichole saw the perfect opportunity to tease Damon.

"So are there any other sports you need me to school you in?"

He playfully bumped her, causing her to giggle.

"You don't have to rub it in. I'll have to admit that you surprised me out there. I would love it if you would pair up with me sometime so we could shut up some buddies of mine. I could probably win back some of the money I lost playing them."

"Are you trying to pimp me?" she asked as she playfully bumped him with her elbow.

He laughed. "No, Nichole. It's just that I recognize talent when I see it. Since you're a female, they won't see the threat until it hits them."

Nichole stopped in her tracks at that comment. "Heeey! What are you trying to say?"

He sighed.

"I'm not being sexist, Nichole. You know I'm speaking the truth."

She could see Damon's sincerity and decided to let him off the hook. "I know you're not being sexist, Damon. So when do you want to run this little scam of yours?"

They started walking again.

Damon smiled and then looked over at Nichole. "You tell me. When are you available again to play?"

"How does next Saturday sound? I don't have anything else to do with my time since I don't have a man anymore."

Damon stopped walking again and grabbed Nichole's arm. She could see he had a frown on his face.

"I wish you would stop saying things like that, Nichole. You don't seem like you're the type of woman who needs a man in her life to define who she is."

Nichole folded her arms and stared up at Damon. "I'm not saying that, but when you've been with someone as long as I've been with Deacon, it's hard to adjust to change, especially when it happens so suddenly and gets so ugly."

"That may be true, but when you make statements like that it's perceived differently."

"I get it," Nichole whispered. "Now can we please change the subject?"

"Sure," he replied as he picked up his golf bag and continued walking.

"You know, Damon," Nichole said as she poked Damon's arm, "speaking of betting, I should've made a bet with you."

He chuckled. "I guess today was my lucky day then, because I can't have you turning my pockets inside out."

"I wouldn't take all your cash, Damon. I'd leave you with at least cab fare." She giggled.

Damon loved seeing her laugh, especially after witnessing her tears. He hoped he would never have to see her like that again.

"I see you have jokes."

"I do," she teased. "And there's more where those came from, too."

"Well, in that case, I'll have to make sure I put on my best game face."

Nichole stopped in her tracks when they reached the parking lot. "What the hell? I don't believe this!" she yelled.

Damon looked at Nichole's truck and all four of her tires had been slashed. He set his golf bag on the ground so he could inspect the damage more closely.

"Damn! It looks like someone used an ice pick or screwdriver."

Nichole was at a loss for words. All she could do was shake her head in disbelief. Damon stood and looked around the parking lot.

"Do they have surveillance cameras around here?"

"I don't know," she whispered. "This is crazy. Why would someone slash my tires? It's going to cost me a small fortune to replace them."

Damon looked around the parking lot to see if any other cars were damaged. Unfortunately, Nichole's was the only one.

"Don't worry about it. I'll have them replaced for you."

"You don't have to do that, Damon."

"No, I want to. Besides, I know somebody who can give me a huge discount."

"That's thoughtful of you," Nichole said as she held his hand, "but I can't let you do that."

Damon gave her hand a soft squeeze before releasing it. "I insist. Let me do this for you. You've been through enough already. This just adds insult to injury."

Nichole paced back and forth beside her vehicle. "No, it's my responsibility."

"Nichole, you're being stubborn," he pointed out to her. "I told you I know someone who could give me a discount."

Nichole paced beside her vehicle. "I can't allow you to pay for my tires, but if you keep insisting, I'll compromise with you."

"What do you have in mind?" he asked as he wiped his hands off with a towel.

"How about half?"

"I'm listening," Damon said as he folded his arms.

"I figured if you're determined to help me, we could split the bill."

He scratched his chin and said, "Come on, Nichole. Why is it so hard for you to accept my offer?"

Nichole put her hand up to silence him. "It's half, or nothing."

"You drive a hard bargain, Miss Adams."

She smiled. "That's what I do. I negotiate all day long."

"What exactly do you do, Nichole?"

She pulled out her cell phone and checked the time. "I'm an investment banker."

"I'm scared of you," he joked to try to lighten the mood.

Nichole was proud of her career, and she was good at her job. "Don't be scared, but I am fierce in the boardroom."

"I bet you are."

Nichole looked down at her tires and cursed. Damon reached over and plucked some grass out of her hair.

"OK, you win. I'll compromise with you. Now let's go find security so you can report what happened and see if they have cameras."

Nichole and Damon put their golf clubs in the back of the truck and made their way to the security office.

Chapter Seven

After returning home, Damon finally got an opportunity to sit down and go over the events of the day. While he was happy that his associate could replace Nichole's tires on such short notice, he wasn't happy that the security guard at the golf course didn't seem too concerned with the vandalism. The guard tried to insinuate that Nichole could've driven through a construction zone, causing the damage to the tires. In fact, he wasn't even going to take a report until Damon threatened to take the matter to his superior if he didn't. The tires were definitely slashed, making it no accident.

As Damon sat there in deep thought, Zel walked into the room and stretched out on the sofa. He noticed that his brother seemed to be a thousand miles away.

"Yo, Damon, why are you daydreaming so hard? Could it be that fine woman that picked you up this morning?"

Damon snapped out of his trance and looked over a Zel. He hadn't even realized he'd entered the room. He sat up.

"I'm sorry. What did you say?"

Zel chuckled. "You like her, don't you?"

"Who?"

Zel sat up. "Stop trying to play dumb. You know exactly who I'm talking about. What's her name? Nichole?"

A faint smile appeared on Damon's face before he replied. "Yes, her name is Nichole."

"So what's up?" Zel asked.

"Nothing's up," Damon said as he stood. "We actually just met a few days ago."

"Bullshit! You know you have that woman on your radar."

Damon folded his arms and said, "I'm not going to stand here and lie to you and say that I'm not interested, but for now we're just friends."

"Why are you putting on the brakes?" Zel asked.

"She has some personal issues she's dealing with right now, and I don't want to be an obstacle for her. I'm a patient man, so if friendship is all I can have with Nichole, I'll take it."

Zel stood and faced his brother. "What am I going to do with you? You played that same sorry-ass game with Arnelle and lost. It's time for you to step up your game, bro. You and I both know you're not getting any younger, and I want some nieces and nephews."

Damon frowned and pushed past Zel. "While you're trying so hard to concentrate on me and my love life, you need to concentrate on graduating. "

Zel laughed. "Here we go again. I'm able to multi task, and you are going to be my special project while I'm here. There's more to life than football, bro. You need a woman!"

"Stay out of this, Zel!" Damon yelled as he walked out into the hallway. "I mean it!"

Zel lay back on the sofa. "No can do, bro," he mumbled. "No can do."

Upstairs, Damon pulled off his shirt and shoes and sat down to remove his watch. He glanced over at the telephone and thought about what Zel had said about his love life. He wanted to call Nichole, but instead, he picked up the telephone and called Arnelle.

"Hello?" she answered.

"Hey, Arnelle," he greeted her.

"Damon Kilpatrick, where have you been? I left you a message this morning to call me."

"On my home phone or my cell?" he asked, surprised.

"It was your home telephone," she replied.

"I'm sorry, Arnelle, I haven't had a chance to check my messages yet. What's up?" he asked.

"You tell me. I was calling to get an update on you and Nichole," Arnelle pried.

Damon couldn't help but chuckle. "Aren't you nosey? Look, I'm just getting in from the golf course. How about we talk about this over dinner tomorrow if you're free?"

Arnelle picked up her PDA and checked her schedule. "Hmmm, let me see. My workload is light so I can probably get off a little early. What time do you want to get together?"

"What about Winston?" he asked.

She punched the dinner date into her PDA and then turned it off.

"What about him? You know Winston doesn't mind us being friends."

"That's what you say. I don't know many men who allow their wives to spend time with other men," Damon replied. "Especially a man who used to have strong feelings for his wife."

"Winston trusts me, Damon. He knows I love him and wouldn't do anything to disrespect him."

"I hear you, but I'm a man and I know how we think, so talk to him and make sure it's OK first."

"OK! OK! So what restaurant do you have in mind?" Arnelle asked.

"It doesn't matter to me. You pick the place."

"OK, what about A Taste of Italy? I love that place, and you know how I feel about pasta."

"How could I forget?" he said and laughed.

Arnelle rubbed her stomach. "I'm getting hungry just thinking about it."

"You always did have a healthy appetite," he added. "Look, I'm not going to hold you any longer. I'm getting ready to jump in the shower, so I'll see you tomorrow."

"Sounds good, Damon."

"Tell Winston and the kids I said hello."

"I will," she replied before hanging up.

Arnelle sat there a minute before picking up the telephone to call her sister-in-law, Meridan. Since Meridan was Nichole's best friend, she could probably give Arnelle some detailed information on what was going on between Nichole and Damon.

Arnelle had to admit that she wanted Damon to find a good woman, because he was definitely a good man. His heart had been bruised on more than one occasion, and having a career as an NFL coach didn't help matters. Most of the women he'd dated were not able to deal with the amount of time coaching took away from his personal life, even though it paid very well. For some gold diggers, that would be ideal, because they could do what they wanted while enjoying his lavish lifestyle. Fortunately for Damon, he could spot a gold digger a mile away. He'd experienced his fair share of groupies and gold diggers when he was actually playing in the NFL. Therefore, finding Miss Right was very important to him.

Arnelle waited as the telephone rang for the third time. A winded Meridan finally answered.

"Hello?"

"What are you up to that has you breathless?" Arnelle asked, joking. "Where's Keaton? Did I interrupt something?"

Meridan giggled. "I wish. Anyway, you can get those nasty thoughts out of your mind because Keaton is at the restaurant, and Jeremiah is taking a nap, so I decided to work out on the elliptical a little bit."

"How's my nephew?" Arnelle asked. "I'm sure he's grown some more since the last time I saw him."

Meridan ran her fingers though her hair, which had become moist with perspiration. "Arnelle, the boy eats like his daddy. He's so greedy, and it seems like every time I turn around he's growing out of his clothes."

"I know exactly what you mean. I'm having a hard time keeping up with both Fredrick and MaLeah," Arnelle replied.

Meridan picked up a towel and wiped the sweat from her face. "How're my babies doing?"

"Good when they're not fighting. MaLeah knows how to aggravate Fredrick, and as soon as he pinches or bites her, she wants to scream bloody murder. I tell you, Meridan, it drives us crazy sometimes. They're loving on each other one minute, and the next they're trying to kill each other."

Meridan laughed. "It'll get better. I'm sure you and Keaton had your moments when you were growing up, too."

"Not like these two. They can be vicious."

Meridan laughed again and then said, "Maybe it's the

Navajo coming out in them, and I don't have to remind you how fiery your husband is."

Arnelle closed her eyes briefly.

"Don't remind me. We've created little monsters."

They laughed together for a moment before Arnelle changed the subject.

"Listen, Meridan, I actually called you to see if you've talked to Nichole lately."

She slowed her pace on the elliptical. "Yes, I have. She's going through so much drama right now, and I'm so worried about her. Since Deacon is a police officer, he could make Damon and Nichole's life hell if he wanted to."

"I hope not. I pray this thing blows over with no drama," Arnelle added. "I'm having dinner with Damon tomorrow. I want to make sure he keeps his head on straight. I think he likes Nichole already."

"It doesn't surprise me. Nichole is very outgoing and has a sweet personality."

"I could tell when I met her," Arnelle agreed.

Meridan glanced over at the baby monitor when she heard Jeremiah whine. He was waking up from his nap, which signaled that she would have to cut this conversation short.

"Hey, Arnelle, I hear Jeremiah waking up. I'll give Nichole a call later to find out how things are going and get back with you. Let me know how your dinner with Damon goes."

"Will do, Meridan. Tell my brother I said hello, and kiss Jeremiah for me."

"I will, and you do the same with Winston, MaLeah, and Fredrick."

As soon as Arnelle hung up the telephone she heard a loud thump and then both Fredrick and MaLeah started screaming. She put her hands over her face in disbelief as MaLeah ran into the room covered in ketchup, and Fredrick followed behind her covered in mustard. She jumped up and grabbed both of them by the arm. As she was pulling them toward the laundry room, she yelled at them.

"I'm getting tired of you acting like wild animals! If you don't stop right now, I'm going to pack your suit-cases and send you to live on a deserted island!"

At that moment Winston entered the house and stopped dead in his tracks.

"What the hell is going on in here?"

Arnelle gave him a disgusted look and said, "Your children are at it again."

Winston sat his briefcase down on the kitchen floor and threw his suit jacket over the kitchen chair. He loosened his tie.

"Wait a second, Arnelle. Let them go."

MaLeah saw the fire in her daddy's eyes. "Daddy, Fredrick squirted me first."

Winston put his hand up to silence her.

"I want both of you to sit right here on the floor and not say a word. Daddy's getting ready to have a talk with you."

Fredrick wiped some of the mustard off his shirt and then licked his fingers. MaLeah looked at him and frowned.

"You're nasty, Fredrick."

"You stink!" he yelled at her.

Winston looked over at Arnelle and shook his head.

"Sweetheart, I got this. You can go ahead and get their baths ready for them, because this won't take long."

Arnelle turned to walk out of the room. "Good luck," she said.

Once Arnelle was out of the room, Winston turned his

attention back to his two young children. He sat down in a kitchen chair and leaned in close to them.

"MaLeah, Fredrick, I don't know what's been going on between you two, but whatever it is, it stops right now, today. You're supposed to love each other, not fight each other. You're driving your mother crazy, and when Mommie's unhappy, I'm unhappy." MaLeah poked out her bottom lip.

"Daddy, Freddie started it."

Winston frowned at MaLeah. "I don't care who started it. I'm finishing it. Look at yourselves! You have mustard and ketchup all over yourselves and the kitchen. Now, Fredrick, I've seen you aggravate your sister on more than one occasion, and if I catch you doing it again, I'm going to spank you until you can't sit down. That goes for you too, MaLeah. Do you guys understand what I'm saying?"

"Yes, Daddy," they said in unison.

He stared at them. "Now stand up and give each other a hug," he said, "and then take off those clothes so you can get cleaned up."

Fredrick stuck his tongue out at MaLeah and she squinted her eyes at him.

Winston elevated his voice. "Don't make me say it again."

MaLeah reluctantly leaned over and gave Fredrick a hug. He wrapped his arms around his sister's neck and returned the gesture before quickly releasing her.

Winston stood. "Good, now stand up and take off those clothes so I can put them in the laundry room. MaLeah, your mother is waiting upstairs for you. Fredrick, you come with me. We need to have a man-to-man talk."

MaLeah stripped down to her panties before running upstairs to meet Arnelle. Fredrick received assistance from Winston as he disrobed down to his Spider-Man undergarments. Fredrick was two-years-old, but was very mature and big for his age. He was already potty trained, and he took great pleasure in irritating his sister. Winston took him by the hand and made his way into the downstairs bathroom to bathe his mustard covered son.

As Winston washed and scrubbed the mustard that was now hardening in his son's hair, he talked to his young son about respecting and loving not only his sister and mother, but all women. Fredrick seemed to understand every word his father was saying as he listened attentively. Once he was clean and wrapped in a towel, Winston led him upstairs where he ran into Arnelle with MaLeah. The couple watched as their two children eyed each other. MaLeah smiled up at her father.

"Hi, Daddy," she said.

His heart melted. "Hello, MaLeah. You and Fredrick go get on my bed. I'll be in there with your pajamas in a second."

MaLeah and Fredrick did as they were told, leaving Arnelle and Winston alone to reflect on the last hour.

Winston sighed. "What is wrong with them?" he asked.

"Sibling rivalry, I guess," she replied.

Winston unbuttoned his shirt.

"This early? They're too young to be at each other's throat so much."

Arnelle smiled and started helping Winston unbutton his shirt.

He stared down at her. "You know it drives me crazy when you touch me like that."

She giggled. "I'm only unbuttoning your shirt, baby."

"With seriousness, Arnelle, all you have to do is walk into the room. It doesn't take much for you to turn me on."

Arnelle helped him out of his shirt and kissed his cheek. "You're so sweet."

He patted her lovingly on her backside. "Don't start anything you can't finish."

"Oh I can finish it, just not right now. Our children are waiting on us."

Winston looked toward the bedroom and sighed. "You're right."

Arnelle kissed him on the lips. "Winston, Damon called today and invited me to dinner tomorrow evening so he could talk to me about something. Do you mind?"

Winston frowned. Arnelle was the love of his life. She had dated Damon a few years ago; however, he still didn't like her spending a lot of time with him.

"What's going on? Why does he need to talk to you?"

"I don't know. I think he wants to talk to me about Meridan's friend, Nichole. I think he likes her."

"Arnelle, I don't have to tell you not to get involved in their business."

She smiled and hugged Winston's waist. "I'm not, baby. Damon said he just wanted to talk to me. You're not still jealous of him, are you?"

Winston held her close to his heart. "He was in love with you. I just don't want you hanging out with him so much."

"You trust me, don't you?"

"Of course I trust you, but I'm a man and I'll never be comfortable with my woman spending time with someone she used to date."

"Winston, you know I was never in love with Damon."

He kissed her on the forehead and said, "I know, but he was in love with you, so that makes him a hazard."

Arnelle put her hands on her hips. "So are you saying you don't want me to have dinner with him?"

"No, I'm saying I don't want you spending a lot of time with him. Listen, baby, I know I still have some insecurity issues when it comes to you, but we've been through so much. My stubbornness almost caused me to lose you, remember?"

Arnelle hugged his waist again and smiled.

"You're still stubborn, but you never have to worry about losing me to any man. You know my heart belongs only to you."

"I feel that in my heart, Arnelle, but my male mind causes me to have a lot of insecurities. You're a strikingly beautiful woman and men notice you. While it makes me proud, I can't help but feel a little jealous at the same time. I know Damon's a co-worker and a friend, so I'm going to try to chill and work on my issues, so feel free to have dinner with Damon, but if he steps out of line, make sure you let me know."

"You have nothing to worry about, sweetheart. Damon is a gentleman and he respects you, me, and our marriage."

He cupped her face, kissed her softly on the lips, and whispered in her ear. "He'd better. Now, let me go put some clothes on your children. We'll be right down for dinner."

"I'll have everything ready," Arnelle said as she descended the stairs.

Chapter Eight

Three weeks passed and Deacon couldn't believe that Nichole never came to visit him and wouldn't take his calls. He was on medical leave and it left him with nothing but time to simmer in his anger. Deacon threw his glass against the wall, breaking it into hundreds of pieces. After sitting in the darkness drinking cognac for over an hour, he couldn't take it any longer. He spent the next hour dialing Nichole's number, but each time he only got her voicemail. When he got out of the chair, he grimaced at the tenderness around his wound. He picked up the bottle of cognac and turned it up, finishing off the brown liquid.

"If this is how you want to play, Nichole, fine."

Drunk, heartbroken, and angry, he grabbed his keys off the table and headed out the door. It took Deacon all of twenty minutes to reach Nichole's house. When he pulled his car into the driveway, he barely took time to put it in park before he swung open the door, marched up to her front door, and started beating on the door with his fists. Inside, Nichole was startled out of her sleep at the sound of loud pounding on her door. She pulled her .38-caliber handgun out of her nightstand and nervously made her way downstairs. Once there, she discreetly looked out the window and found Deacon standing there clearly inebriated and angry.

"Nichole! Open the goddamn door!"

"Go away, Deacon!" she yelled back at him.

"I'm not going anywhere until you talk to me!" Deacon continued to pound and kick on the door.

"Please, Deacon, just go! Don't make me call the police on you!"

Deacon was now kicking the door and screaming at her. "Open the door, Nichole! All I want to do is talk to you!"

Nichole backed way from the door and picked up the telephone. Since Deacon was drunk, she had no idea what he would do if he was able to break down her door, so she decided to dial 911 to be on the safe side.

"Nine-one-one emergency. How may I help you?" the operator asked.

Nichole gripped the telephone as Deacon continued to beat on the door.

"My name is Nichole Adams, and my ex-boyfriend, who's a police officer, is trying to break into my house."

"What is your ex-boyfriend's name, ma'am?" the operator asked.

"Officer Deacon Miles," she replied. "He's not well, and I think he's drunk. He was recently shot on the job, and I don't believe he's thinking clearly.

"Do you know if he's armed, Miss Adams?" the operator asked.

Nichole sighed. "I'm sorry, I don't know. Could you send someone quickly? He's not happy over the fact that I broke up with him, and he sounds like he's about to kick down my door. I have a gun and I might have to shoot him if he gets inside."

"Just stay calm, ma'am, but if he gets in and you feel threatened, by all means defend yourself. We have officers on they way."

Nichole closed her eyes and prayed that the police officers would get there before Deacon kicked down her door. The last thing she wanted to do was kill him. She'd never get over taking his life, but she would if she had to. Nichole could hear the operator recite the fact that the suspect was a police officer and possibly armed. Seconds later she heard sirens in the background and relief swept over her.

"They're coming. Thank God."

"Ma'am, just stay on the line with me until the officers get there," the operator suggested.

Nichole could still hear Deacon yelling her name on the other side of the door. "Deacon, I've called the police! Go home!"

"You're not giving me a chance, Nichole! I love you, and if I can't have you, nobody will!" Deacon yelled back at her.

Nichole felt the hair stand up on her arms. Deacon had never threatened her before, but she never expected their relationship to get to this point either. She gripped the gun tighter and realized it had to be the alcohol in his system that was making him act so crazy. Her heart beat wildly in her chest. She was sweating and her mind was racing at what felt like a thousand miles an hour. The 911 operator interrupted her thoughts.

"Miss Adams, officers are on the scene now, but don't open the door until they give you the order."

Tears fell from Nichole's eyes as she sat the handgun down on a nearby table. "I won't. Thank you."

Nichole could hear several voices at her door. When she peeped out the window she saw that two officers had Deacon in handcuffs and were leading him away from the door. She opened the door when she saw a third officer walking toward her.

"Operator, it looks like they have him in custody and an officer is ready to talk to me. Thanks for all your help."

"You're welcome, Miss Adams. Let me speak to the officer before you hang up," the operator instructed her.

Nichole stepped out on the porch, handed the telephone to the officer, and leaned against the doorframe. As she stood there she noticed a few of her neighbors out on their lawns. She was so embarrassed. She knew that her elderly neighbor, Mrs. Adele, would be over asking questions any minute.

The officer smiled at Nichole and spoke into the telephone. When he was finished talking, he handed the telephone back to Nichole.

"Good evening, ma'am. I'm Officer Hobbs," he said.

"Good evening, Officer Hobbs," Nichole replied.

He glanced over at the table and noticed the handgun. "Do you have a permit for your firearm?"

"Yes. I'll get it for you," Nichole said as she picked up her purse and pulled out her permit. "Would you like to sit down?" she asked as she handed the permit to the officer.

"No, I'm fine," he replied as he studied the permit. "Everything looks to be in order here," Officer Hobbs said as he handed the permit back to her.

Nichole sighed as she sat down on the sofa and put the permit back inside her purse. The officer looked at Nichole and could tell she was shaken from the events of the evening.

"Miss Adams, it's obvious that you're upset, but I need to get a statement from you about what happened here tonight."

Nichole took a deep breath.

"I'm not sure what really happened, officer. All I know is that I was asleep, and I woke up when I heard Deacon beating on my door. He was cussing and screaming at me to open the door. You see, I recently broke up with him, and he won't accept the fact that it's over. I've never seen him like this, officer."

"I understand, Miss Adams," the officer said after he had written down a few notes. "Hopefully Officer Miles realizes his mistake and you won't have a problem out of him again. It's always difficult for us to answer calls when one of our own is involved."

Nichole looked up at the officer with tears in her eyes. "I don't want to press charges against him. I just want him to leave me alone and move on with his life."

The officer smiled. "Unfortunately some people have a hard time moving on with their lives when love goes bad, Miss Adams. If you're concerned about any future misbehavior by Officer Miles, you might want to take out an Order of Protection against him and maybe he'll get the message."

"I don't know about that," Nichole said, shaking her head. "I don't want to make things any worse between us than they already are. I just hope he got the message tonight."

"So do I, Miss Adams. Unfortunately, if you don't want to press charges for trespassing, we still have to charge him with disorderly conduct and public intoxication."

"I just want him gone, and I don't want him back over here."

The officer turned to walk out of the room, but stopped

to repeat his advice. "If that's the case, then it might be in your best interest to get the Order of Protection."

Nichole walked the officer to the door. "I'll think about it. Thanks for all your help. Oh, officer, what about his car? I don't want him coming back over here to get it."

"We'll make sure it's removed from the premises shortly."

"Thanks again," Nichole replied as she watched the officer walk down the sidewalk to his squad car. She closed her door and watched from the window as the officers backed out of her driveway and pulled away with Deacon in the backseat. It was then that Nichole noticed her neighbors returning to the confines of their homes. Nichole turned to set the alarm on her house, and her telephone rang, startling her.

"Hello," she answered.

"Nichole? Are you OK?"

Nichole sighed when she heard the voice. "Yes, Mrs. Adele, I'm fine."

"I heard a lot of noise and yelling coming from your house. What was going on?"

Nichole definitely didn't want Mrs. Adele spreading her business all over the neighborhood.

"It's OK, Mrs. Adele. The police took care of things."

"But what was all that noise?" Mrs. Adele asked as she pushed for details.

Nichole wasn't in the mood, so she told her nosey neighbor the least amount of information possible.

"A drunk man was trying to break into my house. He was confused and at the wrong house. There shouldn't be any more disturbances tonight, so you can go back to bed."

"Are you sure you're OK, Nichole? Maybe you should call Officer Miles to come see about things."

"No, Mrs. Adele, I'm fine, really. Thanks for checking on me. It's late and I'm just going to go back to sleep. Good night."

"Good night, Nichole."

Nichole hung up the telephone, knowing Mrs. Adele would have those few details spread all over the neighborhood by sunrise. Deacon had made her the topic of neighborhood gossip in just one night, and it angered her.

Suddenly, as if the wind had been knocked out of her body, she felt like she was hyperventilating or having an anxiety attack. It took several minutes, but eventually she got her breathing back to normal. This thing with Deacon was starting to affect her health. She couldn't let him get the best of her. Maybe it was time for her to take a stand with Deacon, or maybe she should just leave town for a while until things cooled down. Whatever she decided to do, she needed to do it quickly. Deep down inside, Nichole still loved Deacon, but his lies couldn't be ignored, and she could never forgive him for his stunt tonight.

Down at the police station, Deacon held his head in his hands as he waited to be booked on the charges against him. His head was spinning from all the alcohol in his system, and he felt sick. Riley walked into the room and sat down across from him. Deacon didn't even look up when Riley spoke.

"Deacon, what did you do?"

"I messed up, Riley. She'll never talk to me or give me a chance now," Deacon mumbled.

Riley reached over and put his hand on Deacon's shoulder. He actually felt bad for his friend. "Why didn't you call me? You know I would've been there for you."

Deacon finally looked up at Riley. "I don't know, man.

I started drinking that cognac. Nichole wouldn't answer her phone, so I just snapped."

"You didn't hurt her, did you?" Riley asked.

"Nah, but I'm sure I scared her. I was beating on her door trying to get her to open up."

"Did she?" Riley asked.

"No. She called the boys in blue on me and here I sit," Deacon revealed.

"Listen, Deacon, maybe you should just forget about Nichole. It's not like she's trying to hear anything you have to say right now. Maybe after a few months have passed she'll be a little more receptive to talking with you."

Deacon stared at Riley in silence for a moment. "You've lost your damn mind. Nichole is the best thing that has ever happened to me, and I'm not going to just let her walk out of my life. I just have to get her to understand that my marriage to Lala has been over for a long time. Then she'll forgive me."

"Good luck with all of that," Riley said as he stood to leave. "Are you going to need me to bail you out or anything? Do you know if Nichole is pressing charges against you?"

"I don't know. They said something about charging me with trespassing and public intoxication."

Riley started laughing. "I'll go out there to see what's going on, and from now on, leave the liquor alone because you can't handle it."

"Kiss my ass, Riley!"

Riley laughed again. "The truth hurts, my brotha. Get yourself together. I'll be back in a second."

Once Riley was gone, Deacon's thoughts went back to Nichole and how much he loved her. He'd made a fool of himself today, but he vowed if he got out of the jam he was in now, he would try to prove his love to her, but using a different approach.

In the booking room, Riley approached Deacon's arresting officer. He flashed his badge.

"Officer Hobbs, I'm Officer Riley. I understand you're the one who brought Officer Miles in on a trespassing charge. Could I have a word with you in private?"

"Sure," Officer Hobbs said as he walked away from the booking desk. Once they were in a more private part of the hallway, he asked, "What can I do for you, Riley?"

"You would be doing me a big favor if you gave Deacon a break. He's recovering from a near death experience. He got shot in the line of duty, and he's having a hard time adjusting to his recent breakup with his girl."

Officer Hobbs put his hands up in defense.

"I appreciate your concern for Officer Miles, but as you know, we as police officers are not above the law. Now I hate that Officer Miles is having some difficulties, but you didn't see him like I saw him. He was out of control, and the young woman was scared and very upset."

"Did she press charges against him?" Riley asked.

"No, she didn't want to press charges, but that doesn't keep him from being charged with trespassing, disorderly conduct, and public intoxication. The situation could've turned out badly, not only for the young lady, but for Officer Miles as well. He needs help, and while you're out here trying to get me to drop the charges, you should be trying to talk some sense into your friend so he won't mess up his career and his life."

"You would be doing me a personal favor if you could help him out this one time," Riley pleaded with Officer Hobbs. "I promise I'll get his head straightened out so he can get off medical leave and back on the job right away."

Officer Hobbs stared at Riley for a few seconds, then spoke. "I guess since Miss Adams doesn't want to press charges, I can let him off with a warning, but you'd better get his ass straight, because next time I won't be so understanding."

Riley patted Hobbs on the shoulder. "You're a good man, Hobbs. I owe you."

Hobbs walked down the hallway and said, "You don't owe me. Just get him out of here, and I don't want to see him on the other side of the law again."

"I'll make sure of it," Riley replied as he walked down the hallway to get Deacon.

Chapter Nine

Arnelle walked into Venice's office and sat down in a chair.

"Venice, you're not going to believe what Damon has gotten himself into."

Venice stopped typing on her computer to look up at her business partner and best friend.

"What is Damon involved in that has you so worked up today?"

"Well, I think he's dating Meridan's best friend, Nichole, and she has some serious drama going on with her ex-boyfriend, who just so happens to be a police officer."

"What kind of drama?" Venice asked as she leaned back in her chair.

"Nichole found out her ex was married the whole time they were dating," Arnelle revealed as she crossed her legs. "Nichole broke up with him, but he keeps pressuring her to give him another chance. That's the reason I'm so worried about Damon being a third wheel."

Venice stood and removed a file from a nearby file cabinet. "I'm sure Damon can handle himself."

"I hope you're right."

"Sounds like the making of a TV movie full of sex and violence," Venice commented.

"Don't it? Meridan told me that Nichole is really hurt from all the lies, and that there's no way she's going to hook back up with him."

"So, how does Damon play into all of this?" Venice asked. "Has he fallen for Nichole or something?"

"I'm not sure, but it wouldn't surprise me. They met for the first time at Jeremiah's party. Damon said they're just friends, but you know if Deacon's not ready to let go of Nichole, there could be trouble."

Venice sat there quietly for a few seconds in deep thought.

"I think you're worried for no reason, Arnelle. I don't think Damon is going to fall for a woman he's only known for a few weeks."

Arnelle ran her fingers through her long, wavy hair and sighed. "Are we talking about the same Damon Kilpatrick? Remember how he was with me?"

Venice smiled. "I almost forgot. He was a little crazy about you."

With a smirk on her face, Arnelle stood and walked toward the door. "Damon was very understanding when he found out I didn't feel the same way about him, and that I was in love with Winston."

"Yeah, you and Winston were definitely the poster kids for love," Venice said sarcastically. "Arnelle, was I the only person around at the time? You and Winston were at each other's throats all the time. Craig and I spent half our time trying to keep you two from killing each other. I don't know how in the world you guys ended up married."

Arnelle couldn't help but laugh herself. "You enjoy reminiscing about my drama, don't you?"

"You know I do," Venice said as she looked up from her computer. "It's better than reminiscing about my own."

"Like I said, that's ancient history. Winston finally came to his senses and married me because he realized he couldn't live without me. He knew I was the only woman who could handle his temper, and he's the only man who can handle mine."

Venice laughed loudly this time. "That's the truth, because you would've eaten poor Damon alive with that temper of yours."

Arnelle looked over at Venice and laughed.

Venice typed a few words on her keyboard and giggled. "I knew there was no way Skeeter, a.k.a. Winston was going to let you date Damon for too long," Venice said. "I was a little worried he might try and do something stupid like fight Damon. He was so whipped."

"Come on, you're exaggerating now," Arnelle replied.

"You know I know the truth, and I'm not afraid to use it," Venice joked. "Listen, don't worry about Damon. I'm sure he knows what he's doing in regard to Nichole."

Arnelle stepped out into the hallway and said, "I hope you're right."

Venice pulled out a folder from her desk drawer and added it to the stack on her desk. "I know I'm right, and deep down you know I'm right. Damon's a big boy and can take care of himself. Just stay out of it."

Arnelle stepped back into Venice's office. "Damon's a good man, Venice, and I don't want to see him get in the crossfire and get hurt."

"You've been warned. Remember when you tried to get into Keaton's business when he was dating Meridan? Winston tried to tell you to stay of that, but nooooo. You just had to stick your nose in his business."

Arnelle waved off Venice. "Winston is not the boss of

me. He didn't know Keaton like I did. Keaton was a playa, and I was trying to save Meridan some heartache."

Venice put her hands on her face and acted like she was in shock.

"Oh my God, and look what happened? Keaton and Meridan are happily married with a beautiful son all without your help. Stop feeling like you always have to save everyone, Arnelle, and let nature take its course," Venice advised her.

"It's hard, Venice. I really do care about Damon. He works hard and has a hard time maintaining a social life. In my opinion he needs to wait and let this drama with Nichole and her ex blow over before he gets involved with her in any way."

Venice pulled another folder out of her desk and typed a few words on her keyboard.

"That's not your call, Arnelle," Venice said without making eye contact with her friend. "I know you care about Damon, but I'm going to advise you one last time not to get involved with his affairs. I'm sure he can work through this with Nichole if he wants to."

"I hope you're right, Venice."

Just at that moment Venice's husband, Craig, walked through the door, pushing their twins in a stroller. Venice looked at her watch and then jumped out of her chair. "Hey, baby! Oh my God! I forgot the twins have a doctor's appointment."

Arnelle kissed the twins on the cheek. "I'm sorry, Venice. I've been running my mouth so long about Damon that I forgot about it too. Get out of here."

Venice walked over and kissed Craig on the lips. "Hey, baby."

"Hey, sweetheart. We're good on time. Don't stress." Craig then looked at Arnelle and smiled mischievously. "Hello, witch doctor."

Arnelle pointed her finger at him playfully. "Don't start with me, Craig Bennett."

He chuckled as Arnelle gave the kids another kiss. Arnelle was married to Craig's best friend, Winston Carter III, Attorney at Law.

"What? You are a witch doctor, aren't you?"

Arnelle poked Craig in the chest with her finger. "Be quiet, Craig. Don't you have a doctor's appointment to go to?"

Craig laughed as Arnelle walked past him and out into the hallway. He always called her that nickname after finding out she was half Navajo.

Venice gave her children a kiss and chastised her husband. "Stop giving Arnelle a hard time, Bennett."

"I'm not giving her a hard time, babe. Arnelle knows I'm just kidding around with her. How's Skeeter and the kids?" he asked Arnelle, stopping her in the hallway.

Arnelle squinted her eyes at Craig.

"He's *your* best friend, so you should know since you talk to him every day."

"Ah, Arnelle, don't be like that," Craig said while opening his arms. "Come give me a hug before I leave."

"I'm not hugging you. You know you're wrong for calling me a witch doctor."

"I don't get a hug?" he asked.

"No!" she replied.

Craig laughed. "Aight, I'm sorry. Give me a hug."

"You're so stupid sometimes, Craig," she replied before giving him a hug.

"Now I can make it through the day. Thanks, witch doctor."

Arnelle punched Craig in the arm playfully. "Goodbye!" she said.

Venice grabbed her purse. "Ignore him, Arnelle. Let's

go, Bennett, before we're late. Arnelle, call me if you need me. I'll be back shortly."

"Take your time, sis," Arnelle said as she walked down the hallway.

Damon was running late to his early dinner with Arnelle. It had to be postponed from a previous date because the kids had a stomach virus. By the time he arrived at the table, Arnelle had already eaten two hot, buttered rolls and a bowl of minestrone soup. Damon kissed her on the cheek before he sat down across from her.

"Arnelle, I can't believe you started without me. Are you that hungry?" Arnelle wiped her mouth with her napkin before responding.

"I'm sorry, Damon. When I walked in and smelled that garlic, I couldn't help myself. I tried to wait on you, but I couldn't."

"You're forgiven," he replied as he picked up the menu and began to scan it. "How are the kids?"

"Much better and I'm sorry I had to cancel on you the other week."

He looked up at her and smiled. "Family first, right?"

"Right," she replied with a smile.

"So what are you going to order?"

"Oh, Damon, they have a stuffed pasta misto with shrimp that I have to try. You know I love my seafood."

He glanced up at her from his menu.

"I know. I think I'm going to try their grilled chicken spiedini."

Arnelle looked on the menu and read aloud what was included in Damon's entrée.

"Skewered chicken marinated in Italian herbs with extra-virgin olive oil. Served with Tuscan potatoes and grilled vegetables. That sounds delicious, too. I might try that next time. Today I'm having my seafood."

"Welcome to A Taste of Italy," the waitress said as she approached the table. "Are you two ready to place your orders?"

Arnelle pointed over to Damon and smiled.

"He'll order for me since he's buying."

Damon gave her a surprised look and laughed.

"I beg your pardon?"

They laughed together, leaving the waitress feeling a little awkward. Damon apologized for confusing the waitress and then gave her both of their orders. Before the waitress left the table she removed Arnelle's empty soup bowl and told them she would be right back with more rolls and their entrees.

"How are things at the sports clinic?" Damon asked after taking a sip of water.

"Everything's fine, but we're not here to talk about the clinic. I've been dying to find out what's been going on between you and Nichole. What did you want to talk about?"

Damon leaned back in his chair and put his napkin in his lap.

"Things have been a little crazy since I started seeing her."

Arnelle leaned forward in her chair. "So you are officially dating her?" she whispered.

"Not really. I mean, we sort of went out if you want to count golf, and I've been over to her house, and she's been over to mine."

"Well? Are you saying you want to date her?" Arnelle asked.

Damon picked up his glass of water and took another sip to moisten his suddenly dry throat.

"She is a beautiful woman, but you know me. I have to have a woman with substance and intelligence as well. Nichole seems to have the complete package, and it doesn't hurt that she plays golf like Tiger Woods. She's athletic, strong, and she loves football. What more could I ask for?"

Arnelle knocked on the table with her fist.

"Hello? You could ask for a woman that doesn't have a crazy police officer as an ex-boyfriend. Why would you want to get mixed up in drama like that?"

Damon paused before responding because he noticed the waitress approaching their table with a basket of hot, buttered rolls and two glasses of iced tea. She set the items on the table.

"Your order will be right out," she said.

"Thank you," Damon and Arnelle replied in unison.

Once the waitress was gone, Damon took a sip of tea and smiled. "Delicious! Oh, and just for the record, I'm not mixed up in anything. Right now I'm just a shoulder for her to lean on."

"Call it what you want, Damon."

He sat his glass of tea down and said, "Don't worry about me. I can handle the situation. Besides, I think you're overreacting just a little bit."

Arnelle reached across the table and gave Damon's hand a friendly squeeze.

"I'm just trying to look out for you. I don't want you to get hurt." Damon laughed.

"Stop acting like I'm a little boy who needs his mother to walk him to school. I'm a grown ass man, Arnelle, and cop or no cop, I know what I'm doing. I appreciate your concern, and I promise you if the situation with Nichole and her ex gets crazy, I'll back off. OK?"

She smiled. "Since you put it that way, OK."

The waitress arrived at the table with their entrees a little while later. Damon rubbed his hands together.

"I'm starving and this looks delicious," he said.

Arnelle's eyes widened as her plate was placed before her.

"You got that right. Everything looks so good."

"Will there be anything else at this time?" the waitress asked.

Arnelle looked around the table before replying. "Not at this time. Thank you."

"I'll be back to check on you shortly. Enjoy your dinner."

After the waitress left, Damon blessed the food and they dug in.

Across town, Nichole cautiously entered the parking garage after a long day at work. She quickly activated her car alarm and climbed into her truck, locking the door behind her. She couldn't help but worry that Deacon might try to approach her again. Maybe getting an Order of Protection would be in her best interest after all, in case he decided to come after her again. Before turning on the ignition she decided to give Damon a call.

Nichole dialed Damon's number and was happy that he picked up on the second ring.

"Hello, Damon."

"Hello, Nichole. What are you up to?" he asked.

"Just getting off work. I was headed home and thought I would check with you to see if you wanted to grab some dinner."

"That sounds great, but I'm already having dinner with Arnelle," he revealed.

"Oh, I'm sorry for interrupting your dinner. Tell Arnelle I said hello."

Damon looked over at Arnelle.

"Nichole says hello."

Arnelle picked up the napkin and wiped her mouth. "Tell her hello."

With a gleam in his eyes Damon turned his attention back to Nichole's telephone call.

"Arnelle says hello as well. I'm glad you called."

"So am I. Listen, Damon, go back to your dinner. I'll talk to you tomorrow."

He pulled a buttered roll out of the basket. "How about I call you when we're done? Maybe I'll bring you a carryout order or some dessert."

"That's sweet of you, Damon, but I'll pick up something on my way home. I'm really tired, so after I eat I'm just going to shower and go to bed. I have another early morning tomorrow anyway."

Damon smiled at the visual of Nichole in the shower with suds sliding down her soft, brown skin. "Are you sure?"

"I'm sure. I'll talk to you tomorrow, Damon. Drive safely."

"You do the same, and if you're free tomorrow night and feel up to it, I would love a rain check on dinner."

The tenderness in his voice warmed Nichole's heart. "That sounds wonderful. I'll let you know. Good night, Damon."

"Good night, Nichole."

Damon hung up the telephone and laid it on the table. Arnelle giggled.

"You should see the way your face lights up when you talk to her."

Embarrassed, he leaned back in his chair and tried to deny what was so obvious.

"I don't know what you're talking about. What do you mean my face lights up?"

Arnelle scooped up some food on her fork and replied.

"The face doesn't lie, Damon Kilpatrick. You're falling for her fast."

He picked up his fork and took a bite of his food without responding. Arnelle watched his reaction and body language in silence.

"Oh my God! Have you already fallen in love with her, Damon?"

Once again, Damon was silent as he continued to eat his dinner without acknowledging Arnelle one way or the other. He looked up at Arnelle and just smiled.

She smiled back at him because she didn't want it to seem like she was hating on his happiness. "I hope you know what you're doing."

He nodded and winked at her in response. Arnelle poked her fork into her entrée and took another bite of her food. "OK, I won't say another word about her or the situation unless you bring it up. Deal?"

Damon wiped his mouth and said, "Deal."

At the same time a dark figure bypassed Nichole's security system and moved quietly throughout her house. After looking through Nichole's mail, the shadowy figure slowly climbed the stairs and entered her bedroom.

Chapter Ten

Nichole pulled into her garage and lowered the garage door behind her. The aroma from the large stuffed crust pizza sitting on the seat next to her had her mouth watering all the way home. She couldn't wait to get inside, change into some comfortable fleece sweats and open a cold beer to wash down the pizza. She exited the vehicle and placed the pizza on the hood of the truck so she could grab her purse and briefcase. After gathering the items, she stuck her keys inside the doorknob and opened the door leading into her kitchen. She kicked off her shoes, placed the pizza on the table, and rested her purse and briefcase in the chair. After turning on the small TV sitting on her countertop, she then removed her jacket and skirt.

Standing in the middle of the kitchen in her black lace bra and boy shorts, she caught her reflection in the french doors leading into her dining room. The lingerie set she had on made her legs appear longer than they actually were. Deacon used to salivate and couldn't keep his hands off her when she modeled her lingerie. The reality was that she enjoyed wearing the skimpy pieces of lace and satin for him, especially the crotch-less panties and satin corsets.

Nichole snapped herself out of her trance and made her way inside the laundry room. She opened the dryer and pulled out a pair of sweats and an oversized T-shirt and quickly slid into them. Even though she enjoyed being sexy, she still enjoyed being relaxed and comfortable as well. Before walking out of the laundry room she picked up a pair of thick socks and put them on her feet. When she returned to the kitchen she sat down at the table to enjoy her dinner.

As she sat there she couldn't help but think about Damon. The thought of him made her smile and forget about all the drama she had been through recently. Having Damon with all his sex appeal around kept her sane and confident that there was life after Deacon. Four slices of pizza and two beers later, she was full and ready for a hot shower. Nichole placed her leftover pizza in a Tupperware dish and slid it inside the refrigerator. As she stood there she realized she was low on food and would need to visit the grocery store before the weekend. She pulled another beer out of the refrigerator and yawned before grabbing her suit off the back of the chair and heading upstairs.

As Nichole climbed the stairs an uneasy feeling suddenly came over her. She stopped halfway up the stairs when she smelled an unusual scent in the air. Her heartrate accelerated slightly, but she continued up the stairs cautiously. When she reached the landing she turned on the hallway light and proceeded into her bedroom. Once inside she gasped and dropped everything on the floor. The beer bottle shattered against the hardwood floor as Nichole backed out into the hallway.

She couldn't believe what she saw. Two white candles

illuminated the room, and pink, white, and red rose petals were scattered everywhere. On her bed red rose petals were arranged in the shape of a heart, and from where she was standing, Nichole could see what looked like a note lying in the center of the heart.

Horrified, she ran down the stairs in fear that whoever staged her bedroom was still in the house. She grabbed her keys and purse and frantically raised the garage door so she could get away. She sped out of the garage and down the street to the corner gas station where she used her cell phone to call the police, who arrived in a matter of minutes. Shaking from her ordeal, Nichole tried her best to explain to them what happened before they followed her back to her home to investigate.

The police pulled into the driveway first and instructed Nichole to wait outside. Two officers entered the house with guns drawn, while two more officers covered the back of the house. After a thorough search, the all clear was given and Nichole was allowed to enter the house.

Nichole entered the house and asked, "What do think, officer? Did you find anyone inside? What about the note on my bed? What did it say?"

"You'd better come with me, Miss Adams," he replied as he climbed the stairs ahead of her.

Once upstairs, Nichole gasped again. This time it was because the rose petals, candles, note, everything was gone. Confused, she turned to the officer and stuttered.

"Officer, I-I don't know what to say. Everything was here just a minute ago. I promise you that I wasn't hallucinating."

The officer walked over to Nichole's closet and peeped inside again. "Are you sure, ma'am? I see there's a broken bottle of beer on the floor. Have you had anything to drink tonight?"

This angered Nichole. "I had a couple of beers, but I'm not drunk, if that's what you're insinuating. I know what I saw. Can't you smell the smoke and scent left over from the burning candles?"

The officer looked around the room and said, "I'm sorry, ma'am, but I don't smell anything. Maybe you thought you saw the flowers. I've seen beer affect a lot of people in strange ways."

Nichole stared at the officer. She could hold her alcohol and knew that she would have to be on drugs to hallucinate everything that she saw. Was it possible that Deacon could have other officers helping him harass her?

"Listen, sir, I called you because someone broke into my house. Can't you take fingerprints or something?"

"We would, ma'am, but we can't see where any crime has been committed. Have you looked around to see if anything is missing?"

Nichole scanned the room and took a quick inventory of all her valuables. "It doesn't seem like anything is missing, but I would have to look closer and in other rooms to be sure."

The officer walked toward the door and said, "You're probably just tired and need some rest. I suggest you get some sleep and watch your intake of alcohol. We made sure your home was safe. Lock your doors, set your alarm, and call us if you find out anything is missing or if you need our help."

Nichole followed the officer out of her room and down to the front door. Tears welled up in her eyes as she thought about the mind game that had just been played on her.

"Thank you, officer. I appreciate your help. Good night."

Nichole closed the door and activated her alarm system. It was then that it hit her that she didn't have to de-activate her alarm when she first came home. Someone had bypassed her security system, and without proof that it was Deacon, there was nothing she could do.

Nichole returned to her bedroom and stripped all the linens off the bed. There was no way she was sleeping in her bed after someone had violated her space. She sat down in a chair and thought about her life and the spiral it seemed to be spinning around in. All of this drama because she fell in love and trusted a man? Now he was making her out to look crazy just because she wanted him out of her life.

As she walked around the house checking for missing items, the telephone rang. The loud ring startled her. She picked up the telephone.

"Hello?"

"Nichole, it's Damon. Did I catch you at a bad time?" Nichole stifled her tears.

"You calling me could never be a bad time. I must say that I didn't expect to hear from you tonight."

Damon hesitated before responding. He could hear a touch of sadness in her tone.

"Are you OK? You sound a little down."

Not wanting to worry Damon, she decided to lie. "I'm fine, just tired I guess. It's been a long day."

"Are you sure? You were a lot more cheerful when I talked to you earlier."

Damon knew something was going on with Nichole, but he didn't want to pry or pressure her for information. If she had something on her mind and wanted to talk, he just wanted to be there for her. Most men in his position would love to be involved with a vulnerable woman like Nichole, because the possibility of them ending up in bed together was rather high. He could feel himself falling for her and they hadn't even kissed. Most of the time he'd at least kissed a woman before having any sort of romantic feelings for her. Arnelle was the only exception, because their relationship was platonic, even though he had wanted it to be more.

Nichole's full, sexy lips, her infectious giggle, and the way her hips swayed when she walked were instant turn-ons for Damon. She was easy to talk to and had a sex appeal registering off the charts. It was obvious that his attraction to her also had a thing or two to do with her knowledge of football and her athletic abilities on the golf course. There was something about the way she swung her club that caused a burning desire in his lower body; however, he was able to restrain himself so she wouldn't think his interest in her was purely sexual. Yes, Nichole was exactly the type of woman he'd been looking for, but he had to be patient until things settled down with Deacon.

"I'm OK, Damon. How was your dinner with Arnelle?" she asked, hoping to change the subject.

"Dinner was great. We don't get an opportunity to hang out like we used to since we're both so busy and she has the kids. We had a good time."

"I'm glad. The few times I've been around Arnelle she seems to be genuinely nice."

"She is. So are we still on for tomorrow night?" Damon asked.

"You bet, but would it be OK if I cook dinner for us instead of going out? I've been eating out a lot lately, and I'm starting to see the results in my clothes. I can't afford to gain any more weight."

Damon chuckled. Nichole had a spectacular body, and if she'd gained weight, the pounds had found a home in all the right places.

"You look fine, Nichole. Weight is nothing you should be worried about."

What he wanted to say was that her curvy backside, small waist, and nice, round breasts had him mesmerized, but he couldn't say that, at least not yet.

"Can you cook, Nichole?" he asked.

"Of course I can cook. Actually, I've been cooking since I was about twelve years old," she answered with pride.

"You do know that burning food is not the same as cooking it," he joked.

"I'm going to make you eat those words, literally," she joked back at him.

Damon chuckled again. "Don't get hostile. I'm just asking because a lot of you new age women can't cook. In fact, most of them can't even boil water."

"Well, Mr. Kilpatrick, I'll just have to prove my culinary skills to you, won't I?"

"Yes, you will, Miss Adams, and I'd better warn you, I'm a serious food critic since I have skills myself."

"Well, bring it on because I'm going to bring my best game to the table," she boasted.

"Then we're on?"

"Most definitely, Coach."

"Well, it's late and I didn't mean to keep you on the telephone so long. I look forward to seeing you tomorrow," he said with tenderness.

"Likewise, Damon. Good night."

Nichole hung up the telephone and sat there for a moment. Talking to Damon felt wonderful, but it didn't take long for an uneasy feeling to come over her once again. There was no way she was going to get any sleep in her house tonight, and after what she'd been through, who would? So she got up, packed an overnight bag of clothing, and drove to a nearby hotel. Once she had settled into her room, she called Meridan and told her about the home invasion just in case Meridan tried to contact her at home. She didn't want her to worry and end up sending Winston over in the middle of the night to check on her.

Meridan was obviously worried about Nichole and suggested that she fly to Texas for a visit until things cooled down. Nichole thanked her best friend, but assured her she would be fine, and she would definitely visit in the near future. In the meantime she vowed to be careful and watch her back. Tomorrow she would worry about making changes with her home security company so she could get back to her life.

Chapter Eleven

The next morning Meridan yawned as she entered the kitchen in her bunny slippers and oversized, button-down shirt. Keaton was sitting at the breakfast bar reading the morning paper and finishing off his second cup of coffee while Jeremiah lay asleep in his baby carrier. Meridan walked over and kissed her sleeping son before sliding into the seat next to Keaton. She leaned over and gave him a loving kiss on the lips.

"Good morning, babe. What time did you two get up?"

"You don't want to know," Keaton said, closing the paper. "Why do you think Jeremiah's gone back to sleep?"

Meridan caressed her husband's back lovingly. "He got me up around two. After I put him back to bed I was so sleepy I didn't even know he woke up again."

Keaton laughed. "I knew you were tired, sweetheart, so when Jeremiah woke up again at four-thirty, I didn't expect you to have the strength to get back up."

Surprised, she asked, "You've been up since four-thirty?"

"Once I got up and got him situated, I wasn't sleepy anymore, so I went ahead and worked out."

"Thanks, baby. Mmmm, it smells delicious in here. I hope you made enough cinnamon rolls."

He smiled as he poured her a cup of hot coffee and handed it to her. "You know I did. I know how much you love them. I also knew you were going to be extra tired this morning. You tossed and turned all night long. What's going on? Is something bothering you?"

She sighed. "I'm sorry, baby. I didn't mean to disturb you."

"Don't worry about me. My concern is for you. What's on your mind, sweetheart?"

Meridan picked up a spoon and scooped up a serving of mango, strawberries, cantaloupe, and honeydew fruit salad. She also reached over and picked up a warm cinnamon roll and added it to the fruit.

"Keaton, I'm so worried about Nikki. She called me last night and said someone broke into her house, lit candles, and sprinkled rose petals all over her bedroom. Of course that freaked her out, so she got out of there quick and called the police from down the street. By the time they returned to her house, everything was gone."

Keaton frowned. "What do you mean gone?"

"Just what I said, baby, gone," Meridan said after taking a bite of her cinnamon roll. "This means whoever did it was still in the house when she got home. What's even weirder is that they took the time to clean everything up before the police arrived to investigate. Now they don't believe it really happened."

Keaton walked over to the refrigerator and retrieved the butter so Meridan could butter her cinnamon roll.

"Thank you, sweetie," she said.

He climbed back into the seat next to her and said,

"You're welcome. So, what happened? They didn't charge Nichole with filing a false report, did they?"

"No, but they could've because there was no evidence of her accusations."

Keaton nodded and said, "I see," as he picked up the sports section of the newspaper.

Meridan watched the news on the small TV while she ate breakfast. As she sat there she thought about how nice it would be to have Nikki in San Antonio permanently with her. She had made a few friends since moving there, but none of them were like Nichole. She was worried about her safety, and she missed her dearly. After all, Nichole was Jeremiah's godmother.

"Keaton?"

"Yes, dear?" he replied without taking his eyes off the newspaper.

"Would it be OK with you if I go visit Nikki for a couple of days?"

This got Keaton's immediate attention. He'd almost lost Meridan once before to a deranged individual, and he wasn't about to let that happen again. He placed the newspaper on the counter and looked Meridan directly in the eyes.

"No, it wouldn't be OK. Nichole has too much drama going on with Deacon right now, and I don't want you caught up in the middle of it. Wait until Deacon comes to terms with their relationship and moves on."

Meridan caressed Keaton's arm to try to soften him up. "I'll be careful. Besides, Deacon wouldn't hurt me."

With a scowl on his face, he looked into her eyes. "What makes you so sure?" he asked. "Listen, I'm just as concerned about Nichole as you are, but there's no way in hell I'm going to let you go up there and risk getting hurt or killed because Deacon can't accept the fact that things are over between him and Nichole, so forget it."

Meridan gave Keaton a look that let him know she wasn't happy with his response. "Have you forgotten that Nikki risked her life for me on more than one occasion when Sam was stalking me?"

"No, I haven't forgotten," Keaton said, raising his voice. "And that's the exact reason you're not going up there. There's more at stake now, babe, and I don't want Jeremiah to grow up without his mother. I love Nichole and she's welcome in our home any time, but you're not going up there when there's a chance you could get caught in the crossfire. Did she ask you to come to Philly?"

Jeremiah was awake now and whining. Meridan slid out of her seat and placed her empty dishes in the sink before attending to their son. She picked up Jeremiah to comfort him.

"Did Daddy wake you? Mommy loves you. Are you hungry, sweetheart?"

Keaton walked over to the refrigerator, pulled out a bottle of milk, and placed it in the bottle warmer. He turned to Meridan and made eye contact with her.

"Keaton, I love you and I know you love me and don't want anything to happen to me, but something could happen to me right here in San Antonio. My best friend needs me. She was there for me in my time of need, and I want to be there for her, and to answer your question, no, she didn't ask me to come to Philly."

Keaton removed the bottle of milk from the warmer and handed it to her. "You're right, I do love you, but what I'm trying to get you to understand is that you can be there for Nichole in ways other than physically. We have Jeremiah now, so we have to look at things differently."

"Don't think I'm not concerned about you and our son just because Nikki needs me. And I'm going to be there for her!" she snapped at him. "I'm the one who almost died twice, remember? So, I'm not trying to make the third time a charm. I just feel like I owe it to Nikki to be there to support her."

Keaton kissed Meridan's forehead. "I'm sure Nichole will understand why you can't be there for her. In fact, I don't think she would expect you to come up there since we have Jeremiah."

"I hope you're right, Keaton," she replied as she put the bottle in Jeremiah's mouth.

He caressed her cheek and softly said, "I know I'm right."

Keaton tried to be as gentle as possible in expressing his opinion. Nichole and Meridan had known each other for years and were closer than most sisters. He understood how badly Meridan wanted to comfort Nichole, but Deacon was a police officer who carried a weapon. If he was having a hard time accepting his breakup with Nichole, someone could get hurt. Besides, Deacon was probably the one who broke into Nichole's house, which meant he was already out of control.

"Babe, I need to go by the restaurant for a little while. Why don't you give Nichole a call or something? I'm sure it would make you feel better. In the meantime, I have a stack of paperwork on my desk that I need to take care of. Do you need anything while I'm out?"

"No, I'm going out shortly to look at some office spaces that Zenora told me about."

Keaton was somewhat surprised. They had talked about her opening a practice in San Antonio, but he didn't expect her to want to do it so soon. Maybe she was getting bored as a housewife and mother and missed being a pediatrician.

"I didn't know you had Momma looking for an office for you," he stated.

"I didn't, Keaton. She ran across it one day and just mentioned it to me."

"Meridan, if you're bored around here, I clearly understand you wanting to get out of here and back to work. I told you in the beginning of our marriage to let me know when you're ready."

Meridan giggled. "I'm not bored, silly. I love being here with you and Jeremiah. I can open a practice without spending all my time there. I guess you could say I would be more like a pediatric manager. You know I love being around children. This way, I could set my own hours and still keep my skills fine tuned at the same time."

Keaton knew what it was like to want to stay close to a career you were passionate about. Even though he was retired from the NBA, he still worked with other retired NBA players in organizations that aided student athletics with their educational goals and under-privileged children.

Keaton now owned Lorraine's, a family style restaurant in the heart of San Antonio that served a variety of food. He also owned a sports bar called Hoops, located not far from AT&T Center, the home of the Spurs. Meridan's career as a pediatrician had flourished over the years, and they had a very nice financial portfolio under their belt, so it wasn't about money. He loved having Meridan at home, but he also wanted her to be happy. So if she was ready to open her practice, he would support her all the way.

"So you are ready to open a practice, aren't you?" he asked.

"I'm not going to lie and say I don't miss it. I just want to look at the office space to see if I like it, and if I do, I want to go ahead and get it. I'd hate to lose out on a good location," she explained.

Keaton's heart thumped inside his chest. Meridan was the love of his life, and her happiness meant everything to him.

"I know my mother has good taste, but if you don't mind having company, I'd love to see the office with you."

"I thought you had to go to the restaurant?" she asked.

"I do, but I'd rather be with you. Besides, if you like the space, we might as well go on and get it."

Meridan smiled. "I'd like that, but first you have to do something for me."

His lips were within inches of hers now as he caressed her lower back.

"Anything for you, babe," he whispered.

"Go to the restaurant and do what you have to do, and then meet me at your mom's house in about two hours. Do we have a deal?"

Keaton kissed her without responding verbally. Her lips were soft and sweet and he could never get enough of her. Breathless, Meridan broke the kiss.

"So, I guess that's a yes?"

"Of course it is. Now I have a proposition for you, Mrs. Lapahie."

Meridan sat Jeremiah's bottle on the counter. "I'm listening," she said.

Keaton was a creative man and loved making bets with Meridan. The payoffs were usually something seductive and erotic, but no matter who lost, both parties reaped the benefits.

Meridan placed Jeremiah on her shoulder as she waited to hear Keaton's proposition. Within seconds, the couple heard a loud belch come out of their tiny son. Keaton took Jeremiah out of Meridan's arms and kissed his son's chubby cheek.

"You need some sleep, and I know Momma and Daddy

would love to keep Jeremiah for the day. Besides, they haven't spent a whole day with their grandson in a while, so I know they're itching for the opportunity."

Meridan yawned and then looked up at Keaton, who now had their son giggling. "I'll be fine, Keaton. It's not necessary for you to inconvenience your parents."

"Spending the day with their grandson will never be an inconvenience for my parents," Keaton said. "You're getting the day off, Meridan, so you might as well take advantage of it."

Meridan loved the way Keaton pampered her. She never thought she would find a man to accept her when she didn't think she would be able to have children, but Keaton loved her and saw her for the woman she was. Then a miracle happened and Jeremiah was conceived.

"Keaton, you really do know how to spoil me, but—"

"No buts, Meridan. You're getting the day off and I don't care what you do as long as you take the day off to relax. Go shopping, to the spa, or something. Momma can bring Jeremiah home anytime you want."

Meridan thought for a moment and realized that Keaton was right. A day at the spa would definitely do her some good, especially since she'd been up most of the night worrying about Nikki.

"OK, you win, but only if you take a nap with me after we finish looking at the office space."

He pulled her into his arms and cupped her hips. "If I lay down in the bed with you, I guarantee it won't be for a nap. You just get some rest, because I plan to be the reason for your sleepless night tonight."

She hugged his waist and winked at him. "I'm looking forward to it, chief. Now, if you would turn my backside loose, I can go upstairs and get Jeremiah's diaper bag together."

"Do I have to?" he asked in a whining voice.

Meridan giggled. Keaton was a very affectionate man and loved to show it, privately and publicly. His favorite part of her anatomy was her hips, even though she'd always been very self-conscious about them.

"Yes, you have to if you expect me to start this relaxing day."

Before releasing her from his grasp, he seductively kissed her neck. This excited her and sent shivers all over her body.

"Mmmm, that feels so good."

"The best is yet to come," he whispered, "but you'll have to wait until tonight."

Now it was her time to whine. "Do I have to?"

They laughed together as Keaton released his wife.

She giggled again. "I'll be back down shortly."

"OK, I'll call Momma and set up everything."

Keaton picked up the telephone and called his mother, who was excited that they would have their grandson for the day. Afterward, he put away the leftover food, made Jeremiah some extra bottles, and washed the dishes. When Meridan returned to the kitchen she gave Keaton Jeremiah's bag and other baby items for his day with his grandparents. Once everything was packed and ready to go, they climbed into Keaton's truck and pulled out of the garage.

Chapter Twelve

The next morning Nichole walked into her office after a decent night's sleep at the hotel, but before she could sit her briefcase down, she noticed a large vase with two dozen pink roses sitting on her desk. This was an eerie reminder of what had happened at her house the night before, and it sent shivers over her body. Nichole stared at the roses as if they were going to take on a life of their own and come after her. She slowly backed out of her office and turned to her assistant, Phillip.

"Phillip, where did those roses come from?"

Phillip smiled mischievously, got up from his desk, and walked into her office. He walked over to the vase of flowers and admired them.

"They were delivered this morning. I wanted to take a peek at the card, but I know how much you hate it when I do that. Do you want me to open the card for you?"

Nichole put her belongings down and stood there, not knowing what to do. She didn't want Phillip in her business but she did want to know who sent the flowers, and she didn't know if she had the strength to look. In fact, she'd been on edge ever since her personal space had been violated with the candles and flowers.

"Well?" Phillip asked as he stood next to the flowers with the envelope in hand. "Why are you acting so skittish?"

Nichole let out a breath and said, "I'm not skittish."

"Yes, you are. Anything you want to talk about?"

"No, but thanks anyway."

Phillip was a masculine man with an athletic build. He was very handsome with a strong sex appeal, and no matter how many women threw themselves at him, he never strayed from his marriage. He was also the best executive assistant anyone could ever have. It wasn't a profession most men of Phillip's caliber would choose; however, someone with skills like Phillip could make upwards of forty-five thousand dollars a year. But since Nichole was a successful investment banker, she made sure he was compensated more than the norm, and he was worth every dime.

"Nichole! Do you want me to read the card or not? I do have work to do."

Phillip jarred her out of her trance. She walked over to Phillip and slid the card out of his fingers.

"No, I'll open it, but thanks anyway."

"OK, but if you change your mind, let me know," Phillip said as he walked toward the door. "Don't forget you have a conference call in thirty minutes. I'll have the reports you asked me to compile on your desk in ten minutes, and your coffee in two."

Nichole smiled. "What would I ever do without you, Phillip?"

He glanced down at his watch and then said, "You'd be unorganized, late for all your meetings, and this office would be a wreck."

Nichole burst out laughing because she knew that

Phillip couldn't be more correct. As Phillip turned to walk out, Nichole stopped him. "Phillip, wait."

"Do you need something else?"

"No, but I want you to know that I'm serious when I say this. You are the best assistant in the world, and there's no way I could do this every day without you."

"I know," he said, smiling. "That's why you pay me so much. I'll be back in a second with your coffee."

After Phillip left the room, Nichole looked down at the envelope in her hand. She sat down in her chair and took a deep breath before opening it. She could feel her hands trembling, and it was so unlike her. She'd always been strong willed and never backed down from a fight, but the drama with Deacon had shaken her to her core. He'd sent her flowers before, and sending her two dozen roses of her favorite color was something he did often when they were together. Nichole now imagined him sending flowers to his wife as well. All along, Nichole had been the other woman without knowing it, and it made her angry. If Deacon had sent her the flowers, she was going to hand deliver them to his wife and tell her to keep Deacon away from her. Could she be that bold? Only time would tell.

"Oh, to hell with it," she yelled as she ripped open the envelope, read the card, and found a nice surprise.

Hey Nikki!

I hope these flowers brighten your day. I also want to extend an open invitation to you to come stay with us for a while. Jeremiah would love to see his godmother, and I miss my best friend.

Love Always,
Dee

Tears welled up in Nichole's eyes. She pulled out a Kleenex and dabbed the corners of her eyes just as

Phillip walked back into her office with a hot cup of coffee. He stopped in his tracks when he saw Nichole wiping her eyes.

"What's wrong, Nichole? Did somebody die or something? Who are the flowers from?"

"They're from my friend, Meridan," Nichole said, and smiled.

"That was nice of her," Phillip said as he set the coffee cup in front of Nichole. "I thought they were from that police officer you're dating. I haven't seen him around in a while. Are you two headed to the altar anytime soon?"

Nichole cleared her throat, picked up the coffee cup, and blew the steam.

"If you must know, I'm not dating him anymore," Nichole said without making eye contact.

Phillip smiled. "Well I'm not going to say I'm sorry, because I didn't like him anyway."

Surprised at Phillip's admission, she put down her coffee cup and folded her arms. "Where did that come from?" she asked.

Phillip sighed. "I have my reasons, Nichole, but you are my boss, and there are certain lines I don't want to cross."

Intrigued, Nichole stood and walked over to Phillip, who was now backing out of her office.

"What do you know, Phillip? We're just two friends talking right now, so if there's something you think I should know, you can tell me."

He threw up his hands and said, "You guys have broken up now, so anything I have to say doesn't matter. While I didn't like him, I am sorry things didn't work out for you."

"He wasn't who I thought he was, and I'm so glad I found out before I married him," she admitted.

Phillip could see through Nichole. It was obvious that she was hurt from the breakup.

"Well, as long as you're OK with it, that's all that matters."

She blew on her coffee again to cool it off before taking a sip.

"So you're not going to tell me, huh?"

"No, I'm not," he replied.

"Traitor," she teased.

"Whatever. Now, if you don't need anything else from me, I'll get those reports to you so you can get ready for your conference call."

Nichole eyed Phillip curiously. In a way she wanted to know what he knew, and in a way she didn't want to know. Her heart was already broken. If she started digging around in Deacon's life, she might find more than she could emotionally handle. She decided to let it go after thinking about how much worse things could get.

"Thank you once again, Phillip."

"No problem," he replied as he hurried out of Nichole's office and back to work.

A few minutes later Phillip re-entered the room and placed a folder of reports on her desk. "I have everything in order. You have fifteen minutes until your conference call starts."

Nichole opened the folder and scanned the documents as Phillip walked out of the room.

"Thank you, Phillip."

As soon as Phillip was out of the office, Nichole's telephone rang. She reached over and picked up the receiver.

"Nichole Adams. How may I help you?"

"Don't hang up, Nichole. We really need to talk."

Nichole gripped the receiver when she realized it was Deacon. "How many times do I have to tell you? We have nothing to talk about."

"I love you, Nichole," he said with his voice cracking. "I always have. This thing with my wife is not what it seems. We weren't together."

Nichole could feel herself getting angry, and she was pissed off that Deacon would throw love at her to try to soften her up.

"Deacon, if you really loved me you would leave me the hell alone."

"What do I have to do to prove to you that you're the only woman for me? Do you want me to announce it to the world? Because I will."

Nichole stood, gained control of her anger, and calmly replied. "Baby, you don't have to prove anything to me, because I've moved on, and you need to do the same."

While Nichole's response was calm, Deacon's reply was full of threats.

"You're mine, Nichole, and if I see any man within ten feet of you, his ass will have to answer to me."

"Deacon, I swear to God if you don't stop harassing me, I'll never forgive you. You're the one who ruined what we had, not me. I deserved to be loved without lies and deception. Now I have a meeting to go to. Please, please, just leave me alone and don't you ever threaten me again."

Silence gripped the telephone lines. Seconds later, Nichole heard him reply, but his voice was barely a whisper.

"I'm sorry, Nichole, but I can't."

After that comment the line went dead. Nichole didn't know what to think. She felt numb and needed to escape, even if it was for just a few days. Maybe visiting Meridan and her family would be just what she needed to get her life back on track. Having a stalker wasn't on her menu. She put the telephone back on the receiver and looked at her watch. She recited a short prayer, picked up her reports, and headed toward the door. Just then a text message popped up on her cell phone. She started to ignore it, but decided to check the message in case it was related to her meeting.

Good morning, Nichole. It's Damon. I hope your morning has been pleasant. I just want to let you know that I can't wait to sample your cooking tonight. I have my Pepto-Bismol all lined up. Just kidding! Don't work too hard and have a wonderful day.

All the stress Deacon had just thrown at her immediately melted away as soon as she viewed Damon's text message. It put an instant smile on her face and made her wish the day were almost over.

"Nichole, you're going to be late to your meeting if you don't get going right now," Phillip said in an elevated tone as he walked through the door.

"I'm on my way, Phillip. Calm down," she replied as she typed a reply to Damon while she slowly walked down the hallway. She smiled when she hit the send button on her PDA. She checked her appearance in the mirror and admired her ability to stay focused in her professional life even when her personal life was chaotic. She plucked a piece of lint off her jacket. She was dressed in a stylish black suit with a short skirt, which accentuated her long, shapely legs. It was a power suit, and she wore it well.

"You look great, Nichole, now get going," Phillip urged her as he gently pushed her in the direction of the conference room.

"I'm going. Do you have a breath mint?" she asked.

Phillip hurriedly reached inside his pocket and pulled out a container of Altoids. He opened the lid and popped two mints into Nichole's mouth.

"Now go. I just saw Mr. Joslin look this way."

"Yes, sir," Nichole jokingly replied.

Phillip folded his arms and gave Nichole a frustrated look as she made her way into the conference room. Nichole knew she would be late to every meeting if it wasn't for Phillip. He always made sure she had everything she needed before convening with her colleagues. That's why Nichole always rewarded Phillip with extras gifts of appreciation like concert and sports tickets and restaurant gift certificates for a job well done.

Damon jotted down some notes in the football team's playbook. He tried to keep his mind on football, but knowing he would be sharing dinner with Nichole later that night made it hard for him to concentrate. He quickly picked up his cell phone when it signaled him that he had a text message. Damon opened the text message and a huge grin appeared on his face when he read Nichole's reply.

> Hey Coach,
> I'm really looking forward to seeing you tonight as well. It's been a crazy few days for me (long story). Just for the record, dinner is on me; however, dessert is definitely on you, and it better be good.
> Nichole

Damon leaned back in his chair and stared at the text. Her remark regarding dessert seemed to have a sexual undertone to it, but he could be mistaken and reading more into it than was really there. In reality he wished he could make Nichole his dessert in place of actually bringing a dessert. Of course he realized that he was fantasizing at this point in their relationship, but it might be worth seeing if Nichole wanted more than just a friendship. The last thing he wanted to do was take advantage of her, but he really liked Nichole, and just maybe he could help her get over Deacon. He could already tell she enjoyed his company as much as he enjoyed hers, but whether she wanted anything more remained to be seen. Maybe he would open the door tonight and see what happened.

"Coach Kilpatrick, we're ready to start the film from last season," another assistant coach stated as he stuck his head in the door.

Damon stood, tucked his cell phone in his pocket, and picked up his notebook and pen before following the assistant coach out the door and down the hallway to their meeting.

At the same time and unbeknownst to Nichole, a unique GPS tracking system was being discreetly placed on her truck in the parking garage down the street from Nichole's office. This way Nichole's every move would be tracked, and she would never know.

Chapter Thirteen

Venice stepped out onto the patio and found Craig and Brandon in the pool pulling the twins around in an inflatable boat. Dressed in a navy suit and white blouse, she was just returning from spending a few hours in her office before beginning her two-week vacation. She removed her jacket and laid it across one of the deck chairs before approaching the pool. As a family, they always enjoyed time to themselves before traveling south to visit family and friends. Brandon spotted his mother and yelled, "Momma! Watch this!"

She walked closer and gave Craig a nice view of her shapely legs. He watched her as she slipped out of her shoes and sat down on the side of the pool so she could place her feet in the water. Craig made his way across the pool with the twins so he could watch Brandon's performance with her. She smiled at the twins, who were obviously excited to see their mother as well. She blew kisses at them, and then said, "I'm watching, Brandon, but whatever you're about to do, be careful."

Venice and Craig watched as Brandon did a back flip

off the side of the pool, causing a huge splash of water. Venice and Craig clapped as Brandon swam over to them.

"Did you see me, Momma? I did good, didn't I, Pops?"

"You did great, Brandon," Craig said as he splashed water.

Venice pulled Clarissa, who wore a bright red swimsuit with Elmo on the front, out of the boat and gave her a kiss.

"Yes, Brandon, you did good, but next time try to warn me before you do something like that. You almost scared me to death."

Craig playfully splashed a little water at C.J. and Clarissa.

"Brandon's fine, Venice. I've been helping him practice that move for the past hour. You know I wouldn't let him do anything to hurt himself."

Venice kissed C.J. on the cheek and placed Clarissa back inside the boat.

"I know, Bennett, but you know how I am. He's my firstborn."

Craig looked over at Brandon, who was playing water basketball on the other side of the pool.

"Brandon! Come take your brother and sister around the pool for me."

"OK!" he replied as he swam over, took the rope out of Craig's hand, and proceeded to slowly pull the twins around the pool. Craig climbed out of the pool and sat next to Venice. He glanced down at her thighs as she reached over and handed him a towel so he could dry off. When she turned back around she caught his wandering eyes.

"Stop undressing me with your eyes, Bennett."

He smiled and took the towel out of her hand. "Would you rather I do it with my hands?"

She smiled back at him. "Yes, baby, but later tonight.

Brandon! Don't pull the twins too fast, and don't put the rope around your neck!"

"Yes, ma'am," Brandon said with a roll of his eyes.

Craig was the only one who saw him roll his eyes. Although he understood exactly why Brandon did it, he would have to talk to him later about not doing that again, because it was disrespectful.

"Listen, Venice, I know Brandon is your firstborn, but you also know that I love him as if he was my own son."

She stared out at the children and said, "I know you do."

"Then you also know that I wouldn't let anything happen to him."

Venice turned to Craig. "I know you wouldn't, Craig, but Brandon is the only grandchild of Jarvis's parents. They would never forgive me if I let him get hurt. They lost their son, and I don't think they could handle it if I let something happen to to their grandchild."

"Stop stressing, Venice. If Jarvis were still alive, he would be proud of you and what you've done with Brandon."

This wasn't a subject she wanted to stir up. Jarvis Anderson was her high school sweetheart and first love. She'd fallen for Craig only after attending college with him. Unfortunately for Craig, Venice ended up marrying Jarvis and moved away to Michigan, leaving Craig severely heartbroken. Life was good for Jarvis and Venice, who later had Brandon, but six years later, their lives were forever changed when Jarvis succumbed to death after he was stricken with a terminal brain tumor. It wasn't until months later that fate brought Venice and Craig back together once again. It took a lot of convincing from Craig and Venice's loved ones for her to move on with her life, but the couple eventually married and she moved to Philadelphia to start a new life with Craig. As expected, it didn't take them long to increase their household with the twins, Craig Jr. and Clarissa.

Craig put his arm around Venice's shoulder and gently tilted her face toward him. They were now eye to eye, and Venice couldn't look more beautiful to him. He'd loved her ever since he had laid eyes on her in college.

"You and I both know that in this life, things happen beyond our control. We've both lost people we loved dearly, but as you can see, we turned out OK. The Andersons have to understand that life's circumstances are not always predictable or avoidable. I'm sure they know that we love the children and will protect them with our lives, but the rest is in God's hands."

"You're right, baby," Venice said as she nuzzled his neck. "I'm making myself crazy, huh?"

He kissed her on lips before answering. "You're not crazy for wanting to protect your children, Venice. All we can do is pray for God to watch over the kids and keep them safe."

She smiled. "Thanks, sweetheart, I needed to hear that."

He kissed her again and then ran his finger down to her cleavage. "You also look like you need to cool off."

"Craig Bennett, you bet' not," Venice said as she pulled away from his embrace. A mischievous grin appeared on his face.

"I bet' not what?"

"Craig!"

Seconds later they disappeared under the water. When she resurfaced, Brandon laughed and cheered. Venice swam after Craig.

"You're in so much trouble, Bennett," she yelled.

He tried to swim away from her, but she grabbed his foot.

"OK! OK! Venice! I'm sorry."

"No, you're not!" Venice climbed out of the pool with her clothes dripping with water. She tried to wring out her blouse, which was now practically transparent against her skin.

Craig laughed and also climbed out of the pool. He handed Venice a towel and grabbed another one for himself.

"I didn't know I was going make a wet T-shirt contestant out of you," Craig said as he wrapped the towel around Venice's upper body. "Had I known that, I would've tossed you in the pool when you first came out here."

Venice looked down at her chest and then back up at Craig. "You do know that I'm going to get you back for this, don't you?"

Craig pulled her close and kissed her neck. "Yeah, I know, but I'm looking forward to it."

"I'm sure you are," she responded as she walked toward the back door.

"Hey, baby, before you go inside, I want to ask you something."

She started unbuttoning her blouse as she walked back over to him. Craig couldn't help but glance down at her chest.

"What's up?" she asked.

"I've been thinking about doing something different with my life, and I wanted to talk to you about it."

Venice looked at him curiously. "What did you want to do?"

"I was thinking about teaching my skills to inner city kids. The architectural firms are doing well, and I've even been thinking about selling the office in Japan."

"I think that's great, Craig. You're always thinking of others."

"Thanks, sweetheart. There are so many kids out there with talent. They just need someone to take an interest in them and mentor them. You know, help them bring out their creativity. Your boy Skeeter's been talking about getting into politics, but that's not me. I want to do something less demanding."

Venice knew Craig was a man who needed to stay challenged, and it was obvious that he was getting bored with the architectural firms he owned.

"Craig, you know I'll support you no matter what career choice you choose. If you're ready to sell your interest in the firm and teach, I'm all for it. Lamar might even be interested in buying you out."

Lamar had been Craig's business partner for years.

"He might, but I don't know if Tressa will want him committing to it."

Craig glanced over his shoulder to check on the kids before running his hands through her wet tresses. He cupped her face.

"I'm sorry to spring it on you like this, but I feel like this is something that's calling me."

Venice smiled and saw that Clarissa and C.J. were now swimming in the pool with Brandon. The couple made it a point to make sure their children learned to swim at an early age.

"Then do it, baby."

"Thank you, Venice. I would like to run this by the family and our friends. What do you think about inviting everybody over for a weekend of fun to see what they think about my career change?"

"Sounds good to me, babe. Now it's time for the kids to take a nap, so bring them inside so they can get a bath. While you're doing that, I'll get their lunch ready, but first I need a shower and some dry clothes."

"Need any help?" he teased.

"No, Bennett, I think you've done enough," she replied playfully as she grabbed her shoes and jacket and went inside the house, leaving a trail of watery droplets behind her.

Once she was out of sight, Craig turned to Brandon and the kids and ran toward the pool.

"Cannonball!" he yelled.

Inside the house, Venice shed her wet clothes and stepped into the shower. She always loved her showers and baths extremely hot, and today was no different. As she enjoyed the hot spray in her face she thought about Craig being a teacher. It would be a nice change of pace for him, and it'd give him a chance to do something for their community. As she slowly lathered her skin, the shower door swung open. She turned and found Craig standing there with a mischievous grin on his face.

Venice smiled. "May I help you?" she asked.

"You could if you turn the hot water down a notch or two."

She giggled and continued to lather her body. "No can do. You know how I love hot showers. Where are the kids?"

"Everyone's downstairs, clean and dry. Now, back to you, Mrs. Bennett. Turn the water down a little bit."

Venice reached over and turned down the hot water. "Now are you happy?" she asked.

Craig removed his T-shirt and swimming trunks, stepped inside the shower with her, and immediately pulled her into his arms.

"I will be in just a second." Craig kissed her moist neck, causing a soft moan to escape her lips.

"Craig, what about the kids?"

"The kids are fine, Venice. The twins are downstairs in the baby corral playing with their toys. Brandon's in the room with them playing with his Wii," he replied as his hands slid down her firm backside.

Venice looked up at Craig and smiled. "I'm sorry. It's just that—"

Craig put his finger over her lips to silence her before he leaned down and kissed her passionately on the lips. At the moment it wasn't the temperature of the water heating things up between the loving couple. Instead, it was the love they shared that had steam rising out of the shower. Venice broke the kiss.

"You know we don't have much time."

Craig ran his tongue over her breasts. "Don't worry, baby," he whispered. "I'll make it quick."

Venice smiled at Craig before turning the hot water up at least one notch. Craig gritted his teeth as the hot water splashed on his skin.

"OK, I see how you want to play," he said.

Craig pushed Venice's back against the tile as he covered her lips with his. His kisses were sweet and hot. He raised her leg slowly and meticulously entered her body. Venice gasped each time Craig gyrated his hips against hers. Between the scalding hot water, Venice's gasps, and the heated passion, Craig knew this was going to definitely be a quickie.

In the meantime, he savored the sensual waves of passion that radiated throughout his body. Venice clawed at his back when he lifted her other leg, giving him complete access to her sensual body. Her gasps quickly turned into moans as he quickened his pace and kissed her feverishly. Making love to Venice in the shower had always been a fetish of his. There was something about the hot water, the steam, and the echo of her moans that sent him into overdrive.

Seconds later, Venice loudly moaned his name, signaling him that he had satisfied his woman as usual. He kissed her luscious lips tenderly as he reached his own plateau of satisfaction. As he sprinkled her face with kisses, he released Venice's legs so she could stand.

"That was very nice, Bennett."

Craig picked up the bottle of shower gel and poured a small portion into his hand. He began to slowly lather her body in a circular, seductive motion.

"So you liked that, huh?"

She nibbled on his chin as she rubbed lather onto his broad chest. "You know I did."

"Momma!" Brandon called from outside the shower door as he knocked.

"Oh shit!" Craig yelled.

"What is it, Brandon?" Venice called out to her son as she put her hand over Craig's mouth.

"C.J. stinks and he's crying."

"Thanks, sweetheart. Go back downstairs and look after them for me. I'll be right down."

"OK, Momma. Pops, are you coming, too?" Brandon asked.

Craig shook his head in disbelief. He had hoped that Brandon hadn't noticed that he was also in the shower with Venice.

"Yeah, son," he answered, embarrassed. "I'll be down in a second."

"OK, Pops!" he yelled happily before leaving the bathroom.

Venice turned off the water and burst out laughing. Craig wiped the suds off his mouth and opened the shower door. He grabbed a towel as he stepped out of the shower.

"That's not funny, Venice."

Venice picked up a towel and giggled. "You should've seen your face. If I didn't know any better, I would say you turned red."

Craig wrapped the towel around his waist and picked up his wet clothes. "I probably did turn red. That was embarrassing."

She stood in the mirror and dried her hair. "He didn't see or hear anything, Craig. Lighten up."

Craig put his wet clothes in the hamper and disappeared into the walk-in closet. "I can't believe you're telling me to lighten up. You and I both know that children talk during the most inopportune times and places."

"So what if he does? We're married, unless you've forgotten," she yelled out to him. "We're entitled to make love when and where we want to."

Craig walked out of the closet with a pair of shorts and a T-shirt in his hands.

"You're right, baby, but it's still embarrassing."

Venice pulled the blow dryer out of a drawer and turned to Craig. "It'll be OK, sweetheart, I promise. Now, forget we ever got busted."

Craig chuckled. "If you say so. By the way, I can't believe C.J. messed on himself. I just took him to the bathroom before I came up here."

"Maybe he didn't have to go when you took him, baby," she replied as she turned on the blow dryer.

"Clarissa's doing better than he is with potty training," Craig pointed out.

"Stop comparing them, Bennett. Boys are usually harder than girls, and we have been upstairs for a long time."

"I know," Craig replied. "I'll go get him cleaned up . . . again."

Venice continued blow drying her hair. "OK, baby. I'll be down in a sec."

Chapter Fourteen

Damon stepped up on Nichole's doorstep and rang the doorbell. He was anxious to see her and to taste the dinner she'd been bragging about all day. As he stood there with two bottles of wine and a box containing a strawberry cheesecake, he heard a strange noise coming from inside the house. The door swung open and Nichole appeared dressed in a short, satin robe.

"Damon! Come in!" she yelled frantically. "I need your help!"

Damon hurried through the door and was immediately faced with a house full of smoke and an ear-piercing smoke alarm. He sat the wine and cheesecake on a table in the foyer and raced toward the kitchen.

"Damn, Nichole! Is the house on fire?"

"Almost!" she answered, coughing. "I fell asleep in the bathtub and burnt the hell out of dinner."

Damon opened a window and the door leading out into the garage to ventilate the room while Nichole removed the charred meat from the oven.

"Give me that before you burn yourself," Damon instructed as he took the meat outside into the backyard. When he came back in he took a towel and started fanning the smoke detector in hope that it would stop going off. As he waved the towel in the air he glanced over at Nichole, who looked perplexed as she coughed.

"Nichole, go outside for a while and get some air."

"I'm fine," she replied as she coughed a couple more times.

He frowned. "Nichole, go sit out on the porch so you can catch your breath."

She nodded and coughed all the way out the door. Once the smoke alarm ceased beeping, Damon joined Nichole on the back steps.

"Are you OK?" he asked softly.

She lowered her head. "Not really, Damon. Nearly burning down my house is nothing compared to what happened the other night."

"What happened?"

"Somebody broke into my house the other night and did some weird stuff."

"Why are you just now telling me?" he asked, frowning.

She sighed. "I don't want you pulled into all my drama, Damon."

He put an arm around her shoulder. "Why don't you let me decide what I want to get involved in? Now tell me what happened."

Nichole proceeded to tell Damon about the candles and flowers doing a disappearing act in her bedroom. Damon's heart rate accelerated as he listened.

Once she was finished, Damon let out a breath and said, "I'm worried about you, Nichole. A person who does something like that is obviously crazy, and there's no telling what he'll do next. Do you think it was Deacon?"

She knocked some dust off her shoes and said, "Who

else? I can't do anything about it, though, because I don't have any proof it was him."

Damon reached over and softly touched her cheek. "I hope you're taking precautions coming in and out of the house?"

"I am, but it still didn't stop him from showing up at my door. He was beating on the door like a mad man. I had to call the police. They took him away, but I didn't want to press charges. I didn't want to provoke him any further."

Damon was angry now. He realized that Nichole had been living a nightmare all by herself.

"Nichole, I would appreciate it if you would stop hiding these things from me. I wish he would come over tonight. I'll show him what it feels like to be victimized. Do you have a gun?"

"Yes," she whispered.

"Most importantly, do you know how to use it?" he asked.

She pointed her fingers like a gun and said, "Just like Clint Eastwood. I'm good. I also upgraded my security system, so there's no way he's getting back in."

"Nichole, be serious."

She tugged on his ear playfully. "OK, Coach. I'll be serious."

"Good. One thing I've learned about a determined person is that they won't let anything stop them from getting what they want. I think I need to talk to him."

Nichole reached over and touched Damon's hand with hers. "No, it's OK. I'm sure he'll back off. Listen, I don't want to talk about Deacon anymore. What are we going to do about dinner? I can't believe I burned it, especially after I went on and on about my culinary skills."

Damon gently bumped his shoulder against hers and tried to cheer her up.

"It's OK, Nichole. I like my meat well done."

Nichole smiled. "I see you have jokes."

"Seriously, though, you could've killed yourself tonight. How did you fall asleep in the tub?" he asked.

"I haven't slept very well since the whole candles and flowers thing. I guess it freaked me out more than I'm willing to admit."

"You can stay with me for a while if you like," he said without hesitating. "Or I could stay here."

She played with the belt on her robe, thinking over his suggestion. "That's sweet of you to offer," she said without making eye contact, "but I have to be a big girl, Damon. I can't let him win."

He turned to her so he could observe her facial expressions.

"Being safe is not giving in to him, Nichole. I hate that he's doing this to you. I should pay him a visit."

Nichole reached over and gently touched Damon's arm to calm him.

"Damon, please, don't . . . I'll be fine. Scout's honor."

Damon wasn't convinced. He could tell that Nichole wasn't as brave as she tried to pretend.

"Nichole, look at me."

She turned and looked at him. Damon never looked as serious as he did at that moment. He was positive that his heart was past the friendship stage, and he didn't want anything to happen to her.

"I'm here for you. I mean that."

Nichole smiled. "It's sweet that you care about me, and if I really thought I was in any kind of danger, I would take you up on your offer. He's just trying to shake me."

"I hope you're right," Damon added. "If he's stupid enough to break into your house again, he'll have to answer to me."

"This is not your battle, Damon."

Damon's heart thumped in his chest. The thought of someone breaking into Nichole's home to terrorize her, or worse, made him fearful for her safety.

"I know it's not my battle, but I'm trying to be a friend and help you. Right now Deacon could show up on your doorstep, at your job, or anywhere else you go. What's stopping him from harming you?"

"He'd never hurt me."

"Are you a hundred percent sure about that? Deacon's a desperate man who doesn't take rejection very well. If you want to feel a little safer, it might be a good idea to take out a restraining order against him."

Nichole shook her head in disagreement. "Nah, I don't think so. Those things only anger men and get women killed."

"I'd never let him hurt you."

"Be realistic, Damon. You can't be with me twenty-four, seven. Besides, Deacon is aware that we know how the other thinks, which means he knows I'd kill him in a heartbeat if he stepped to me like a psycho."

He shook his head in disbelief. "If you say so, but if anything like this ever happens again, you'd better call me. Understood?"

Nichole leaned over and kissed Damon on the cheek. "Understood. You know, you always seem to say the right things. Why aren't you married, Damon Kirkpatrick?"

He looked into her eyes before answering. "Not many women can put up with me."

Nichole coughed. "You're not so bad, unless you haven't shown me your true colors yet."

Damon stood, smoothed down his jeans, and held out his hand. "You definitely haven't seen all my qualities; however, they're all good, so you don't have anything to worry about."

Nichole put her hand inside his and stood next to him. "Are you sure you're ready to go back inside? There's nothing to eat now."

"Get dressed. We're going out to dinner, my treat."

"Is that my reward for burning your dinner?" she joked.

Damon winked at her mischievously.

"Now what does that wink mean, Coach?" she asked.

"I plead the fifth, Miss Adams. Besides, you'll know when I reward your good deeds," he explained.

She giggled at Damon's remark as they walked back into the house together. The house was almost free of smoke. Nichole waved the remnants of smoke out of her face.

"It stinks in here."

"We're going to start smelling just like the house if we don't hurry up and get out of here. By the time I bring you home, the house should smell much better."

Nichole released his hand and said, "Give me ten minutes to get dressed, and I'll be right back."

"With that said, I'm going to clock you, Miss Adams," he said, looking down at his watch.

Nichole giggled as she turned to walk out of the room. Damon couldn't help but notice the way she swayed her hips as she climbed the stairs.

Upstairs, Nichole decided to open the window in her bedroom, and one in each spare bedroom. She thought it'd be safe for her to crack her windows just a little bit. As high as her windows were, there was no way anyone could get inside her house that way.

She quickly chose a pair of jean capris she had recently purchased and a pink oxford-style shirt. Before leaving the bedroom she slid into some pink wedge-heeled sandals and fluffed her hair. As she descended the stairs, she pulled a tube of lipstick out of her purse and applied it to her lips.

"You don't need any makeup, Nichole," Damon said as he saw her coming down the stairs.

She closed the lipstick and dropped it inside her purse.

"That's sweet of you to say, but I can't be walking around with dry, crusty lips."

Damon looked at Nichole's luscious lips and had to struggle to resist the urge to kiss her. "Your lips are fine. Are you ready to go?"

She grabbed her keys off the table and said, "I'm ready when you are, Coach."

At Zanzibar Blue, Damon and Nichole placed their orders. While they waited on their entrees, they enjoyed the sounds of a very talented jazz band.

"Damon, I want to apologize again for burning dinner."

"It's no big deal," he said as he took a sip of wine. "I'm just happy you didn't kill yourself."

She picked up her glass and before taking a sip said, "I hope you let me make it up to you."

"You already have. Stop stressing about dinner."

Nichole's cell phone rang, interrupting their conversation. She looked at the number on the ID and then ignored the call.

"Was that him?" Damon boldly asked.

She turned up her wine glass, completely draining the liquid before answering. "Yes, that was him. I'm thinking about changing my number, but I use it for business as well."

"I'm sure you can work through it. Changing your number is one way to stop Deacon's phone harassment."

At that moment the waitress returned to their table with their entrees. The couple thanked her and proceeded to eat their dinner as they continued to listen to the smooth sounds of jazz.

After dinner, Damon drove Nichole around town to admire the city lights.

"I can't believe how hungry I was," she said.

"Me neither. You ate your food and half of mine."

Nichole giggled. "I'm sorry, but your steak looked so tender. I had to taste it."

He understood exactly how she felt, because he was at the point where he had to taste her lips. Restraining himself, Damon pulled up in front of a coffee shop and looked over at Nichole.

"Do you have room for coffee and dessert?"

Nichole looked at the coffee shop. "I do, but I'd rather go back to my house and have that delicious dessert you brought with you. That was a cheesecake I saw in your hands, wasn't it?"

Damon put his SUV in drive and pulled out into traffic. "Yes, it was, and that sounds like a great idea."

"Well, I hope that cheesecake is just as delicious as the caramel pie you brought the last time."

He looked over at her and smiled. "Don't worry, it is."

Thirty minutes later Nichole and Damon were back at her house. Nichole climbed out of the vehicle and pulled her keys out of her purse. As they walked up to her front door she linked her arm with his.

"Thanks again for dinner," she said.

Just having Nichole's hands on him in this simple gesture immediately aroused him.

"You're very welcome. Besides, it was the least I could do after your Food Network debut."

Nichole opened her front door and deactivated her

alarm. "I see you have jokes and will never let me live this down."

Damon laughed as he stepped inside the foyer and sat his keys on the table. "You know I'm just having a little fun at your expense. Let me help you make the coffee."

"Are you saying that because you're afraid I might burn the coffee, too?" she joked back at him.

"Of course not," he replied. "I said it because I want to help."

She smiled.

"I'm glad the smoke is gone."

"The smell is still here, though," Damon added.

Nichole slipped out of her shoes, lit several scented candles, and walked barefoot into the kitchen. Damon followed her and pulled the cheesecake out of the refrigerator. As he sliced the cheesecake, he saw Nichole retrieve the coffee pot and fill it with water. While standing at the sink a bird flew into the closed kitchen window, causing Nichole to scream and drop the coffee pot in the sink where it shattered into hundreds of pieces.

"Don't move, Nichole," Damon yelled as he hurried over to her. He picked her up into his arms and said, "I don't want you to cut your feet. There's broken glass on the floor."

Nichole buried her face against his warm neck and sobbed. "It's OK, Nichole. It was just a bird."

Damon carried Nichole into the family room and sat down on the sofa with her still in his lap. He hugged her.

"This scene seems very familiar," he said.

He was referring to the infamous plane ride they shared back to Philadelphia from Texas when they got caught in the turbulence storm. Damon loved the way Nichole's soft, yet firm body felt in his lap; however, now was not the time for his body to defy him. He was trying to comfort her, not seduce her. Nichole tightened her arms around his neck and cuddled even closer without responding.

"We're going to have to stop meeting like this, Nichole," he whispered into her ear, trying to lighten the mood.

She sat up and said, "I'm sorry. I guess I'm still a little freaked out about the break-in."

He smiled. "That's understandable. However, you won't hear any complaints from me. I actually enjoy having you in my lap."

Embarrassed, Nichole climbed out of his lap, grabbed a Kleenex out of a nearby box, and wiped her eyes.

"This is so stupid! Deacon did me wrong and I'm the one living in fear."

Damon stood up and took Nichole's hands into his. "Then do something about it, and stop giving him power over you."

"I don't have any proof that Deacon was the one who broke into my house."

He cupped her face. "Who else would do it unless he got that partner of his to do it? You can be certain it wasn't a typical burglary."

"I agree with you on that one."

Damon lowered his head. "Nichole, what would it take for you to have peace of mind and a good night's sleep?"

She lowered her head and softly replied, "I don't know."

Damon tilted her chin and looked into her beautiful, brown eyes.

"Well I do, and I have the perfect solution."

"You do?" she asked.

He kissed her forehead. "Yes. Just leave everything to me."

Chapter Fifteen

Damon didn't have to twist Nichole's arm too hard to get her to fly to Miami with him for a long weekend of rest and relaxation at his condo. He knew he was taking a chance when he asked her to spend the weekend with him, but he also knew this trip would be exactly what Nichole needed. She called Meridan and told her where she would be and why she was going, just in case Meridan called looking for her. Meridan was glad Nichole was moving on with her life and gave her blessings.

After buckling into their seats on the plane, Damon looked over and noticed that Nichole seemed to be a little nervous.

"Are you ready?" he asked.

She fanned herself with her hands and said, "As ready as I'm going to be."

Damon reached up and turned on the fan above Nichole's seat.

"How's that?"

She closed her eyes and leaned back against the seat.

"That feels wonderful. Thank you, Damon."

"You're welcome."

Silence fell on them as they taxied to the runway and waited to take off. Damon felt a little awkward, and for the first time he didn't know what to say. Maybe now was not the time to say anything to Nichole. He just wanted to make this weekend the best she'd ever had. Once they landed in Miami they both could finally unwind. Challenging her to a game of golf might be the first thing on the itinerary since it was her first love.

The plane sped down the runway, and in moments they were airborne and climbing in altitude. Damon looked over at Nichole again and noticed that she still had her eyes closed, but didn't appear to be asleep. Just as he was about to lean over and whisper into her ear, she opened her eyes. She turned to him and smiled.

"May I help you, Coach?"

Damon glanced down at Nichole's lovely lips.

"I was just going to ask you if you were OK."

Their lips were within inches of each other's. Nichole could feel Damon's warm, sweet breath against her face, and it was then that she really looked at him. He was absolutely gorgeous. She'd been so fixated on all her drama with Deacon that she hadn't realized what was directly in front of her. Of course when they first met she recognized him as a handsome and sexy man; however, looks can be deceiving. But the more time she spent with him, the more she'd been able to experience his generous nature, sense of humor, and of course, his golfing abilities.

"I'm fine. Just ready to hit the beach. How about you?"

He shook his head and said, "You look a little tired to me. Are you sure you don't want to get some rest first?"

"I will after I hit a few waves. You're so sweet to rescue me from all the mess in my life. That's why I want to make the most of this weekend. Tell me about your beach house."

Damon reached over and played with a straggling curl dangling in her eyes. He pushed it back in place, then spoke.

"It's just a house on the beach. I've had it for a while. It's where I go to unwind between seasons."

"Speaking of seasons, when do you have to report to work?"

"Well, I've actually gone back to work. We're already having meetings, reviewing film, and other stuff, but the vigorous schedule with the guys won't start for a few more weeks."

"Sounds like you're going to be a busy man, huh?"

He reached over and caressed her cheek, "I guess."

Nichole stared at him for a minute. "Damon, can I ask you something?"

"Sure," he replied.

"Remember when I asked you why you weren't married and you said because women can't put up with you?"

"Yes."

"What did you mean by that, because I don't want to speculate."

He sighed. "Well, because of my work schedule, when the season started most of the women I dated would leave because I didn't have a lot of time to spend with them."

"Are you serious?" Nichole asked.

"All I can say is that's what I've been told, but what I meant was they can't put up with me and my work schedule."

"I'm sorry, Damon," she whispered, lowering her head.

"There's no reason for you to be sorry. My career means a lot to me, and I'm a good coach, but I can sort of understand where they were coming from."

"Did these women have jobs, too?" she asked.

"Some of them did."

Nichole pulled some hand lotion out of her purse and poured some into the palm of her hand. "Would you like some?"

"No, thanks."

Nichole put the lotion back inside her purse and proceeded to rub the lotion over her hands.

"You'd think those women would understand that your coaching job has a demanding schedule."

"A few of them did, but a lot of them didn't. It didn't matter, though, because no matter how much time I spent with them, it was never enough," he explained.

Damon couldn't take his eyes off her beautiful face. She was the first woman in a long time that understood him. Nichole was stunning and he couldn't understand how Deacon or any man could ever hurt her.

"Well, those women were idiots. I would love the chance to travel and see the Eagles up close and personal."

What a nice thought. Having Nichole on the road with him would be a dream come true. They stared at each other for a few more seconds, and then Nichole cupped his face and kissed him lovingly on the lips. Damon thought he had died and gone to heaven. He'd planned on kissing her this weekend, but he didn't expect it to happen this soon. When Nichole released him, she giggled.

"Yes, those women were definitely idiots, and you are a great kisser, Coach."

"Thanks, and for the record, you're not so bad yourself."

"I was hoping you would say that," she answered.

"While we're on the subject, Miss Adams, what inspired you to kiss me?"

She blushed. "Because you've been a great friend to me, and I like you, Damon. I like you a lot."

"Really?" Damon teased.

"Yes, really," Nichole admitted.

Damon winked at Nichole. "Well just for the record, I like you, too."

"That's nice to hear, especially since Deacon's turned me into damaged goods."

He caressed her cheek and said, "You're not damaged goods, so stop saying that. Deacon's an idiot, and none of this is your fault."

"I still can't believe I was so naïve and trusting."

Damon looked out the window of the plane. "It happens to the best of us," he said. "I've been there, so I know what you're going through. Just remember, people have been through a lot worse than what we have."

"I'll drink to that," she said jokingly as she noticed the flight attendant approaching their row.

"Do you want a drink?" he asked.

She shook her head. "No, I was just kidding, but once we land I would like a glass of wine or something to unwind."

"I think I can arrange that. I told my housekeeper to make sure the house was fully stocked for the weekend."

"Housekeeper? I hear you, high roller."

Damon burst out laughing. "I'm not a high roller, but I do appreciate having nice things."

"That you do. Your home in Philly is beautiful and I can't wait to sample some of your culinary skills while we're in Miami," she hinted. He took her hand and kissed the back of it.

"I think I can arrange for that and a lot more."

The sensation of Damon's lips on her hand sent shock waves over her body. If this was any indication of what he had to offer, she was in for a long weekend.

"You're spoiling me, Damon."

He released her hand. "What's wrong with that?"

She linked her arms with his and said, "Nothing at all. Seriously, though, you've been the best thing that has happened to me in a long time, and I don't know what I would've done without you."

Damon leaned back and closed his eyes. "It feels great to have a beautiful woman boost your ego like that."

She playfully pinched his arm.

"Ouch! I see you're dangerous, too," he joked.

"You're so bad," she replied.

"I know, but in the best way possible. Seriously, Nichole, I like having you on my arm like this," he revealed.

"Does that mean I can come to some of the home games and cheer for you?"

Nichole's question surprised him, and then he remembered that she was a huge sports fanatic.

"Of course you can. You're welcome to come along on the away games too, if you want."

"And just where would I sleep?" she asked curiously.

He caressed her cheek and said, "We'll work it out."

She gave him a quick kiss on the lips. "Sounds like a lot of fun."

"Oh, I'd make sure you have the time of your life," he replied.

Deacon sat at the table while Lala poured two cups of coffee. It was obvious there was a lot of tension in the air. She set a cup of coffee in front of him and took her seat.

"Deacon, I'm glad you came over to talk to me."

He picked up the cup and took a sip. She'd remembered exactly how he liked his coffee, not that he thought she would forget. He rubbed his eyes.

"What do you want to talk about, Lala?" he asked.

She ran her finger around the rim of her cup before answering. "I want to talk about that woman that you've been seeing."

Deacon made eye contact with Lala. "Why? We've been separated for a couple of years now."

"Exactly! Separated. Do you love that woman, Deacon?"

"Her name is Nichole," he said angrily.

"I guess that answers my question."

Deacon put his hands over his eyes and sighed. "Listen, Lala, I care about you. I always have, and there was a time I loved you, but you and I both know that's gone and we need to move on with our lives."

"So are you saying you want a divorce?" she asked with tears in her eyes.

"I'm saying I want to be happy, and you and I haven't been happy together in a long time. It's time we faced it and moved on."

The tears that were lingering in Lala's eyes dropped into her coffee. She wiped her eyes.

"I'll have to admit, I didn't expect you to say that. In fact, I thought that you would've taken a second look at our marriage after you got shot. I know I did, especially when I thought I might lose you for good."

"We lost each other a long time ago, Lala. We were both just too stubborn and lazy to admit it," Deacon explained.

Lala reached across the table and covered Deacon's hand with hers. "I still love you, Deacon."

"I love you, too, Lala, but I'm not in love with you."

She leaned back in her chair and folded her arms. "So are you saying you're in love with that woman?"

"Do you want me to keep it real?" he asked.

"As hard as this is for me, yes, I want you to be honest with me."

Deacon stood up and placed his empty coffee cup in the sink. He turned to Lala. "Yes, I'm in love with her. I was in love with her the moment I laid eyes on her."

Angry, Lala stood up so fast she knocked over her chair. "What does she have that I don't?" Lala asked.

"It's not like that for me, Lala. I can't help who I fall in love with, and I never meant for any of this to happen. When you lost our child you went into a shell. I tried everything in my power to help you. I was hurting just as badly as you were, but instead of us coming together, you pushed me away from you emotionally and physically. How long did you expect me to stick around?" he yelled.

"We took vows, Deacon! You were supposed to stay with me for better or worse, but what did you do? The first time we have a crisis you did what you do best—disappeared."

Deacon lowered his head. Bringing up the painful memories of losing their child wasn't something he wanted to do. What he did want to do was put an end to his dead end marriage so he could concentrate on getting Nichole back.

"I'm sorry, Lala. I'm sorry for abandoning you, and I'm sorry things turned out like they did, but I'm only human."

Lala picked up her coffee cup up and threw it against the wall, shattering it into hundreds of pieces. "So am I, Deacon! So am I!"

Lala ran past Deacon, but he grabbed her arm and pulled her into his arms. As she sobbed, he hugged her.

"Lala, I'm sorry, baby. I never wanted things to end like this between us. You'll always be special to me, and I'll always love you. I just can't love you like you want and need me to."

She hugged his neck and completely broke down in

his arms. Seeing Lala like this broke Deacon's heart, but he knew he couldn't prolong the inevitable any longer. He cupped Lala's face and looked into her teary eyes.

"You're a good woman, Lala, and I'm sure you're going to be the perfect woman for the right man. I'm just sorry I can't be that man."

Lala looked up into Deacon's eyes. Her face was stained with tears.

"I guess it wasn't meant to be, huh?"

He kissed her on the lips and lingered there for a moment. "We were meant to be together, Lala, it just so happens that life's unfortunate circumstances tore us apart. I thought I was strong enough to deal with everything, but I wasn't. I still want us to be friends, because you are a wonderful woman."

Lala stepped out of his embrace and wiped her eyes with a napkin. "I'd like that, but you're going to have to give me a little time to get through all of this. It's going to be hard for me to accept that it's really over."

He turned and started picking up the pieces of the shattered coffee cup.

"I understand. In the meantime, if there's anything you need, and I mean anything, don't hesitate to call me. OK?"

"OK," she replied as she opened her pantry and retrieved a broom and dust pan.

Chapter Sixteen

Winston hung up the telephone and turned toward Arnelle.

"Well, Craig's going to do it," he said.

"Do what, baby?" she asked as she pulled back the linens on the bed.

"Sell part of his firm and start teaching architecture in the inner city. Remember? I told you he was thinking about changing his career a few weeks ago," he reminded her as he untied his shoes.

"Yeah, but I didn't know he was thinking about teaching," Arnelle said as she fluffed a pillow.

"Well, while we're on the subject, I'm thinking about doing something different, too," he announced before walking into the bathroom.

"What do you want to do, counselor?"

He walked over to her and pulled her into his arms. "Don't freak out on me, but I want to run for mayor."

Winston's announcement totally caught her off guard. "Mayor? What's going on with you and Craig? You're both too young to be going through a midlife crisis."

She stepped out of his embrace, walked over to the window, and looked out onto their back lawn. Winston joined her.

"Does this mean you're against it?" he asked softly.

Arnelle reached over and took his hand. "Politics can be very unforgiving, Winston. You see all the drama my dad has to deal with as San Antonio's mayor."

"I understand, sweetheart, but Herbert knew what he was getting into when he decided to run for mayor. He's been a judge for years, so he's quite familiar with the state government, and correct me if I'm wrong, but he is making a difference in the city with education, crime, jobs, and so many other things. That's what I want to do, baby, make a difference."

"I'm not saying I'm against it, Winston. I'm saying it's a big step and I don't want you to get hurt. Being mayor will put all our lives under a microscope, and throw us in the spotlight."

Winston kissed her cheek. "If you think it's going to be too much for you and the kids, I won't do it, but I know I will be an asset to the city, and I also want to complete the work our present mayor started as well."

Arnelle stared into Winston's eyes and saw his strong desire and seriousness in running for the mayor's office.

"Are you sure about this?"

He kissed her forehead. "Only if you're behind me and cool with it."

She thought for a moment and realized that Winston would be a great mayor. He was driven, always down for the cause, hardworking, outspoken, intelligent, fair, and compassionate. It didn't hurt that he was already friends with the present mayor and some of his staff. In reality he was already in the political circle.

Arnelle walked past Winston, giving him a bird's eye

view of her shapely body. He stared at her in silence. She turned around, catching him in his seductive gaze.

"What are you staring at, counselor?"

He looked her body up and down and said, "You. You get sexier each and every day."

She walked over to him and he immediately caressed her thighs and hips. Arnelle tilted his chin up so she could look him in the eyes.

"I support you, Winston, and I should've never hesitated when you asked me my opinion. I love you so much, honey, and if you want to be mayor, I'm there for you in any way possible."

"Thank you, Arnelle. I couldn't do this without you beside me."

Winston slowly raised the short, white satin nightgown she wore, exposing her thick, sexy thighs. He gently kissed her thighs and abdomen, and then looked up into her eyes.

"You are so beautiful," he whispered. "You're going to be a fine first lady."

Arnelle caressed his face. "You sure do know how to flatter me, sweetheart."

"I know," he replied softly right before he flicked his tongue against her sweet folds.

"Winston!" she yelled as she stumbled backward, nearly falling to floor. "You know I can't take that standing up!"

He quickly steadied her and then leaned back in the chair and laughed.

"I know, sweetheart. That's why I did it."

Arnelle smoothed down her nightgown. "You're so nasty."

"You like it," he replied as she stood and removed his watch.

She couldn't do anything but smile because Winston was right. She did like it. She never knew when he would strike, which kept the spontaneity in their marriage.

"Craig and Venice are going to have a casino night party in a few weeks on a Friday and a dinner party the following Saturday to talk about him teaching and me running for mayor."

"That sounds like fun," Arnelle replied as she sat down at her vanity and started brushing her hair. He unbuttoned his shirt and removed his T-shirt.

"It does. I'm going to help Craig put it together. It'll be great to see everybody. We haven't done that in a while."

Arnelle smiled with admiration for her husband. Winston winked at her as she continued to undress.

"I'll make sure Camille is free that weekend so she can keep the kids," she announced as she swung her hair over her shoulders. That simple gesture caused Winston to lose his thoughts once again. She twirled around in her chair and noticed his seductive facial expression once again.

"Winston, are you listening to me?"

"Huh?" he asked, snapping himself out of his trance.

She smiled and said, "Never mind."

Winston stood, walked over to his beautiful wife, and started massaging her shoulders. With her hair blown straight it hung down to her waist, which drove Winston crazy.

"You distracted me when you swung your hair over your shoulders. Baby, you look so hot tonight, not that you don't every night."

Arnelle giggled. "I thought we were talking about Camille."

"Really?" he asked as he kissed her neck. "You make it hard for me to concentrate on anything when you're walking around in front of me half naked."

She stood and ran her hands over Winston's backside. "I know it drives you crazy, baby. Why do you think I do it?"

Winston scooped up Arnelle into his arms and playfully tossed her on the bed.

"You do it for this," he said as he quickly removed his remaining clothes.

"You know me so well, and you know what I like," she purred.

His hands disappeared under her nightgown so he could touch her.

"Winston," she moaned, dragging out his name.

While kissing her greedily, he caressed her center. As his kisses trailed lower to her ample breasts, Arnelle's breathing became shallow with anticipation.

"Winston," she called out again, but this time breathlessly.

"I know, baby, be patient," he whispered as he ran his lips and tongue over her firm, ripe peaks.

Winston kissed his way down a little farther to her navel and lingered there momentarily to heat her up even more. She massaged his shoulders and wiggled beneath him as he trailed his kisses to his final destination.

"I love you so much, Arnelle," he whispered as he gripped her hips and dipped his head to taste her sweet nectar. When he flicked his tongue against her feminine flesh, Arnelle lost it emotionally, causing tears to flow from her eyes. She writhed and moaned as he slowly feasted on her feminine core. Winston's erotic torture stripped Arnelle of any inhibitions she might have been experiencing. Once his seductive foreplay had ceased and he positioned himself between her legs to finally make love to her, they were interrupted by a tiny knock on the bedroom door.

"Damn!" Winston whispered as he rolled off Arnelle. "Is that Fredrick?"

"Yes, dear," she replied as she climbed out of bed.

"I thought they were asleep," he said as he made his way into the bathroom.

"They were asleep, counselor," she called out to him as she climbed off the bed and walked over to the door. When she opened it Fredrick was standing there rubbing his tiny eyes.

"I'm thirsty, Mommie."

"You know I don't like giving you anything to drink after you've gone to bed," she said as she picked him up. "I'll make an exception this time, but only if you promise to go back to sleep."

Fredrick snuggled against his mother's neck and nodded in agreement. She heard the shower turn on as she sat Fredrick on the bed. She'd have to ask Winston if he took a cold or hot shower when he returned to the bedroom.

"Fredrick, you've gotten out of your bed three nights in a row asking for something to drink. Your daddy's not happy about it, and neither am I. This is the last night we're going to do this. OK?"

He rolled over onto his stomach, laughed, and started playing with the pillows.

"Fredrick, this is not playtime," she gently scolded him as she slipped into her robe. She held her arms out for Fredrick, who happily dived into his mother's arms. Winston returned to the bedroom and frowned at Fredrick.

Fredrick smiled at his father and yelled, "Daddy!"

"Don't Daddy me, Li'l Man."

Arnelle noticed Winston's scowl as she slipped into her shoes. "Winston, he's just a baby."

He sighed, walked over to her, and took their son out of her arms. He sat down on the bed and kissed Fredrick on the cheek.

"Son, you have no idea what you interrupted tonight."

Fredrick patted Winston's cheeks and laughed as if he understood exactly what Winston was talking about. Arnelle put her hands on her hips.

"Winston, be nice to your son. Besides, it's not like we can't pick up where we left off."

"I've heard that before. Fredrick is the only man I have to compete with," he joked. "Seriously, Arnelle, he's starting to make this a pattern, and we need to nip it in the bud now."

"You're so silly, Winston. You're not competing with your son, and he'll outgrow this soon."

"I hope so," he replied as he laughed and tickled Fredrick, who was now wide-awake.

"Winston, he'll never get back to sleep with you tickling him like that."

He picked up Fredrick up and placed him on his shoulders. "Get in bed, sweetheart. I'll take care of Fredrick."

Arnelle didn't hesitate as she smiled and removed her robe before climbing back into bed.

"Make sure you look in on MaLeah before you come back to bed. I'll be waiting."

"In that case, I'll make this quick," he replied as he walked out the door with Fredrick on his shoulders.

When Winston returned to the bedroom he had two glasses and a bottle of champagne. Arnelle was waiting for him just like she said she would be.

"What do you have there, counselor?"

"A bottle of your favorite champagne."

She sat up and asked, "What's the occasion?"

"Being in love with you is the only occasion I need," he said. "By the way, your son and daughter are now fast asleep."

He sat the bottle and glasses on the nightstand and closed the bedroom door. After removing his robe, Winston climbed into bed next to his wife and filled their glasses. Arnelle took a sip and closed her eyes to savor the flavor.

"Delicious. Thank you, baby."

"You're welcome," he answered after taking a large sip of the bubbly liquid. The loving couple laughed, talked, cuddled, and kissed as they finished off the last of the champagne. Shortly afterward the lights went off and they picked up exactly where they left off before Fredrick interrupted them.

Chapter Seventeen

Nichole woke up to the smell of bacon, coffee, and other breakfast delicacies, and the sound of the ocean waves. She rolled over and realized she'd slept in until nearly eleven o'clock. She'd had a great evening with Damon, and wished she could make it last longer.

The previous day they took a swim together in the warm coastal waters and relaxed on the beach. Later that evening they enjoyed dinner on the deck and spent the rest of their time together watching the sun set into the clear blue water. Nichole smiled as she reminisced about her first day in Miami. She sat up on the side of the bed and yawned before making her way to the bathroom. After showering, brushing her teeth, and combing her hair, she made her way back into the bedroom. As she made up the bed, Damon knocked on the door.

"Nichole, are you awake?"

"Yes, I'm up," she replied.

"Are you decent?" he asked.

"Open the door and find out," she teased.

Damon opened the door and walked into the room. "I see you woke up with a sense of humor."

Nichole couldn't help but notice how Damon's presence excited her. He possessed a broad chest, a very pronounced eight pack, and large, muscular legs. Nichole had a hard time concentrating after seeing him shirtless and in swimming trunks the day before. Today he was dressed in a pair of khaki cargo shorts and a bright orange golf shirt. Nichole finally snapped herself out of her trance.

"Yes, I feel quite frisky after my relaxing night. I haven't slept that well in a long time."

Damon was a little disappointed that Nichole was fully dressed when he entered the room. He was hoping to catch her in at least a robe. Needless to say, her outfit still showed off every sexy curve she owned. She had on a pair of red terrycloth shorts and a matching hoodie. Her legs were shimmering with baby oil, and her perfume caressed his nostrils and gave him a partial erection. He walked over and gave her a hug. When he released her he noticed she had a swimsuit on underneath her attire.

"Nichole, is that a bikini strap?"

She unzipped her jacket and revealed her bikini top. "Of course it is. I'm in Miami and I'm going to make the most of it. I'm ready to hit the beach. Are you game?"

Damon laughed. "I'm up for whatever. I was hoping that we could get in a round of golf sometime today."

Nichole's eyes immediately lit up. "Are you serious?"

"Of course I am, but not before we have breakfast," he announced.

Nichole clapped her hands together and said, "Sounds like a date, and speaking of breakfast, what is that heavenly smell downstairs?"

Damon quickly scooped her up into his arms, causing Nichole to scream.

"Damon! What are you doing?"

He smiled. "I'm taking you to breakfast."

She held on to his neck. "I think I can walk on my own."

"I know you can, but I want to carry you. Do you mind?"

Nichole hadn't been this close to a man since she broke up with Deacon, and it felt heavenly. In fact, she savored Damon's scent and the heat of his body. Damon carried Nichole down the stairs in his arms and sat her in the chair across from him.

"You keep treating me like this, and I'm never going back home."

"You won't hear any argument from me. Would you like coffee or orange juice?"

She held out her glass. "Orange juice, please. Wow, look at all this food. Are we having company?"

She couldn't believe the amount of food Damon had cooked for just the two of them. It also amazed her that he had the mindset to place a bouquet of fresh yellow roses on the table.

He laughed and poured orange juice in their glasses. "No. I've seen you eat, so I wanted to make sure you had plenty of food."

She put her napkin in her lap and said, "Ha! Ha! Damon. When did you cook all of this?"

He held out his hands to her. "I'm an early bird. Now, do you want to bless the food or should I?"

Nichole was stunned. He was a religious man, which was a major plus in her book. Could Damon have any flaws, or was it possible that he was the perfect man?

She blushed, placed her hands in his, and gave them a soft squeeze. "No, you can do it."

Damon proceeded to bless their food. Once he finished the prayer, they filled their plates with bacon, eggs, pancakes, fruit, sausage, and pastries. Nichole savored the delicious food.

"I'm going to need a nap after I finish with this buffet," she said.

"No, you're not, because I'm going to make you work it off on the golf course," he responded as he put a crispy piece of bacon in his mouth.

"You sure are talking a lot of trash for someone who's zero and one against me."

Damon chuckled. "I hear you, Tigress Woods. In that case you need to hurry up and finish eating, because I've lost my last game against you, young lady."

She leaned forward and seductively stated, "Sounds like you're planning on teaching me a lesson, Coach."

With his glass halfway to his mouth, he froze. Was this a come-on from Nichole, or a legitimate challenge? Whatever it was, her tone of voice aroused him to the fullest. She had no idea how badly he wanted to teach her all sorts of erotic lessons, and at the moment golf was the furthest thing from his mind.

"Well?" Nichole asked. "What are you going to do?"

He finally took a sip of orange juice. "I've played against you, and there's no way you need any lessons."

"Maybe not in your eyes, but in mine I do. You're a great golfer, and I've seen you putt. That's something I desperately need to work on. So are you going to give me a few lessons or not?"

Damon leaned forward. "OK, you twisted my arm," he whispered. "I'd love to give you a few lessons, Nichole."

A warm sensation ran through her body and settled in her lower region. She crossed her legs when she felt a tingling sensation between her thighs. Nichole gathered her thoughts.

"Damon Kilpatrick, if I didn't know any better, I'd think you were flirting with me."

"You think?" he asked innocently as he stood and carried his empty plate over to the sink. "Seriously, Nichole, you make it hard for a man not to flirt with you. You're a sexy woman."

Nichole blushed as she also stood. Damon took her empty plate out of her hand and placed it in the sink.

"Damon, I don't know what to say."

"You don't have to say anything," he replied as he pulled her into his arms and kissed her firmly on the lips.

Nichole felt like she was in heaven as she kissed Damon's ample lips. She loved the way he made her feel, and at the moment his tongue and lips were doing a number on her.

"What are you doing to me, Damon?"

He broke the kiss and said, "Whatever you want me to do."

She backed away from him to give herself some breathing room.

"Everything is telling me yes, but I'm scared."

Damon felt terrible, but he couldn't help himself. Here they were in Miami with blue skies, sandy beaches, and Nichole's sweet fragrance. It didn't help that she had a smile that shook him down to the bone.

"I'm sorry, Nichole. I didn't mean to pressure you."

"It's not your fault, and don't worry, you're not pressuring me. I enjoy kissing you, Damon, and believe me I do want more. When I say I'm scared, it's not of you. It's of me. I'm afraid of falling in love again."

He walked over to her and tilted her chin upward.

"You don't have to explain anything to me. I understand. It's hard to get back up on that horse after you've fallen off, but I will tell you this: You will ride again. On another note, I just want you to know that I'm into you. Not just physically either. I feel like I'm already emotionally attached to you, Nichole, and I would never hurt you. So when you feel like you're ready for us to take our relationship to another level, just let me know. OK?"

She nodded in agreement. Damon kissed her cheek.

"I didn't bring you here to take advantage of you. I only did it so you could get some rest, have fun, and for us to get to know each other better."

"I appreciate that you're trying to help me get past everything that I went through with Deacon, and I know it's only a matter of time before I'm able to let go."

"Sounds good," he responded as he cupped her face. "In the meantime, if anything happens between us it'll be because you're ready and nothing else. Agreed?"

Nichole saw the spirit of a man that was tearing down the wall she'd built around her heart.

"Thank you, Damon," she said with her voice cracking.

He kissed her cheek and said, "Give yourself time to heal. I promise you, things will get better."

"I hope you're right," Nichole whispered.

He lowered his head and kissed her slowly on the lips. "I'm not Deacon, and I can back up every promise I make to you. Just trust me."

She laid her head on his chest and felt another wall crumbling down around her heart.

"I do trust you, Damon."

He caressed her back. "Good. Now are you ready to lighten the mood around here and play some golf?"

Nichole smiled and wiped a stray tear off her cheek. "Yes, and when we get back can we go for a swim?"

"Sure we can. Now before we go, would you like to make a small wager to make it interesting?"

She laughed as she helped Damon clear the table. He'd made her feel 100 percent better, and now she was actually ready to have some real fun with him.

"Not again. Damon, I'm going to beat you like you stole something. Do you honestly want to lose to me again?"

"Ouch, I guess I should be afraid, huh?" Damon asked as he put the dirty dishes into the dishwasher and turned it on. Nichole put what was left over from their breakfast into the refrigerator.

"No, don't be afraid. OK, if you want to give your money away, I'll take it."

"Who said anything about money?" he asked with a raised brow.

"What do you have in mind, Coach?" she asked.

Damon thought long and hard and then said, "You go first."

Nichole smiled. "I see you need to get your thoughts together. OK, I'll go first. Whoever loses has to pay for the next two games?"

He folded his arms and leaned against the counter. "That's reasonable."

She put up her finger up and said, "Not so fast, Coach. Also, if I win I would like an Eagles jersey autographed by all the players."

"Done. What else?"

Nichole paced back and forth across the kitchen floor as if she was negotiating with one of her multimillion-dollar accounts.

"I would also like Sunday dinner prepared by you personally, and a foot massage whenever I request it."

Damon smiled. "I'd lose on purpose if that's all you

want. You're not making this hard at all, Nichole. You'd better reconsider before I list my demands."

Nichole put her hands on her hips. "Those are my requests. Now whatcha got?"

Damon knew what he wanted to request, but once again, he didn't want to pressure her. In his heart he wanted to tell her that if he won, he would like to hold her in his arms all night, every night—nightly massages, morning kisses, mind boggling sex, and lastly her everlasting love. What he did say made her gasp.

"If I win, Miss Adams, you are hereby ordered to mend your broken heart, with my help of course, be insanely happy twenty-four hours a day, and finally I want you to call me at sunrise every morning so I can start my day with a sound mind and happy heart. Deal?"

Nichole couldn't believe how perfect Damon was. She held her hand out to him and it was at that moment that she knew she would give herself to him at the next available moment. So to seal their bet, she kissed his lips and lingered there momentarily.

"Deal, now let's get out of here."

Nichole surprised Damon by jumping on his back for a piggyback ride as he walked out of the kitchen and into the hallway.

He laughed. "What are you doing?" he asked.

He loved the fact that Nichole was being so physical with him. She was a tomboy when she wanted to be, and a sexy vixen when she needed to be.

"You carried me in your arms downstairs, so I figured you could carry me out to the car on your back," she said as she mocked him.

"Nichole, you're torturing me. You're going to have to get off my back."

Teasing him further, she said, "I don't think so."

Without responding, Damon flipped Nichole over his

shoulder, causing her to scream. She had no idea how he maneuvered her over his shoulder. All she knew was that her head was spinning and Damon now held her body in a compromising position. Now it was his turn to taunt her. He stared into her eyes seductively.

"What were you saying?" he asked.

Nichole had never felt so stimulated. Her breathing was shallow and her center was throbbing once again. Damon had taken control of Nichole's sensual playfulness once again. She cleared her throat.

"I wasn't saying anything," she whispered. "You can put me down now."

"What if I don't want to?" he teased as he held her body in mid air. To keep from falling, Nichole had to lock her legs around Damon's hips. This simple gesture allowed her to feel Damon's aroused lower body, which left no question to his physical attraction to her. Stunned, she was unable to look him in the eyes.

"You might not want to, Damon, but . . ."

Damon released her before she could finish her sentence.

"Stop whining, loser," he whispered.

Nichole's knees were weak, her body was on fire, and her core was moist. Straddling Damon's large physique ignited something inside her. She watched him get his golf clubs out of the closet and softly asked, "How did you do that?"

He casually opened the front door and winked at her.

"Oh, Nichole, I have all kinds of tricks up my sleeve. Let's play golf."

Nichole silently grabbed her purse and walked out with Damon to his awaiting car. From that moment on she would never look at him the same way. She realized he was a man with some hidden qualities that could possibly turn her world and body upside down.

Chapter Eighteen

Deacon couldn't believe that Nichole still wasn't answering her telephone. He was getting desperate and had to decide how he was going get Nichole to listen to his side of the story.

"Where are you, Nichole?"

He drove over to her house and pulled into the driveway. As he got out and walked up to her door, Nichole's nosey, elderly neighbor was outside watering her flowers. When she looked up and saw Deacon, she yelled, "She's not home."

"I'm sorry, Mrs. Adele, what did you say?" he asked as he walked over to the gate separating the two houses. She met him at the gate.

"How are you doing, Officer Miles?"

"I'm fine, Mrs. Adele. How are you?"

"Besides this arthritis in my hip, I'm doing well."

"If that's the case, then you need to be taking it easy."

She patted his hand and laughed. "I guess you're right."

"Mrs. Adele, I didn't hear what you said when I got out of my car."

"Oh, I said Nichole's not home. I saw her leave a few days ago with a couple of suitcases. I guess she needed a vacation after that man tried to break into her house."

Deacon was glad that Mrs. Adele didn't know he was the man who had tried to kick down Nichole's door. He had to keep her as an ally as long as possible in order to gain more information.

"Was she alone when she left?"

Mrs. Adele thought for a moment. "I'm not sure. It could've been a taxi picking her up. You know Nichole travels a lot with her job, so I'm used to seeing her leaving with suitcases. You haven't talked to her, son?"

"No, ma'am. Nichole just recently came back into town from visiting a friend, and I've had some health issues, so we haven't had much time to catch up with each other."

Mrs. Adele frowned. "You work too much, Officer Miles. You should always keep in touch with Nichole. When are you two going to get married anyway? You've been playing around much too long. She's a good girl, you know?"

"I know she's a good girl, Mrs. Adele." He pulled his business card out of his pocket and handed it to her. "Do you mind giving me a call when she comes home?"

Mrs. Adele smiled and then pinched Deacon's cheek. "Of course I don't mind. You be safe now, OK?"

Deacon walked toward his car and said, "I will, and you take care of that hip."

"Oh, I will," she said as she limped up the steps to her house. "Good-bye."

Deacon climbed into the car and slammed the door. He started the engine and backed out of the driveway. As he drove down the street, he pulled out his cell and dialed.

"Hello?" the voice on the other end answered.

"Meridan, it's Deacon. You got a moment?"

"Not really. What can I do for you, Deacon?"

"I know Nichole's told you what happened between us, and I'm sorry things turned out this way. Meridan, I would never hurt Nichole because I love her, but I can't seem to get her to talk to me so I can explain things to her. Can you talk to her for me?"

"Deacon, I'm not going to get between you and Nichole. I don't have to remind you that she is my best friend. The best advice I can give you is to back off and give her some time to absorb everything that's happened."

"I've given her nothing but time," he said, frustrated. "Now her neighbor tells me she went out of town a few days ago. Do you know where she is?"

"Deacon, please," Meridan pleaded with him. "Wherever Nichole went, I'm sure she's doing a lot of thinking so she can figure things out."

"All I want to do is to talk to her," he reiterated. "I love her."

"Deacon, she had to call the police on you. That's not love."

"I was drunk, Meridan. None of that would've happened if she had just talked to me."

"You and I both know that Nichole is not a woman you force into anything. Like I said, leave me out of it and give her some time."

"All right, Meridan, I'll leave you out of it, but I will get Nichole to listen to me one way or the other," he said before he hung up the telephone.

Meridan hung up the telephone and yelled, "Shit!" She quickly dialed Nichole's cell phone, but it went directly to voice mail, so she left her a message.

"Hey, Nikki, it's Dee. Give me a call as soon as you get

this message. By the way, I hope you're having a great time."

Deacon arrived at the police station and found Riley. He sat down at his desk and abruptly said, "I need a favor."

Riley looked up at him and asked, "Well hello to you, too. Why are you here? You're still on medical leave."

Deacon leaned forward.

"I'm sorry, Riley. Listen, I need you to pull Nichole's cell phone records."

"You've lost your damn mind," Riley replied as he leaned back in his chair. "You know I can't do that without approval from the captain."

"Bullshit! You can get it done. I'm your partner, remember? I also need you to get a ping on her cell and see where she is. She's out of town somewhere and I need to know where she is."

"Why? Nichole travels all the time with her job. Why is it so important this time?"

Deacon wadded up a piece of paper and threw it at Riley. "Because I have a gut feeling it's not for her job, and I swear if she's with that coach, I'm going to—"

Riley put up his hands to stop Deacon from talking. "Stop right there! Don't say another word, Deek. You can't talk like that around me, or here at the office, and you know it. You're going to have to chill with this obsession you have with Nichole. Damn!"

Deacon slammed his fist down on the desk, causing other officers in the squad room to look at them. He leaned forward and whispered, "You don't understand, Riley."

Riley stood and poured Deacon a cup of coffee. "Yes, I do. You're obsessed."

Frustrated, Deacon jumped out the chair. "Go to hell, Riley. Just get me the records. I'm out of here."

Riley shook his head in disbelief and watched help-
lessly as Deacon walked out of the office.

Damon and Nichole returned to the house after playing eighteen holes of golf. Nichole walked into the
house ahead of Damon, who was obviously in a great
mood. He followed Nichole into the kitchen and
watched as she opened the refrigerator and retrieved two
bottles of Heineken beer. She opened them and handed
Damon one before taking a sip.

"I can't believe I let you come back and beat me. I lost
by two strokes!" Nichole said.

Damon held his bottle of beer out so Nichole could tap
hers against it. "You can't win them all, sweetheart. I'm
definitely going to savor this victory."

Nichole sat down at the kitchen table and pouted.
"Enjoy your victory while you can, coach. I want a re-
match."

Damon set his beer down on the kitchen table and
started massaging her hand. She smiled.

"That's feels great, Damon."

"Thank you. Now, what do you want to do for dinner?
Do you want to go to a restaurant, or do you want to put
something together here?"

"I really don't want to be around any crowds, Damon.
If it's OK with you, I'd rather stay here and throw a couple of steaks on the grill."

Damon stopped massaging her hands.

"Let me see what I have."

He opened the refrigerator, pulled out two T-bone
steaks, and placed them in the sink before returning back
to his seat.

"I found some T-bones," he revealed as he continued
to massage her hands.

Nichole finished off the rest of her beer and allowed Damon to massage her other hand as well.

"I want to help. What can I cook to go with the steaks?" she asked.

"You decide. Look in the fridge and see what looks interesting," he answered as he opened the door to the deck. "I'm going to start the grill. I'll be right back."

Nichole looked inside the refrigerator and found two large potatoes and a variety of vegetables to stir fry. Damon walked back into the kitchen and closed the patio doors.

"The grill is on. What did you find?"

"Oh, I found a little something, something," she said as she pulled some aluminum foil out of a drawer. "You just make sure my steak is tender and juicy."

"Don't worry, I will. Would you like another beer?" Damon asked as he opened the refrigerator.

She wrapped the potatoes in foil and said, "Not right now. I'm trying to stay sober so I won't burn dinner again."

He chuckled as he seasoned their steaks. "You're not going to burn anything. Now, tell me how you like your steak. Medium well?"

She unzipped her jacked and removed it, revealing her bikini top. "Exactly."

Damon stood there for a moment gazing at Nichole's voluptuous chest. He licked his lips.

"These steaks will be ready in no time, so step it up on the side orders."

"Just because you beat me at golf doesn't mean you get to boss me around, Coach," she joked as she followed him out onto the deck with the potatoes. She placed them on the top shelf of the grill. "They'll be ready to come off the grill in a little while. Will you watch them for me while I get the veggies ready?"

Damon placed the two large steaks on the grill and smiled without answering. Nichole disappeared into the kitchen and started stir-frying zucchini, squash, peppers, broccoli, and carrots in extra virgin olive oil. Once the steaks and vegetables were done, Nichole and Damon finished their meal in no time. After cleaning the kitchen they sat on the beach and watched the orange glow of the sun set into the clear blue water.

It was nearly eight o'clock when the pair finally made their way back to the beach house. Tired and wet, they showered and met back up in the living room to watch a movie. Nichole wore a pair of short satin pajamas with large SpongeBob SquarePants slippers. When she walked into the room Damon looked down her long, shapely legs to her feet and laughed.

"What the hell?"

"Leave my slippers alone. I like SpongeBob and they're comfortable."

Damon flipped through a stack of DVDs and said, "I bet they are."

Nichole sat down on the sofa and watched Damon in silence. He was built like a chiseled African warrior, and the T-shirt and shorts he wore accented his well-toned physique. She was still fascinated and turned on by the way Damon had flipped her over his shoulder earlier that day. Nichole came to the conclusion that Damon would be an exceptional lover, and she challenged herself to explore her suspicions further.

"Found one," Damon announced before popping the movie into the DVD player.

Nichole stood. "Are you thirsty?" she asked.

"Yes, another beer would be nice. Bring the pretzels and that can of mixed nuts in the cabinet too, if you don't mind."

Just as Nichole was about to walk into the kitchen, Damon heard a key turn in the front door. Startled, he hurried over to the door, but before he could get to it, Zel walked in with a huge smile on his face.

"What's up, bro?"

"Zel! What the hell are you doing here? I've told you a hundred times that you are not to use my house without my permission, and why aren't you at school anyway?"

Zel sat his duffel bag on the floor next to the door.

"I'm sorry, bro, but I kind of had to get away for minute and do some early graduation celebrating, if you know what I mean. I didn't expect to find you here, though."

Confused, Damon looked over Zel's shoulder and noticed a young woman standing behind him. Damon backed away and let Zel's female companion enter. She wore a pair of skintight jeans and a cut-off shirt which exposed and flat stomach with a pierced navel.

"I'm sorry for my outburst, young lady. You are?"

The young lady moved around in front of Zel and shook Damon's hand while Zel walked over to Nichole and gave her a hug.

"Nichole, it's great seeing you again. Nice PJs."

Embarrassed, Nichole picked up a pillow and held it in front of her body.

"Oh, bro, my bad. That's my shorty, Mia. Mia, this is my big brother, Damon, and his lady, Nichole."

Nichole noticed a vein protruding in Damon's neck. She could tell by the look on his face that he was about to snap. Damon slammed the door.

"Zel, you never cease to amaze me. Mia, I'm sorry we're meeting under these circumstances but—"

"Damon, could I see you in the kitchen for a second?" Nichole interrupted him.

"In a minute, Nichole," he replied. "Zel, I don't know where your brain is sometimes. I've—"

"Coach!" she yelled to get Damon's attention. "Please, it'll only take a minute."

Damon pointed his finger in Zel's face and whispered, "Don't you move, and I mean it."

Mia was clearly taken aback by Damon's presence, but she noticed that Zel didn't seem to be shaken by his aggressiveness at all. Inside the kitchen, Nichole took Damon's hands.

"Take a breath. You need to calm down before you give yourself a stroke."

"I'm going to kill my brother, Nichole. I can't believe he came down here without calling me first. He's got to go, Nichole."

She smiled. "He's your brother, Damon. He's young and he's having fun. I called you in here because I didn't want you to embarrass him in front of his girlfriend."

"That's not his girlfriend. Zel has a different woman every day of the week."

"In any case, I don't think you should scold Zel in front of her. I'm just telling you how it looks from a woman's perspective. Just talk to him and discreetly take the keys from him. Then when you guys can talk in private, tell him that the beach house is off limits until further notice. Explain to him that he has to respect you and your things."

He put his hands over his face. "Nichole, I've said it until I'm blue in the face."

Nichole reached up and removed Damon's hands. "Don't worry. I got this."

Before Damon knew what was happening, Nichole was back in the living room, talking to the young couple. He followed behind her.

"Mia? Is that your name?"

"Yes, ma'am," Mia answered

"Do you mind waiting for Zel in the kitchen?"

"No, ma'am," she replied before making her way into the kitchen. Zel, Damon, and Nichole waited for Mia to enter the kitchen before speaking. Just as Damon was about to say something, Nichole put her finger up to his lips.

"Hold on, Coach."

Damon smiled and stood to the side. "Go right ahead."

Nichole walked up to Zel. "Zel, you and I haven't had the chance to get to know each other yet, but I think I know your type very well."

"Hold up, Nichole," he responded.

"No, you hold up," she replied with her voice slightly elevated.

Zel looked at Damon. "Bro, you going to let her talk to me like this?"

Damon stared at Zel without responding. Nichole grabbed Zel's chin and made him look at her.

"Zel, Damon loves you, and there's nothing he wouldn't do for you. I think you know that, too, and that's why you take advantage of his kindness. Now, according to Damon, you didn't ask his permission to use the beach house. Correct?"

"Correct," Zel said as he rolled his eyes.

"You and I also know that the best thing you could do right now is apologize to your brother and hand over the keys."

Zel shoved his hand into his pocket and pulled out the keys. "I'm sorry, bro," he apologized as he dropped the house keys into Damon's hands. "Nichole, you got a lot of balls talking to me like that, but I deserved it, so it's cool. Damon, I promise I'll chill. I do appreciate everything that you have done for me, and all I was doing was trying to have some fun. You'll do good to keep Nichole on your side. She's no joke. Seriously, though, I love you, man, and I'll try not to make any more stupid decisions."

Damon hugged Zel.

"I love you, too."

Nichole clapped her hands together and said, "Good! Now, Damon, do you mind if Zel and Mia go ahead and stay since they're already here?"

Damon stepped up and wrinkled his forehead. "I'm not that forgiving. Zel, you and your *shorty* can't stay here."

"I understand. It's cool," Zel said as he picked up his duffel bag. He walked over to Nichole and gave her a kiss on the cheek. Before releasing her, he whispered in her ear. "You're perfect for my brother."

Nichole was shocked at Zel's statement. She stepped out of his embrace and blushed.

"Mia!" Zel yelled. "Let's roll."

"I thought we were staying here for the weekend," she said as she re-entered the living room.

He took her bag out of her hand and said, "Change of plans."

"It was nice meeting you guys," Mia said as she passed Damon and Nichole. "Sorry we can't stay."

"Likewise," Nichole answered. Damon didn't say anything. Just as Zel was about to close the door, Damon stopped him.

"Zel?"

"Yeah?"

"Take her over to The Palms in South Beach. I'll call and take care of everything."

Zel smiled. "Thanks, bro, but I got it this time."

"Are you sure?" Damon asked.

"If there's one thing I learned from you, bro, it's to treat your lady like a queen. I got it, seriously," Zel replied.

Damon was impressed. He was watching Zel mature right in front of his eyes. "Good night, Zel."

Zel looked at Nichole and then Damon, and said, "Sweet dreams."

Zel closed the door leaving Damon and Nichole alone once again. Damon let out a loud sigh before dropping his exhausted body down onto the sofa.

"What a night," he said.

"Are you still up for a movie?" Nichole softly asked as she sat down next to him.

He patted her gently on the leg and said, "You bet I am."

She hugged his neck. "Start the movie, I'll get your Heineken."

Chapter Nineteen

An hour into the second movie, Nichole fell asleep. After a full day of golf and swimming, she was wiped out. Damon was fighting sleep himself until he decided not to fight it anymore. He turned off the TV and woke up Nichole.

"Nichole, it's time to go to bed."

"What time is it?" Damon looked at his watch and stood.

"It's one o'clock."

Groggy, Nichole held out her hand so Damon could help her up from the sofa. She slid her feet into her gigantic SpongeBob slippers and slowly made her way up the stairs ahead of Damon. When they reached the landing, Nichole did something totally unexpected. She turned and entered Damon's bedroom instead of her own, kicked off her slippers, and crawled under the comforter. Damon froze, not understanding what had just happened. He didn't know whether Nichole was incoherent, or if she knew exactly what she was doing. This put Damon in a strange predicament. He walked over to the bed and sat down.

"Nichole?"

"Huh?" she answered, mumbling and still groggy.

"You're in my bed, sweetheart."

She rolled over. "It's OK, I won't bite."

Damon smiled. "I'm not worried about you biting me, Nichole. I'm worried about something else."

Nichole rolled over and sat up putting her face to face with Damon. She noticed he had an odd look on his face.

"Damon Kilpatrick, what does a girl have to do to get you into bed?"

"I thought you were delirious, so I just wanted to be sure that you knew what you were doing," he announced.

"Coach, I'm in your bed because I want to be with you. You make me feel safe and loved. I haven't felt like that in a long time."

Damon reached up and caressed her cheek. "What exactly are you saying?"

Nichole wrapped her arms around Damon's neck and kissed him firmly on the lips. Damon's body instantly responded as he shared the loving kiss with Nichole. They continued to kiss as they slowly began to remove each other's clothing. Once Damon had Nichole stripped down to her natural attire, all he could do was stare at her beautiful body. Nichole had never been ashamed of her body and actually loved the fact that Damon took pleasure in gazing at her assets. She lay back on his fluffy pillows and gazed up at him.

"Do you see something you like?"

He gently ran one finger across her thigh. "Without a doubt."

She sat up, wrapped her arms around Damon's neck,

and began to kiss his neck, lips, and chest. Nichole paused when she heard Damon suck in a breath.

"Are you OK?" she asked as she leaned back.

"I'm cool," he replied after clearing his throat. He ran his hands down her back and pulled her closer.

Nichole nibbled on his earlobe. "I want you, Damon," she whispered. "When are you going to take off those shorts and get between the sheets with me?"

Damon nearly lost it at that point. The only reason he was hesitating was because he was trying to remember if he had any condoms in the house. He hadn't had the luxury of bringing a woman to his beach house in a long time, and he didn't want to mess up the night with Nichole because of that reason. Nichole continued to torture Damon with her butterfly kisses.

"Nichole, I don't have any condoms in the house."

"Really?" she asked. "Don't worry. I have some in my bag."

Nichole climbed out of bed and leisurely walked across the hallway to her room. "You'd better be out of those shorts by the time I get back," she yelled from across the hall.

Damon now wondered if Nichole had packed condoms for the weekend, or if they were left over from her nights with Deacon. Either way, she was in his bed now, and she obviously wanted to be with him. He stood and happily let his shorts fall down around his ankles.

When Nichole walked back into the room she found Damon standing beside the bed waiting on her. When she saw his assets, she stopped in her tracks and said, "Have mercy." Nichole was taken aback by Damon's physique. He was significantly larger than she had imagined, and his toned body clearly showed that he took pride in his appearance. Damon took note of Nichole's obvious admiration.

"Do you see anything you like, Miss Adams?" he asked.

Without answering, she walked across the room and slowly looked Damon up and down. After sizing him up, she smiled.

"I see a lot of things that I like."

Damon pulled Nichole into his arms and held her there so she could feel the hardening of his body. Nichole closed her eyes and pressed her face against his warm neck. Damon slid his hands down to her derriere, cupped her hips, and lifted her into his arms, laying her down on the bed. He trailed kisses from her lips down to her navel and back up again.

"Relax, Nichole. I'll never hurt you."

She ran her tongue across his lips. "Thanks, Damon, she whispered. "I needed to hear that."

"I also think you need this," he replied as he methodically dipped his head between her thighs and feasted on her for several minutes. Nichole closed her eyes and moaned as Damon tongue danced against her tender flesh. He wanted Nichole to remember their weekend together for the rest of her life and he wanted her to feel what true love really felt like. He reached up and took the small packet she had clutched in her hand. While he continued to sprinkle her body and breasts with light kisses, he quickly covered his rigid shaft. Nichole opened her eyes and looked up into Damon's sensual eyes.

"I'm ready," she breathlessly whispered.

He responded to her request systematically as he immersed himself into her soul. Damon gyrated slowly against Nichole's hips as she held on tightly to his large frame. Soft whimpers escaped Nichole's lips as her body melted into Damon's in complete ecstasy.

The next morning Deacon couldn't wait for Riley to call him with information. Unfortunately, when he received it, it wasn't what he wanted to hear. He yelled at Riley through the telephone.

"What do you mean Nichole's in Miami? What the hell is she doing in Florida?"

"I don't know, Deek. I'm just telling you what I found out. Once again, if you care anything about your career, you'd back off Nichole before she goes to Internal Affairs and has you brought up on charges for stalking," Riley replied.

"Nichole wouldn't do that. She'd never hurt my career. She knows how much I love being a cop."

Riley laughed. "Am I the only one looking at this situation with clear eyes? She's moved on, Deacon."

"I might end up losing Nichole in the end, but until that happens, she has to know the truth, and she has to hear it from me. One way or the other, I will get her to talk to me."

Riley closed his eyes. He was becoming more frustrated with his friend by the second.

"Deacon, for the last time, Nichole needs more time. If you keep pushing up on her like this, she'll never talk to you," Riley pointed out.

"Bro, I don't have the luxury of waiting. That Eagles coach is already putting the full court press on Nichole, and I swear to God if he's touched her, I'm not going to be responsible for my actions."

"She's not your wife, Deacon! You need to concentrate on the woman that is your wife," Riley yelled.

Deacon sighed. "Lala and I are getting a divorce. We've already discussed it."

Riley laughed. "Just like that, huh?"

"You damn right! I could kick myself in the ass for not divorcing Lala sooner. Nichole will come back to me once she knows the truth. She loves me. You can't stop loving somebody overnight."

"If you say so, bro. Listen, I have to run and do some police work. It would do you some good to go somewhere for a few days to get your head together because I can't keep covering your ass."

Deacon frowned. "My head is together. My heart will be back together once I get Nichole back."

"Whatever you say. I'll holler at you later," Riley replied before hanging up the telephone.

Damon and Nichole lay in each other's arms until late morning. They'd made love off and on throughout the night, and eventually collapsed from exhaustion. If it weren't for the ringing of Damon's telephone, he would've slept longer. The phone was on the third ring by the time he reached across Nichole's body and answered.

"Hello?"

"Damon? It's Arnelle. I'm sorry if I woke you, but is Nichole with you?"

He gently kissed Nichole's neck. "Yes, she is," he whispered. "And why do you want to know?"

That subtle contact with Nichole's skin caused his lower body to awaken. He didn't know how it was possible after everything they'd done the night before, but he was once again ready for some more.

"I'm asking because Meridan was concerned about her. She said she'd been trying to call her cell, but it's going straight to voice mail."

Damon kissed Nichole's neck again, causing her to squirm and spoon her hips against him.

"Let Meridan know she's fine. She turned off her cell because she didn't want Deacon calling."

"I understand," Arnelle replied. "Well, tell her to call Meridan when she has a chance."

"I will," he whispered as he gently brushed his hand across Nichole's breasts. "I'll talk to you later."

"Damon?" Arnelle called out to him.

"Yes?"

"I guess it's safe to say that you and Nichole are getting along OK?"

He chuckled under his breath. "Something like that. Now if you don't mind, I would like to get back to bed."

"Sure you would. Anyway, enjoy your day and tell Nichole I said hello."

"Consider it done. Good-bye," he said before hanging up the telephone. Nichole was sound asleep, but she wouldn't be for long. Damon ran his tongue over her brown peaks and lingered there. Seconds later, Nichole's eyes slowly opened.

"Good morning to you, too, Coach."

Damon stopped pleasuring her only to reply, "Good morning." He kissed her firmly on the lips, sampling the sweetness of her tongue as well. Nichole loved kissing Damon, and she now loved making love to him. Damon grabbed the last condom off the nightstand. Nichole anxiously watched and waited as Damon applied the latex barrier.

Her body was already on fire and anticipated feeling Damon's skin against hers once again. Needless to say, he didn't disappoint her when he rolled her on to her stomach and moved in between her hips. The intensity of his loving was greater than the night before. Nichole was sure her screams of pleasure could be heard by swimmers on the beach. The problem was that she couldn't control her cries of passion, and Damon wasn't showing any signs of weakening. In fact, his thrusts became stronger, causing Nichole's body to finally climax uncontrollably beneath him.

Drenched in perspiration, the couple fell on to the bed. Nichole's legs trembled as Damon stroked her hair and kissed her lower back.

"Damn, Nichole, you're driving me crazy."

She gathered what little strength she had left and said, "I can't move. I think I'm paralyzed."

Damon laughed and caressed every curve of her body. "You're not paralyzed, Nichole."

"I'm serious, Damon. I can't move."

"That's because I was on top of you, woman," he said as he rolled off her body. "You're fine, and I mean that in every sense of the word."

"You sure know how to flatter a girl after you tried to kill her, don't you?"

Damon laughed again and then kissed her. "In that case, I'm glad I held back."

Stunned, Nichole looked into Damon's eyes to figure out if he was serious. When he fell back on the bed laughing, she knew he was just kidding. She pinched his arm and climbed on top of him to pin him down. Damon tickled her.

"I have you right where I want you," he said.

"If we're going to go another round, I need to do some stretching exercises or something first," she joked. "I thought I was going to pull a muscle."

He sat up and held her in a sensual embrace. "You don't need to stretch, baby, because you did just fine. Are you hungry?"

She kissed his chin. "Thanks to you, I'm famished."

Damon gave Nichole a quick kiss on the lips before climbing out of bed. "Don't put all the blame on me. Correct me if I'm wrong, but weren't you involved?"

Nichole giggled without answering. She couldn't help but admire his beautiful body as he made his way into the bathroom. When he returned, he put on his shorts and a shirt.

"Sit tight. I'll fix breakfast."

"Don't you mean brunch?"

"I'll think of something," he answered as he walked across the room. "By the way, don't get dressed, and give Meridan a call."

"Is something wrong?" she asked.

He kissed her on the forehead. "Not that I know of. Arnelle called and said Meridan had been trying to reach you, but she's getting your voice mail. I told her why you had your phone turned off."

Nichole threw the comforter off her body, giving Damon a clear view of her body. She posed provocatively.

"Thanks, Damon."

He cursed under his breath and did his best to keep his body under control; however, Nichole wasn't making it easy for him to leave the room.

"You're playing dirty, Nichole. You know we're out of condoms."

"I know, but I can't help it. I love seeing that ravenous expression on your face."

"I bet you do," he said as he turned toward the door. "I'll be back shortly, so don't move."

"Don't you want me to come down and help you?" she asked.

"No, I can handle it by myself. Call Meridan and put her mind at ease," he insisted. "I'm sure she'd love to hear your voice."

Nichole walked over to Damon, wrapped her arms around his neck, and kissed him lovingly.

"What was that for?" he asked as he embraced her.

"Don't you know?" she replied softly as she stared into his eyes.

Damon gazed into Nichole's eyes. He knew exactly what he wanted to say, but he didn't want to get ahead of himself.

"I have my suspicions, but I've been wrong before, so this time I'll keep my speculations to myself, at least for now."

"I understand," Nichole said as she nuzzled his neck.

Damon patted her firm, round backside. "I'd better start breakfast. Save me some hot water," he said.

Nichole nodded and disappeared inside the bathroom.

Chapter Twenty

After showering and putting on one of Damon's T-shirts, Nichole changed the sheets on the bed and crawled between the linens as instructed. She turned on her cell phone and was immediately alerted that her mailbox was full. Ignoring it, she dialed Meridan's number. Nichole smiled when she heard Damon humming from downstairs. Three rings later, Meridan answered.

"Hey, Dee, what's up?"

"Nichole! Don't you ever turn your cell phone off again! I was worried sick about you," Meridan scolded her. "Do you have any idea how many messages I left on your phone? I mean I know you're in Miami with Damon, but you still don't cut yourself off from the outside world. If you were going to do that, you could've at least given me a courtesy call each day so I wouldn't worry!"

Nichole giggled and said, "Are you finished?"

"No, I'm not finished, Nikki. What are you and Damon doing down there anyway?"

Nichole laughed. "You know I'm not one to kiss and tell, but I will say that Damon is an unbelievable man."

"What the hell does that mean, Nikki? I want details!" Meridan demanded. "Have you slept with him?"

Nichole looked toward the door and then whispered, "Yes."

"Already, Nikki? Couldn't you have held out just a little while longer?"

"Listen to me, I'm in sunny Miami. I'm listening to waves crashing on the beach, we're playing golf on some unbelievable courses, and this man is unbelievably handsome and his body is awesome. It doesn't hurt that he's also sensitive, attentive, and thoughtful. He looks me straight in the eyes when he talks to me, and he's a fabulous kisser. I could go on and on, and did I mention how fine he was?"

Meridan laughed at Nichole's explanation. "You're a nut!"

"Dee, I have to say that I have never in my life experienced anything like him. I thought I was going to start talking in tongues."

"It's like that, is it?" Meridan asked.

"That and more, Dee. Damon is amazing, and did I say how fine he was? You should see this man's abs. Girl, yesterday he flipped me over his shoulders and the next thing I knew I was straddling his waist. I almost burst into flames. Did I mention how fine and handsome he was?"

Meridan was rolling in the bed from laughing so hard at Nichole. "OK! OK! You're so stupid. Forget I even said anything. Have fun and I'm happy for you. Damon is a nice guy, but I don't want you to rush things."

"Thanks, Dee, but I wouldn't have made it this far without him. I'm starting to feel normal again after Deacon."

"Listen, Nikki, speaking of Deacon, he called me looking for you. Of course I wouldn't tell him where you were, but you're going to have to be extra careful. He's determined to get you back."

"What did he say?" she asked.

Meridan filled Nichole in on her conversation with Deacon. She also told her that she should share this news with Damon because the nature of their relationship had changed.

"I just don't understand. Why can't he let go?" Nichole asked.

Meridan sighed. "I'll tell you two possible reasons. He's either obsessed or really madly in love with you. Don't forget you guys were talking marriage, and I know you were in love with him, too."

Nichole hated that Meridan had brought up her possible engagement to Deacon.

"My feelings are not the same. Deacon has done some foul things since I've broken up with him, and I suspect him of doing a few other things. What I felt for him is gone."

"Nikki, do you remember what Daddy used to always tell me when we were in school? 'Don't open another door until you close the one behind you.' Speaking of the other door, where is Damon?"

"He's downstairs cooking breakfast for me."

"Are you still coming back tomorrow?" Meridan asked.

"Yes. I have to be back at work on Tuesday, and Damon does too."

"Well, give him my regards, but remember what I said. You already have enough drama going on. Don't add Damon in the mix until you clear things up once and for all with Deacon. Do you agree?"

Nichole shook her head in disagreement. "It's not that easy, Dee. Damon's already in the mix, and there's no turning back now."

"I hope you know what you're doing."

"I believe with all my heart that I do, Dee. I'll call you before we leave for the airport. Give Keaton and Jeremiah a kiss for me."

"I will. I love you, Nikki."

"I love you, too, Dee. I'm getting ready to run. I think Damon's on his way back to the bedroom. I'm going to be his breakfast in bed."

"You are so nasty!" Meridan teased. "Don't be down there acting like a freak-a-zoid."

"Stop it, Dee! You know I'm a lady."

"Whatever you say, sis. Seriously, Nikki, have a safe flight and call me when you land."

"You'll be my first phone call," Nichole assured her. "Good-bye."

"Good-bye, Nikki."

Nichole hung up the telephone just as Damon walked into the bedroom. He pulled off his T-shirt and instantly stimulated her.

"Breakfast is served, but I want to take a shower first, if you don't mind."

"Go right ahead. Something smells delicious downstairs," she mumbled as she stared at his physique.

Damon opened his dresser and pulled out some clean clothes. When he turned to go into the bathroom, Nichole closed her eyes.

"If you don't hurry up and get out of here, I'm not going to be responsible for my actions. Your abs are unbelievable."

He laughed. "Are you saying you like my body, Nichole?"

"Yes! Now go!" she pleaded with him as he walked slowly toward the bed.

He leaned over her. "Do you want to touch them?" he whispered.

Nichole closed her eyes. "We don't have any more con-doms, Damon, so you need to back off."

He moved even closer. "Is that why you don't want to touch me?"

"No, I can't because I'm afraid of what might happen if I do. We can't afford to lose control of ourselves," she responded softly.

Damon leaned down and whispered into her ear. "Well I guess we'll just have to make sure we have an ample supply of condoms from here on out then, won't we?"

Nichole could feel his warm breath on her face and it sent shivers all over her body. She turned to him. "I guess so," she said.

He kissed her ever so lightly on the lips and said, "Give me a few minutes in the shower and I'll be right out."

"I'll be waiting," Nichole answered as she leaned back on the pillows and thought about her conversation with Meridan. Damon was the answer to her prayers, but in no way did she want him going toe to toe with Deacon. She'd definitely have to kept things on the low until Deacon agreed to let go of the relationship they had together once and for all.

After breakfast, Damon was able to convince Nichole to go out and explore Miami.

She wanted to be comfortable, so she put on a short lavender halter-top and denim shorts. Damon had on some black cargo shorts and a green T-shirt. They visited a large market with all sorts of vendors selling food, cloth-ing, jewelry, and other exotic items. Damon watched as Nichole's eyes widened when she saw a vendor selling handbags. She'd set her eyes on a large, red purse with silver buckles.

"How much is this one?" she asked the vendor.

"Seventy-five dollars," he replied in a Jamaican accent.

"Seventy-five dollars? I'll give you sixty for it," she negotiated.

"Seventy-five," the vendor repeated.

Nichole sat down the bag and walked off. Damon knew she was bluffing, because he'd seen the look on her face when she spotted it. It was clear to him at that point that you could take the woman out of corporate America, but you couldn't take corporate America out of the woman. Nichole walked over to another booth. All the while the vendor with the handbags was calling out to her.

"Ma'am! Ma'am!"

Nichole pretended not to hear him as she looked at a pair of sunglasses.

"Ma'am! Ma'am! I'll sell the purse to you for sixty dollars," he announced.

She turned to him and slowly walked back over to his booth. She pulled some bills out of her wallet and held them out to the vendor.

"I'll buy it right now for fifty dollars. No more, no less."

The vendor dropped his head in defeat and handed Nichole the bag.

She smiled. "Nice doing business with you," she said.

Nichole giggled and stuck her new purse inside her shopping bag before walking off. Damon smiled at her.

"I'm scared of you," he said.

"Don't be scared, baby. I didn't go overboard, did I?" she asked as she hugged his waist.

"Nah. It was obvious you knew what you were doing. It was also obvious that you enjoyed negotiating with him over that purse."

"You're right. I get a thrill out of getting what I want. I

knew I could get him to go lower if he thought he was going to lose the sale altogether. It was a steal at seventy-five, but I never pay the asking price. Do you see anything you want me to get for you?"

"No. I'm happy just seeing you happy," he replied as he stopped at an ice cream vendor. "Do you want a popsicle?"

"Sure. Cherry if they have it. Thanks, Damon."

Damon bought a cherry-flavored popsicle for Nichole and selected an orange one for himself. "Here you go."

Nichole opened the popsicle and immediately stuck it in her mouth. Damon watched her for a second until a slight groan escaped his lips. She looked over at him and smiled.

"What was that for?"

"What?" he asked innocently.

She found a bench under a canopy and sat down. "I heard you grunt, Coach. What was that all about? Are you OK?"

He licked his popsicle and smiled.

"I'm fine. I was just admiring the way you ate your popsicle."

Nichole playfully pushed him. "You are so nasty, Damon. I could say the same thing about you, but my mind is not on sex right now. My mind is on food and shopping."

"Your mind is always on food. I don't know how you keep that hot body the way you eat."

She wiped her mouth with a napkin. "I have a high metabolism, and I work out five days a week."

"I'm sure you have to, because you can put away some food, sweetheart."

Nichole turned to Damon and giggled. "I can't help it.

I love trying new food. I watch the Food Network all the time. I love to eat. Maybe I was a chef in my previous life or something."

"Or a pig," he teased.

Nichole playfully pushed him again, nearly knocking him off the bench. "Speaking of food, Mr. Comedian, why don't we invite Zel and Mia over for dinner tonight? We can get some lobsters and hang out."

The mention of Zel's name made Damon wrinkle his brow. He continued to eat his popsicle as he thought about Nichole's idea.

"Lobsters, huh?"

"It doesn't have to be lobster, Coach," she said as she cuddled up to him. "It could be hotdogs and marshmallows. I don't care. I just thought it would be nice to invite them over."

Damon finished his popsicle and then lowered his head and kissed Nichole. His cool lips covered hers for several seconds before he broke the kiss.

"Mmmm, you taste good," he said.

"You taste good, too," Nichole responded as she tossed their empty popsicle sticks and wrappings into a nearby trash bin. She knew Damon was trying to distract her, and at the moment he was doing a good job. He kissed her again, this time deepening his kiss. For a split second it made her reconsider her idea, but she knew what he was up to. She slowly pulled away and looked up into Damon's eyes.

"Oh, you're good."

"What are you talking about?" he asked innocently.

She stood and put her hands on her hips. "Don't think I don't know what you're trying to do. So, are you going to invite Zel and Mia to dinner? I think it would be a nice gesture to make up for last night."

Damon reached up and grabbed Nichole's hips. He pulled her closer and kissed her exposed abdomen.

"I don't want to think about Zel right now. Besides, I've already made up with that knucklehead. I wanted to be alone with you on our last night here."

She tilted his chin upward. "We can still be alone. I didn't say they had to stay all night. Just for dinner."

He leaned back and let out a loud sigh. Nichole sat down on his lap and massaged his neck.

"I promise I'll make it up to you after they leave."

"Yeah?" Damon asked with a raised brow.

Nichole wrapped her arms around his neck and whispered every erotic detail of her plan into his ear. Without saying another word, Damon quickly pulled out his flip phone and invited Zel and Mia over for dinner. He closed the phone and looked over at Nichole.

"Are you happy now?" Nichole kissed his cheek.

"I'm very happy. You won't regret inviting them."

"The sooner they come, the sooner they can get the hell out of there," Damon said as he looked at his watch.

Nichole giggled. "What am I going to do with you?"

He gently pushed her off his lap and stood. "You already told me, remember? And I'm going to hold you to everything you said."

"I always keep my word, Coach, so I have no problem following through."

He adjusted his sunglasses and said, "Good! Now let's go to the pharmacy because what we need is more important than some lobsters."

She smiled and shook her head in disbelief, because Nichole realized that she was in for a long night of passion with Damon, and in all honesty, she was looking forward to it.

Nichole smiled mischievously and then linked her arm with his.

"OK, calm down. You'll get your chance to go to the pharmacy, but first I need to get some T-shirts for souvenirs."

"Cool, let's go," he replied as he led her through the crowded aisles of the market before finally making their way back to his car.

Chapter Twenty-One

After stopping at the pharmacy and the seafood market, Damon and Nichole made their way back to the beach house. Nichole was looking forward to dinner with Zel and Mia, but Damon was still walking around the house acting grumpy. Nichole put the lobsters into the refrigerator.

"Damon, if you don't stop pouting, I'm afraid I'll have to punish you, and you don't want me to punish you, do you?"

He placed a couple of bottles of wine inside the refrigerator and then turned to her.

"I just want my knucklehead brother and his girl to hurry up and get here, so they can eat and leave."

Nichole laughed. "You are so wrong."

"I know. Anyway, do you want me to start on the roasted red potatoes? They'll be here in about an hour and a half."

"No, I'll do the potatoes," Nichole said as she washed her hands. "If you want, you can put the corn on the grill and start the water for the lobsters."

Damon pulled the fresh ears of corn out of the bag and began to shuck and wash them. Before long the food was prepared and Zel and Mia had arrived. Damon invited them in and they proceeded out to the deck where they ate the delicious meal. Damon poured Mia a glass of wine.

"You are over twenty-one, aren't you?" Damon asked sarcastically.

Nichole kicked Damon under the table.

"Ouch!" he yelled.

"What's wrong, bro?" Zel asked.

He squinted his eyes at Nichole before answering Zel. "Muscle spasm. I'm all right."

Mia smiled. "Yes, Damon, I'm over twenty-one. Actually, I'm twenty-seven."

"Good, then I guess you can have some," Damon said as he handed Mia the glass of wine.

"So, Mia, what do you do?" Nichole asked. "Are you in school with Zel?" Mia took a sip of wine before answering.

"No, I'm a dancer," she said.

"Dancer?" Damon chimed in. "What kind of dancer?"

"What difference does it make what kind, bro? She's a dancer," Zel interrupted.

Mia reached over and touched Zel's arm lovingly. "It's OK, baby. I'm not ashamed. I dance in a gentleman's club."

Nichole lowered her head in silence. She had no idea how Damon was going to react after hearing that bit of information; however, he surprised her.

"So is stripping the only kind of employment you think you can get, Mia?" Damon asked.

"No," she replied. "Stripping is paying my tuition. I'm going to a small technical school to get certified as a medical assistant."

Damon briefly closed his eyes and let out a loud sigh. "What else do you do on the side?"

Zel put his hand up. "Hold up, Damon. I don't appreciate you talking to her like that."

"I asked a legitimate question," Damon said as he wrinkled his brow and looked over at Zel.

"I know what you're insinuating, bro. Mia's cool people and I like her."

Mia wiped her mouth with her napkin. "It's OK, Zel. I get this all the time. Damon, I'm not a whore if that's what you're thinking."

"She's not Momma, Damon, so you need to chill," Zel said in an elevated tone.

"Shut your mouth, Zel," Damon warned him.

"It's OK, baby. Maybe we should just leave," Mia suggested.

Nichole didn't know what to think of the angry exchange between the two brothers. Whatever it was, it had something to do with their mother.

Zel finished off his wine and said, "Sounds good to me, Mia. You know what, Damon, you can be so judgmental sometimes. You're not perfect, so stop looking down on other people just because you don't agree or believe in the same things they do."

Nichole was seeing a different side of Damon, but she was sure he had his reasons.

Agitated, Damon rubbed his head and stood. He pointed toward the door. "Dinner is over," he said.

Zel stood. "With pleasure! Mia, let's go."

"Zel, wait," Nichole said. She looked over at Damon and said, "Don't let Zel leave like this."

Frustrated with Damon's attitude, Zel helped Mia out of her chair. He kissed Nichole on the cheek. "Thanks for dinner, Nichole."

"You're welcome, Zel," she replied before they hurried out the door.

Once they were gone, Nichole turned to Damon, who

was standing in the middle of the kitchen with his head down. She walked over to him.

"What was that all about?" she asked.

"I don't want to talk about it," he answered as he walked into the living room and sat on the sofa. Nichole followed him and sat down beside him.

She wrapped her arm around his shoulder. "What's really going on, Damon?"

"It's nothing, Nichole," he replied softly.

"I know you don't want to believe it," Nichole whispered as she caressed Damon's neck, "but Zel is a grown man. He's allowed to date whomever he wants."

"No, he can't," Damon replied. "He's supposed to want more."

"Listen, Damon, you have to let Zel make his own decisions and his own mistakes. Otherwise, how else will he learn anything?"

"What could you possibly know about it?" he asked with an agitated tone.

"I know I was once his age, and so were you," she answered.

Damon sat there in silence. Nichole cuddled her body against his.

"It's OK, baby. I'm sorry. I didn't mean to pry. I'll go put up the food."

Just as Nichole was about to get up, Damon grabbed her wrist and pulled her into his lap. She could tell that whatever was bothering him was very stressful for him to confront. He kissed her.

"I'm sorry. I didn't mean to yell at you," he whispered.

She caressed his face and said, "You don't have to apologize to me."

"Zel was right. I am judgmental, but I have a reason to be."

"We're all judgmental to some degree," Nichole admitted as she laid her head on Damon's chest. "Don't be so hard on yourself."

"No, I need to explain this to you, and I need to come to terms with it as well."

Damon proceeded to tell his story as Nichole lay in his arms. When he was finished, Nichole could tell that a huge burden had been lifted, and her heart went out to him. Damon revealed that his mother was somewhat of a loose woman who hung out in bars with any man who would pay her some attention. Unfortunately, their grandmother was unable to save her daughter because she was drawn into the street life by a smooth talking gambler. The only time she came home was when she was pregnant. After each son was born, she returned back to the smoke-filled slums of dark bars with loud music and plenty of drinking. Their mother loved her sons dearly, but she just wasn't able to care for them like they needed to be cared for. Things went from bad to worse the wife of a man she was having an affair with stabbed her. Therefore, when Damon found out that Mia was a stripper, it brought up painful memories of his childhood and his mother's dark, dingy lifestyle.

"I'm sorry, Damon," she whispered.

"So am I. I loved my mother and I believed she loved us, but she just couldn't care for us."

"Is Zel aware of her lifestyle?"

"Yes, he knows. That's why I don't see why he's drawn to women who hang out in bars."

"That might be the exact reason that he does it, Damon. Maybe it reminds him of your mother and he's looking for that affection. Damon, take your own advice. Don't let the past screw up your present. You were blessed with loving grandparents who made up for everything you didn't have with your mother."

Damon kissed her forehead. "You're right, but it's not

that easy. None of us know who our fathers are. My
grandfather asked around, but no one would talk, so he
just dropped it."

"Damon, Mia is not your mother, but I think when you
looked at her that's who you saw."

"You couldn't be more right. I'm still angry with my
mother for not being there for us. It's a wonder any of us
made it."

Nichole sat up. "Have you and your brothers ever sat
down and discussed your feelings about all of this?"

"Not really," he revealed. "I think we all just tried to
forget about it. My grandfather didn't want us to dwell
on the ugly side of our lives, but he didn't want us to forget where we came from either. He said that knowing the
truth about our family could only make us stronger."

"Your grandfather is right, Damon. Where do they
live?" He smiled when he talked about his grandparents.

"They're in Huntsville, Alabama."

"So you're a southern boy, huh?"

"I am. My grandmother sings in the church choir and
she keeps babies while my grandfather runs a small store
there. I'm able to take care of them, so I tried to get him to
retire, but he loves that store. It's sort of a gathering place
for him and his friends. He has a small deli inside where
they make sandwiches. So they sit around all day talking,
eating, and playing cards. They are some special people. I
love them very much, and I owe them a lot. My brother,
Anthony, lives in Atlanta where he teaches at Morehouse."

"They all sound wonderful. You might not think you
did, but you had a good life, Coach, with some very loving grandparents."

He sat there for a moment and then quickly stood. "I'll
be back."

"Where are you going?" Nichole asked as she also
stood. Damon kissed her passionately.

"To apologize to Zel."

Tears welled up in Nichole's eyes. "Be careful and take your time."

Damon found Zel and Mia at the Palms getting dressed to go out. Damon apologized to Zel and pleaded with him to sit down and talk about the way he reacted in regard to Mia. Zel agreed and they called their brother, Anthony, and put him on speakerphone so they could all express their feelings about their mother. Damon felt good about his conversation with his brothers. They were able to let go of a lot of hostility toward their mother, and they finally expressed their honest feelings about her to each other. As the oldest, Damon loved his brothers deeply and didn't want to see any harm come to either one of them, emotionally or physically. That was why he was so hard on them and protective of them. Their mother's legacy would live on through them, but not the dark side of her life. Their grandparents worked very hard to see that they succeeded in life in spite of the drama surrounding their mother and the life she led when she was alive.

By the time Damon returned to the beach house, Nichole was sound asleep. It was nearly three AM, and she looked like an angel. She'd cleaned up the kitchen and put away all the food. He quietly made his way into the bathroom where he removed his clothes and climbed into bed. Damon snuggled up next to Nichole's warm body and kissed her softly on the neck. Still groggy, she turned to him.

"Did you work out everything with Zel?" she asked.

"Yes. Now go back to sleep," Damon instructed. "It's late."

"May I have a kiss first?" she asked.

Without hesitating, he kissed her tenderly on the lips.

Nichole buried her face in his neck and said, "Good night, baby."

He held her securely in his arms and said, "Good night, sweetheart."

At that moment, Damon realized that he was in love with Nichole. He started having feelings for her a few weeks ago, but now he was sure without a doubt. He loved her with all his heart, and she was everything he'd been praying for in a woman, and then some.

The next morning Nichole made good on her promise to Damon and fulfilled every erotic dream he'd ever had. In between their erotic rendezvous, they spent time in the hot tub and out on the beach. Before packing for their flight home, they made love one more time and shared a sensual bubble bath. Damon caressed her hips and covered her breasts with his mouth as the suds danced around them. Nichole panted as Damon's strong body moved deeper and deeper inside her body.

"I love you, Nichole," he moaned as he climaxed.

She fell against his chest and kissed him. "I love you too, baby," she whispered breathlessly.

As far as Damon was concerned, the deal was sealed and he would never let her go. Nichole Adams would be his forever, and while their relationship had become a whirlwind romance, he planned to make it official as soon as possible.

Nichole finally climbed out of the Jacuzzi tub and wrapped a towel around her body. Damon followed her into the bedroom with an alluring expression on his face. As she sat on the bed and dried her body, she looked up at him.

"Damon, we'd better get dressed so we'll have time to get to the airport."

"I'm not ready to let you go yet," he replied as he stood completely naked in front of her.

She pulled out a bottle of lotion and started rubbing it onto her skin. "You can hold me all the way home on the plane if you'd like, Coach."

He looked down at her. "Agreed, but I need one more taste before we go."

Before Nichole could react to his request, he flipped her backward on the bed and dipped his head between her thighs. His oral, sensual assault caused Nichole to let out loud, unrecognizable moans as he held her hips hostage in his grasp. She was helpless and totally at his mercy. There was nothing she could do but lay back and savor the ripples of pleasure that consumed her body. When her body finally defied her and revealed her contentment to Damon, she whimpered and softly called out to him.

He kissed his way up to her lips. "I love it when you make those sounds," he said.

Nichole was too weak to react or respond to anything he was saying or doing to her body, especially when he looked at her with a sly grin and whispered, "One more time."

After one last vigorous love making session, the couple finally got dressed and made it to the airport with only minutes to spare. Nichole succumbed to her exhaustion and slept the entire flight home. Damon, on the other hand, replayed the entire weekend in his head and flew home with a huge smile on his face because he knew in his heart that this was beginning of his life full of true love and sincere joy.

Chapter Twenty-Two

The next few weeks flew by, and Nichole and Damon spent as much time as possible together. The couple had even started leaving extra clothes at each other's houses, since they never knew whose house they would end up at on any given night. Their schedules were very hectic, so to be able to spend any time together was a treasured gift. Nichole usually worked ten-to-twelve-hour days, and Damon was putting in about the same amount of hours at the football office.

One particular night when Damon got home from practice he sat down on the sofa and went through his usual ritual of scanning the mail. He noticed what looked like an invitation in the stack, and decided to open it first. Once it was opened he saw that it was an invitation to a casino night and dinner party at Craig and Venice Bennett's home. He immediately picked up the telephone and called Nichole, who answered after the second ring.

"Hello, stranger," she answered before putting him on speakerphone.

"Hello, yourself. Are you still at work?" he asked lovingly.

"I just pulled out of the parking garage and I'm so tired. If I never go to another meeting, I'll be happy. These twelve-hour days are getting old," she admitted. He chuckled.

"But you're getting paid, babe! You know that putting in a lot of time is the trade off for making the big bucks."

"I guess you should know," she teased. "Seriously, though, I don't care about the money. I just want to make sure I have a fulfilling life."

"Sweetheart, I agree, and I know exactly what you mean. Have you eaten?"

"No, and I don't know if I have the energy to even hold a fork."

He tossed his mail onto the coffee table, walked into the kitchen, and opened the refrigerator. "Come on over. I'll have something waiting for you, and if you're a good girl, I'll feed you and then give you a full body massage to relieve all that tension I hear in your voice."

Nichole smiled and felt her lower body begin to throb. Damon always knew what and how to say something to get her juices flowing.

"That sounds like a winner. Give me thirty minutes, baby."

"I'll be waiting. Drive carefully," he softly replied before hanging up the telephone.

Inside his refrigerator he found a small tray of chicken breasts. He quickly seasoned them with lemon pepper and a few other seasonings before sliding them into the oven. Next he mixed together lettuce, cucumbers, tomatoes, and shredded carrots and tossed them together in a red wine vinaigrette dressing. He placed the salad inside the refrigerator and decided that he would wait to bake the buttery croissants. He then looked at clock on the wall.

Nichole should be there in ten minutes, giving him plenty of time to jump in the shower so he could change into something more comfortable. Just as he was about to head up the stairs, the telephone rang. Thinking it was Nichole calling back, he quickly answered.

"Hello?"

"Hey, bro, feel like having some company?" Zel asked.

"Not tonight, Zel. Nichole's on her way over for dinner," he said.

"Damn! Nichole is always over there. Are you two living together or what?" he asked jokingly.

Damon looked at his watch and laughed as he ran up the stairs. "Funny, Zel. I guess it does seem like that sometimes. Seriously, though, I don't have to tell you that Nichole is a sexy woman and that I really, really like her."

He wasn't ready to tell Zel that he had fallen in love with Nichole, because Zel would've called everybody in their family to announce it before giving him a chance to do so.

"Damon, don't you think that is somewhat of an understatement?"

Damon laughed. "I guess you could say so."

"Well, I hope I don't have to tell you to use protection, young man," Zel teased.

Damon laughed again at Zel's comment.

"Good-bye, Zel. I'll call you tomorrow. I need to jump in the shower before Nichole gets here."

"OK, I'll let you slide this time. Tell Nichole I said hello."

"I will. Now go hit those books. Graduation is just around the corner."

Nichole hit the dial on her radio and changed the station from R&B over to smooth jazz for the thirty-minute drive out to West Chester. Her life seemed to finally be at peace, and she was glad that Deacon had seemed to move on with his. Her cell phone rang a little while later, and she quickly hit the speaker button.

"Hello?"

"It's so wonderful to hear your voice, Nichole. It's been such a long time."

She nearly ran off the road when she heard his voice. "Hello, Deacon."

"I can tell you're in your car, which means you're still working those long hours."

Nichole frowned and wondered how he could know that. Was he following her? She went into a slight panic, but did her best to remain calm.

"You could say so."

Nichole wanted to keep her answers short, in hopes of ending their conversation as quickly as possible.

"Listen, Nichole, I know you're tired, but do you think you could meet me somewhere for a cup of coffee or a drink? I really need to talk to you."

Nichole bit down on her lower lip. "Tonight is not a good night, Deacon. Why don't you just tell me what you need to talk about now?"

He sighed. "Nichole, I know I made a stupid mistake showing up at your house the way I did that night, but you have to understand why. I love you and when you told me it was over, I lost it, especially since you never gave me an opportunity to explain my side of things."

Nichole began to tear up. "I loved you, too," she said softly, "but you hurt me, Deacon. I felt like I'd been made a fool of and that you used me. I'll never let anybody double cross me again."

It hurt Deacon to hear the pain in Nichole's voice.

"I'm so sorry, Nichole, and I didn't double cross you. I haven't been with my wife in years. Yes, we should've gone through the process of divorce, but after a while neither one of us stepped up to take the initiative to contact an attorney."

"All of that is irrelevant to the situation now, Deacon."

"Is it? I talked to my wife and she agreed to the divorce."

Nichole let out a breath and said, "Just like that, huh?"

"Yes! I told you we haven't lived as husband and wife in years. She did her thang and I did mine."

Nichole was getting angry. "Is that what I was to you? A thang? You didn't even have the respect to be honest with me. If your marriage was so dead when we met, why was it so hard for you to tell me about it?"

"I don't know. Looking back, I see how wrong I was for keeping that information from you," he said with frustration in his voice.

"It doesn't matter to me anymore. Everything that happened is water under the bridge now. The damage is done, and I'm focusing on moving on with my life."

"Are you saying there's no way we can get past this and repair our relationship?"

"I'm saying again for the hundredth time that it's over, Deacon. I hate being lied to. That's one thing I will never tolerate in a relationship."

Deacon was silent. He wasn't getting anywhere with Nichole, and he had hoped that she would be a little more forgiving by now.

"Nichole, there's a lot of things I should've done that I didn't, but here I am trying to make things right between us. You can't just walk away from love."

Nichole pulled into Damon's driveway, shut off the engine, and picked up the telephone.

"I'm not saying it was easy to walk away. I cried my eyes out over you, Deacon. My heart is finally on the mend, and I'm not going to let you or what happened between us ruin my life. I think about you and what we had together sometimes, but only as a memory. My hope is that you and I can remain friends, but anything more is definitely out of the question."

Deacon held the telephone in silence. "Is it because you're seeing someone else?"

Nichole realized that it was seriously possible that Deacon had been following her, which meant he knew where Damon lived. She lowered her head and thought carefully before she answered him.

"Deacon, I wish you the best and hope you have the same wish for me. Whether I'm seeing someone has nothing to do what we're discussing. Like I said, you're a wonderful man and I want us to try to be friends. Please don't make this any harder than it already has been."

He laughed. "I guess at the moment I have no choice, huh?"

"Deacon," Nichole called out to him. "At any moment you have no choice when it comes to me."

"One day you'll change your mind, sweetheart, and you'll see just how much I really love you. I'll talk to you later, Nichole. Good night."

"Good night, Deacon."

Nichole hung up the telephone, but she continued to sit in her car, playing back the conversation. Seconds later Damon knocked on the driver's side window, startling her. She slowly opened the car door.

"You scared me," she said.

Damon opened the car door wider so she could get out of the car. He pulled her briefcase off her shoulder and noticed the strange look on her face.

"What's wrong?" he asked.

She climbed out of the car and hugged his waist. "Nothing. I'm just glad I'm here."

"I'm glad you're here, too, but why were you sitting in

the car in a daze? You didn't notice me walking toward the car or hear me calling your name."

"I'm OK," Nichole said as she locked her car. "Let's go inside."

He took her keys out of her hand. "Let me pull your car into the garage first. Go on inside and get comfortable."

Damon unlocked her car, pushed the button on the garage door opener he'd given her, and started up the Mercedes. He sat and watched Nichole walk into the house before pulling into the garage. Damon was well aware that something had happened to Nichole after their telephone conversation, because her demeanor was totally different. He hoped to find out what it was after she had a chance to unwind.

Venice hung up the telephone and grabbed her hair in frustration.

"I can't believe every caterer I've called this week is booked. I love you, Bennett, but I'm not cooking for this dinner. It was too much on me the last time."

Craig smiled and poured himself a cup of coffee. "I know, sweetheart. Why don't you ask Arnelle's mother? She's a big time caterer in Texas, isn't she?"

"Yes, but I can't ask her to come all the way up here."

Craig picked up a knife and poured some grape jelly on a piece of toast. "Why not? Just call her and see what she says."

Venice shook her head and took a sip of coffee. "Not yet. If all else fails, she can be my last resort. It's asking a lot for her to come up here and do a catering job out of her element."

He took a bite of his toast. "OK, then let me take care of the catering. I know this is your busy time of the year, and you don't have a lot of time on your hands."

She closed her planner and turned on the TV to catch the morning news. "You're just as busy as I am."

He grabbed a plate and put a spoonful of eggs and two pieces of bacon on it before sitting down at the table across from her. "You're right, I am busy, but I have Francine, remember? Now, when I went over the guest list I came out with sixteen people, but we might as well round it out to twenty. Do you agree?"

"Yes, Craig, but Francine's your secretary, not your personal assistant. I don't want to tie her up with something like this. You keep her busy enough as it is."

He winked at Venice. "I said I got this. You know Francine won't mind helping. She loves you."

Venice giggled. "She loves you."

He wiped his mouth with a napkin. "She actually tolerates me. I do rely on her a lot."

"Stop being so modest, Bennett. Francine would walk over hot coals for you, and you know it."

He thought for a second and said, "You know, you're right. She's the best and I wouldn't trade her for anyone. Listen, Francine handles all the catering arrangements for our office. Let me run it by her and see if she can help. "

"Are you sure about this?" she asked. "I could make a few more calls."

Craig held up his coffee cup. "You've spent enough time on it already," he said.

She picked up the newspaper and handed him the sports and business sections, which were his favorite parts.

"Since you insist, it's best to plan for twenty. Thank you, baby."

He sat down, started reading the paper, and blew her a kiss. "Thank you. Now put a menu together for me and we're done."

Seconds later, Brandon, C.J., and Clarissa walked into

the kitchen. Clarissa ran over, climbed up in her daddy's lap, and immediately picked up a piece of his bacon and stuck it in her mouth. He laughed.

"Well good morning to you too, young lady."

Venice frowned. "Clarissa, I have your plate over here. Stop eating your daddy's food."

Craig kissed Clarissa's cheek. "It's OK, Venice. I'll just take her plate."

Brandon hugged Craig's neck and said, "Good morning, Pops."

"Good morning, son."

Brandon walked over and kissed his mother on the cheek. She hugged him and wiped dried toothpaste off his face.

"Thank you for helping me with the twins this morning, Brandon. You help your mother so much, and because you are such a big help to us, you can have that electric scooter you've been looking at."

His eyes widened in surprise. "I can, Momma?"

Craig gave Clarissa his other piece of bacon and said, "It's for real, Brandon, but you have to wear a helmet when you ride it. We can go pick it up after breakfast if you want."

Brandon ran over and hugged both his parents again.

"Thank you!" he yelled. "I promise I won't ride my scooter without my helmet, and I'll be real careful not to fall."

"I wanna ride!" C.J. yelled.

"Me too!" Clarissa yelled before grabbing a fistful of Craig's eggs and jamming them into her mouth.

Venice pointed at the twins. "You two can forget about it. You already have foot-powered scooters. Brandon, the twins are not allowed to ride on your scooter, no matter how much they beg you or cry."

"OK, Momma," he answered as he put a couple of sausage links and eggs on his plate.

Clarissa reached over and tried to take Brandon's sausage. He popped her hand, causing her to scream out in pain.

"These are mine, Clarissa!" Brandon yelled as he scolded her.

Tears filled Clarissa's eyes as she looked up at her daddy for assistance.

"Don't look at me. You should've asked before trying to take your brother's food. Now tell him you're sorry."

"I'm sorry, Brandon," she apologized as she lay back against her daddy's chest. He looked down at her and smiled. Clarissa had a large appetite, so he picked up his fork and retrieved a sausage link. He held it out for her, and she pulled it off the edge of his fork and took a bite.

"Thank you, Daddy."

He kissed the top of her head and said, "You're welcome."

Craig and Venice loved their children dearly. They kept them on their toes and were the source of a lot of headaches, but they wouldn't trade them for all the tea in China.

Venice closed the newspaper. "OK, today is our last day of vacation, so what do you guys want to do?"

"Ice cream!" C.J. yelled.

Craig frowned at C.J. "Not so loud, son."

"I wanna go to the park," Clarissa added. "I want to see the tigers!"

Venice turned to Brandon. "What about you, Brandon?"

He sat down his fork and said, "I wanna stay home and ride my scooter."

She looked up at Craig. "What do you want to do, babe?"

He sat down the paper and sighed. "I'm with Brandon. I just want to chill and relax, and maybe go for a swim or something later."

Venice looked at the twins. "Well, kiddos, it looks like it's just you and me. I'll take you guys to the zoo, and then we can get some ice cream. How does that sound?"

"Yay!" was the response from both twins.

Craig looked at Brandon and gave him a high five.

"Wait a minute. Were you two trying to get rid of us?" Venice asked.

"No, Momma," Brandon answered with a sly grin. "I just wanna ride my scooter and hang out with Pops."

Craig winked at her and laughed. She stood and put her hands on her hips. "Bennett, what are you two up to?"

He laughed and also stood. After sitting Clarissa in his chair, he walked over to Venice and embraced her.

"I'm up to this," he answered as he gave her a passionate kiss on the lips.

C.J. and Clarissa covered their eyes and yelled, "Ewwwww!"

Brandon kept eating without being distracted. He looked at C.J. and Clarissa and said, "Stop screaming. They kiss and stuff all the time."

Venice and Craig continued to kiss as though they were the only people in the room. C.J. and Clarissa continued to cover their mouths and eyes in embarrassment.

Craig broke the kiss and said, "That was nice. Why don't we take it back upstairs?"

With her arms linked around his neck, she snuggled up to him. "That sounds wonderful," she whispered, "but we've already told the munchkins our plans. You know they won't let us off the hook that easily."

Craig glanced at his watch and said, "Meet me back here no later than five o'clock. The rest of the evening, you're all mine, so make sure you bring some of that ice cream home so we can play."

She smiled and kissed him again. "You bet. I'll see you at five."

Chapter Twenty-Three

Later that night, Craig alerted Venice that Francine had come through for them and booked a caterer for their parties. Pleased with the results, Venice rewarded Craig by incorporating the ice cream she'd brought home into their prelude to making love. He slowly licked the ice cream off her chest,

"Strawberry, yummy, my favorite."

She kissed him. "I thought butter pecan was your favorite."

"Strawberry is my favorite on you," he admitted. "As a matter of fact, any ice cream smeared over your body is my favorite."

"Bennett, you are a freak and you're sticky."

He trailed kisses down to her navel and then traveled lower. "It's your fault. You turned me into one. Now be quiet. I have something I want to do."

Venice gasped and then let out a soft moan. Craig had her right where he wanted her: in total submission to his desires. He knew he was working his magic when Venice started mumbling in Spanish.

"¡Te quiero! Quiero estar contigo para siempre."

He stopped for a moment and kissed her thigh. "I don't know what that means, but it sounds very sexy."

"It means I love you and I want to be with you forever," she translated with pleasure.

"I'll drink to that, Mrs. Bennett."

Venice smiled and then dipped her finger into the bowl of ice cream, rubbed it on Craig's lips, and immediately kissed and licked it away.

"I love you, Bennett."

"You already told me, sweetheart," he replied before rolling over onto his back and pulling her naked body on top of him. "Can you believe we haven't been interrupted by any of our children tonight?"

"They're exhausted. I wore the twins out today at the zoo," she responded.

"Brandon's wiped out too," Craig said. "He almost road that scooter until the wheels fell off."

Venice smiled and then dipped two fingers into the bowl again. Craig raised his eyebrows with curiosity.

"What are you going to do with that?"

Smiling mischievously, she ran her fingers over his lower body and watched Craig's reaction.

"That's cold."

"I know," she whispered. "Don't worry, baby. I'll heat you up in just a second."

He closed his eyes as Venice lowered her head and consumed him until he cried out for mercy. She fell back onto the bed and giggled. Craig lay there unable to move for a few seconds, but when he did move, Venice was the recipient of some intense, vigorous loving that took them to incredible heights of unbridled passion.

Meridan looked at the small picture in her hand one more time. She couldn't believe it and she couldn't wait to share the news with Keaton.

Keaton walked into the house and found his mother, Zenora Lapahie, feeding Jeremiah. He walked over and kissed her on the cheek.

"Good morning, Momma. When did you get here?"

"I got here about an hour ago. I thought I would come by and see if Meridan needed any help with my grandson, and she did. Keaton, Meridan looks exhausted. I don't think she's getting enough rest. Are you helping her with the baby at night?"

Keaton poured himself a glass of orange juice and frowned. "Yes, Momma, I'm helping her as best I can. You know Meridan's nursing him, so there's not a whole lot I can do."

"Yes, you can," Zenora replied with an irritated tone. "Meridan is pumping her milk so there are bottles in the refrigerator that you could give him at night. It's not like you can't set your own hours at the restaurant, or better yet, not go in at all. What had you out so early this morning anyway?"

He sat down across the table from his mother.

"I had an early morning meeting."

"Humph," Zenora grunted. "Your manager can conduct meetings for you. He's done it before, and correct me if I'm wrong, but didn't you set up conference call capabilities with your home telephone when Meridan was pregnant?"

Keaton realized he wasn't going to win this discussion, and his mother was not happy with him at the moment. As he sat there drinking his orange juice, he studied her facial expression and body language. Zenora Lapahie was clearly angry.

Keaton sighed. "Yes, Momma. I'm sorry, I'll do better."

"You'd better, son, because Meridan needs your help. A baby is a huge responsibility, and she can't do it alone," she replied as she put Jeremiah on her shoulder to burp him.

"I said I'll do better, Momma. I'm sorry. Where is Meridan anyway?" he asked.

Jeremiah burped.

"That's my boy," Zenora yelled proudly. "If you must know, I sent her upstairs to take a nap. She was walking around here like a zombie."

Keaton finished off his orange juice and stood. He put his glass in the sink, leaned over and kissed Jeremiah, and then kissed his mother.

"I love you, Momma. I'm going upstairs to check on Meridan. Are we cool?"

Zenora smiled. "Yes, we're cool, and we will stay cool as long as you get up off your ass and help your wife."

He laughed. The only time he ever heard his mother curse was when she was really angry. This was one of those times.

"I will, Momma. I'll be back shortly."

Zenora got up out of her chair and put Jeremiah in the stroller. "I'm getting ready to take Jeremiah on a walk."

"Take your cell phone and the hybrids with you," Keaton said as he walked out of the room.

She opened the french doors leading out into the backyard, and Keaton's hybrid dogs immediately stood up. Zenora gave them a gentle pat on their heads.

"You know they would go anyway," she said.

"Enjoy, Momma," he replied as he hurried up the stairs.

Keaton walked into the bedroom and found Meridan sitting on the side of the bed.

"Hey, sexy. Momma said you weren't feeling well. Are you OK?"

"I'm fine," she replied softly.

He sat a stack of mail on the dresser. "We got an invitation from Venice and Craig. They're having a casino night and dinner party at their house next weekend. We haven't been up there in a while, and this would give us a chance to visit with the family and Nichole. Also, I wanted to talk to you about opening another restaurant. What do you think about that?"

"Uh-huh," she answered robotically. "Sounds nice."

Keaton turned and noticed the strange look on her face. He took off his watch, placed it on the dresser, and walked over to where she was sitting.

"You didn't hear a word I said, did you?"

"I'm sorry, Keaton," she said as she looked up at him. "What did you say?"

"What's wrong?" he asked with a frown on his face.

She held out the piece of paper and photograph. "Nothing's wrong, baby, except that the adoption agency found us a little girl."

Keaton became weak in the knees. In complete shock, he sat down on the bed and took the letter and photo out of her hand.

"Are you serious? I didn't expect it to happen this quickly. Some people say it takes years."

Meridan burst into tears. "It's true, Keaton. Jeremiah's going to have a little sister."

He stared down at the photograph and said, "She looks like MaLeah. How old is she?"

"The letter says she's eleven days old."

Tears fell out of Keaton's eyes. Meridan reached over and lovingly wiped them away. After a grim diagnosis from her ObGyn and a difficult pregnancy with Jeremiah, Keaton and Meridan decided not to try again. Instead, they decided to adopt.

"I know. Isn't she beautiful?"

Keaton hugged and kissed Meridan.

"Momma's going to flip out."

Meridan eased her way onto Keaton's lap and wrapped her arms around his neck. "So will my entire family, especially Daddy and Gwendolyn. You know how crazy they are, and we're not even going to mention my Aunt Glo. Once she knows, everyone will know, so is it OK if we hold off telling the family until she's officially ours?" she asked.

"I'm already claiming her. God wouldn't have blessed us with her if she wasn't already ours. He hasn't failed us yet, and it's going to be hard for me to keep this kind of news to myself," he admitted. "Momma has built-in radar for stuff like this."

Meridan kissed his cheek. "If it gets too hard on you, baby, let me know, and we can go ahead and tell everybody. I just don't want them to get excited if things don't work out."

Keaton looked down at the photograph one more time. "I'm not worried one bit, because she's ours."

Meridan took the photograph out of Keaton's hand. "We need to start thinking of some names," she said.

"You're right, and I have the perfect name. What about Nizhoni?"

"That's beautiful. Is it Navajo?"

"Yes, and it means beautiful, just like you and our daughter."

Meridan smiled and repeated the name.

"Nizhoni, I love it. However, I would like to give her my mother's name as well."

Keaton held Meridan's hand and linked his fingers with hers. "Nizhoni Rosa Lapahie."

"Perfect!" Meridan responded. "My mother would be so proud."

He kissed her hand. "I have no doubt that she's looking down on us, sweetheart, and that she's very proud."

Keaton gently laid Meridan back on the bed. "You make it hard for me to keep my hands off you, Meridan," he admitted as he slid his hand up her thigh. "As a matter of fact, why don't we celebrate the news about Nizhoni right now?"

"Now? Your mother's downstairs."

He sprinkled her neck with sweet kisses. "She took Jeremiah for a walk, so she's not even in the house."

Meridan giggled. "Isn't this also your poker night?" she asked.

Keaton lifted her shirt and kissed her stomach. "They won't see me tonight. I'm spending the evening with my babies."

"You're going to blow off your poker game with the boys for me?"

He started unbuttoning her blouse. "Without a doubt. Besides, I can take their money from them next week."

"What excuse are you going to give them for not showing up?" she asked. "You can't tell them about Nizhoni."

Keaton opened her blouse, exposing her black lace bra. "I'm going to tell them the truth, which is that I wanted to stay home and make love to my wife."

"You're serious, aren't you?" she asked. "You've never missed a poker game."

He straddled her body, unsnapped her bra, and covered her breasts with his hands. He loved touching her breasts, and since Meridan had given birth to Jeremiah and started nursing him, she'd gone up two cup sizes. Keaton looked her in the eyes.

"Have you ever known me to joke about making love

to you, especially when you have assets like these?" he whispered.

She closed her eyes and exhaled. Keaton knew exactly how and where to touch her, and he was causing her body to simmer.

"No, you'd never joke about it, and, baby, that feels so good."

Keaton leaned over and ran his tongue ever so gently across her nipples. He could hear Meridan suck in a breath from the subtle contact.

"I have something even better for you."

Meridan looked at the clock. "I told your mother I was coming upstairs to take a nap."

"You can take your nap after we're done. I want to celebrate."

"But, Keaton, she could come back with Jeremiah any minute."

He quickly removed her jeans, lacy boy shorts, and the rest of his clothing. "They just left, leaving us just enough time. Let's not waste another second. Show me what you got, momma."

Meridan wrapped her legs around his torso and said, "OK, chief. You asked for it, so now bring it on."

A half hour later, Meridan pulled the sheet over her nude body and smiled. Before climbing out of the bed, Keaton gave her another kiss.

"I feel the same way, baby. I'll be back shortly."

She watched him as he strolled into the bathroom to take a shower. The telephone rang just as Keaton turned on the water. She reached over and answered.

"Hello?"

"Meridan, did I wake you?"

She lay back in the bed and smiled. "No, Arnelle. I was just lying down to take a nap."

"I'm sorry. I didn't mean to wake you," she apologized. "I should've called Keaton's cell."

"He wouldn't have heard it. He's in the shower right now. Do you want me to have him call you back?"

"No. I was just calling to see if you guys received the invitation to Venice and Craig's party."

"The invitation just came in the mail today, but we haven't had a chance to talk about it yet," Meridan revealed. "More than likely we'll be there."

"Well give me a call and let me know for sure. You know you guys can stay with us. How's my nephew doing?"

"Jeremiah's growing like a weed. Zenora took him out for a walk a little while ago. They should be coming back any moment. She's been a big help since I had Jeremiah."

Arnelle chuckled. "I'm glad Momma's helping you, Meridan, but send her home to Daddy when she starts getting on your nerves. She means well, but I know what it's like, and Momma can be a little overbearing at times when she doesn't mean to be." Meridan giggled.

"I'll keep that in mind, Arnelle, but your mother's great."

At that moment Keaton exited the bathroom with a towel wrapped around his waist. He sat down next to her and pulled the sheet off her body. Meridan playfully smacked his hand.

"Stop, Keaton," she whispered.

"Who's on the phone?" he whispered.

"Arnelle. Now behave."

"Is that Keaton?" Arnelle asked.

"Yes, it's him. Do you want to talk to him?"

"Thank you, Meridan. Get back to your nap. It was nice talking to you. Kiss Jeremiah for me."

"I will. Here's Keaton."

Meridan handed Keaton the telephone, but before speaking into it, he kissed Meridan's soft lips.

"Damn, you taste good. I love you, Meridan," he said softly.

She happily returned the kiss. "I love you, too, baby."

"Hello? Hello? Is anybody there? Keaton? What is going on with you two?" Arnelle yelled through the phone.

Keaton put the telephone up to his ear. "Calm down, sis. I was just giving my wife a kiss."

"I hope that's all you were giving her while I was on the phone," she joked.

"Nah, I took care of that before you called," he admitted.

"Y'all are nasty," Arnelle teased. "No wonder she needs a nap."

"I know you're not talking about me, Arnelle. I lived with you and Winston for several weeks. If anybody's nasty, it's you two. I have nothing on you two freak-a-zoids."

Arnelle knew Keaton was right. She and Winston never held back their emotions when they were intimate with each other, and she knew there was the possibility that Keaton could've heard them when they'd made love on one occasion or another.

"Let's leave that alone for now. Anyway, I was just calling to see if you guys were coming to Venice and Craig's parties, but we can talk about it later. Go take care of your wife and Jeremiah, and we'll talk this evening."

Keaton caressed Meridan's cheek while he talked to his sister.

"Kiss the kids for me, and tell Winston hello. I'll call you later. Love you, sis."

"I love you too, Keaton," she replied. "Good-bye."

Chapter Twenty-Four

The week had finally come for Damon and his team to start practicing for the upcoming season. It was also the week of Venice and Craig's parties. It was nearly nine o'clock in the morning when Damon picked up his clipboard and walked out onto the practice field alongside the other Eagles coaches. He helped coach different parts of the defensive team, but was mainly in charge of the cornerbacks, a position he used to play himself. He was anxious to start working with his unit so he could get them ready them for the upcoming season. The pre-season was a few weeks away, and having Nichole in his life was going to make this year much sweeter for him. One thing he looked forward to was spending his nights with her soft body curled up next to his.

It was a nice, sunny day and spectators had gathered to watch the first of many practice sessions. There were a lot kids on the sidelines praying they would get the autographs of their favorite players. Damon blew his whistle and called the cornerbacks over so they could start going over zones as well as drills on man-to-man coverage. It

was going to be a long but exciting day for Damon and
the Eagles.

Nichole finished off her third cup of coffee and worked
vigorously on her computer. She had been trying to play
catch-up on her work since returning from her fun-filled
weekend in Miami with Damon. She twirled around in
her chair and opened one of her file drawers. When she
turned back around, Deacon's wife, Lala, was standing
in her office. Stunned, Nichole stood. Phillip wasn't one
to let anybody in without checking with her first. Now
she wondered how this woman had made it past him
and into her office.

"May I help you?"

Lala walked farther into Nichole's office and sat down
without an invitation to do so. "Yes, you can," she
replied as she crossed her legs. "You can stay away from
my husband."

Phillip walked into the office with an angry look on his
face. He reached for Lala's arm. "Ma'am, I believe I
asked you to wait until I could see if Miss Adams could
see you. Come with me."

Nichole put her hand up. "It's OK, Phillip."

He released Lala's arm. "I'm sorry, Nichole. I was distracted by a telephone call and she walked in before I
could stop her."

Nichole smiled at Phillip to assure him it was OK.

"Don't worry about it. Just hold my calls until my
meeting with Mrs. Miles is over."

Phillip could feel the tension in the room. "Can I get either one of you anything before I leave?" he asked, smiling.

"No, we're fine. This won't take very long," Nichole
announced.

Phillip closed the door, leaving the two women alone. Nichole turned her attention back to Lala.

"Contrary to what you think, I have no interest in your husband."

Lala burst out laughing. "Don't play with me, Nichole. We're grown women, which means that I'm fully aware that you were having an affair with Deacon. I saw you at the hospital and you saw me."

Nichole sat down.

"I'm not having an affair with your husband," Nichole said angrily, "and I never see people in my office without an appointment, so it's best that you leave before I call security."

Lala leaned forward and picked up a crystal dolphin paperweight and inspected it. "Please, Nichole! Stop with the innocent act. It's not becoming, and if you want to call security, go right ahead, because if they drag me out of here before I'm finished talking to you, I'll make sure I announce to your entire office on the way out how you're a homewrecker."

Nichole thought for a moment and realized that the last thing she wanted was her personal business all over the office. She sighed.

"I had no idea you existed until that night at the hospital," Nichole explained. "I've been with Deacon for over two years and he never told me he had a wife."

"Would it have mattered?" Lala asked as she set the paperweight back down on desk with Nichole's eyes following her movements.

"Of course it matters. I don't knowingly date married men. Besides, what Deacon and I had is completely over," Nichole answered as she repositioned the paperweight.

"And just what exactly did you and Deacon have?"

Nichole stacked up some paperwork and looked across her desk at Lala. "Why don't you ask him, and while you're at it, tell him to stop calling me."

Lala smiled. "I'm interested in what you have to say about it."

Nichole stood and walked over to the door. "Well, you're not going to get a response, and I would appreciate it if you would leave."

Lala stood and pulled her purse strap over her shoulder. Nichole looked her up and down and couldn't help but notice that she had on a pair of Dolce and Gabbana jeans worth about six hundred dollars. Lala walked over to Nichole and paused at the door.

"Listen, Nichole, it's obvious that we didn't know about each other, but the truth is that I still love Deacon, and if my senses are correct, so do you. Look, I'm not mad at you. Deacon is a passionate man, but he's mine, so back off!"

"Good-bye!" Nichole firmly stated as she pointed toward the door.

Lala walked out the door, but left Nichole with one parting comment. "Remember what I said, Nichole. Stay away from Deacon."

Nichole slammed her door without responding. Lala had a lot of nerve to walk into her office and confront her about Deacon. She made her way back over to her window and looked outside. To say she was angry was an understatement. Phillip came in to check on Nichole.

"Are you OK? Who was that diva?"

"That was Deacon's wife," she revealed. "I don't know how she found out where I worked."

"Do you want me to call security?"

She turned, picked up her telephone, and dialed. "No, it's OK. She won't be back. Thanks for offering."

Phillip smiled. "Well, call me if you need anything."

She put the telephone up to her ear and said, "I will."

Phillip left the office and went back to his desk. Nichole sat down in her chair, and after about two rings, the baritone voice on the other end answered.

"Hello?"

"Deacon, we need to talk."

Deacon was happy to hear Nichole's voice. "Hey, sweetheart, it's so good to hear your voice."

Nichole rolled her eyes and then said. "Listen, I don't know what you told your wife, but I don't appreciate her coming into my office confronting me."

"She did what?" he asked, infuriated.

"You heard me. She rolled up in my office and told me to back off you because you belonged to her," she reiterated. "Deacon, like I told you before, what we had is over, but obviously your wife thinks otherwise. What did you tell her?"

"I'm sorry she did that. I've already served her with divorce papers. I don't know why she's acting so crazy."

"That doesn't concern me. Did you tell her where I worked?"

"No! You know I wouldn't do that."

"Well she found out somehow," Nichole yelled into the telephone.

Deacon held the telephone in silence for a few seconds. Lala had crossed the line and Deacon was furious.

"Like I said, I'm sorry Lala came to your job. I'll make sure she doesn't bother you again. I have to go, Nichole. I'll call you later."

"Don't bother, Deacon!" she yelled before hanging up the phone.

"Good-bye, Nichole," he whispered even though she was already gone.

Nichole felt like the office was closing in on her after

Lala's visit, and she needed some fresh air. After deciding to escape, she grabbed her purse and headed out to an early lunch. Once outside, she felt so much better. Now all she felt like doing was driving, and before she knew it she was at the Eagles' practice field. Nichole climbed out of her truck, put on her sunglasses, and made her way over to the field where all the rest of the fans were lined up on the fence. Nichole knew she wasn't exactly dressed for watching a football practice in her gray business suit, but she did the best she could while walking across the grass in her three-inch heels.

The football field was full of activity with the coaches yelling and whistles blowing. With so much activity, it took a minute for Nichole to spot Damon. It wasn't that she didn't recognize him. He just seemed to blend in with the players he was coaching. Seconds later she heard his booming voice and watched him demonstrate the next drill to his players. As she stood there two boys around ten-years-old in age joined her on the fence with footballs in hand and started yelling out the names of one of the players who was drinking from a cup of Gatorade nearby. Nichole smiled upon seeing the joy on the boys' faces as the star running back autographed their footballs. When she looked out toward the field again, she noticed Damon walking in her direction with a clipboard in his hand.

With a huge smile on her face she greeted him.

"Hey, Coach."

He smiled back at her.

"Good morning, Nichole. What a nice surprise. What brings you all the way out here? Aren't you supposed to be at work investing somebody's money somewhere?"

"Sort of. I snuck out for a couple of hours so I thought I would see you in action."

Damon looked over his shoulder at his players, and then at his watch. "Can you stick around for a few more minutes? We're wrapping up our morning practice now, and I could use some lunch. Would you like to join me?"

"Sure, but it's my treat."

Damon couldn't resist the urge. He leaned over the fence and gave Nichole a quick kiss on the lips.

"You won't get an argument from me. I'll be right with you, and by the way, you look beautiful."

Nichole blushed and looked down at her suit. A white silk blouse complemented her gray suit jacket. The matching skirt fell just at the knees, giving an expansive view of her sexy legs.

Once the morning practice was dismissed, Damon motioned for Nichole to join him on the field. She helped Damon gather his belongings before walking off the field and toward his office.

"What time do you have to be back?" Nichole asked as she looked around at the football players' photographs on Damon's wall. He glanced over at her long, beautiful legs and finally answered.

"This afternoon. Why?" She turned to face him and seductively replied.

"Oh, I just wanted to know how much time we possibly had together."

Damon's head turned quickly toward Nichole. "What exactly do you have in mind?"

She walked over to him, wrapped her arms around his neck, and nuzzled his neck. "Oh, I could think of a couple things, but it involves a lot less clothes than what we have on now."

Damon walked across the room, opened his door, and put a do not disturb sign on the doorknob. When he turned around, Nichole already had her jacket and skirt off. Damon frowned.

"Wait, I wanted to do that."

She put her hand over her mouth and smiled.

"Well, get over here then."

Damon greedily kissed Nichole as he slowly unbuttoned her blouse. He looked down and noticed that she had on a pink lace bra and panty set. "Hmmm, my favorite color."

"I think all of my lingerie is in your favorite color, Coach."

He gently gripped her soft, yet firm hips and grinned mischievously. "You got that right."

The rest of Nichole's attire was quickly removed and placed on a nearby table. Within minutes they were on his leather sofa in each other's arms.

"What if someone comes to your door?" Nichole whispered. She could hear voices in the hallway as Damon kissed his way from her lips down to her abdomen.

"They know when I put my do not disturb sign out not to come anywhere near my door. If they do, there will be hell to pay," he revealed breathlessly.

Nichole squirmed beneath him. "I didn't know you had it like that around here."

He put his finger over her lips and said, "You damn right. Now relax because we're cool." A sad look appeared on Nichole's face.

"What's wrong?" Damon asked.

"I guess you've done this a lot."

He smiled and kissed her forehead. "Never. None of the women before you would be caught dead here. All they cared about was shopping and getting their hair and nails done. This place would've been too dirty for them to hang out."

Embarrassed, Nichole said, "I'm sorry, I—"

He cut her off. "It's OK. I like it when you're jealous."

Nichole looked up in Damon's eyes. "I've fallen hard and fast for you, Damon," she said softly.

"I second that motion, Nichole," he admitted as he

played in her hair. "I'll even take it a step further and admit that I have a hard time concentrating during the day because you're always on my mind. I love you, Nichole."

Nichole nuzzled his neck and closed her eyes. "I love you, too, Damon." She caressed his back lovingly and tilted his chin. "I'm so glad we met."

Damon rolled off her body and sat up. "So am I. Get dressed."

Confused, Nichole sat up next to him and asked, "I thought we were—"

He handed over her clothes and said, "Not right now. You're going to have to wait until tonight. There's not enough time for me to do what I want to do to you. Besides, they'll think I'm killing you in here if I get started."

Nichole stood and hugged Damon's waist. "So you're not a quickie man after all, are you, Coach?"

He ran his hands over her naked body. "Oh, I'm more than a quickie man, sweetheart. When I'm done with you tonight, you'll see and you'll thank me for making you wait."

Nichole ran her tongue across Damon's lips and whispered, "Kiss me."

Damon did what he was told and kissed Nichole firmly on the lips. This went on for several seconds until Damon pulled back and looked down at his body. "I see you're playing dirty."

Nichole looked down as well. "You know, I could take care of that for you if you want me to," she whispered with a raised eyebrow.

A man only has so much willpower, and Nichole had just stripped Damon of any trace he had left. Therefore, in one swift motion, Damon had her suspended in his arms with her back against the wall. Nichole gasped the moment their bodies joined together. Instantly she was overcome with passion and emotion as he made love to her and clarified his position in her life. The rapid motion of his hips caused Nichole to cry out feverishly and beg for mercy.

"Damon," she pleaded.

"I'm sorry, Nichole," he responded breathlessly, "but I can't hear you."

Nichole could feel her body defying her and waves of gratification overtook her soul.

"Damon, I'm about to scream," she announced breathlessly.

Ignoring her, he tried his best to kiss every sensitive spot of her hot flesh. Seconds later, Nichole let out a sound that was a cross between a loud moan and a scream. She was unaware if anyone heard her, but if they didn't they were deaf. Damon followed with an incoherent groan of his own as he leaned into Nichole, totally spent. Before allowing her to stand, he kissed her firmly on the lips. Nichole was weak and needed assistance standing.

"Damon, I can't walk."

He carried her over to the sofa and sat her down. "I warned you, but you didn't want to listen. Now look what you made me do to you."

Nichole lay down on the sofa and closed her eyes as Damon got dressed. She still hadn't reached for any of her clothes.

"Nichole, do you need help getting dressed? I thought we were going to lunch."

She opened her eyes and smiled. "I love you, Damon."

He chuckled and gathered the rest of her clothing before joining her on the sofa. "I love you, too, and I like undressing you a lot more than dressing you."

Nichole grabbed his arm and pulled herself up to a sitting position. Then as if he were dressing a child, Damon helped Nichole into her clothes. Once they were done he looked into her eyes and frowned.

"Are you going to be able to drive?"

"I don't know what's wrong with me. It's not like we haven't done this before, but for some reason I'm totally exhausted this time."

He shook his head and walked across the room to his dorm-size refrigerator. He opened the door, pulled out a bottle of Gatorade, and handed it to her.

"Drink this, Nichole."

She took it out of his hand and unscrewed the top. "Thank you, Coach."

Damon watched Nichole drink the entire bottle of Gatorade all in one breath. She sat the bottle on floor and burped. Damon laughed.

"Was it that good?" She put her hand over her mouth.

"I'm sorry. That slipped out, but, yes, it was delicious."

"Yeah, right. Come on and let me get some food in you before you pass out or something on me."

Chapter Twenty-Five

Lala opened the front door and found a FedEx delivery-man on her porch.

"I have a delivery for Lala Miles," he announced.

"I'm Lala Miles."

She signed for the package and thanked the delivery driver before closing the door. Sitting down at the kitchen table, she opened the envelope. Inside was a petition for divorce from Deacon's lawyer. As she read the documents, she whispered, "Son of bitch."

Lala set the papers on the table and covered her eyes with her hands. "Deacon, Deacon, Deacon. If you won't listen to reason, I'll have to help you," she whispered to herself. "You will not leave me for that woman. I'll see to that."

Lala quickly picked up the telephone and placed a call to her attorney.

Deacon stepped onto the porch and rang the doorbell. As soon as the door opened, he grabbed Lala by the neck so she couldn't scream and pushed her into the house.

He closed the door behind him and pressed Lala's body against the wall.

"What the hell is wrong with you? Why did you go to Nichole's office? Have you lost your damn mind? I told you to stay away from her! I told you we were through! Why can't you get that through your thick head?"

Lala clawed and struggled to get Deacon's hands away from her throat, but he held on with a tight grip until he saw that Lala was about to pass out. He released her and she fell to the floor.

"I can't believe you!" Deacon yelled.

She coughed and gasped for air as Deacon paced in front of her. Lala crawled across the floor, grabbed a chair, and pulled herself up. She stumbled into the kitchen coughing and made her way over to the sink.

"You brought this on yourself, Lala," Deacon yelled. "Stay the hell away from Nichole!"

Lala turned on the kitchen faucet and tried her best to get some water down her throat. Deacon followed her into the kitchen and continued to pace the floor.

"I don't know what's wrong with you, Lala. I thought we had an understanding. Are you crazy or just stupid?"

Lala backed away from Deacon before answering. "You're still my husband," she whispered.

He walked toward her. "Not for long, and it's time you faced that fact and moved on."

"I can't believe you would try to kill me over that bitch!" Lala yelled. "I'm not handing you over to her, Deacon! Never! You married me!"

He laughed. "We'll see about that, and if you contest this divorce, you'll be sorry."

"No, *you'll* see. I should call the police and let them see your hand print on my neck. Looks like assault to me. That should get you a little time in jail."

Deacon knocked a chair out of his path and stalked

over to her. He grabbed her by the chin. "Sending me to jail won't make me take you back."

"It'll keep her from having you," Lala whispered as she glared at him.

When he turned and walked away, he picked up the chair and sat down with his head in his hands.

"Lala, our marriage has been over for a long time. Let it go."

She walked over to him and caressed his neck. "I'm sorry, Deacon, but I'm not ready to give you up. Not to Nichole or any woman."

Deacon jumped out the chair without responding and stormed out of the house.

Once inside his car, Deacon dialed Riley's cell phone.

"Riley, I lost it, man. Can you meet me somewhere?" he asked once Riley picked up.

"What have you done now?" Riley asked. "You haven't been back over to Nichole's house, have you?"

"Worse. I jumped on Lala and nearly choked her to death."

"Is she OK?" Riley asked, concerned.

"She's fine. She just don't want to let it go. Can you believe she confronted Nichole at her office?"

"That's foul, but you'd better be careful as far as Lala is concerned. You put your hands on her and that could get you locked up. You know you're halfway there after you pulled that stunt at Nichole's house. Take a vacation, Deacon, and get yourself together. Forget Lala and forget Nichole."

Deacon listened to Riley and sighed. "What I need is Nichole back in my life and Lala out of it."

"I don't think either one of those things are going to happen anytime soon, Deacon."

"I hope you're wrong, Riley. Boy, do I hope you're wrong."

Riley chatted with Deacon a while longer and told him where to meet him for lunch so they could talk.

The Gatorade Nichole drank helped her gain some of her energy back, making it possible for her to follow Damon in her truck to lunch. Once inside the restaurant they found a cozy table and placed their order within minutes. While they waited on their meal, Nichole took the opportunity to check her messages and e-mails on her handheld PDA. Damon watched her for a moment.

"I hope you still have a job when you get back to your office," he said.

"I'm the boss, Damon. I thought you knew."

He laughed and then got up to get a newspaper so he could read the sports section to pass the time. Nichole glanced up at him and smiled. He looked so fine in his green shorts and white shirt. When he returned to the table and sat down, he opened the newspaper, then looked over at Nichole.

"What are you smiling at?" he asked.

"I'm smiling at you and your muscular legs."

Confused, he looked down at his legs and asked, "What's wrong with my legs?"

She put her PDA into her purse and leaned closer to him. "There's nothing wrong with your legs. I was just admiring the view," she whispered.

"Is that right?" he asked before kissing her softly on the lips. When they finished kissing, Nichole turned to find Deacon and Riley standing beside their table.

"Hello, Nichole," Deacon greeted her.

She shook her head in disbelief. "Hello, Deacon. Hello, Riley," she replied.

Riley nodded at Nichole. "Hey, Nichole."

Nichole pointed to Damon and said, "Riley, I'm sure you remember Damon from the hospital."

Riley stared at Damon. "Yeah, I remember him," he mumbled.

"I'm sorry, Deacon. You and Damon haven't been introduced," Nichole announced. "Damon, this is my ex, Deacon Miles. Deacon this is my dear friend, Damon Kilpatrick."

Damon stood and extended his hand, but neither Riley nor Deacon shook it. Instead, Deacon frowned.

Damon lowered his hand and then firmly said, "Deacon, I'm glad to see you've recovered from your injuries. I'm sure you're anxious to get on with your life now."

Deacon stared at Damon without responding. He definitely had plans of moving on with his life but not without Nichole. The next few seconds felt like an eternity until Nichole said, "I hope you guys enjoy your lunches."

Deacon smiled and said, "Whatever, Nichole. Riley, are you ready to eat?"

"Yeah, man, I'm ready."

Before walking off Deacon said, "Later, Nichole."

"Deacon, I hope you took care of that problem we talked about earlier," she called out to him as he walked off.

Damon sat down. "So that's Deacon?"

"Yeah, that's him."

"You talked to him today?" Nichole lowered her head.

"Unfortunately I had to. I called him after his wife showed up at my office this morning threatening me about staying away from her husband."

"Threatening you? What did she say? Is that why you came out to the field so early this morning?" Damon asked, clearly distressed.

"I guess so. I was pissed. She walked up in my office acting all arrogant and smug."

The waitress interrupted them when she arrived at their table with their lunches, which consisted of a turkey club sandwich and fries for Nichole, and a sirloin steak burger and fries for Damon. After making sure they had everything they needed, the waitress left. Nichole revealed to Damon the rest of her conversation with Lala. Damon picked up the pickle on the side of his plate.

"This is getting out of hand, Nichole," Damon said before taking a bite of his pickle. "I'm worried about you. You could get hurt."

She sprinkled some pepper on her fries. "I can take care of myself. That's why I called Deacon and told him he'd better handle it so I won't have to. I can't have that woman or anybody showing up at my job acting ignorant, because that'll make me have to show my tail, and that's not going to look good on my resume."

Damon couldn't help but chuckle. "Hmmm, a catfight. So what did your lover boy say he was going to do?"

Nichole rolled her eyes at Damon. "He's not my lover boy, so stop saying that. Anyway, he apologized and told me he would handle it."

"Did he say what he was going to do about it?"

She took a sip of water. "I didn't stay on the phone long enough with him to find out."

Damon stood. "Why don't we go over there and ask him? We need to know that his wife is not going to be a problem."

"Damon!" Nichole yelled as she grabbed his arm to make him sit down. "I don't want to talk to him any more than I have to."

He sat down and fed her one of his fries. "Call him."

"What?" she asked.

Damon pointed to her cell phone. "I said call him. I need to know for my peace of mind, too. I don't hit women, but if his wife tries to come at you again, I'll beat her like a man."

Nichole giggled. "Don't say that, Damon."

"I'm serious. Now call him."

Nichole picked up her cell phone and dialed Deacon's number. He picked up on the first ring.

"Listen, Deacon, I'm sorry to interrupt your lunch with Riley, but I wanted to check in with you to see if you handled that problem I had earlier at my office."

"I told you I would handle it, Nichole," he replied, clearly agitated.

Nichole looked over at Damon, who was staring at her.

"Yes, Deacon, I know you said you would take care of it, but I would feel better if I knew exactly what you were going to do to handle it."

"Everything's cool, Nichole, so you can get back to lunch with your boyfriend."

Nichole sighed. "Come on, Deacon, can't we try to be civil with each other without all this hostility?"

Deacon laughed. "Whatever you say, Nichole. Now if you don't mind, I would like to get back to my lunch."

"OK, Deacon. I'm sorry I interrupted your lunch. Good-bye."

Nichole hung up the telephone and picked up her sandwich. "Are you happy now?"

"What did he say?" Damon asked.

"He said what I told you before. He said he would take care of it."

"I hope for his sake, he does," Damon replied before taking a bite of his sandwich.

Deacon picked up a slice of pizza and asked, "Is that the Philly coach you was telling me about?

Riley sprinkled extra cheese on his pizza and said, "The one and only."

"Look at them over there," Deacon said. "I almost lost my appetite when I walked in and saw him all over her."

"Give it up, Deacon!" Riley answered as he wiped his hands on his napkin. "Nichole has made her choice."

Deacon took a bite of his pizza and mumbled, "We'll see about that."

"What did you say?" Riley asked.

"Nothing. I didn't say anything."

"Don't do anything stupid, Deacon. I'm all out of favors," Riley announced.

Deacon continued to eat his lunch and stare at Damon and Nichole from across the room.

Before going their separate ways after lunch, Damon gave Nichole a fiery kiss and reminded her that he would be over later so they could pick up where they left off in his office. Nichole reluctantly returned to her office and Damon drove back out to the practice field to prepare for the afternoon practice.

Inside the restaurant while Riley paid for lunch, Deacon spied on Nichole and Damon through the window. It made his blood boil to see Damon's arms wrapped around Nichole's body. Riley picked up a toothpick and joined Deacon at the window to see what he was looking at. As they stood there witnessing Damon kissing Nichole, Riley looked over at Deacon.

"Let it go, bro. You act like Nichole is the only female on this earth. Do you know how many women down at the precinct have been trying to get with you? No, you haven't noticed because you can't get your head out of your ass."

Deacon turned to Riley. "You know what, Riley? Kiss my ass!"

Riley laughed and walked out the front door. As they walked across the parking lot Riley deactivated his car alarm.

"The writing's on the wall, Deek. Are you blind or did you see what I saw? Nichole and that coach are all over each other."

"Maybe for now, but we'll see how devoted she is to him," Deacon replied as he leaned against his car.

Riley laughed. "What do you mean by that?"

"Nothing. I'm just thinking out loud, Riley."

"You just don't get it, Deacon. Have you ever considered that Nichole might not have ever been *the one*? If you keep acting like this, you're going to mess around and let the real Miss Right get away."

Deacon opened his car door. "Like I said, kiss my ass," he said as he climbed inside.

Riley laughed. "I love you, too, bro. Remember what I said. Don't do anything stupid. I'll holler at you later."

Lala pulled down the ladder to the attic and climbed inside. Once in the attic she shuffled through several boxes of items stored on a shelf. As she searched the boxes she stopped when she came across some pictures of her and Deacon that were taken when they first started dating.

"We were so happy back then," she said.

She closed that box and then came across another box that had baby clothes in it. They still had the tags on them and were in pristine condition. She pulled the pink and blue footy pajamas out of the plastic covering and held the small outfits up to the light. Before putting them back into the plastic bag, she held them up to her face and took a deep breath. After staring at the baby clothes a few more seconds, she carefully placed them back into the box and sealed it.

Nichole got back to work and was immediately summoned to a meeting. The meeting lasted nearly an hour, and by the time she made her way into her office she was ready to call it a day, but she knew she couldn't. She had some accounts to work on after obtaining new information in the meeting. When she walked into her office she was greeted with a large vase of purple roses on her desk. She set down her purse and opened the card.

Nichole,
> *This is just a small example of how I feel about you.*
> *I'll show you exactly how much I love you tonight.*
> > *Love,*
> > *Damon*

Nichole smiled and sniffed the roses. Damon always knew how to make her feel sexy and special. She quickly picked up her phone and dialed his number; however, it went straight into his voice mail. Nichole looked at her watch and realized that Damon was probably on the field with the team. She waited patiently for the tone so she could leave him a message. As she listened to his greeting she leaned over to smell the roses again. Damon's baritone voice was very sensual, and that was only one of his many assets. The fragrance of her roses gave her office a sweet, summer smell, and they happened to be her favorite color. Seconds later Nichole got the beep tone so she could leave Damon her message.

"Coach, I know you're probably out on the field, but I wanted to call and thank you for the beautiful roses. I don't know when you had time to order them, but I wanted to call to let you know that I love them and I love you, and I can't wait to see you tonight. Kiss, Kiss."

Chapter Twenty-Six

Venice walked into the house and found Craig and the kids sitting at the table already eating dinner.

"I'm sorry I'm late. Something smells delicious in here," she said.

Craig stood and kissed her. "Brandon cooked dinner."

Surprised, Venice walked over and hugged her son's neck. "I can't wait to taste your cooking, Brandon."

He smiled proudly and said, "Pops helped me."

Venice took off her jacket and hung it on the chair.

Craig walked over to her and folded his arms. "Aren't you forgetting something?"

Venice thought for a moment. "I can't think of anything."

"Where's my kiss?" Craig asked right before he grabbed her around the waist and quickly dipped her.

Venice yelled out in shock. Brandon and the twins cheered and clapped. Craig kissed Venice firmly on the lips.

Venice smiled. "I kissed you when I came in," she said.

He poured himself a glass of apple juice. "That wasn't a kiss."

"Well, I'm sorry my first kiss wasn't good enough," she joked. "I'll make sure to really lay one on you next time."

Brandon got out of his chair and hugged his mother. "I'm glad you're home, Momma."

She kissed Brandon's cheek and then the twins, who happened to be playing with their food.

Venice washed her hands and then sat down at the table with her family. "I'm glad I'm home, too, sweetheart."

Craig took a glass out of the cabinet. "What do you want to drink, Venice?" he asked.

"I'll have whatever you're drinking," she said as she scooped some mashed potatoes, green peas, and chicken tenders onto her plate.

He poured her a glass of apple juice and set it next to her plate.

"Thank you, baby. You know the casino party is in two days, which means that Bernice and J.T. will be here tomorrow, and so will Joshua and Cynthia."

"Who's staying with us?" he asked.

"Just Joshua and Cynthia. I told Bernice that we had room for them, too, but she said they would stay in a hotel."

"My sister loves her privacy. When are Bryan, Galen, and Keaton coming in?" Craig asked as he sat down.

"They'll be here Friday morning. I'm starting to get excited," she admitted.

He looked over at her and said, "You should be. This is big."

She leaned over and puckered her lips, and Craig happily kissed her.

"I know, baby, and I'm so proud of you," she said.

"Thank you," he replied with a smile and another kiss.

"Now listen, Craig, I know all you guys haven't been together like this in a long time, so pace yourself."

He laughed. "I know you're not talking about me. Once Joshua and Bryan walk through that door, it's going to be on. You're the one who's going to need to pace herself."

Venice had to laugh along with Craig, because he was right. Her relationships with her best friend, Joshua, and oldest brother, Bryan, were very unique and special. She loved all her friends and family members, but those two were the ones who understood her the most.

"OK, OK, you got me there. We both need to pace ourselves this weekend. I want to make the most of our time together while they're here. Casino night is going to be off the chain," she said.

"I'm actually looking forward to that myself."

Brandon got Craig's attention. "Can I go to casino night, Pops?" he asked.

"You can hang out for a little while, Brandon. I might even let you deal a few hands, but once everyone arrives, you have to go to bed. OK?"

"OK, Pops. Thanks!"

Craig put his fork up to his mouth and calmly said, "Look at your twins."

Venice glanced over at Clarissa and C.J. and noticed that they had honey mustard and ketchup all over their faces. She playfully punched Craig in the arm.

"Why are they my twins when they're messy?" she asked.

He pointed at her blouse and drew her attention to the honey mustard staining her own blouse.

"Funny, Bennett," she said as she picked up her napkin and wiped the honey mustard off her blouse. Craig laughed and stood. He pulled a couple of baby wipes out of the diaper bag and cleaned the twins' faces and hands.

"Like momma, like children," he joked when he sat down. Venice pinched him gently.

"I see you're full of jokes tonight. Just for that, you're giving the twins their bath tonight, and you're doing the dishes."

Craig widened his eyes at her. "I have to do both?"

She smiled as she got up to put her plate in the sink.

"Yes, you do. I'm going up to relax in my own bubble bath. I need peace and serenity before Friday."

"You're serious, aren't you?" Craig asked.

She wrapped her arms around his neck. "You bet. I love you, and don't forget to double check our order at the liquor warehouse and make sure they deliver everything Friday morning."

"Yes, dear," Craig teased.

"Keep it up, Bennett," she replied as she kissed him. "Good night, my loves!"

"Good night, Momma!" Brandon yelled.

"Good night, baby. I'll be in to kiss you good night after I finish my bath."

"OK, Momma."

Craig was stunned. He actually thought Venice was joking. He looked over at Brandon.

"Hey, Brandon, will you help your old man clean up the kitchen?"

Brandon jumped out of his chair and said, "Sure, Pops."

Craig stood and started removing the dishes from the table while Brandon loaded them in the dishwasher. When Craig walked over to the twins he noticed that they had food all over their lap and in their chairs. He sighed and in the voice of Elmo said, "You messy little monsters."

Brandon, Clarissa, and C.J. all burst out laughing.

Damon's telephone rang just as he was leaving his office. He opened the door to his truck and climbed inside.

"Hello?"

"Hello, son."

Damon smiled. "Hey, Daddy. How are you and Nanna doing?"

It was Damon's grandfather, Ryan Kilpatrick. Since neither he nor Zel knew their fathers, their grandfather had been and always would be daddy to them.

"Oh, we're doing fine. Zel tells us you've met a young woman."

Damon gritted his teeth and made a mental note to kick Zel in the ass when he saw him. He wanted to be the one to tell his grandparents about Nichole.

"Yes, Daddy, I met a young woman named Nichole. What exactly did Zel tell you?"

His grandfather chuckled. "Ah, you know Zel."

"That's what I'm afraid of," Damon said as he pulled out of the parking lot. They laughed together. "Seriously, Daddy, Nichole is a wonderful woman and I'm in love with her. I hope to bring her down so you and Nanna can meet her real soon."

"Make sure you let us know when you're coming. Your grandmother will want to cook all your favorite dishes for you."

Damon looked at the time and asked, "Is she already in bed?"

"Yeah, you know she gets up early. I'll let her know that we talked, but make sure you call her yourself. She will want to hear about this young woman herself."

Damon pulled out onto the expressway. "I will, Daddy. Do you or Nanna need anything?"

Damon's grandfather chuckled again. "Now what could me and your grandmother need that we don't already have? We have you boys and each other, and that's good enough for us. That is until we get some daughters-in-law and great grandchildren in here."

Damon smiled. His grandfather was actually thinking along the same lines as he was. Giving the people he loved most in the world a daughter-in-law and great grandchildren was something he wanted to do very soon, but only with Nichole.

"How's the store doing, Daddy?"

"Oh, the store's doing great. We sit down there and watch you on the sidelines all the time. You're doing a good job, son."

Damon was like any young man who wanted to please his parents. For him he wanted to make sure he pleased his grandparents and always carried himself in a way that would make them proud of him.

"Thank you, Daddy. By the way, I checked the bank account the other day and you and Nanna never spend any money. I set that up for you so you can do some things you've always wanted to do."

His grandfather burst out laughing. "Damon, me and your grandmother don't want for anything."

"I know, Daddy, but I know you and Nanna would like to travel or get something new."

"Son, you buying us this fabulous house with all the furnishings and my truck was more than enough. I think your grandmother got herself some new cookware the other day, but that's about it. The store is paid for and you know I'm OK on the inventory."

Damon smiled. "OK, Daddy. Give Nanna my love and let her know that I'll be calling her tomorrow."

"Will do, son. I can't wait to me your young lady."

"I can't wait for you to meet her. I love you, Daddy.

"I love you, too, Damon. Good night."

"Good night, Daddy."

Damon arrived at Nichole's house around ten o'clock. Nichole met him at the door dressed in a lime green nightgown that exposed her shapely thighs. He looked so handsome in his jeans and red, button-down shirt. Nichole reached over, took his overnight bag out of his hand, and frowned.

"You look exhausted. I think you work just as hard as your players do."

He closed the door behind him, looked up and down her shapely body, and smiled. "I'm all right."

Concerned, she touched his head and cheek. "You don't look all right. Are you hungry?" she asked.

Damon laid his keys on the hallway table and pulled Nichole into his arms. "I said I was fine, but I appreciate your concern, and you are right about one thing, I work just as hard as my players."

Nichole hugged his neck and softly said, "Your job is so stressful. I'm worried that you might overdo it."

He kissed her forehead. "I'm used to my rigorous schedule. I can handle it."

Nichole led him farther into the house. "It's not going to make me stop worrying about you."

Damon tilted her chin. "Thank you. Listen, I'm sorry I got over here so late."

"It's not really late to me," she said as she caressed his back. "I'm a night owl anyway, so it's no big deal. I was upstairs working on my laptop while I waited for you."

He patted her backside lovingly. "Good. Now you can put it away."

Still clinging to Damon's large frame, she looked into

his eyes. He was sinfully handsome with his cocoa complexion, white teeth, and dimples.

"Well, since you're not hungry, Coach, let me get you upstairs so I can tuck you in."

He picked up his overnight bag. "That's what I'm talking about," he replied as he followed her up the stairs to her bedroom.

Once upstairs, Nichole saved the work she was doing on her laptop and shut it down. After putting it into its case, she turned her attention back to Damon and immediately started unbuttoning his shirt.

Damon laughed. "You don't waste any time, do you?"

"It's your fault. You shouldn't be so damn sexy."

Damon's hands went to her backside. "You're the one who's sexy. Look what you have on. That color against your skin is an aphrodisiac to me."

Nichole pushed off his shirt and started unzipping his jeans. She looked up at him seductively. "Your smile is my aphrodisiac," she said.

"Really?"

"Really," she replied as she lowered his jeans, allowing him to step out of them. Dressed in only his snug-fitting boxer briefs, he kissed her. Damon's large hands caressed her neck and face as he deepened their kiss. Nichole's hands roamed all over Damon's muscular physique, especially his firm, round derriere. He was about as fit as any man she'd been with. His abs, pecs, and biceps were nothing short of amazing. Damon flicked his tongue against Nichole's, causing her to moan. She pulled back momentarily and nibbled on his lower lip.

"I could do this all night," she admitted.

Damon kissed her cleavage. "I might have to put you to the test if you keep that up."

"I'm game if you are," she taunted him. "I'm addicted to you, Damon Kilpatrick."

He stared into her eyes in silence as he ran his hands through her hair.

"I'm addicted to you, too, Nichole."

She kissed his chin and breathlessly replied, "Prove it."

Before she could get the words out of her mouth, Damon tossed her onto bed and covered her body with his.

"What did you say?" he asked as he kissed her neck.

"I said prove it," she said softly.

"No problem," Damon responded as he massaged her foot. As he massaged it he noticed that she'd recently had a pedicure and her toenails were painted with a glossy, red nail polish.

"Nice feet."

"They're not my best assets."

He kissed her foot and raised his eyebrows. "You don't have to sell me, Nichole. I love everything about you."

Nichole slid her foot up his thigh and massaged his groin. Damon quickly removed her nightgown. For the next few minutes Nichole screamed, whimpered, and moaned as she writhed beneath him. What she was feeling left her totally exposed and helpless. Damon had entered her soul and took control. Nichole felt her body trembling, and Damon only stopped because it was his body that was about to defy the both of them. As he towered over Nichole, he looked down into her eyes and whispered, "I love you, Nichole."

Tears spilled out of her eyes. Damon's proclamation of love overwhelmed Nichole. She lost track of time after he entered her body with a force to be reckoned with. The room was instantly filled with sensuality and sizzling passion. Damon branded her physically and emotionally, and Nichole would never be the same. She held onto Damon, a man who had trusted his heart to her and accepted her love in more ways than one. Never in Nichole's wildest dreams did she think she could ever get past all the hurt and drama she had experienced after her messy breakup with Deacon. It left her afraid to fully trust her heart, but somehow God had sent Damon to her in the most unlikely way and convinced her to trust in him and herself.

The couple continued to kiss and devour each other's lips. Nichole was at Damon's mercy as he showered her body with waves and waves of pleasure before he collapsed on top of her. Out of breath and overcome with emotions, Nichole sobbed. Reality hit her like a ton of bricks. This was it for her. There would never be another.

For Damon, it seemed like a fantasy or a dream. He was a little skeptical at first, but at that moment he realized that God had answered his prayers and sent him an angel named Nichole. His search was over, and even though Nichole hadn't confessed the same feelings for him, he knew without a doubt that she loved him. He felt it every time she kissed him and saw it every time she smiled. Then, as if it was scripted out of a romantic movie, Nichole snuggled close to him and softly said, "I love you, too, Damon."

He kissed her, turned out the light, and closed his eyes. All that was left to take care of were the formalities of making their union official. Minutes later the couple drifted off into a deep and satisfied slumber.

Parked outside in the shadows of the moonlight a dark figure sat staring up at Nichole's bedroom window and realized when the lights went out that her visitor was going to be there for the duration of the night. With that knowledge, the driver turned on his ignition and drove off into the night.

Chapter Twenty-Seven

Casino night had arrived, and so had all of Craig and Venice's guests for the event. The house was buzzing with activity, music, and laughter. Craig had two poker tables set up, a craps table, a roulette table, and several slot machines. The catering service had all sorts of delicacies for everyone to sample, and an endless supply of beer, wine, champagne, and mixed drinks were available as well. To make sure all their guests would be safe, Craig had hired several limo drivers to transport guests to and from their homes. This way no one would have to worry about driving if they consumed a little too much alcohol.

At the poker table, Craig, Winston, Keaton, Damon, and Bryan were engrossed in a heated game of Texas Hold'em, while Craig's business partner, Lamar, Venice, Nichole, Joshua, and Arnelle battled at the craps table. At the other poker table, Manley, the husband of Craig's secretary, Galen, Venice's brother, challenged, Meridan, along with Venice's sister-in-law, Sinclair, and Craig's brother-in-law, J.T. Tressa, Lamar's wife, Francine, and Joshua's wife,

Cynthia kept the slot machines ringing while Sidney, Galen's wife, and Bernice placed bets on the roulette wheel. It was one big family affair, and long overdue. Venice looked up from her cards and glanced over at Craig's table.

"Baby, keep your eye on Skeeter. You know he cheats."

With a smirk on his face, Winston retaliated. "You're the one who has tricks up her sleeve. Worry about your own game. We got this over here."

"Talk to the hand, Skeeter!" she replied back to him playfully.

Winston always went head-to-head with Venice. They'd known each other since college, and every opportunity they had, they would antagonize each other in a playful manner. Winston was Craig's best friend, and he just laughed when they started battling with each other.

Nichole crapped out on the dice table and decided to check on Damon. She walked over to the poker table and hugged and kissed his neck.

Keaton looked up and frowned. "Don't come over here jinxing me."

Nichole walked around the table and hugged Keaton's neck to aggravate him. "Stop whining, you big baby, and play cards."

"I know that's right," his lovely wife Meridan chimed in from her card game.

"Oh, I see. You two are going to gang up on me," Keaton pointed out.

Nichole playfully smacked the back of his head. "Be quiet, Keaton. Nobody's ganging up on you."

Damon laughed and motioned for Nichole. She walked over to him and put her arm around his shoulders. "See, Keaton? Damon doesn't see me as a jinx."

With a smirk on his face, Keaton set his cards down. "That's because he's blinded by the booty," he joked.

Everyone at the table burst out laughing, even Damon.

Without a colorful response, Nichole instead stuck her tongue out at Keaton and then turned her attention to Damon.

"What can I get for you, baby?"

He kissed her hand. "Do you mind bringing me another Heineken, baby?"

"Of course not, sweetheart," she replied as she walked over to the bar.

"See what I mean?" Keaton said. "Damon, you are finished, dude. You might as well burn your playa's card right now."

"I'm sorry, Damon, but I'll have to agree with my brother-in-law," Winston said as he threw a chip out on the table. "It shows all over your face."

Bryan threw his chips in and looked over at Damon as well. "I'll have to agree with Keaton and Winston. Dust off your tuxedos."

Craig put up his hands and said, "Hold on, guys. Give Damon a break. Besides, why shouldn't he hook up with Nichole? I think she's perfect for him."

"Thank you, Craig," Damon replied.

"Who was the man who vowed he would get married when hell froze over, huh?" Craig continued, looking over at Keaton. "And, Skeeter, you can't talk. Arnelle broke you down so bad you jetted off to Florida like a mad man to get her when you thought she was about to marry Damon. You were pitiful."

Winston just shook his head as he listened to Craig, because everything he said was the truth. Then Craig looked at his brother-in-law, Bryan. Bryan laughed.

"You don't have to crack on me, Craig. I know Sinclair is a piece of work, but she's my piece of work, we complement each other, and I love her to death."

Craig laughed. "So with that said, y'all need to lay off Damon. I'm happy for you, man."

Damon accepted Craig's touching words by bumping his fists together with Craig's fists.

"You're right, Craig," Keaton intervened.

"I know I am," Craig responded before taking a sip of beer.

Keaton held out his fist and said, "Then let's do this right."

At that moment, Craig, Winston, Keaton, Bryan, and Damon all held out their fists and gave each other dap, and Nichole walked back over to the table.

"What are y'all doing?" she asked.

Damon smiled. "Nothing, baby, just showing each other a little brotherly love. Thanks for the beer."

She leaned down and gave him a kiss. "Great. Look, I'm going back over to the craps table. Have fun."

"Go get that money, baby," Damon joked.

All the fellows laughed upon hearing Damon's remark. Craig threw his cards in and asked, "Do any of you think you'll have enough energy to play golf in the morning?"

Damon's hand quickly went up, and so did Bryan's. Craig stood and made an announcement.

"If any of you squares are not too worn out from tonight, we're going to play a friendly game of golf in the morning at ten."

Nichole's eyes lit up. "I'm there!"

Damon shook his head and looked at Craig and Bryan.

"I'd better warn you guys. Nichole is the female version of Tiger Woods. I've only beat her once."

"Is that so?" Bryan asked. "We might have to make this golf game interesting when we hit the green."

Damon laughed. "I'm already out of about five hundred dollars."

Keaton looked over at Damon and folded with his cards. "Damn, Damon, you're talking to us like we're punks or something."

"Don't say I didn't warn you," Damon replied before turning up his Heineken.

The night was a huge success, and when all was said and done, it was nearly two AM when Craig and Venice said good night to everyone. Joshua and Cynthia stayed up and helped Craig and Venice clean up before retiring for the night. When everything was in place, Craig and Cynthia turned in for the night; however, Venice and Joshua stayed up a while longer to catch up on each other's lives.

Outside the gate to Craig's house, the same car that was previously parked in front of Nichole's house took note of the last limo that exited the property before speeding off down the street into the night.

Back inside the house, Joshua poured two glasses of champagne and sat down next to Venice on the sofa.

"Niecy, you and Craig really know how to put on a party."

Venice took a sip of champagne, kicked off her heels, and rubbed her feet. "Thanks. It wasn't that hard to plan. Once I got my caterer, the hard part was over."

"Well, it was fun. I had a great time."

She smiled. "I'm glad. I don't get to see you guys as much as I want. I know you're busy, but damn."

Joshua put his hands up in surrender. "I know, I know. My mom said the same thing. I'm going to do better."

She playfully punched him in the arm. "You'd better. You know you're my best friend, and talking over the phone or e-mailing doesn't do it for me."

Joshua took another sip of champagne and looked at the glass. "This is delicious," he said.

"I know. Winston recommended it. It's that Bollinger champagne."

Joshua laughed. "I guess it doesn't always take Dom Perignon, huh?"

"You have expensive taste, Joshua. You know I could drink some Cold Duck and be happy," Venice revealed.

Joshua put his arm around her shoulder and said, "That's funny. Here I sit next to a millionaire and no one would ever know it."

She kissed his cheek. Venice had been left very well off after the death of her ex-husband, Jarvis Anderson, who had played several years in the NFL.

"That's how I like it, but I don't look at myself that way. You know we don't live the life of the wealthy, but I do like splurging every now and then."

"No, you don't, and that's a good thing. You want the kids to grow up as normal as possible. Just because you got it, don't mean you have to flaunt it in public."

"I agree. I love doing unique and special things for my family and friends. A casino party is something we've been thinking about having for a while, and I love having all of you here."

They sat in silence for a moment. Venice held out her glass so Joshua could refill it. He sighed.

"Jarvis has been heavy on my mind lately. I mean I think about him all the time, but some days I think of him more than others. I still can't believe that he's gone."

Tears formed in Venice's eyes. She took a large gulp of champagne. "I know."

Joshua studied her expression. "You know it's OK for you to still cry over him, don't you?"

She wiped a tear off her cheek. "I guess."

"Craig understands, Niecy. Jarvis was your first love, and he was Brandon's father. Craig met him and he understands the connection you two shared."

"It doesn't seem fair to Craig that my love for Jarvis is still so strong."

"Why not? You loved Jarvis just as hard as you love Craig now. He knows what that feels like, and I'm sure he realizes that your feelings for Jarvis will never go away, God rest his soul."

"If you say so, Joshua."

"I know so," Joshua replied with a wrinkled brow. "Listen, Niecy, Jarvis was your husband. He got sick with a brain tumor and it took his life. Your mourning has no time limit, so stop trying to make yourself be over him, because you're not."

Venice sighed. "I'm not trying to make myself be over him."

"Yes, you are. You've done everything Jarvis wanted you to do. You married Craig, you're happy, and you have three wonderful kids. Just because you've moved on doesn't mean you're not allowed to think about him and the life you had together," Joshua explained.

Venice finished off the rest of her champagne and then curiously looked over at him. "What do you mean I did everything Jarvis wanted me to do?"

Joshua stood and walked over to the window without replying. Consuming so much alcohol tonight had caused him to let his defenses down. He had allowed something to slip out of his mouth that he promised Jarvis he would never reveal. Jarvis knew that Craig was the only other man who truly loved Venice, and he was the only choice to raise Brandon. Jarvis had made Joshua promise to make sure that Venice and Craig found their way back to each other after his death and without their knowledge. This was because he didn't want Venice taken advantage of by gold digging men once she inherited millions of dollars.

Venice walked over to Joshua and touched his arm.

"What are you talking about, Joshua?"

Angry with himself, he put his arm around her shoulders and they slowly walked back over to the sofa and sat down. He put his head in his hands.

"I didn't mean anything in particular, Niecy. I'm just tired and I've had a lot to drink tonight. My words are not coming out like I want them to."

She removed his hands and asked, "Are you sure?"

"Of course I'm sure," he said, smiling. "I'm the one who said it," he answered after regaining his composure. "Jarvis used to talk about you and Brandon to me all the time. He loved you guys and just wanted you to be happy after he was gone. Do you have any idea how hard it was for me to have those morbid conversations with him about you?"

Venice studied his body language as she listened to him. Joshua smiled and playfully bumped his shoulder against hers.

"Why are you staring at me like that?" he asked.

"I'm sorry. I know it was hard for you to lose Jarvis, too."

"You damn right it was," he answered. "We had some weird conversations, and Jarvis always talked about how he wanted you to find some guy to fall in love with."

"Who would've thought it would be his rival?" she asked.

Joshua laughed. "They weren't really rivals. They were actually cool with each other, and Craig was your booty on the side."

Venice couldn't help but giggle at Joshua's comment, and he couldn't help but laugh along with her.

"Niecy, all Jarvis wanted for you was a good husband and a good father for Brandon. That's all."

Venice looked at Joshua and asked, "And that's all you meant?"

He hugged her lovingly and said, "Of course that's what I meant."

Venice looked at Joshua and saw that he was struggling with his own emotions as they reminisced about

Jarvis. Joshua reached over and wiped a tear from Venice's cheek.

"Is it OK with you if we change the subject?" he asked softly as he grabbed the champagne bottle off the table and finished it off.

As Venice sat there she remembered how she ran into Craig in Ocho Rios, Jamaica nearly six months after Jarvis passed away. Venice linked her arm with Joshua's. He laid her head on his shoulder.

"You're right. Jarvis did want me to be happy. I'm so blessed that Craig was the man I ended up with."

Joshua kissed the top of her head. "I couldn't say it any better than that."

For the longest time they sat there in silence. Venice felt even more at peace than she had before. Her conversation with Joshua had allowed her to finally stop feeling guilty about loving Craig.

"Thanks, Joshua. I love you."

Joshua stood, grabbed her arm, and pulled her up from the sofa. "I love you, too, but I'm drained. Let me help your drunk tail up the stairs so you can go to bed."

Venice gave him a big hug before walking hand in hand upstairs to their respective spouses.

Damon and Nichole were the last couple the limo dropped off. Nichole couldn't keep her hands off Damon as he fumbled with the key.

"Nichole, you're going to make me drop the keys."

"Well you need to hurry up, Coach."

Nichole was spending the weekend with Damon since his house was located closer to the Bennetts' home. Since the Bennetts were providing transportation for the weekend, Nichole and Damon wanted to make it more convenient for the limo drivers.

Damon finally got the door open and they practically

fell into his foyer. As soon as they disappeared into the house a car came to a halt outside and turned off the engine. The couple started undressing each other the moment Damon locked the door and set the alarm. There was a trail of clothing leading from the foyer, up the stairs, and down the hallway to his bedroom. It would be nearly four o'clock in the morning before Damon and Nichole fell asleep, sated within each other's arms.

Chapter Twenty-Eight

The next morning, Craig and the gang, including Damon and the only female, Nichole, all met at the golf course to play golf. As Nichole positioned herself so she could practice her swing, Damon elbowed Bryan.

"Watch," he whispered.

Nichole took several powerful swings, causing Bryan to mumble, "Damn!"

"I told you," Damon replied. "Now you see what I've been dealing with."

"Well, I'm not scared." Bryan reached into his pocket and pulled out a one-hundred-dollar bill. "I want to see what she's got."

"She's a hell of a golfer," Damon responded. "So, if you don't mind losing your money, you're cool."

Bryan held up his C-note. "Would anybody like to make this game interesting?" he asked.

Keaton patted his pockets and frowned. "I didn't bring any money. I thought this was going to be a friendly game."

Winston quickly pulled out two one-hundred-dollar bills. "I got you, brother-in-law."

Keaton slapped hands with Winston and said, "Thanks, bro."

Craig pulled out his money and so did Damon, Lamar, and Joshua. Next they all looked over at Nichole, who reached down into her bra and pulled out her money. She handed it to Bryan.

"I'm in! I'm going to enjoy taking everybody's money."

All Nichole heard next was rumbling and trash talk from the men. Confident with her abilities, she took a few more swings to try to intimidate them. With her muscles loosened up and satisfied with her swing, Nichole turned and found several pair of eyes staring at her. She smiled.

"You guys ready?"

Everyone grabbed their clubs and said, "Let's go."

While the friends played golf, an odd package was placed in an inconspicuous place on Damon's truck.

Hours later, Nichole found herself counting off seven hundred dollars while six ego-bruised eyes stared at her. Damon was used to losing his money to her, so he wasn't the least bit embarrassed. Nichole had kept at least a three-stroke lead the entire game, finishing six under par. She smiled at her competitors.

"Lunch and drinks are on me at the club, guys."

Damon pulled her into his arms and kissed her. "You did great, baby."

"Thank you, Damon. Come on, fellows, I'm hungry!" She motioned as she led the way back to the clubhouse. There, the guys gave Nichole her props before ordering. Their lunches consisted of a variety of food, which included salads, sandwiches, and light entrees. No one wanted to overdo it because they knew they would be eating a full course meal later that night at the Bennetts'. They shared great conversation by talking about golf, football, and basketball. Nichole blended right in with guys, and was able to intelligently participate in each discussion.

A short time later, they all went their separate ways. Most of them were still tired from the previous night of gambling.

Craig yawned. "I'm going home to take a nap before Venice puts me to work. I'll see everyone tonight. Don't forget the limos will pick you up again."

A nap sounded like music to everyone's ears. Damon loaded up their golf clubs and then started up his truck. Before he could hit the expressway, Nichole was fast asleep. She'd played a strenuous game of golf with the fellows, and now she needed to recuperate. Damon, on the other hand, was not sleepy, so after dropping Nichole off at his house so she could rest, he decided to run a few important errands.

At the precinct, Riley noticed that Deacon seemed to be in an unusually upbeat mood. He was back to work, and hadn't mentioned Nichole's name one time. Curiosity got the best of Riley, so he decided to inquire about the change in his behavior.

"Yo, Deacon, what are you so happy about?"

Deacon smiled. "Nothing, really. It's a new day and life couldn't be better."

Riley chuckled. "That's a big difference from the other day when you were all broken up over someone that I won't mention by name."

Deacon waved him off. "I know, but I have a feeling things are going to change in a few days, so I'm good."

Studying him carefully, Riley asked, "What do you mean?"

Deacon laughed. "I don't mean anything. I'm good, Riley, so leave it alone. What's on the agenda today?"

Still leery of Deacon's new revelation, Riley decided to go along with him. "I'm glad you're back, Deacon, in more ways than one."

"Me too," Deacon replied as he waited for Riley to fill him in on the events of the day.

"How are things between you and Lala?"

Deacon picked up a file and opened it. "Lala is Lala. I haven't talked to her in a few days, so since I'm not locked up for choking her, I guess we're cool. My attorney hasn't received the divorce papers back from Lala, but at least I got the ball rolling on my divorce."

Riley leaned back in his chair. "For real? So you're really going to do it?"

He looked up at Riley. "I told you I was serious about making it official. I just hope Lala gives me the divorce without any hassle. It's not like we've been together for years."

"I hope for your sake she goes along with it, too. Being divorced is not the same as being separated. Divorces make everything final, and it can make some people go a little nuts."

Deacon picked up the telephone. "Lala knows not to do anything stupid."

"Does she?" Riley asked.

"If she don't know, she'd better ask somebody. I want out of this marriage for good."

The sun had set and the Bennett house was once again buzzing with laughter and good friends. Tonight's event was a semi-formal affair, and everyone had dressed accordingly. Craig had a big surprise for his friends and family, but he could be upstaged before the night was over.

The menu consisted of savory pork tenderloin, grilled salmon, and crispy herb chicken. Accompanying the meat were twice backed potatoes with mushrooms, roasted carrots, zucchini, corn, and peppers, as well as scalloped green beans, and a few other delicious side dishes.

With everyone gathered around the table, Craig tapped on his wine glass.

"May I have everyone's attention for a second, please?"

The chatter that filled the room quickly died down.

"First, I want to thank all of you for coming to share this weekend with us," Craig began. "We need to make our gathering a quarterly tradition; however, we can talk about that later. I hope you've all enjoyed yourselves, and with that said I'll get to the real reason I asked all of you to come. I've been doing a lot of thinking about what I wanted to do next with my life, and as you know, I love helping others, especially children. So after talking things over with Venice, I figured it wouldn't be right if I didn't get your thoughts and opinions on the next chapter in my life as well. What I want to do is sell the Japan office and take a leave of absence from the office here so I can teach architecture to inner city kids."

Applause filled the room, and so did joyful congratulations. Craig raised his hands to get the group's attention again.

"I take your applause to mean that you all support my decision. I know it's going to take a lot of work, and I have some challenges ahead of me because some of these kids have never had anyone to take an interest in their lives. I want to change that because so many of them are full of potential. It just needs to be brought out."

Everyone at the table gave Craig their individual congratulations and opinions on his career move. After receiving unanimous approval, he turned the floor over to Winston.

Winston stood. "Before I go any further, this announcement calls for some champagne."

He reached over to a nearby champagne bucket, popped opened two bottles of Dom Perignon, and prepared for his toast. After everyone's glasses were filled, he proceeded with his speech.

"Thank you, Craig. I just want to let you all know that Craig is not the only man who's been doing some soul searching. I've been thinking about doing something with my life to make a difference as well. With that said, I want to let you all know that I've decided to put my hat in the ring and run for mayor."

The entire room erupted in applause and surprise.

"Craig, I'm confident in saying that I believe the children of Philly couldn't have a better man to give them the tools they need to show them that they are not a statistic. And when I'm mayor, you'll have my complete support in making sure programs are established in the inner city in order give children a head start in life. So if you would raise your glasses, I propose a toast to Professor Craig Bennett, and to myself as the future mayor of Philadelphia."

Cheers sounded throughout the room as the guests toasted Craig and Winston.

Everyone offered their congratulations and accolades to Venice and Arnelle because their lives were going to be changed by the new careers their husbands were taking on.

Champagne glasses continued to clink together. There were also a lot of hugs for Venice, Craig, Winston, and Arnelle. After the initial celebration was over, they finished up their dinners and concluded with dessert and coffee.

As the night wore on, everyone gathered in the family room. Champagne was still being served, and Nichole noticed Damon anxiously looking at his watch while he was talking to Bryan. She walked over to him and wrapped her arms around his waist.

"Damon, are you OK? You look a little nervous."

He leaned down and gave her a kiss. "Not really."

Bryan took a sip of champagne. "You do seem to be sweating a little bit," he said.

Nichole felt his face and asked, "Are you sick?"

Damon smiled. "No, I'm not sick, and, Bryan, you're not helping matters."

Bryan chuckled and said, "I'll leave you two alone for a second."

Nichole looked at Bryan curiously. "What was that all about?" she asked.

"Forget about Bryan. Can I talk to you alone for a second?"

She stepped back and said, "Sure."

As they walked out the French doors into the Bennett backyard, Damon took a deep breath.

"You really look beautiful tonight," he said.

Nichole linked her arm with his. She was dressed in a silver tea length dress with matching shoes, which was a good contrast to Damon's navy blue suit and silver tie. Her hair was extra curly, and her makeup was natural and flawless. Nichole walked alongside Damon until they reached the opposite end of the pool and sat down on a bench.

"What do you want to talk about, Damon?"

Damon reached into his pocket and sat a black velvet box in her lap. "Open it."

Nichole picked up the box and slowly opened it. She gasped when she saw the square, four-carat, diamond platinum ring. Damon pulled it out of the box and placed it on her left hand.

"Nichole, I love you. Will you marry me?"

Nichole stared down at the shimmering diamond in total shock. She heard what Damon had asked her, but she couldn't believe her ears. She was overwhelmed, and even though tears were running down her face, she looked over at him and smiled. Her voice was scratchy when she asked, "Are you sure about this?"

"Of course I'm sure about this. Do you love me, Nichole?"

Unable to answer him verbally, she nodded as her tears increased.

He smiled. "I guess that's a yes?"

Still unable to speak, she nodded again.

Nichole flung her arms around his neck and finally blurted out, "Yes, Coach. I'll marry you. I'll marry you right now if you want me to."

Damon picked her up in his arms and kissed her lovingly on her rose-colored lips. "Too bad there's not a preacher in the house, huh?"

Nichole giggled and kissed Damon some more. He moaned. "I'm ready to take you home," he whispered.

She nuzzled his neck and purred. "I'm ready for you to take me home."

"Should we let them in on our news?" he asked as he held her in his arms.

"Do you want to?" she questioned him.

"It's up to you, baby."

"They *are* our friends, Damon. We can tell them, and then I want to go home so I can properly congratulate you," she revealed as her hand slowly slid down to his groin. Damon sucked in a breath in response to her sensual contact. He took her by the hand and quickly led her back into the house to make their announcement. When the newly engaged couple walked through the French doors, Nichole held up her left hand without saying a word.

Meridan was the first one to spot the ring, and she let out a loud squeal, startling everyone in the room. Arnelle followed Meridan's squeal with one of her own, and the rest was history. The couple was quickly separated as the women surrounded Nichole so they could see her ring, and the men punched and patted Damon on the shoulders and back to congratulate him. Craig motioned for Winston to retrieve more champagne. As Winston filled everyone's glasses, Craig pulled Venice over to his side.

"Damon, Nichole, I want to congratulate you guys on your engagement. I know we haven't known each other long, but you already feel like family. We wish you a long life of love, happiness, and the pitter patter of little feet in the near future."

Everyone laughed and then Craig continued.

"With all seriousness, I can tell it's true love when I look at you guys, and I hope your life is constantly filled with as much love and happiness as I have with Venice."

Nichole blew a kiss at Venice and Craig and mouthed the words thank you because she was too choked up to speak. Damon, however, did speak, even though his heart was about to burst.

"Thanks, Craig, and to all of you here. I've never felt as comfortable with people as I do with you guys. You all do feel like family, and with this beautiful woman beside me I know the sky's the limit. I love Nichole with all my heart, and I plan to do everything within my power to make her happy. Also, if I have anything to do with it, this will be a very short engagement, so look for wedding invitations in the mail real soon."

Laughter and applause filled the room once again as Damon gave Nichole a passionate kiss in front of everyone.

Arnelle hugged Damon's neck. "Congratulations,

Damon. I knew it the moment I introduced you guys in Texas."

He kissed Arnelle's cheek and whispered, "So did I, Arnelle. Thank you."

Tears had welled up in Arnelle's eyes by the time she released Damon. Winston handed her his handkerchief so she could wipe her eyes before she hugged Nichole.

"Congratulations, Nichole. You have yourself a good man." Nichole hugged Arnelle back.

"I know. Thank you."

Damon looked at his watch and walked over to Craig and Venice.

"I hate to leave so soon, but I want to get my fiancée home so I can congratulate her properly. I want to thank you guys for a great weekend, and congratulations on your new ambitions. If there's anything I can do to help either one of you, just let me know."

Craig shook Damon's hand.

"No problem. I'm glad you had a great time. Nichole, Venice and I expect to see more of you."

"Oh, you will," she replied as she hugged Venice and then Craig.

The couple walked hand in hand toward the front door.

"Good night, everyone," they said.

Everyone waved good-bye to Damon and Nichole before they disappeared out the door for a special night of hot passion.

Chapter Twenty-Nine

The next morning while Nichole slept in, Damon headed out to the practice field to take care of a little business, but as soon as he got off the exit, blue lights flashed in his rearview mirror. Damon had no idea why he was being pulled over, but he did as instructed as soon as he was able to maneuver through traffic. The officer cautiously approached his car.

"License and registration, please."

Damon pulled out his registration and insurance card from his glove compartment and handed everything to the officer.

"Why did you pull me over, officer?"

The officer studied Damon's information. "I noticed that you weaved out of your lane."

"Excuse me? I think you're mistaken, officer," Damon replied.

"I know what I saw, Mr. Kilpatrick. Sit tight. I'll be right back."

Damon couldn't believe what was happening to him. As he sat there he wondered how long it was going to take for the officer to write his ticket so he could be on his way. He wanted to hurry up so he could get back to Nichole. Minutes later he noticed the officer returning to his vehicle.

"Could you step out of the car, sir?"

Damon frowned, but did as he was told. The officer had Damon walk back to the front of his patrol car and patted him down. A few minutes later a K-9 unit arrived.

"Officer, could you please tell me what is going on?" Damon asked, frustrated. "I haven't broken any laws."

"We'll see about that. You just keep your hands on the hood."

Damon watched as the police dog started barking at his rear passenger side wheel.

"What the hell?" he mumbled.

That's when it hit Damon that this whole fiasco could be the work of Deacon Miles. A few seconds later, Damon watched as the officer pulled a large package out of his wheel well. They opened it and then looked over at Damon. The patrol officer walked back over to Damon, set the package down on the hood of his patrol car, and pulled out his handcuffs.

"Mr. Kilpatrick, you're under arrest for the possession of narcotics. You have the right to remain silent. Anything you say or do can be used against you in a court of law. You have the right to an attorney. If you can't afford one, one will be appointed to you. Do you understand these rights as I have told them to you?"

Damon was fuming in anger, but he knew he shouldn't do anything to provoke the officer further. He couldn't believe he was being arrested for drugs, drugs that had been planted on his vehicle. And he knew there was only one person who could be behind it—Deacon Miles.

Once at the police station, Damon was allowed to make a phone call. He knew he was in big trouble, but he was innocent. He dialed his house and prayed that Nichole would answer the telephone. After the third ring, she answered in a groggy voice.

"Hello?"

"Nichole, it's Damon. I need your help."

Nichole sat straight up in bed. Her heart started beating wildly in her chest. She immediately panicked. "What's wrong?"

"Somebody planted drugs in my car and I've been arrested. Call Winston and see if he can come down here and help me straighten this mess out."

Nichole jumped out of bed and frantically searched for her shoes.

"I'm on my way, baby. I'll be there in a second."

"Drive carefully, baby," he said before hanging up.

It took Winston nearly an hour to get to the police station. When he arrived, Nichole was nearly in tears. She stood.

"They won't let me see him, Winston."

He put his hand on her shoulder and said, "Calm down, Nichole. I know Damon's innocent. I'll go see what's going on. Wait here."

Nichole sat down and waited patiently; however, her stomach was turning flips As she sat there she tried her best to hold her composure and was doing a great job until she looked up and saw a familiar face.

"Nichole, what are you doing here?" Deacon asked.

She stood. "Like you don't know," she angrily replied. "Why did you do this, and don't lie because I know you set Damon up."

"I'm hurt that you think I would do something like that. I didn't know that Damon was here. What's he in for?"

Nichole folded her arms and walked closer to Deacon. "You know exactly why he's here, because you put him here. If you ever cared anything about me, Deacon, you would put a stop to this. Damon's never done anything to you. These charges against him could ruin his life."

"I'm not going to admit to anything, because I haven't done anything." Deacon looked down at Nichole's left hand. "What's that?" he asked.

"It's a ring and it's none of your business," Nichole responded nervously.

Deacon briefly closed his eyes and his jaw twitched. "Are you engaged to him, Nichole?" he asked calmly.

"That's none of your business, Deacon."

He turned to walk away. "In that case, I guess Damon's trouble is none of my business either, huh?"

"Wait, Deacon!" Nichole yelled. "Please, do it for me."

He caressed her arm and asked, "What do I get in return?"

She frowned. "My forgiveness. I don't owe you anything, Deacon."

"Here you are worried about your precious Damon's life being ruined, and you didn't have a problem ruining mine."

"You ruined your own life, Deacon, so don't put the blame on me. You're the one who lied to me about your marriage, so stop trying to make me out to be the bad guy."

He reached up, touched her cheek, and softly responded. "I still love you, Nichole, and there's nothing I wouldn't do for you, except this. He doesn't deserve you, and he's right where he should be, in jail for stealing you away from me."

Nichole pulled away from him. "Don't touch me, Deacon."

He stared at her in disbelief. "Oh, I can't touch you now?"

Nichole shook her head without answering. All she wanted him to do was go away if he wasn't going to help Damon.

"Are you going to help Damon or not?"

He took Nichole by the arm and walked over to a part of the hallway that was more private.

"I can make all of this go away, and your boyfriend's career will be unblemished. He could be out of here in an hour, but you have to do something for me in return."

"What?" she asked curiously.

He took her left hand into his. "Give him back that ring and break off the relationship, and he's a free man."

Nichole jerked her hand away. "You've lost your damn mind."

Deacon laughed and said, "OK, it's your life, but you'll be visiting your husband in jail for a long time. A large amount of cocaine is not just possession. Your boy is looking at some serious time."

Nichole was furious. She smacked Deacon hard in his face. "Go to hell!"

He chuckled and rubbed his cheek. "I see you still pack a mean punch. You've made your answer clear. Just remember it's Damon's life that you're playing with. Have a good evening."

Nichole angrily watched as Deacon disappeared around the corner.

Minutes later, Winston returned with information on Damon's arrest.

"Nichole, I'm not going to lie to you. This doesn't look good. Even though it's a first offense, it's still a felony. What we have in our favor is that Damon's fingerprints were not found on the package, and he doesn't have any priors. Right now he's being held without bail and he can't go before a judge until the morning."

"I can't leave him here, Winston! You have to do something to get him out of here," she pleaded. "He didn't do anything wrong."

"You and I know that, but the police don't see it that

way. There's a war on drugs, and it doesn't exempt anybody."

Nichole shook her head in disbelief. "No way, Winston. You have to do something because I'm not leaving him here."

Winston stood. "I'm sorry, Nichole, but you don't have a choice."

"You can't let this hit the newspapers. He'll lose his job."

Winston scratched his head. "Let me see if I can call in a few favors. Go home and I'll get back to you."

"I can't leave here without him. If I have to sit here all night, I will. Can you get me in to see him?" she asked.

"They're only letting me see him for now. I'm sorry."

Nichole grabbed Winston's hand. "Did you tell him I was here?"

"Yeah, he knows, and he's worried about you believing in him."

She put her hand over her heart. "Winston, please tell him I know he didn't do this. I don't want him back there worrying about me."

Winston saw someone walk by that he wanted to talk to regarding Damon's arrest.

"I'll tell him, and he's doing fine, considering. Listen, just stay here. I'll be right back. I see somebody that might be able to help."

Nichole couldn't believe what was happening. Even though Deacon didn't admit to setting up Damon, she knew he was involved in some way. He had gone too far, and she would never forgive him for this. While she waited, she was surprised once again, but this time by an unlikely source.

"Well, what a nice surprise. Are you here to see Deacon?"

Nichole looked up and found Lala standing before her.

She sighed. "Don't flatter yourself. I could care less about Deacon right now."

This got Lala's attention. She was actually interested in this bit of news, because she thought Nichole was still her competition.

"Is that so?" she asked.

"Listen, Lala, I've been over Deacon for a long time, so go on and live happily ever after with him. I wish I'd never met him," Nichole replied angrily.

Lala studied Nichole's expression and realized she was telling the truth. That's when she noticed the huge diamond resting on her finger.

"Nice ring. Are you engaged?"

"Yes," Nichole replied in a robotic like manner.

"Congratulations. Who's the lucky guy?" Lala inquired.

Nichole turned to her. "It's not Deacon, if that's what you're thinking."

Lala sat silently next to Nichole for a moment. "I believe you. I didn't mean to pry, Nichole. It's not like you and I are friends or anything."

"You got that right," Nichole replied as she crossed her legs. "Lala, if you don't mind, I'd rather be alone."

Lala pulled her purse strap up on her shoulder and said, "I understand, and I just want to say that I'm sorry I came to your office and confronted you about Deacon. I actually thought you were a home wrecker, but I now know differently. I misjudged you, Nichole, and I hope you can forgive me."

Nichole looked over at Lala and saw sincerity in her eyes. "You're forgiven, Lala. I honestly didn't know about you when I was dating Deacon, and I'm sorry if you got hurt because of me."

"It wasn't your fault. Deacon hurt a lot of people with

his lies, and it's time he got a little taste of his own medicine."

"If you want to take some type of revenge on Deacon, go right ahead, but count me out. I just want him to leave me alone."

Curious, Lala took a chance, reached over, and touched Nichole's hand. "I know Deacon better than anyone. I can help you, Nichole, especially if he's harassing you. I know Deacon's weaknesses."

Nichole squirmed in her seat. "Thanks, but no thanks."

"I'm really sorry, Nichole." Lala stood and dropped her business card into Nichole's purse. "If you change your mind or ever want to talk, give me a call. I hope you and your fiancé have a happy life together."

Nichole watched as Lala quietly disappeared into the crowd just as quickly as she had appeared. What Nichole didn't see was Lala talking with one of the female officers she'd known for sometime. When she found out that Nichole's fiancé had been arrested, she understood why Nichole was so upset. If Deacon had anything to do with it, he needed to be stopped.

When Winston returned Nichole could tell by the look on his face that he didn't have any good news to report.

"I didn't have any luck, Nichole. No one will hear his case until tomorrow morning."

Nichole's head was throbbing and she felt her world crumbling down around her.

"You can go home, Winston. There's no sense in you hanging around any longer."

"Come on so I can walk you out," he said, putting his hand on her arm.

"No, you go ahead. I'm going upstairs to see a friend while I'm here."

Winston frowned. "Are you sure?" he asked.

She smiled and said, "I'm sure."

Winston was very frustrated that he was unable to get Damon released.

"Why don't you go home and get some rest? I'll be back first thing in the morning."

Nichole hugged Winston's neck. "Thanks for all your help, Winston."

"You're welcome." Winston exited the precinct.

Nichole said a little prayer, proceeded over to the elevator, and reluctantly punched the button.

It was nearly midnight when Damon was finally released from jail; however, when he picked up his belongings, Nichole was nowhere to be found. Instead he found Winston waiting for him in the corridor.

"Where's Nichole?" he asked.

"I was going to ask you the same thing. She called and told me you were being released and to meet you here," Winston revealed. "I was looking for her myself."

Damon dialed Nichole's number but got her voice mail. Now it was his turn to worry.

"When was the last time you saw her?" Damon asked. Winston looked at his watch.

"I left her here this afternoon."

Damon tried to dial her number again. "Something's wrong, Winston. Did she say anything else?"

Winston thought for a moment. "When I told her there was nothing I could do to get you out tonight, she mentioned something about going upstairs to see a friend before going home to get some rest."

"Wait a minute. You didn't get me out of jail?" Damon asked.

"No, the arresting officer dropped the charges. He said a colleague told him that an informant revealed that you and your vehicle were mixed up in a case of mistaken identity, and you were targeted in error. The drugs were supposed to be left in someone else's vehicle. Besides, your fingerprints were nowhere on the package, so the case would've been thrown out anyway. Your record's clean and you're good to go," Winston announced.

"There's no way. Something doesn't sound right. Shit!" Damon yelled.

"What's wrong?" Winston asked.

"I hope Nichole didn't go meet up with Deacon."

"Deacon? You mean the police officer that Nichole used to date?" Winston asked.

"Yeah. In fact, I think he was the one who set all this up in the first place. He hasn't been able to let go of Nichole since she found out he was married and broke up with him. Nichole even suspects that he broke into her house and did some weird stuff in her bedroom. Another time she had to call the police because he showed up at her door drunk in the middle of the night. Personally, I think he's dangerous."

Winston shook his head. "I hope you're wrong. Come on, Damon, let me get you out of here so we can find Nichole. This is possibly bigger than I thought it was."

Damon walked past Winston. "Not before I talk to Deacon. He has to be around here somewhere."

Winston grabbed him by the arm to stop him. "You're too upset. Go home. I'll see if I can find out when and where he works, and call you later. I doubt he's still here this time of night, and you can't afford to get locked up for assaulting an officer."

Damon thought for a moment. "You'd better call me the minute you know something."

"Will do," Winston acknowledged before walking toward the elevator.

Chapter Thirty

Winston found out that Deacon was not at work, and that he worked the day shift. He called Damon and filled him in, and in doing so he found out that Nichole was still missing in action, but she didn't stay missing for long. By the next afternoon Damon was ready to call the police and file a missing persons report, but just as he picked up the telephone, his doorbell rang. He opened the door and found Nichole standing on the porch. His heart sank and he immediately pulled her into his arms.

"Nichole, where have you been? I've been looking all over for you. I was worried sick!"

She hugged him. "I'm sorry I wasn't there for you when you got out, but I had something very important to take care of."

Damon closed the door and led her into his hearth room. He immediately started kissing her, but she slowly pulled away. Nichole had never pulled away from his kisses, and it puzzled him.

"What's going on, Nichole? Why the disappearing act?"

She sat down on his leather sofa and sighed. "Sit down, baby. We need to talk."

Those words never meant anything but misery. He sat down next to her. "About what?"

Nichole threw her arms around Damon's neck and whispered, "About us. Listen, Damon, I hate to do this to you, but I can't marry you right now."

He looked into her eyes. "What are you talking about? What's really going on, Nichole?"

"Nothing's going on. I just can't marry you right now," she repeated as she took off the ring and held it out to him.

"Why not?" he asked with a scowl on his face. "It's Deacon, isn't it?"

"No, it's not Deacon. It's me," she replied as she stood. "I don't want to give the ring back, but I have to. Just trust me, Damon, please."

Damon stood and looked down at the ring in her hand. "Trust you? You've been lying to me the whole time, haven't you?"

"No, Damon!"

"Yes, you have, because if you loved me, and I mean really loved me like you said you did, you wouldn't be doing this. How can I ever trust you when you tell me one thing and then do another?"

Nichole's heart was aching. She couldn't look into his eyes, because she would see the pain she was inflicting on him. "Just take the ring, Damon," she whispered.

He refused to take the ring. Instead he backed away from her. "This is some bullshit! I want to know why you're doing this to us."

She set the ring down on the table and walked toward the door without answering. When she got to the door she turned and mouthed the words I love you.

Confused, he frowned and started to say something, but she stopped him by putting up her hand.

"Good-bye, Damon," she whispered before walking out the door.

Damon slowly walked over to the door and watched Nichole as she backed out of his driveway and drove off. He slammed the door.

"Son of a bitch!"

Craig and Venice were just about to bid Joshua and Cynthia farewell when Winston arrived. He shook Joshua's hand.

"Are you guys getting ready to head out?" he asked.

"Yeah, we're ready to hit the road. I need to get home so I can recuperate from all this fun."

They all laughed together.

Winston looked at Cynthia. "Can I borrow your old man for a second?"

"Of course, Winston. It just gives me a reason to stay here a little longer."

Venice folded her arms and asked, "What's wrong, Skeeter, and don't lie to me because I know when something's wrong."

He looked at Venice and kissed her on the cheek. "Nothing's wrong, Oprah. Craig, can you join us?"

"Sure," Craig replied as he motioned for the guys to follow him into his office. Once inside he closed the door and sat down. "OK, I'm like Venice now. What's going on?" Winston sat down.

"Don't say anything to any of the females, but Nichole gave the ring back to Damon."

Craig shuffled some drawings around on his desk.

"That was quick," he said.

Joshua laughed at Craig's comment.

"It's not funny," Winston yelled. "He called Arnelle a little while ago hysterical."

Craig walked over and poured himself a glass of wine.

"Well, if the witch doctor knows about it, it's only a matter of time before the rest of the women know about it. You know she's like Venice, nosey as hell."

Joshua burst out laughing again. Winston paced across the floor.

"This thing is deep. Damon got arrested yesterday for having drugs in the wheel well of his car. But I believe him when he said he didn't know how it got there."

This revelation got Joshua's and Craig's attention.

"Arrested for drugs? I'm with you, Skeeter, that's not Damon. He's a fitness guru and he barely drinks. I know he's not going to put that stuff in his body, and he's not going to risk his job over something so stupid," Craig said.

"Exactly!" Winston pointed out as he walked over to the window.

"I can tell he's a cool guy, and I don't even know him," Joshua said.

"He is, Joshua. I think all of this happened because of Nichole's deranged ex-boyfriend. He's a cop and he's giving her hell because she's dating Damon, so at this point I wouldn't put anything past him."

"What do you mean?" Joshua asked. "What did he do?"

"OK, check this out. Damon got arrested. I used all my connections and skills and I couldn't even get him out on bond. His fingerprints were not on the package, but they were ready to charge him with a class A felony for possession with the intent to sell. Damon was looking at some serious time, even as a first offender. Then all of a sudden the charges got dropped. When I talked to the arresting officer he said a colleague said it was a case of mistaken identity and that Damon was targeted in error. Then this morning, Nichole gives the ring back," Winston explained. "Damon thinks this cop is dirty and was behind the whole thing, and so do I now that I see how everything's playing out. Joshua, what do you think? Can you use your contacts at the F.B.I. to find out what what's going on?"

"I'm sure I can. If this cop is dirty, he needs to be locked up," Joshua added.

Craig twirled around in his chair. "What I don't get is why Nichole gave the ring back. Does she think he's guilty?"

"No, no! She loves him. I think that cop got to her some kind of way. Damon is a wreck," Winston said.

"I know too well about blackmail. That crazy witch Katrina did it to Venice and convinced her to run, but luckily my boy Joshua took care of her. Maybe this cop is doing the same thing to Nichole," Craig suggested.

Winston pointed his finger at Craig. "You know, you could be on to something. Damon did get out of jail with ease after I was told he couldn't go before the judge until the morning."

"What's this cop's name?" Joshua asked as he pulled out his cell phone.

Winston pulled a notepad out of his jacket pocket and said, "Deacon Miles."

Joshua called someone on his cell phone and put in several requests. He stopped talking for a moment and asked, "Craig, what's your fax number here?"

Craig twirled around to his fax machine and read off the number. Joshua hung up the telephone and walked toward the door.

"Where are you going?" Craig asked. Joshua opened the door.

"To tell Cynthia to chill because we're not leaving until I see if I can help Damon and Nichole."

Winston walked over to Joshua and shook his hand. "Thanks, Joshua."

"No problem. I'll send you my bill later."

Venice pushed open the door at that moment and walked into Craig's office. She looked at Winston.

"Are you guys meeting about Nichole giving Damon back the ring?" Venice asked.

Craig made his way over to Venice and gave her a kiss before walking her to the door.

"Not really, sweetheart. Why don't you and Cynthia go shopping or to the spa and relax? Camille won't be bringing the kids home until this evening, so the clock is ticking."

She wrapped her arms around his waist. "You guys are just trying to get rid of us."

Joshua walked back into Craig's office and said, "You're right. Now go. We have some business to take care of."

Cynthia joined them in the office.

"Come on, Venice. I saw a pair of shoes I want to get. Let the guys play cops and robbers all they want."

Venice giggled and gave Craig one more kiss before walking out with Cynthia.

"OK, you don't have to be pushy. We're out. Don't do anything stupid, and whatever's going on with Damon and Nichole, I hope you all can fix it."

Nichole pulled her car into a parking space in the park and exited the vehicle. Before meeting Deacon she decided to put her truck in the shop to be serviced. After dropping off her truck she had the repair shop take her home so she could get her Benz. She was anxious to get her meeting with Deacon over with, so Damon would be safe. She was trying to come to terms with what she'd done to Damon and find peace with her decision, but she was unsuccessful. At that moment she received a call from the auto shop. What they told her totally stunned her. The mechanic revealed to her that some type of GPS tracking device had been discovered on her vehicle. She asked the mechanic to hold onto the device until further notice. This information angered her even more as she sat in the parking lot to get her thoughts together.

With a cup of coffee in hand, she exited the Mercedes, walked over to a nearby bench, and took a seat. As she sat there looking around she could hear the birds chirping in the trees. They sounded so happy and were a far cry from the emotions she was experiencing at the moment. Over her shoulder she noticed children playing on playground equipment while the groundskeepers mowed the grass. Within minutes, Deacon joined her on the bench, smiling.

"I see you're in your Roadster. Why aren't you driving your Escalade?"

She frowned, but what she wanted to do was punch him in the throat. "What difference does it make to you?"

He shrugged his shoulders. "It doesn't to me. I just think you look sexier in your truck."

"I know about the GPS system, Deacon," she revealed.

Deacon laughed. "I don't know what you're talking about," he said.

Nichole reached inside her bra, pulled out the small recording device, and slammed it in his hand. "Here's your other spy wear. You're sick, Deacon, and you need help, and you know what? I don't care that you know where I've been, because I'll tell you myself. I've been with Damon. There! Now you know."

Deacon picked up the microphone and smiled. "You don't have to be so hostile, Nichole. Everything I do, I do out of love. By the way, you did real good with Damon. I must say you were very convincing. I didn't think you would actually go through with it, though. Dude was pretty broken up when you gave that ring back to him. You must really love that guy."

Nichole stood. "You know what? You're right, I do love him," she said angrily, "because he's nothing like you. I never in my life thought you could ever stoop so low as to frame someone for a serious crime. And blackmailing me into your scheme is a new low for you."

Deacon stood and grabbed Nichole by the arm. "I don't appreciate you making this sound so shady."

Nichole gritted her teeth. "You're hurting me, Deacon. Furthermore, I call it as I see it. Now let go of my arm. You're making a scene."

He looked around at the patrons in the park. "I don't give a damn about these people! What I do give a damn about is you, and keeping you away from Damon!"

Nichole jerked her arm away from him. "You need to forget about me because I will never be with you again." He grabbed her chin.

"Are you sure about that?"

"I'm not afraid of you, Deacon, so threaten me all you want. What I did was for Damon, not for you! Payback is hell, and you deserve everything you get."

He laughed and then a serious look appeared on his face as he slowly ran his finger down her chest.

"Stay away from him, Nichole, or you'll find his ass right back behind bars. Next time the stakes to get him out will be much higher, so be careful what you say to me."

"Stop thinking you're God over people's lives, Deacon."

He laughed again. "I like the way you put that. I guess in a way I am like God, huh? You'll do what I say or else."

Challenging him, she stepped up to him and yelled, "Or else what, Deacon?" He walked closer to her.

"You don't want to know."

"That sounds like another threat," she pointed out.

"Call it what you want. You gave me no choice but to do what I did. You never gave me a real opportunity to explain my situation to you," he explained.

"None of it would've mattered anyway, Deacon, because you are married and you didn't have the balls to tell me, so I don't care what the circumstances are. I'm out of here," she announced as she stepped around him.

Deacon reached over and grabbed her arm again. "Before you run off, let me remind you that I was able to have your boyfriend, Damon, locked up. I was also able to persuade you to break up with him in return for his freedom. So as long as you do what I say, everybody will be happy. Don't try to grow a brain and do something stupid, or you'll be crying right along with your boyfriend."

Nichole pulled away from him, flipped him the finger, and walked back to her vehicle.

"See you tonight, baby!" he called out to her. "Put on something sexy!"

She heard him laughing all the way back to her car. Nichole climbed inside her car and screamed before speeding out of the park.

Joshua pulled the paperwork off the fax machine and read it. "Deacon Miles has an unblemished record on paper; however, that makes me curious about his background even more."

"Why?" Winston asked.

"Almost every cop has something or some type of something on their record. None of them are boy scouts, not even me."

Craig laughed. "Well, I know that's right. We would probably be shocked at some of the things you've done."

Joshua popped open a beer. "I plead the fifth, but I will

admit that I'm no angel. I just do what I have to do when I have to do it. I almost killed a guy over Venice a few years back."

Craig's eyes widened in disbelief. "Are you serious?" Craig asked.

"Hell, yeah," Joshua admitted. "This was after Jarvis died. One of his teammates thought she was alone in her house and he tried to rape her."

Winston smiled. "So is this guy buried in a shallow grave somewhere?"

Joshua laughed. "Thanks to me he's not, but had it been Bryan or Galen, he would've been. They don't know about it to this day, so don't ever tell them. I did put the fear of God in dude, though. I made him piss all over himself when I shot right over his head. I know he felt the heat of the bullet. I'm just glad I was there because the outcome could've been a different story."

Craig walked over and hugged Joshua. "I love you, Joshua. You're a great friend to us, especially Venice."

"Me and Venice go way back. She's my sister. You know how I am with her."

Winston shook his head. "You are a scary guy, Joshua," he said.

"That's putting it mildly, Winston," Joshua replied with laughter.

Just then the doorbell rang, breaking up their conversation. Craig opened the door and found a sick looking Damon standing on the porch. Craig shook Damon's hand.

"Come in, Damon. I'm sorry about Nichole."

"So am I, Craig. Is Winston still here?"

"Yeah, he's right there in my office with Joshua. Go right in," Craig replied as he closed the door and followed him back into his office.

Damon shook Joshua and Winston's hands before sitting down. "Winston, please tell me you have good news for me."

Winston sighed. "We're working on it, Damon."

"We?" Damon asked.

Joshua opened another beer. "Yes, we, Damon," Joshua said. "If Deacon had anything to do with planting those drugs on you, we'll get to the truth and put him behind bars."

He nodded and then asked, "What about Nichole? I don't want her to get hurt even though it seems she doesn't want to have anything to do with me."

"Let me worry about that," Joshua said calmly. "I won't let Nichole get harmed in any way."

"Well, my history with women continues," Damon said as he stood. "I must be the biggest fool in the world."

Craig smiled. "No, you're not a fool, Damon. You're a decent guy who has a history of falling for the wrong women. However, this time I think you got it right with Nichole. Unfortunately it seems you have the interference from a rogue cop that we have to put away. I know it's heartbreaking to hear the woman you love tell you to get lost. I've been there, so I know."

"You're not by yourself," Winston said as he crumpled a piece of paper. "Arnelle got me good when she ran off to Miami with you, Damon. I was physically sick."

"I'm sorry about that, Winston. I didn't know about your history with Arnelle, but I did love her."

Winston patted Damon on the shoulder. "That's all in the past, Damon. I'm here to help you in any way possible."

"I appreciate that, and I pray Deacon gets whatever he deserves if he is in fact dirty," Damon responded. "I'm going to try to work. Call me if you find out anything."

Winston acknowledged Damon's request and told him good-bye before Craig and Joshua walked him to the door.

Chapter Thirty-One

Nichole checked into a downtown hotel. She decided to grab a bite to eat in the hotel restaurant as she thought about everything that had happened to her that day. She knew that Deacon was the only one capable of planting the GPS system on her Escalade, and he was the only one who had that type of interest in her personal life. Nichole realized that Deacon now had a record of her whereabouts. Everywhere she had driven in her truck had been at his fingertips. Saddened and angry, Nichole took a deep breath to gather her senses. She had given Deacon too much power over her life, and it was time she got it back and then some.

Hours later Nichole woke up crying. She sat up on the side of the bed and wished she could call Damon and apologize for breaking his heart, but she knew she couldn't, not yet. He'd left several messages on her cell phone, and she could clearly hear the pain in his voice. Nichole hated that she had added another stab to his already damaged heart.

Nichole pulled her exhausted body across the floor

and into the bathroom. She looked in the mirror and didn't recognize herself. Turning on the cold water, she splashed her face, trying to revitalize her mind and body. Never in her life had she let someone kick her when she was down, and she was allowing Deacon to do just that.

It was then that she got angry—very angry—and she slammed her fists against the mirror, shattering it. The pain of her injury was nothing compared to the pain in her heart. The blood oozing out of her hand was mesmerizing as she stared down at her wound. She calmly reached over, pulled a hand towel from the towel rack, and wrapped it around her hand. After inspecting her hand again, she ran some cold water over her cuts. Without a first aid kit, she was forced to call the front desk for bandaging supplies. After bandaging her hand, she made an important telephone call. Then she got dressed, packed her bags, and checked out of the hotel. She drove off into the night, hoping to get her life back.

Riley and Deacon drove through an area of Philadelphia known for high gang activity. Riley looked over at Deacon.

"Why are you so quiet?" he asked.

"No reason. I just don't have much to say."

Riley shrugged his shoulders and turned down another street. They saw a few men around the ages of eighteen to mid-twenties loitering on brownstone stoops.

"Look at these guys. They don't have a care in the world except making money the easy way," Riley pointed out.

Deacon pulled out a twenty-dollar bill and flashed it. "It is the root of all evil."

"I thought women were the root of all evil," Riley responded.

Deacon smacked the dashboard. "Them too! Riley, I swear, they make me crazy."

He chuckled. "Are we talking about anybody in particular?"

Deacon put the money back in his pocket and sighed. "Something like that."

Riley laughed. "You're a sick man, Deacon. Nichole is going to be your downfall if you're not careful."

"She's like a drug to me, Riley. I have to have her. Hell, I do have her," Deacon revealed.

Riley pulled into the parking lot of an all-night diner and hit his brakes hard. He threw the car in park and as calmly as possibly asked, "What have you done?"

"Nothing!" Deacon responded as he opened the car door.

Riley stepped out of the car as well. "I know you, Deacon. What have you done?"

Deacon walked toward the diner. "The less you know, the better off you'll be."

When Deacon tried to open the diner door, Riley grabbed Deacon by the arm and pushed him away from the door.

"You're foul, Deacon! You know I've watched you mistreat Lala for years. You're my partner and like a brother to me, but I can't sit back and watch you hurt Nichole, too."

Deacon burst out laughing. "What is this? You're turning on me now?"

Riley shook his head in disbelief. "I'm trying to help you and keep you from throwing away your career over a piece of tail."

Deacon pushed past Riley. "Whatever, Riley. Thanks, but no thanks. Contrary to what you might think, I know what I'm doing, so stay out of my life."

Riley walked into the diner behind Deacon, sat down on a barstool, and picked up a menu. "Don't ever say I didn't try to help you, Deacon."

Deacon chuckled and looked over at him. "Don't worry, I won't."

Nichole stepped onto the small porch of the brownstone and rang the doorbell. Lala opened the door dressed in a white terry cloth robe and smiled.

"I'm glad you changed your mind, Nichole."

Nichole hesitated. "Listen, I'm still not sure about this, but at the precinct you seemed genuine about helping me in spite of the circumstances."

"I meant every word, Nichole. I think we can help each other and give Deacon what he deserves in the end."

Nichole stood there contemplating Lala's offer. Lala reached out and took Nichole by the hand, causing her to flinch.

"I'm sorry," she apologized as she looked down at her hand. "What happened to your hand? Did Deacon do that?"

"No, I just had a little accident. It's OK. Just a little sore."

"Come on in so I can get you something for the pain."

Nichole took a step backward instead. "This is a bad idea."

"No, it's not, otherwise you wouldn't be here, Nichole. It's late, so come on in so I can get you that medicine. I already have a pot of coffee waiting on us."

Nichole entered Lala's house, sat down with Lala over a hot cup of coffee, and they mapped out their road to revenge.

When the sun finally came up, Nichole yawned and sealed two small envelopes before standing.

"I hope this works, Lala."

Lala put their empty coffee cups into the sink.

"Don't worry, it will. I've learned a lot from being married to Deacon, which means I've learned from the best. Come on, I'll walk you out."

Lala walked Nichole to the door and opened it. "I'm so glad you came over, Nichole. I got a chance to know you, and I see why Deacon fell in love with you."

Nichole felt a little awkward. She stepped out on the porch and inhaled a breath of fresh morning air. She looked back at Lala.

"It seems so peaceful."

Lala touched her arm. "It is, Nichole, and it will be from here on out. You'll see."

Nichole made her way down the stairs to the sidewalk and turned to Lala. "Wish me luck."

Lala smiled. "Good luck, Nichole."

"The same goes for you too, Lala, and please be careful."

"Don't worry," Lala said as she patted the pocket of her bathrobe. "I have everything I need right here in my pocket. Now get out of here and go handle your business."

Nichole climbed inside her car and drove off while Lala jumped in the shower and dressed as quickly as she could. She looked at her watch and hurried out the door.

Winston stepped into his office and immediately started looking over his messages. His secretary walked in with fresh flowers.

"Good Morning, Winston."

He glanced up and smiled. "Good morning, Celia. Nice flowers."

She put the flowers on his conference table. "I love the smell of fresh flowers."

Winston turned on his computer and noticed a small package on his desk. "So do I. Thanks for making sure I have some every day."

She walked toward the door and said, "You're welcome. Do you need anything before I get to work?"

He looked over at his coffee pot and noticed that it was filled with fresh, hot coffee. "No, I think you've made sure I have everything that I need. Thank you."

"Call me if you need me," Celia said as she reached for the doorknob.

"I will," he replied as he turned the package over and noticed that it was from Nichole. He hurriedly opened it and found a small cassette tape inside with a note. Winston opened the note and began to read the letter accompanying the mysterious tape. As he began to read the words, he instructed his secretary to hold all his calls and appointments until further notice.

Winston,

By the time you get this package I will hopefully be free of Deacon, who's holding my heart hostage. Before I explain, I want to first thank you for everything you did to help Damon when he was in jail. I'm sure by now you've probably heard about me breaking off my engagement to him. Believe me when I say that giving Damon back that ring was the hardest thing I've ever done, and it wasn't something I wanted to do. It was something I had to do. I love Damon very much, and there's nothing I wouldn't do for him. With that said, I'm sure that once you listen to this tape everything will become clear to you on why I had to leave him. I did it not only to protect Damon and his career, but also to get my life back as well. I pray Damon will forgive me and ultimately understand why I chose to handle things this way. Hopefully he'll give me a second chance and forgive me for all the pain I've caused him once all of this is over. In the meantime, I wanted you to have a copy of this tape in case something happens to me. If it does, please tell Damon that I never stopped loving him and I wanted nothing more than to be his wife. I trust you will make sure this tape gets into the proper author-ity's hands so justice can prevail.

Friends always,
Nichole

Winston put the tape into his small cassette player and listened. What he heard was nothing short of amazing, and he nearly fell out of his chair. What he was listening to was clearly a crime. Nichole had somehow made a recording of her meeting in the park with Deacon where he admitted framing Damon and threatened to continue black-mailing Nichole. Once he finished listening to the tape, he quickly dialed Craig's number and asked him and Joshua to meet him at Damon's house right away. After giving them Damon's address, he grabbed his keys and quickly headed out the door.

Nichole said a little prayer before pushing the door-bell. A few seconds later Damon opened the door. It was immediately evident that he was surprised to see her. He was gorgeous as he stood there in denim shorts and a wife beater undershirt. He folded his arms and frowned.

"What are you doing here?"

She swallowed before speaking, but was unable to re-move the lump in her throat. "I was hoping that we could talk."

Damon leaned against the door and studied Nichole's body language. She was obviously nervous, but even so she was still breathtaking. He noticed the lines under her eyes and sensed that she'd had about as much sleep as he had. It was taking the strength of ten horses to keep him from pulling her into his arms.

"What else do we have to talk about, Nichole? You made your point very clear the other day when you gave back the ring. What's left to talk about?"

Nichole looked around her surroundings and then looked up at him with weary eyes. "You need to know why. If you give me a chance, I'll try to explain everything to you."

Trying to be hard, he refused. "I don't think so. I've given you nothing but chances, Nichole. I've left you a hundred messages, but you refused to return any of my calls. Now you show up on my doorstep wanting to talk. I've been a fool long enough, so thanks but no thanks. "

Damon's words cut her deeper than the glass that had cut her hand. Tears spilled out of her eyes upon hearing Damon's harsh words.

"I'm sorry I hurt you, Damon. I love you and never meant for things to go down like they did, but I didn't have a choice. You have to believe me."

He laughed. "Why should I believe anything you have to say to me anymore? I trusted you with my heart, Nichole, and you stomped all over it. Good-bye," he said before quickly closing the door in her face.

Devastated, Nichole slowly walked to her car. Damon's heart thumped in his chest. Just the sight of her in those form-fitting jeans aroused the maleness in him and made him want to run after her and sweep her up in his arms. But he was a man with pride, and his heart had been damaged for the last time. He knew he would never again love another woman like he loved Nichole.

Chapter Thirty-Two

Craig and Joshua arrived at Damon's house a few minutes after Winston. Inside, they found Winston pacing the floor and yelling at Damon in the worst way.

"Damon, how could you sit here and let Nichole walk right out of your life? She came here to tell you everything that went down. That woman went to bat for you and this is how you pay her back? So what if you got your heart kicked around a little bit. Who hasn't? It wasn't that long ago that I was sitting right where you are now, remember? So I know exactly how it feels when you're about to lose the only woman you've ever loved and you're too goddamn stubborn to admit it!"

Craig and Joshua pulled Winston away from Damon because he was screaming. Craig sighed.

"Calm down, Skeeter. Can't you see the man's in agony? What happened?"

Winston reached into his pocket, pulled out his cassette player, and slammed it down on the table. "You guys don't understand. I got this in the mail from Nichole this morning, and it explains everything. Listen," he instructed them before pushing the play button.

Winston turned on the cassette player and they all began to listen to the tape recording. When Damon heard Deacon's voice arrogantly admitting to framing him, he was furious. Damon became even more irate when he heard him blackmail Nichole and threaten her to stay away from Damon or else he would have Damon thrown back in jail. Once they finished listening to the entire tape, Winston turned if off, looked over at Damon, and shook his head.

"How did that make you feel, Coach? You need to get off your ass, go find Nichole, and apologize to her before it's too late."

"Damn," Craig mumbled. "I can't believe he put a GPS on Nichole."

"And that's only what we know about," Winston replied.

Joshua frowned. "This guy is reckless and very manipulative. Do you think he's capable of hurting her?"

Damon looked up with sheer terror on his face. "You heard him grab her, didn't you?" Winston reminded them. "She said he was hurting her. I don't put anything past him, not after the GPS and the blackmail. He's obsessed with her."

Joshua nodded. "What are you going to do with that tape?"

"I don't know yet. I can have him brought up on coercion, false imprisonment, and a few other things. He's definitely dirty, and he needs to be dealt with, but I can't move too fast. I need to talk to Nichole first," Winston responded. "I want to make sure she's safe."

"Make me a copy," Joshua requested. "I hate cops like him. He needs a kick in the ass even if you don't prosecute him."

"Damon, you weren't too hard on Nichole, were you?" Craig asked.

He covered his face with his hands. "Yeah, I was pretty tough on her. I basically slammed the door in her face. What can you do about this guy, Winston?"

"Personally, I would like to see him locked up, but I'll know more after I talk to him." Winston picked up the cassette recorder. "You get your ass out of here and go find your woman, and you better fix this before you lose her."

Damon picked up his car keys. "They way I treated her, she probably won't even talk to me."

Craig patted him on the shoulder. "I'm sure she'll talk to you. You might have to do some serious begging and apologizing, but you know how to talk to your woman."

"I don't know, guys. I've never been involved in anything like this. I've never given a woman an engagement ring, and the one time I took a chance and did it, I got it thrown back in my face. That shit hurts," Damon admitted.

"Do you love her?" Joshua asked.

"Of course I love her, but she should've told me what was going on so I wouldn't have been blindsided by this whole mess."

Craig stepped up and said, "You're right, she could've told you, but she didn't, and now you know the whole story and why she did it. Let me ask you something, Damon, is Nichole worth sucking up your pride and going after her, or are you going to sit around here bitter and alone?"

Damon sighed. "You know the answer to that."

"OK! You gave her that ring for a reason, now if you're the man I know you are, be that man and go get your woman," Craig demanded.

All eyes were on Damon as he stood there thinking about everything the guys had said to him.

"OK, I'm going. I just hope you guys know what you're talking about."

"Duh, we're married, aren't we? We didn't get our wives from dial-a-wife. Go!" Winston yelled.

Damon walked out into the hallway. "Lock up when leave. I'll catch up to you guys later. Wish me luck."

They wished Damon good luck in unison before he walked out the door.

L ala found Deacon and Riley at the precinct going over paperwork. When Deacon saw her coming, he shook his head in disbelief.

"I don't believe this," he mumbled.

Riley looked up, saw Lala, and knew why Deacon had made his comment. Lala walked over and greeted them.

"Hello, Riley, and you, too, Deacon."

Riley stood and gave Lala a kiss on the cheek. "Hey, Lala, you look great."

"Thank you, Riley, so do you. Deacon, may I talk to you for a second?"

Without looking up from his paperwork he said, "I'm busy, Lala. It's not a good time."

"I don't care how busy you are," she whispered as she leaned over him. "We need to talk . . . now."

Deacon looked up at her angrily and then pushed back from his desk.

"Riley, I'll be ready to go in five minutes. This won't take long."

"Take your time, Deek," Riley replied as he watched the two disappear around the corner.

Deacon escorted Lala through the squad room and into one of the interview rooms. He pulled out her chair and then sat down across from her. "What do you want, Lala?"

She reached into her purse, pulled out the divorce papers, and laid them on the table.

"I got these divorce papers in the mail the other day. I really didn't think you would go through with it, but you proved me wrong. I honestly thought you were going to give us another chance, but I was wrong."

Deacon reached over and picked up the documents to see if Lala had signed them. "Why aren't these signed?" he asked.

Lala took the documents out of his hand.

"I'll sign them as soon as your attorney amends them with the items I've notated in red ink."

"What are you talking about?" he asked as he flipped through the papers.

Lala wanted complete ownership of their brownstone, alimony until he retired, and then thirty percent of his pension. Deacon slid the paperwork over to her and glared at her.

"You're pushing it, Lala. You've got to be crazy if you think I'm going to give you complete ownership of the brownstone. It's worth nearly five hundred thousand dollars, and I want out, so you'll either have to buy me out or sell it and split the proceeds."

She leaned forward and smiled. "You haven't lived there in over two years, and I'm the one who's been paying the mortgage. You were quite happy living elsewhere while you were whoring around in the streets, so don't start acting like the brownstone means so much to you. I'm keeping it, period!"

Deacon made fists as he sat there. He hated not being in control of a situation, especially where Lala was concerned.

"You don't know what my life was like when I wasn't with you, and what makes you think you deserve alimony? We don't have any kids, and I'm the one who worked for my pension, not you, so you can forget getting your hands on a penny of it."

Lala pulled out a pen. "You know, you're right, sweetheart. I'll cross that one out, and I'll even cross out the alimony request, but in return you will pay off my car and you'll sign the brownstone over to me and pay the mortgage on it until it's paid off."

Deacon slammed his fists on the table; however, Lala didn't even blink. He was furious to say the least.

"Why the hell would I do any of that, Lala, especially pay the mortgage when I don't even live there?"

Lala pulled a small tape recorder out of her purse and sat it on the table. "Because you once loved me, and because if you don't meet my terms, I'll turn this in to your captain and anybody else who will listen."

Deacon looked down at the tape recorder and smiled. "What do you think you have, Lala?"

Lala pushed the play button and calmly sat back and filed her fingernails. She glanced up a few times and watched Deacon's facial expressions as he sat there listening to voice on the tape. After about a minute of listening to the tape, he turned it off.

"Where did you get this?"

She waved him off. "That's not important, baby. What's important is finding out how much it's worth to you."

Deacon jumped up out of his chair. "Where did you get the tape?" he yelled.

"Oh, I didn't tell you?" she taunted him. "Your girlfriend gave it to me."

Deacon almost passed out. He'd been double-crossed by Nichole, and she had ultimately beaten him at his own game. Never in a million years did he think she would team up with Lala. Lala saw the look of defeat on Deacon's face and started laughing.

"Isn't it ironic, baby? While you had her wired to benefit you, she wired herself for insurance. How could you, Deacon? I never thought you could be so low down. To make that woman break up with her fiancé was foul. It's not like you had a chance with her. She doesn't love you anymore, so you need to get that through your thick head."

"What are you going to do with that tape, Lala?" Deacon asked softly as he sat back down.

Lala put the tape recorder back into her purse.

"Oh, I don't know. I'm going to hold on to it for a while until I decide what to do with it. I gave my lawyer a copy for safe keeping, as well as a few other people, so don't get any bright ideas."

"This is some bullshit, Lala. I can't believe you would roll up in here and blackmail me."

She burst out laughing.

"I don't know why you're surprised. I learned from the master."

Lala proceeded to inform Deacon that Nichole didn't want anything else to do with him. Deacon laughed.

"Oh, I see you don't believe me." Lala reached into her purse, pulled out another tape. She placed it inside the tape recorder and pushed play.

Deacon was stunned when he heard Nichole's voice.

Hello, Deacon,

I'm sorry our relationship got to this point, but you left me no choice. All of this started because you lied to me, and for some reason you don't think you did anything wrong. Explaining why you lied doesn't excuse the lie,

Deacon. I just wish you had been honest with me from the beginning. Then maybe I wouldn't have been forced to do this to you. You are a married man and have been for a long time. I deserved to have been told the truth. I don't want to hurt you, Deacon, but it seems you're doing everything within your power to hurt me, so I had to protect myself by making the tape.

What did I do to you, Deacon, for you to turn my life into a living hell? I hope you ask yourself that question and really think about the answer. I love Damon. I love him, Deacon, and I pray I can salvage what's left of our relationship so we can move on with our lives. Deacon, you have all the capabilities of a great police officer. Use your gifts for good, not evil, and try to make amends with all the people you've hurt along the way. As far as that tape of you blackmailing me, I would just as soon forget about it as long as you behave yourself and stop trying to control other people's lives. I did love you, Deacon, and you are a wonderful man. It just wasn't meant for us to be together, and I hope and pray you find someone special to love just like I have in Damon. Good luck, and be careful. Good-bye. Love always, Nichole.

Lala turned off the tape and watched tears well up in Deacon's eyes. She softly called out to him.

"Deacon? Are you OK?"

He wiped his eyes and said, "I'm fine."

"Nichole told me to tell you to please leave her and her fiancé alone. If you do that, no one will ever hear the tapes, and everyone will live happily ever after."

Deacon was backed into a corner with nowhere to go.

"Am if I don't?" he asked.

"Then copies of the tape will be released to your captain and the media, and then you'll go to jail. This tape can end your career and your life. Are you willing to risk everything because of your obsession over her? She doesn't love you anymore. Get over it."

Lala slid the divorce papers back over to Deacon and stood. "I assume I'll be getting a revised copy of these in the mail real soon?"

"Whatever, Lala," Deacon mumbled.

She pulled her purse strap up on her shoulder and walked over to Deacon. "Good luck, Deacon," she said after kissing him on the forehead. "I'm sorry things didn't work out like either one of us wanted. No matter what, I'll always love you. You were my first love. Be careful out there, OK?"

"Good-bye, Lala."

Deacon returned to his desk and threw the divorce papers down. Riley picked up the papers and scanned them.

"Is this what I think it is?"

He sat down and sighed. "Yeah, those are my divorce papers."

"Did she sign them?" Riley asked. "Why the long face?"

Deacon looked around the room and whispered, "You're not going to believe it when I tell you."

This piqued Riley's curiosity. "What happened? Lala left out of here with a huge smile on her face."

"She got me, Riley. I mean she really got me," Deacon revealed.

"What did she do?" Deacon stood.

"I'll tell you over lunch. Let's get out of here. I need some fresh air."

At the bistro around the corner from the precinct, Deacon told Riley everything. He told him about framing Damon, blackmailing Nichole, breaking into Nichole's house with rose petals and candles, and lastly installing a GPS system on her truck. Riley sat there in disbelief. He picked up his glass of raspberry lemonade and shook his head.

"You've outdone yourself this time, Deacon. When do you sleep, man?"

"What's wrong with me, Riley?" he asked.

Riley sipped his lemonade and then sat down the glass. "You need help. I'm serious when I say that. Maybe the shooting had something to do with it. I don't know, but you really need to talk to somebody. Do you realize how many criminal offenses you've committed? Do have any idea how much time you could get for all that you've done?"

Deacon pushed some fries around on his plate with his fork and nodded. "Yeah, I know. I guess it's really over, huh?"

"I'm afraid it is. You'll feel so much better once you sit down and talk to someone that can help you with all of this. I'll go with you it you want me to."

Deacon looked over at Riley and said, "I'd like that, Riley. Thanks."

Chapter Thirty-Three

Damon had been driving around for nearly two hours, but he couldn't find Nichole and her phone was going directly into voice mail. He'd been to her house and job, but he couldn't find her anywhere, and he was beginning to panic. He pulled into the parking lot of a fast food restaurant and put his car in park.

"Where are you, Nichole?"

He pulled out his cell phone and made a call. As soon as Arnelle heard his voice she lit into him worse than Winston had. It was evident that Winston had filled her in on Nichole, and now he was paying for it. He leaned his head against the steering wheel and sighed as he took Arnelle's scolding.

"You'd better find her, Damon, and pray she forgives you for the way you treated her!"

Meridan took the telephone out of Arnelle's hand and was a little more sympathetic to him.

"Damon, Nichole is my best friend. Please find her before something happens to her. She loves you and I know you love her. You men with your pride kill me. I want you to call us the minute you locate her."

"I will, Meridan. Listen, I'll call you guys back later. OK?"

"OK, Damon, and please be careful," Meridan replied.

He raised his head and put the car in drive. "OK, I'll find her. Call me if either one of you hear from her. I'll holler at you later. Good-bye."

Damon hung up the telephone and drove to the last place he figured Nichole would be. In reality, it should've been the first place he checked.

Just as Nichole was about to putt, she remembered that she had turned off her cell phone when she arrived at Damon's house so they wouldn't be disturbed, however she had forgotten to turn it back on after he dismissed her. As soon as she pushed the power button the cell phone rang. She answered, and it was Lala on the other end.

"Nichole, it's over! I got what I wanted with my divorce, and then some!"

"Good for you, Lala," Nichole replied solemnly.

"Oh! You don't have to worry about Deacon ever bothering you again. I played the tape of him blackmailing you and I thought he wet his pants," Lala announced as she laughed hysterically. "What really got him was when I played your tape to him. I think he teared up. Hell, I almost felt sorry for him."

"Thank you, Lala," she said as she let out a breath. "I'm glad things worked out for you."

"You too! Don't get me wrong, because I still love Deacon. He was my first love, but he's changed. He's not the same man I married."

Nichole listened without responding.

"So how did things go with you and your fiancé?" Lala asked.

"Not so good. He wouldn't even let me explain what happened. I think I've lost him for good," Nichole revealed. "That's why I decided to come to the golf course and get my head together."

"He'll come around, Nichole. Just give him a few days and go talk to him again. He didn't ask you to marry him for the hell of it," Lala responded with encouragement.

"I hope you're right, Lala. In the meantime, I'm just going to chill and give him some space."

"Keep me posted, Nichole. Well, I'll let you get back to your golf game and I'll check on you tomorrow. Maybe we can meet for coffee or dinner or something."

"Sounds good, Lala."

"I appreciate all your help, Nichole, and for what it's worth, I'm so sorry we had such a rocky start."

"Me too. Good-bye."

Nichole hung up the telephone and tucked it back in her jeans. She completed her putt and decided to take a break before heading up to the next hole. In the distance she spotted a tree, so she put her golf club back into the golf bag and made her way over. She sat down and listened to the wind as it rustled the leaves. Minutes later she watched as a couple of butterflies flew past her and rested on some flowers around the pond. She leaned back and closed her eyes as several birds chirped away at each other on the upper branches.

The peacefulness of the area almost made her forget about the pain that was settling into the pit of her stomach and her heart. The last several days had been nothing but a nightmare, and she wished she could wake up to find out that it had all been a dream.

"Nichole?"

Nichole opened her eyes and found Damon standing directly in front of her. She quickly stood and knocked the leaves off her jeans.

"Damon, what are you doing here?"

He smiled and Nichole's heart nearly burst out of her chest. She never thought Damon would ever speak to her again, let alone smile at her.

"I've been looking all over this city for you," he replied as he stepped closer to her.

"You have?"

"Yes. Listen, I'm sorry I didn't give you a chance to explain everything to me when you stopped by my house. I was hurt and seeing you intensified all the pain I was feeling from you breaking up with me. It was déjà vu all over for me from women past."

Nichole lowered her head. "You should know by now that I'm not like those women, Damon. I would never intentionally hurt you, and I wasn't about to let Deacon ruin your life."

Damon tilted her chin so he could see her eyes. As he looked in her eyes, he could see how the light had dimmed.

"Winston told me what you did. I'm sorry I doubted you."

"I'm sorry I didn't tell you what was going on."

"You've could've gotten hurt."

She smiled and said, "I was careful."

He glanced down at her hand, which was heavily bandaged.

"What happened to your hand?" he asked with a touch of tenderness in his tone.

Nichole raised her hand and looked at it. "Nothing important. I'll live."

Damon swallowed the lump in his throat. "Did Deacon do that to you?" he asked.

She lowered her head and softly said, "No, it was an accident."

"I'm glad. I thought I was going to have to kill him if he had hurt you like that."

The couple stared into each other's eyes for the longest time until Damon couldn't take it any longer. He leaned down and kissed her ever so slowly on the lips. Nichole melted as Damon's sweet mouth caressed hers. The air became thin, making it hard for Nichole to breathe. She leaned into Damon for support without breaking the kiss. Several minutes passed before either of them considered stopping. Damon finally pulled back and chuckled.

Nichole nibbled on Damon's lower lip.

"Will you ever be able to forgive me?" she asked.

He sprinkled her neck with kisses. "Of course, but you should've told me, or at least Winston what you were planning."

"I didn't think about it, Damon. I just reacted. I wanted you out of jail because I knew you were innocent."

Damon cupped her hips and kissed her once more. "I think we'd better leave before we get arrested."

Nichole nuzzled his neck. "Where do you want to go?"

He reached down and picked up her golf clubs. "Home, let's go home."

"What home?" she asked as she followed him out onto the green of the golf course.

He turned around and faced her with a huge grin on his face. "Oh, I forgot. There's something missing out of this conversation, huh?"

Nichole blushed. Damon sat the golf clubs down on the ground and reached inside his pocket. He pulled out the diamond ring he'd put on her finger days earlier. Nichole's eyes lit up as he walked toward her and took her hand into his. Before sliding the ring on her finger, he kissed her ring finger.

"Nichole Adams, will you marry me?"

Without hesitation and with tears streaming down her face she whispered, "Yes, Damon Kilpatrick, I'll marry you."

He picked her up in his arms and kissed her lips. Nichole locked her legs around his waist and sobbed.

"I didn't think you would ever forgive me, Damon."

"That's funny. I thought the same thing about five minutes ago," Damon revealed. "Now can we go home, baby?"

With her forehead resting against his, she asked, "I'll go anywhere with you, Coach."

"Do you mind if we make a stop first?"

"Where?" she asked curiously.

He winked at her and said, "You'll see."

Meridan dialed Nichole's cell phone and got her voice mail once again.

"Nichole, I don't know why you're not answering your phone, but if you don't return my call in the next fifteen minutes, I'm going to hurt you when I see you."

Keaton massaged her shoulders and whispered, "Calm down, sweetheart. "

Meridan sighed. "I can't believe neither Damon nor Nichole has had the common courtesy to call us. They have to know we're worried about them. I don't even know if he found her."

Craig stepped out into the backyard with a pan of ribs and steaks. Brandon and MaLeah ran out of the house behind him continued out to MaLeah's playhouse.

"Stop running you two before you fall and hurt yourselves."

The kids neither stopped running nor acknowledged Craig's request.

"Keaton, open up the grill for me."

Keaton raised the top of the grill and watched as Craig lined it with the meat.

"Where's Venice?"

Craig fanned the smoke out of his face. "She went to get the twins. She should be here shortly."

Meridan walked over and frowned. "What's wrong with you? I thought all farm girls liked beef."

"I do like beef, just not today," she revealed. "Did you see any chicken breasts in Winston's fridge?"

Craig laughed and then closed the top of the grill. "If you name it, he has it. Winston needs to hurry up and get back because I've served my time feeding you guys this week."

Just then, Craig's cell phone rang. He put down the pan and answered it.

"Hello?"

"Hey, Craig, it's Joshua. Damon called Winston and said he found Nichole on the golf course. She's fine, and Winston and I should be there in about an hour."

Craig covered the telephone and whispered the news to Keaton and Meridan. She immediately ran into the house to broadcast the news to Arnelle, Cynthia, and Venice. Craig put the phone back up to his ear.

"That's great, because I'm ready to get off this grill. Have you guys talked to Deacon yet?"

"We just got here. I'll fill you in when we get there."

"Tell Winston to hurry up," Craig yelled into the telephone. Joshua chuckled.

"OK! Later."

After Joshua hung up the telephone he looked over at Winston, who was still on the telephone with Damon.

"Great! I knew things would work out. Listen, we need to talk so we can tie up a few things. I know it's short notice, but everyone's over at my house right now. Craig's working the grill for me until I get there. Why don't you guys swing by so we can talk over some ribs and beer? I'm sure Arnelle and Meridan would love to see for themselves that you guys are back together," Winston suggested.

"You're right. Otherwise our phones will ring nonstop until we do. We'll see you guys shortly," Damon acknowledged.

Damon hung up the telephone and turned his attention back to Nichole, who was comfortably stretched out on top of his body. He ran his large hands down the length of her statuesque body before cupping her firm hips. She leaned down and kissed his chest.

"What did Winston want?"

He kissed her neck. "Winston's having a cookout and wants us to come. I think he also wants to talk to me about some other stuff too."

"Do we have to go?" she purred as she ran her tongue over his brown nipples. Damon sucked in a breath and let out a loud groan. Nichole smiled and did it once again, causing his entire body to immediately respond. "My, my, Coach. By all the evidence in front of me, I'll have to say that you enjoyed that," she teased as her eyes roamed over his body.

He smiled, flipped her over onto her back, and immediately towered over her. "You think?"

She cupped his face and looked into his loving eyes. "Yes, I think, and I know for a fact that I love you, Damon. I couldn't be any happier than I am right now."

"Is that right? What about when we have kids?" he asked.

Nichole nibbled on his lips and chin and breathlessly said, "I'm ready whenever you are. Bring it on."

He kissed her feverishly on the lips as he moved his hips between her thighs. Nichole moaned loudly with each thrust as Damon consummated his relationship with her. The couple vigorously made love to each other. Nichole felt her body heating up as Damon placed her leg over his shoulder. She muttered his name as her legs trembled and her body shuddered beneath him. Damon let out a loud groan as he followed her into a mist of sheer ecstasy. He collapsed on the bed next to her and almost immediately he caught a cramp in his thigh. Nichole giggled as she applied pressure to his thigh and massaged it.

"Are you OK, baby?"

Damon balled up his fist and gritted his teeth, indicating that he wasn't. The cramp was not letting up, and it wasn't until Nichole gently kissed his thigh that the cramp began to ease up. She continued to kiss and massage the area until she was able to work the knot out of his muscle. Successful, Nichole climbed on top of his body and smiled down at him.

"Is that better?"

He opened his eyes and grinned. "That was the best physical therapy I've ever had in my life. Thank you, baby."

"I'm glad you enjoyed it," she replied as she slid her hand under the sheet and gently grasped his lower body. "You can expect a lot more where that came from, and then some."

With a strained tone, Damon said, "Nichole . . . sweetheart . . ."

"Yes, dear?" she replied mischievously as she tightened her grip on him.

"If you keep that up, we won't make it to Winston's cookout, or even out of this bed."

"You think?"

Before he could respond, she winked at him and dipped her head. Damon screamed out her name and then mumbled something incoherent.

Nichole giggled. "What's wrong, Coach?"

She could see the vein in his neck pulsating, so she released him from her sensual torture.

"Get up, you big baby," she teased him as she sat up and threw back the sheets. As she made her way into the shower, she announced, "I let you off the hook for the moment, but when we get home I'm going to pick up exactly where I left off, so be ready."

Damon couldn't move.

"Damon! I'm waiting!"

"I'm coming, baby!" he yelled back at her as he slowly sat up on the side of the bed to regain his composure.

"Damon!"

He laughed and joined Nichole in the hot, steamy shower.

Chapter Thirty-Four

Joshua and Winston were finally led into a small office so they could meet with Deacon. When they walked into the office they saw that he wasn't alone. Deacon closed the door and said, "Gentleman, have a seat. This is my partner, Riley, who I've asked to sit in on the meeting."

Winston shook Riley's hand before sitting down.

"Since we're doing introductions, this is my friend, Joshua, who I invited to sit in on the meeting as well. Listen, Deacon, I'll get right to the point. As you probably know, I'm Damon Kilpatrick's attorney, and I represented him on his recent misfortune that was luckily dropped. Do you know anything about that?"

Deacon laughed. "Look, I already know that you know I was involved, so let's stop the bullshit. Why are you here?"

Winston frowned and then sat up closer to Deacon. "OK, since you want to do it like that, I'm game. Stay the hell away from Damon and Nichole or you won't see the light of another day."

"Wait just a goddamn minute," Riley said as he stepped forward. "You can't talk to him like that."

Joshua quickly blocked Riley's forward progress. "Yes, he can, and there's not a damn thing you can do about it, so you need to back down."

Riley stared at Joshua for a few seconds and noticed a glimmer in his eye that told him Joshua was more than just Winston's friend, but who was he?

"Who are you anyway? Internal Affairs?" Riley asked.

Joshua smiled. "You wish, but believe me, you don't want to know."

Winston continued his conversation with Deacon. "I have a copy of the recording Nichole made at your last meeting, and I must say it's very incriminating."

Deacon smiled. "Damn! It seems like everybody has a copy of the infamous tape. So what?"

Winston gritted his teeth and said, "Don't let the suit fool you, bro. I wasn't always a lawyer. I'll do whatever it takes to protect my clients, so if you want to take me on, go right ahead."

Deacon waved him off. "You can tell your clients to have a nice life. No piece of ass is worth my career. I don't care how good it is."

Winston stood. "I'm glad you've come to terms with that revelation, and it would be in your best interest to put in for a transfer out of Philly. My associate here could make that happen for you with just one phone call. You have one choice. Otherwise he picks the location and you might not like the location he selects. So are we clear?"

Deacon thought to himself for a moment. "Yeah, we're clear."

"Then you know what I can do with this tape if you ever bother Nichole or Damon again, right?" Winston asked.

"Yes, I know what you can do with it," Deacon answered.

Winston smiled. "Great, then I guess this meeting is over and the tape can stay locked away for safe keeping. It was a pleasure doing business with you."

Joshua and Winston left the police precinct feeling confident that Damon and Nichole were finally free from Deacon's reign of manipulation.

Back at Winston's house Venice and Cynthia arrived with the twins. She put the twins down so they could play.

"Something smells good."

Craig walked through the door wearing Winston's kiss-the-cook apron. He slid the cooked meat into the oven to keep it warm.

"Thank you."

Venice giggled and asked, "What are you doing?"

He kissed her. "Grilling. Winston and Joshua had to take care of some business, so he asked me to start the grill until he made it back."

"Where's Arnelle?" Cynthia asked.

Craig pulled some hotdogs out of the refrigerator. "She and Meridan are outside watching the kids."

Venice took C.J. and Clarissa by the hand and walked them out into the backyard while Cynthia pulled a couple of bottles of water out of the refrigerator and followed closely behind.

Damon and Nichole arrived at Winston's house and found some great looking food simmering on the grill. Arnelle ran over and gave Nichole and Damon a big hug and some welcomed encouragement after which Meridan pulled Nichole to the side.

"Nikki, what is going on?" she asked as they sat down on the garden bench.

Nichole smiled. "Dee, this has been the week from hell, but it's over now."

"What did Deacon do to you?"

"Not just me. He did some terrible things to Damon, too."

Meridan took Nichole's hands and looked down at them. "Why is your hand bandaged?"

Nichole sighed. "I was careless and cut my hand on a mirror."

Concerned, Meridan asked, "Did you have to get stitches?"

"No, it's OK. It's not that sore anymore."

"That's good. Nikki, your ring is beautiful. Damon has good taste."

Nichole held out her hand. "He does have good taste, doesn't he?"

"I was talking about you, Nikki. Damon picked the perfect girl."

Nichole hugged Meridan and whispered, "Thank you." They wiped each other's tears away.

"I can't wait to be your matron of honor. You are going to be a beautiful bride."

Nichole smiled and stood. "I'm starving. I hope Craig has the food ready. Come on, Dee, let's eat."

Meridan looked at Nichole curiously before following her back over to the others. As soon as they joined the others, Winston and Joshua stepped out into the back-yard.

"You would get back after all the food is ready," Craig said as he looked up. "Get everybody to the table so we can eat."

Winston hugged Craig. "Thanks for holding things down for me, Craig. You're the man."

"Yeah, I'm always the man when it comes to cooking. Joshua, round up the kids so I can serve them first."

Winston walked over to Nichole and pulled her to the

side. "I received your package, so Joshua and I decided to pay Deacon a little visit after listening to the tape. You don't have to worry about him anymore. He's going to be going on a little trip real soon."

"He's not going to jail is he?" she asked.

"No, but I'm pretty sure he'll be transferring to another city."

"I never wanted to hurt Deacon," she admitted.

He put his hand on her shoulder and said, "I know you didn't. Now let's forget about it and try to enjoy ourselves."

Nichole hugged his neck. "Thank you," she whispered.

Winston smiled. "You're welcome. With that settled, I'd better get over there and give Craig a hand."

"Thanks for inviting us over, Winston."

"I wouldn't have had it any other way," he answered as he removed his tie and unbuttoned the top buttons on his shirt.

Winston walked over to Craig, who was placing some food on a couple of plates. "Let me help you with that, partner."

"No, you go change your clothes, because I don't want to hear your mouth if you get some barbecue sauce on your expensive suit. I got this out here."

Winston smiled. "You're my boy, Craig!"

Without answering him, Craig walked toward the table with two plates filled with hotdogs and potato chips.

Once everyone was seated and ready to eat, Winston blessed the food so his guests could partake in some delicious ribs, chicken, steaks, burgers, and hot dogs. Along with the meat, potato chips, salad, and baked beans were also served.

After everyone had their fill of food, Keaton kissed Meridan on the cheek and said, "Hey guys, this week has been great. Meridan and I always enjoy coming up here to hang out with you guys. It was a weekend of fun and surprises, so we thought we would add to all the excitement. First, I want to announce that I've decided to open a restaurant here in Philadelphia. We spend a lot of time here, so it's only fitting that we expand out business here."

Congratulations were showered upon the couple, but that was nothing compared to what Meridan announced next.

"While Keaton's announcing his new addition, I want to announce mine. The adoption came through, and we're going to have a little girl!"

Nichole screamed and jumped up from her chair. She ran around to Meridan and nearly pulled her out of the chair with excitement. Damon laughed.

"Do you think Nichole is happy for them?" he asked.

Everyone laughed, but everyone else was just as excited as Nichole since they knew of Meridan's difficulties in having children. When Nichole finally sat down, Damon leaned over and whispered something into her ear, causing her to nod in agreement. Damon took a sip before standing up.

"Hey, guys, I just want to thank all of you for everything that you've done for us, and I don't have to tell you how stressful this week has been. But we're happy to let you all know that it did end on high note after all, especially after we said 'I do' to each other earlier today."

Everyone seemed to look at the couple with a dumbfounded look on their faces. You could actually hear a pin drop because everyone was so stunned.

Nichole stood and put her hands on her hips. "Good Lord, people. We married!"

Now it was Meridan's turn to scream. "Married?"

Arnelle was so happy for Damon and Nichole. She felt

like her prayers had been answered as she hugged and kissed both of them.

Brandon and MaLeah had enjoyed clapping their hands to all the news so he thought it was only fair that he get in on the excitement as well. He stood up in his chair and yelled, "Me and MeLeah's getting married when we grow up."

Craig lifted his glass and said, "OK, that caught me off guard a little bit, but there are as close to each other as all of us are."

Everyone laughed. Craig continued his speech and said, "If everyone would lift their glasses I would like to do a little toast."

All the guests lifted their glasses, including the children as Craig said, "It's obvious that God places people in our lives for a reason and before I go forward, I have to take you all back. When I was lost, I vowed that I would love again when hell freezes over. Sorry, Keaton, I had to borrow your infamous and outdated line."

Keaton smiled at Craig.

"Anyway, no matter how many times I tried, I couldn't move on with my life because I knew I had been there, done that, and considered myself done in the category of love. Funny thing was that God had a different plan for me and brought Venice back into my life. As you look around this table, you can see that we've all been put together by various and sometimes unexplainable circumstances. At the end of the day, you realize that all we need to keep us together is love because what goes around, comes around. Now we've heard some fantastic news today and I have no doubt that more blessings are on the horizon for all of us. I just want to take this opportunity to let you know that I love all of you and I know you feel the same about me and my family. So after all the food is put away and we head back to our homes, instead of saying good-bye, I would rather say until next time because life is all that and a bag of chips and the best is yet to come."

There wasn't a dry eye at the table as everyone toasted to Craig's speech and then applauded him.

Epilogue

A couple of weeks later, Damon and Nichole had an official wedding. It was small, yet elegant, and all their family and friends were around them to share in their joy. Meridan and Arnelle stood by Nichole's side while Zel and Damon's other brother, Anthony, stood by Damon's side. Damon's family couldn't have been happier for him, especially his grandparents. They fell in love with Nichole the moment they met her. She was a beautiful bride, and MaLeah was the cutest flower girl ever.

The happy couple honeymooned for a week on the Caribbean island of Antigua before returning back to Philadelphia. Damon had to quickly return to the football field while Nichole took some time off to put her house on the market. Damon also put his house on the market. He recognized the fact that they needed more space not only for their vehicles, but for the children he couldn't wait to have with Nichole. It didn't take them long to sell their homes and find the house of their dreams. The couple quickly moved in and settled into married life.

Nichole loved traveling to and attending all the games with Damon. Nichole especially loved spending time with Damon during the off-season, and it was during that time that they took advantage of starting a family.

Deacon had gotten further and further from Nichole's mind. After Winston's suggestion, he'd put in for a transfer. He now lived in New Orleans and was busy helping the city restore order and rebuild after Hurricane Katrina.

Lala contacted Nichole months later to inform her that she'd met someone and was considering marriage. Riley had been promoted and now worked cold case files. He kept in touch with Deacon and visited him often. Upon his last visit he was happy to see that Deacon had met someone and was seriously dating.

Once fall rolled around again and the football season kicked off, Nichole geared up for another year of traveling with Damon. Unfortunately, she was sidelined the first week of the season with a terrible case of what she thought was the flu, but instead she was diagnosed with morning sickness. Seven and a half months later Nichole made Damon the proud father of a son they named Nicholas Ryan Kilpatrick. They named him Nicholas after Nichole, and Ryan after Damon's grandfather.

About the Author

Darrien Lee, a native of Columbia, Tennessee, attended Tennessee State University in Nashville, which is where she picked up the love of writing. Majoring in Business Administration, she started out writing various works of poetry. It wasn't until 1999 that Darrien began to take her writing seriously after feeling unfulfilled with her job at United Parcel Service. She found writing was the perfect setting in which to unwind while entertaining her friends. Her experience on her college campus was the inspiration for *All That and a Bag of Chips,* her first novel, published by Strebor Books Int'l in 2001. Since the release of that novel, Darrien's sequel, *Been There, Done That,* released in 2003, made *Essence* Magazine Bestseller's list. Darrien's third novel, *What Goes Around Comes Around,* which was released in July 2004, has also made *Essence* Magazine Bestseller's list. She released of part four of her series and her fourth novel, *When Hell Freezes Over* in July 2005.

Since then, Darrien has written *Talk to the Hand*, *The Last Chance*, and *The Denim Diaries*, a series for teens.

Darrien lives in LaVergne, Tennessee, with her husband and their two daughters. In her spare time she loves reading, watching sports, and listening to jazz.

NOW AVAILABLE

The baddest woman in town is not a gangster girl or a ride-or-die chick. She's a third generation assassin who has plans to change the world.

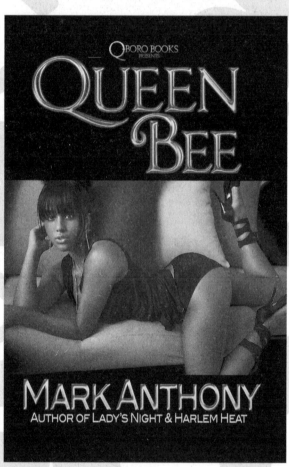

Q-BORO BOOKS
PRESENTS

Freak of the Week

MadameK
Author of *Freak in the Sheets*

Malina's mother throws a wrench in every relationship she engages in. If she can't have love, what's a girl to do to satisfy her needs in the meantime?

AVAILABLE
DECEMBER 2008

Brittani Williams

Q-BORO BOOKS
PRESENTS

BLACK
Diamond

Black Diamond proves why some details are meant to be kept secret. The result of simple pillow talk will leave two best friends fighting to survive.

MORE TITLES FROM

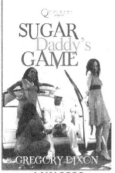